Harriet Martineau

Biographical Sketches

Harriet Martineau

Biographical Sketches

ISBN/EAN: 9783337014599

Printed in Europe, USA, Canada, Australia, Japan

Cover: Foto ©Raphael Reischuk / pixelio.de

More available books at **www.hansebooks.com**

BIOGRAPHICAL

SKETCHES

BY

HARRIET MARTINEAU

NEW YORK
LEYPOLDT & HOLT
TORONTO, CANADA
ADAM, STEVENSON & CO
1869

LITTLE, RENNIE & CO., Stereotypers,
NEW YORK.

PREFACE.

IT has been suggested to me that these Sketches should be reproduced in a convenient form for readers who may wish that they were more accessible than when hidden in the files of a newspaper. Such a proposal, made by a judgment which I respect, is gratifying to me; and I can have no hesitation in accepting it. I have therefore collected all the Memoirs I have written for the *Daily News*, from my first connection with the paper in 1852. It is from one of the gentlemen connected with that Journal, Mr. J. R. Bobinson, that the suggestion has proceeded; and it was accompanied by a generous consideration which obviates all difficulty in complying with it. Aware that my state of health renders all literary exertion impossible, Mr. Robinson desired to charge himself with all the trouble and responsibility, while leaving me all the advantages, of the publication. I have therefore had nothing to do but to put the material into his hands, duly arranged; and it has been carried through the press, and presented to the public, under his care and judgment.

As for my own share in the business, it was evident to me at the first glance over my material that the Sketches must be presented unaltered. In the few which relate to persons then living, there may be sentences or expressions which would have been different if the Memoirs were to be written now; but to alter these now would be to tamper with the truth of the sketch, and to produce something more misleading than the forecasts of a time which has gone by.

There is no such question in regard to the nine-tenths of the Memoirs which relate to the dead. Slight as they are, they convey the impression which the completed life left in each case upon my own mind, and, as I believe, on that of the society of its time. As the impression was final, the first record of it should remain untouched in order to remain faithful. I therefore simply reproduce the Sketches, making no other change than in the headings announcing the death, in each case. For convenience of reference, and for the sake of something like order in the presentment of materials so various, the personages are classified. In each group, however, there is no other precedence than the date of departure.

These few words of explanation being given, I have only to leave the Sketches to produce their own impression, whether on the minds of those who from peculiar knowledge carry a corresponding picture in their own breasts, or of those to whom the personages were historical while they lived. The records are true to my own impressions; and, secure in this main particular, I have no misgiving in offering them to readers whose curiosity and interest about the distinguished dead of their time claim such satisfaction as any survivor may be able to give.

H. M.

The Knoll, Ambleside,
December, 1868.

CONTENTS.

I. LITERARY.

II. SCIENTIFIC.

III. PROFESSIONAL.

IV. SOCIAL.

V. POLITICIANS.

CONTENTS.

VI. ROYAL.

I.

LITERARY.

I.

AMELIA OPIE.

DIED DECEMBER 2D, 1853.

ANOTHER of that curious class of English people—the
provincial literary lion—has left us. Mrs. Opie is dead.
The young, and most of the middle-aged, of our day
will say, "What of that?"—or "Who was Mrs. Opie?"
—or will think of her only as a beneficent Quaker lady,
whose conversion to muslin caps and silent meetings
made a noise some good many years ago. But the
elderly generation are aware that a good deal more
than that is connected with the name and fame of
Amelia Opie.

The long wars of George III.'s time largely influenced *One effect of*
the fate of this lady, as they did, indeed, that of most *long wars.*
people in England. One effect of those wars in an in-
sular kingdom like ours was to shut up our towns with
their peculiarities, and to preserve a state of manners
which has disappeared from the world, unless it be in
some remote German districts, or in some primitive
communities in New England. Lichfield is still renowned
for its departed literary coterie, and their conceits and
pedantries: and Norwich was very like Lichfield—only
with less sentimentality, and with some additional
peculiarities of its own. It had its cathedral; but

[I]

Norwich in the time of the war.

neither the proverbial dulness nor the all-conquering High-Churchism of most cathedral towns. The liberality of good Bishop Bathurst prevented the latter during the long course of his episcopate : and the manufactures of Norwich preserved it from stagnation. It is true that when invasion was expected, the Church and Tory gentry set a watch upon the cathedral, lest the Dissenters should burn it for a beacon to "Boney ;" and the manufacturers who were of Liberal opinions were not accepted as volunteers, but were simply intrusted with the business of providing for the conveyance of the women and children into the interior whenever the French should land at Yarmouth or Cromer. But still, while Bishop Bathurst touched his hat to the leading Dissenters of the place, and Norwich goods were in demand for the Spanish and Portuguese markets, the old city could not stagnate, like some other cathedral towns. The weavers, descended from the Flemish and French immigrants who had sought refuge in our Protestant country, were growing more and more peculiar, narrow, and obstinate—smaller in mind and body with each generation, and sure to ruin the trade of the city by their pedantry about their work, and obstinacy about wages, whenever the time should come for the world to be thrown open by a peace. The French taught in schools was such as was found to be unintelligible when the peace at length arrived—taught as it was by an aged powdered Monsieur and an elderly flowered Madame, driven from France long before, and rather catching their pupils' Norfolk pronunciation of French than conveying the Parisian to them. But it was beginning to be known that there was such a language as German, out of the counting-houses, and that Germany was

beginning to have a literature : and in due time there was
a young man there who had actually been in Germany,
and was translating "Nathan the Wise." When William
Taylor became eminent as almost the only German
scholar in England, old Norwich was very proud, and
grew, to say the truth, excessively conceited. She was
(and she might be) proud of her Sayers ; and Dr. Sayers
was a scholar. She boasted of having produced several
men who had produced books of one sort or another
(and to produce a book of any sort was a title to reverence
in those days). She boasted of her intellectual supper-
parties, where, amidst a pedantry which would now make
Laughter hold both his sides, there was much that was
pleasant and salutary : and finally, she called herself the
Athens of England. If Mr. Windham's family could be
induced to publish all of his papers, there would, we
believe, be found some curious lights thrown on the
social condition of old Norwich in the time of the war.
And some lawyers and politicians—Sir James Mackintosh
for one—who went that circuit in their early professional
days, used to talk of the city and its illustrious citizens
in a strain of compliment which had much amusement,
if not satire in it. They kindly brought fresh ideas to
Norwich, and in return were duly venerated, and extremely amused by so perfect a specimen of a provincial
city up in a corner, which called itself Athens.

Amidst these influences, Amelia Alderson grew up,
to be formed by them, and to renovate them, as far as it
was in the power of a clever woman to do so. She was
the only child of Dr. James Alderson, a physician of no
great mark professionally, but of liberal tastes, and fond
of literary society. Amelia lost her mother in infancy ;
and her childhood and youth were superintended by a

[I]

*Norwich
and her
literary
men.*

*The child-
hood of
Mrs. Opie.*

[I]

lady of considerable ability and book-knowledge. While she was thus training for literary ambition, John Opie, the painter, was among the tin mines in Cornwall, sketching with ochre on barn-doors, like Lawrence, and manifesting the ability which made Dr. Wolcot (Peter Pindar) bring him up to London, and prophesy his turning out one of the greatest painters the world ever saw. It takes more, however, to make a great painter than Dr. Wolcot supposed, or than the generality of persons could imagine before the continental world of Art was opened to us; and before that happened Opie was dead. After the few first of his pictures, painted in London, there appears in almost all of them a remarkable female face—singular in profile, and, as a front face, so waggish that when used for tragic purposes it moves more mirth than sympathy in the observer—a face with merry twinkling eyes, and a mouth either saucily laughing or obstinately resolute against a laugh. This is Amelia Alderson, presently become Mrs. Opie. During their few years of union, she was at her husband's elbow at his easel, or sitting for some of his historical personages, or, no doubt, obviating by her own knowledge some of the mischief arising from his defective education. We see, by some of his pictures, how much this was wanted; as, for instance, in the "Jephthah's Daughter," where the sacrifice is actually supposed to be performed by the High Priest, who stands there in full official array, as if human sacrifices were permitted by the Jewish law!

Her marriage, and her assistance to her husband.

Her first works.

And now came the time when Amelia Opie was herself to achieve fame by her tale of the "Father and Daughter." The edition on our table (the second) bears date 1801, and is illustrated by a most woeful frontispiece, designed by her husband. Her Poems appeared

the next year, adorned in like manner. The most [I]
celebrated of them—and it was very celebrated at the
time—is "The Felon's Address to his Child;" one
cannot but wonder why, in regard to the poems and the
tale alike; and especially when we see that the motto in
the title-page is taken from Mrs. Barbauld, whose fame
would have been, we imagine, considered at the time
inferior to that of her young friend Amelia. Time has
long rectified the judgment—determining that Mrs. Opie
was a jejune Mrs. Inchbald, while Mrs. Barbauld wrote
the little she did write out of a full and glowing mind,
trained to a noble mode of expression by a sound
classical education. Mrs. Opie had other accomplishments, however, than any manifested by her pen. She
sang finely—ballads sung with heartfelt impulse and *Her vocal*
pathos, and without accompaniment. Those who, as *ability.*
children, heard her sing "Lord Ullin's Daughter," will
never forget it. They cannot now read the "Come
back" of that ballad, without feeling again the anguish
conveyed in those heart-rending tones. The Prince
Regent heard them. He went to a supper somewhere
to hear Mrs. Opie sing—not long before the change
which stopped her singing everywhere but beside her old
father's chair. When she began to grow elderly, Amelia
Opie became *dévote.* Her life had been one of strong
excitements; and dearly she loved excitement; and
there was a promise of a long course of stimulation in
becoming a Quaker, which probably impelled her unconsciously to take the decided step which astonished all
her world. During Mr. Opie's life, excitements abounded.
After his death, and when her mourning was over, she
wrote little novels, read them to admiring friends in
Norwich, who cried their eyes out at the pathetic scenes,

[I] read in her dramatic manner, and then she carried them to London, got considerable sums by them, enjoyed the homage they brought to her feet, sang at supper-tables, dressed splendidly, did not scruple being present at Lady Cork's and others' Sunday concerts, and was very nearly marrying a younger brother of Lord Bute. Lord Herbert Stewart's carriage appeared, and made a great clatter in the narrow streets of Norwich ; and the old gentleman was watched into Dr. Alderson's house ; and the hours were counted which he spent, it was supposed, at Mrs. Opie's feet. But it came to nothing. For a while she continued her London visits ; and her proud father went about reading her letters about her honors.

Joins the Friends. But she suddenly discovered that all is vanity : she took to gray silks and muslin, and the "thee" and "thou," quoted Habakkuk and Micah with gusto, and set her heart upon preaching. That, however, was not allowed. Her Quaker friends could never be sufficiently sure how much was "imagination," and how much the instigation of "the inward witness;" and the privileged gallery in the chapel was closed against her, and her utterance was confined to loud sighs in the body of the Meeting. She tended her father unremittingly in his decline ; she improved greatly in balance of mind and evenness of spirits during her long and close intimacy with the Gurneys ; and there never was any doubt about her beneficent disposition, shown by her family devotedness, no less

Her benef- icent disposition. than by her bounty to the poor. Her majestic form moved through the narrowest streets of the ancient city ; and her bright face was seen lighting up the most wretched abodes. The face never lost its brightness, nor the heart its youthfulness and gayety. She was a merry laugher in her old age ; and even, if the truth be spoken, still a bit of a romp—ready for bo-peep and hide-and-seek, in the midst of a morning call, or at the end of a grave conversation. She enjoyed showing prim young Quaker girls her ornaments, plumes, and satins, and telling when she wore them : and, when in Paris, she ingenuously exhibited in her letters to her Quaker friends the conflict in her feelings when Louis Philippe, attended by his staff, stopped to converse with her in the streets of Paris, and when the Queen of the French requested her to appoint an evening for a party at the Tuileries. She made a pleasant joke of the staring of then Parisias at her little gray bonnet ; and sighed and prayed that she might not be puffed up by all the rest. She was not really spoilable ; and her later years were full of grace and kindliness. She suffered much from rheumatic lameness ; but with great cheerfulness, on the whole—almost merrily. She was cordially respected, and will be vividly remembered for life by many who have long forgotten her early fame, or perhaps had scarcely heard of it. She was a striking picture in the childhood of some who are now elderly, when her stately form was seen, half a century ago, among the old elms in her father's garden ; and she will ever be a picture in the minds of such young people as saw her seated, as upright as ever, but with her crutches behind her, at her sofa-table in her cheerful room in the Castle Meadow, any time within the last few years. The Taylors, the Sayerses, the Smiths, the Enfields—the old glories of the provincial Athens—have long been gone ; and now, with Amelia Opie, dies the last claim of the humbled city to the literary prominence which was so dear to it in the last century. The period of such provincial glory seems itself to be passing away. A lady, yet more aged than

[1]
Her cheerfulness.

The last of the Norwich celebrities.

[I]   Mrs. Opie, one who had for nearly a century scarcely left the old city, was of opinion that the depravity of the age was owing to gaslights and macadamisation. It does not require her years to show some of us that railways, free trade, and cheap publications have much to do with the extinction of the celebrity of ancient Norwich, in regard both to its material and intellectual productions. Its bombazine manufacture has gone to Yorkshire, and its literary fame to the four winds.

II.

PROFESSOR WILSON

("Christopher North").

Died April 3d, 1854.

On Monday morning died Professor Wilson, the "Chris-[*]
topher North" whom probably none of his readers ever
thought of as dead or dying, or losing any of the intense
vitality which distinguishes the ideal "Christopher North"
from all other men. The "Christopher North" and
John Wilson are separated now, and forever. The one
will live very long, if not always, and without losing an
atom of his vigor; but the other, after long sinking,
after grievous depression, and gradual extinction by paralysis, is gone; and none of the many who loved and
worshipped him could wish that he had lived another day
in the condition of his latter years.

Yet he was not very old. He was born at Paisley, in *Born in*
1788, his father being a wealthy manufacturer there. *1788.*
He entered Glasgow University at the age of thirteen,
and in four years more went to Magdalen College,
Oxford, where his extraordinary quality was recognized
at once. He was the leader in all sports, from his great
bodily strength, as well as his enthusiasm for pleasure of
that kind; and he gained the Newdegate prize for an
English poem of sixty lines. On leaving College he

[II]

Kindness of Sir Walter Scott.

bought the Elleray estate, on Windermere, which will ever be haunted by his memory; for there is not a point of interest about it or the neighborhood which he has not immortalized. So early as the beginning of 1812, we find Scott writing to Joanna Baillie of the extraordinary young man, John Wilson, who had written an elegy upon "poor Grahame," and was then engaged in a poem called the "Isle of Palms,"—"something," added Scott, curiously enough, "in the style of Southey." "He seems an excellent, warm-hearted, and enthusiastic young man; something too much, perhaps, of the latter quality places him among the list of originals." A short time after this, and in consequence of loss of property, he studied Law, and was called to the Scotch bar. So early as that date, before any of the Waverley novels appeared, the grateful young poet, who deeply felt Scott's kindness in encouraging his muse, gave him the title of the Great Magician, by which he was soon to be recognized by all the world. This was in some stanzas, called the "Magic Mirror," which appeared in the *Edinburgh Annual Register*. When John Kemble took leave of the stage at Edinburgh, and was entertained at a very remarkable dinner, where all the company believed they were taking leave of dramatic pleasure forever, Jeffrey was in the chair, and John Wilson shared the vice-presidentship with Scott. Scott's kindness to his young friend was earnest and vigilant. We find him inviting Wilson and Lockhart from Elleray to Abbotsford, the next year, fixing the precise day when he wished them to arrive; and the reason turned out to be, that Lord Melville was to be there; and it was possible that something good might turn up in the Parliament House for the young men in consequence of the interview.

For Wilson this sort of aid was soon unnecessary. He became Professor of Moral Philosophy at Edinburgh in 1820, and had already done more than any one man toward raising the character of periodical literature by his marvellous contributions to *Blackwood's Magazine*, and the stimulus his genius imparted to a whole generation of writers of that class. We all know his selection from those papers—the three volumes of "Recreations of Christopher North." There is nothing in our literature exactly like them; and we may venture to say there never will be. They are not only the most effective transcription of the moods of thought and feeling of a deeply thinking and feeling mind—a complete arresting and presentment of those moods as they pass—but an absolute realizing of the influence of Nature in a book. The scents and breezes of the moorland are carried fairly into even the sick-chamber by that book; and through it the writer practised the benevolence of the ancient rich man, and was eyes to the blind, and feet to the lame. Mr. Hallam, the calmest of critics, has declared Wilson's eloquence to be as the rushing of mighty waters; and it was no less the bracing of the mountain winds. His fame will rest on his prose writings, and not on his two chief poems, the "Isle of Palms" and the "City of the Plague;" and of his prose writings, his "Recreations" will, we imagine, outlive his three novels, "Lights and Shadows of Scottish Life," the "Trials of Margaret Lyndsay," and "The Foresters." If the marvel of his eloquence is not lessened, it is at least accounted for to those who have seen him,—or even his portrait. Such a presence is rarely seen; and more than one person has said that he reminded them of the first man, Adam; so full was that large frame of vitality, force, and sentience.

[marginal notes:]

[II]

The "Recreations of Christopher North."

Poems and novels.

His tread seemed almost to shake the streets, his eye almost saw through stone walls; and as for his voice, there was no heart that could stand before it. He swept away all hearts, whithersoever he would. No less striking was it to see him in a mood of repose, as when he steered the old packet-boat that used to pass between Bowness and Ambleside, before the steamers were put upon the Lake. Sitting motionless, with his hand upon the rudder, in the presence of journeymen and market-women, with his eye apparently looking beyond everything into nothing, and his mouth closed under his beard, as if he meant never to speak again, he was quite as impressive and immortal an image as he could have been to the students of his class or the comrades of his jovial hours.

His temperament and faults. The tendencies of such a temperament are obvious enough; and his faults arose from the indulgence of those tendencies. A few words from a friendly letter of Scott's, written when Wilson was a candidate for his professorship, will sufficiently indicate the nature of his weaknesses, and may stand for all the censure we are disposed to offer. "You must, of course," writes Scott to Mr. Lockhart, "recommend to Wilson great temper in his canvass; for wrath will do no good. After all, he must leave off sack, purge, and live cleanly as a gentleman ought to do, otherwise people will compare his present ambition to that of Sir Terry O'Fag when he wished to become a judge. 'Our pleasant vices are made the whips to scourge us,' as *Lear* says; for otherwise what could possibly stand in the way of his nomination? I trust it will take place, and give him the consistence and steadiness which are all he wants to make him the first man of the age." He did get his election; and it was not very long after that he and

Campbell, the poet, were seen one morning leaving a
tavern in Edinburgh, haggard and red-eyed, hoarse and *Wilson and*
exhausted—not only the feeble Campbell, but the mighty *Campbell :*
Wilson—they having sat *tête-à-tête* for twenty-four hours, *a scene.*
discussing poetry and wine to the top of their bent : a
remarkable spectacle in connection with the Moral Philosophy Chair in any University. But, if the constituents
of such an office crave a John Wilson to fill it, they must
take him with all his liabilities about him.

His moods were as various as those of the Mother Na- *His various*
ture he adored. In 1815, when all the rest of the world *moods.*
was in the dark about the Scotch novels, he was in excessive delight at receiving from William Laidlaw the
evidence that Colonel Mannering was Scott himself ; and
deep in proportion was his grief when he saw that genial mind going out. The trembling of his mighty
voice when he paid his tribute to Scott's genius at the
public meeting after his death moved every heart present.
He could enter into the spirit of Lake scenery deeply
with Wordsworth when floating on Windermere at sunset ;
and he could, as we see by Moore's Diary, imitate Wordsworth's monologues to admiration under the lamp at a
jovial Edinburgh supper-table. He could collect as
strange a set of oddities about him there as ever Johnson
or Fielding did in their City lodgings ; and he could
wander alone for a week along the trout streams, and by
the mountain tarns of Westmoreland. He could proudly
lead the regatta from Mr. Bolton's, at Storr's, as "Admiral
of the Lake," with Canning, Scott, Wordsworth, Southey,
and others, and shed an intellectual sunshine as radiant
as that which glittered upon Windermere ; and he could
forbid the felling of any trees at Elleray, and shroud himself in its damp gloom, when its mistress was gone, leav-

ing a bequest of melancholy which he never surmounted. The "grace and gentle goodness" of his wife were bound about his heartstrings ; and the thought of her was known and felt to underlie all his moods from the time of her death. She loved Elleray, and the trees about it ; and he allowed not a twig of them to be touched till the place grew too mossy and mournful ; and then he parted *Wilson in the Lake District.* with it. He was much beloved in that neighborhood, where he met with kindness whatever was genuine, while he repulsed and shamed all flatteries and affectations. Every old boatman and young angler, every hoary shepherd and primitive dame among the hills of the District, knew him and enjoyed his presence. He was a steady and genial friend to poor Hartley Coleridge for a long course of years. He made others happy by being so intensely happy himself, when his brighter moods were on *His last years.* him. He felt, and enjoyed too, intensely, and paid the penalty in the deep melancholy of the close of his life. He could not chasten the exuberance of his love of Nature and of genial human intercourse ; and he was cut off from both, long before his death. The sad spectacle was witnessed with respectful sorrow ; for all who had ever known him felt deeply in debt to him. He underwent an attack of pressure on the brain some years before his death ; and an access of paralysis closed the scene.

It is curious that, whereas it is universally agreed that it is by his prose that he won his immortality, he argued with Moore that the inferiority of prose to poetry was proved by the fact that there is no such thing as a school of prose, while literary history consists of a succession of schools of poetry. It may be that his prose is something new in the world. At this moment, under the emotion of parting from him, we are disposed to think it is. Nowhere can we look for such a combination of music, emotion, speculation, comment, wit, and imagination, as in some of his "Noctes Ambrosianæ," and in hundreds of the pages of "Christopher's Recreations." In them we rejoice to think the subdued spirit is revived that we have seen fail, and the dumb voice reawakened for the delight of many a future generation.

[II]

III.

JOHN GIBSON LOCKHART.

DIED AT ABBOTSFORD, NOV. 25TH, 1854.

A man of note.

HE was a man of note on various grounds. He was an author of no mean qualifications; he was the son-in-law of Scott; and he was the editor of the *Quarterly Review* after Gifford. Without being a man of genius, a great scholar, or politically or morally eminent, he had sufficient ability and accomplishment to insure considerable distinction in his own person, and his interesting connections did the rest. He was a man of considerable mark.

The younger son of a Glasgow clergyman, he was destined for the Law—more as a matter of course than from any inclination of his own; for he never liked his profession. He went to school, and afterward to the University at Glasgow, whence he was enabled to proceed to Balliol College, Oxford, by obtaining an exhibition in the gift of the Senatus Academicus. He was subsequently called to the Scotch Bar; but from the first his dependence was on literary effort; for his professional fees never amounted to 50*l*. a year. After the Peace he

Visit to Germany.

went to Germany—a not very common undertaking at that time—and saw Göthe; and his account of this incident seems to have struck Scott, when they who were to become so closely related met for the first time in private society, in May, 1818. A few days after the dinner-party at which this happened, the Messrs. Ballantyne sent to Lockhart, to propose that he should undertake a task which Scott had delayed, and wished to surrender: the writing the historical portion of the "Edinburgh Annual Register" for 1816. When he called on Scott to talk it over, the great novelist, who was then receiving 10,000*l.* a year from the new vein he had opened, assigned a characteristic reason for giving up the Register. He said that if the war had gone on, he should have enjoyed writing the history of each year as it passed; but that he would not be the recorder of Radical riots, Corn Bills, Poor Bills, and the like. These things, he said, sickened him; and he thought it fair to devolve such work upon his juniors. Mr. Lockhart first saw Abbotsford the next October, when he was sent for from Elleray, with his friend John Wilson, to meet Lord Melville, and take the chance of some professional benefit arising from the interview with the First Lord of the Admiralty, if their sins in *Blackwood* could be overlooked by him. This shows that *Blackwood's Magazine* was already rising under the re-enforcement of Wilson's strength. The strength which raised it was not Lockhart's. His satire had, then and always, a quality of malice in it, where Wilson's had only fun; and he never had Wilson's geniality of spirit. Wilson's satire instructed the humble, and amused the proud who were the objects of it; but Lockhart's caused anguish in the one case, and excited mere wrath or contempt in the other. Scott confessed that it might be from complacency at Lockhart's account of this visit to Abbotsford that he judged so favorably of "Peter's Letters to

[III]
First meeting with Sir Walter Scott.

Blackwood's Magazine.

[III]

his Kinsfolk," which appeared a few months afterward. He called its satire lenient; but all the Edinburgh Whigs were up against it as a string of libels; and Lockhart himself tells us candidly that it was a book which none but a very young and a very thoughtless person would have written.

Sophia Scott, the elder daughter of the novelist, and the one who inherited his genial and amiable spirit, his good sense, and his royal tendencies, and who was naturally the delight of his life, had just before manifested singular fortitude for so young a creature, when her father's fearful malady — cramp in the stomach— seized him in the country, alone with her and a set of distracted servants. This was an indication of what she was to be through her too short life. She married Mr. Lockhart just a year after that illness of her father's, in April, 1820; and it was her function for the seventeen years of her marriage to heal the wounds inflicted by those less amiable than herself, and to soothe the angry feelings excited on every hand, sooner or later, by the conduct of the *Quarterly Review* when in her husband's hands. As Scott recovered his strength, after that fearful illness, he busied himself in improving, for the reception of the young couple, a sequestered cottage within a short ride of Abbotsford; and he, with his own hands, transplanted to Chiefswood the creepers which had hung the old porch at Abbotsford. It was for her child that he wrote the "Tales of a Grandfather;" and that precocious boy, who died of spinal disease at the age of eleven, was the object of as passionate an attachment as Scott had perhaps ever known.

In 1820 Mr. Lockhart published his first novel, "Valerius, a Roman Story," which immediately took its

Lockhart's marriage.

place among the secondary Scottish novels, as those
were called which would have been first but for Scott's
series. That book was full of interest, and of promise
of moral beauty which was not fulfilled. The influences
then surrounding the author were eminently favorable.
He always said that the happiest years of his life were
those spent at Chiefswood. During those few years of
domestic peace he seems to have had a stronger hold of
reality than either before or after. The inveterate skep-
ticism of his nature was kept down, and he found dearer
delights than that of giving pain. Other novels followed,
—"Reginald Dalton," "Adam Blair," and "Gilbert
Earle." All are more remarkable for power in the
delineation of passion, and for beauty of writing, than
for higher qualities. Carlyle has described Lockhart's
style as "good, clear, direct, and nervous :" and so it is ;
and with genuine beauty in it, too, both of music and
of pathos. And of all he ever wrote, nothing is probably so dear to his readers as his accounts, in his Life
of his father-in-law, of the pleasures of Chiefswood,
when Scott used to sit under the great ash, with all the
dogs about him, and help the young people with their
hospitable arrangements, cooling the wine in the brook,
and proposing to dine out of doors, to get rid of the
inconvenience of small rooms and few servants. It is a
curious instance of Lockhart's moral obtuseness that,
while writing thus, he could make some most painful
and needless disclosures in regard to Scott himself in
that Life, to say nothing of his foul and elaborate misrepresentation of the Ballantynes throughout. To that
evil deed it is necessary only to refer ; for the confu-
tation immediately published was so complete, and the
establishment of the fair fame of the Ballantynes so

[III]
His novels.

*Lockhart's
Life of
Scott.*

[III] triumphant, that their libeller had his punishment very soon. Some lovers of literature and of Scott still struggled to make out that the Ballantynes and their defenders, as tradesmen, could know nothing of the feelings, nor judge of the conduct, of Scott as a gentleman. The answer was plain :—the Ballantynes were not mere tradesmen ; and if they had been, Scott made himself a tradesman, in regard to his coadjutors, and must be judged by the laws of commercial integrity. The exposures made by the Ballantynes and their friends of Scott's pecuniary obligations to them, were forced upon them by Mr. Lockhart's attacks upon their characters, and misrepresentation of their conduct and affairs. The whole controversy was occasioned by Lockhart's spontaneous indulgence in caustic satire ; and the Ballantynes came better out of it than either he or his father-in-law.

The Ballantynes.

After the publication of his novels, Mr. Lockhart was summoned, one spring day of 1825, to a conference at Abbotsford, to which Constable and James Ballantyne were parties. The project to be discussed was that memorable one of Constable's, to revolutionize "the whole art and traffic of bookselling." From that conference sprang the cheap literature of the last quarter of a century and one of the first volumes produced under the new notion was Lockhart's "Life of Burns," which appeared early in Constable's Miscellany. It was in the same year, 1825, that he succeeded Gifford in the editorship of the *Quarterly Review*, and of course removed to London. If he had not Gifford's thorough scholarship, he had eminent literary ability,—readiness, industry, everything but good principle and a good spirit. These immense exceptions we are compelled to make ; and

A conference at Abbotsford.

Becomes editor of the "Quarterly Review."

they are not a new censure. All the world was always
aware of the sins of the *Quarterly*, under Lockhart's
management; and the best-informed had cause to view
them the most severely. Everybody knows what
Croker's political articles were like. Everybody knows
how the publisher was now and then compelled to re-
publish as they had originally stood, articles which had
been interpolated, by Croker and Lockhart (whose
names were always associated in regard to the *Review*),
with libels and malicious jokes. In their recklessness
they drew upon themselves an amount of reprobation in
literary circles which thin-skinned men could never have
endured. Now, the young author of a father's biography was invited by the editor to send him early proof-
sheets, for the benefit of a speedy review, and the
review did what it could to damn the book before it was
fairly in the hands of the public; and now, the vanity of
some second or third-rate author was flattered and drawn
out in private intercourse, to obtain material for a caricature in the next *Quarterly*. As an able man, a great
admirer of the literary merits of the *Review*, and no
sufferer by it, observed, "The well-connected and vigorous and successful have nothing to apprehend from the
Quarterly; but, as sure as people are in any way broken
or feeble—as sure as they are old, or blind, or deaf, or
absent on their travels, or superannuated, or bankrupt,
or dead—the *Quarterly* is upon them." It was the
wounds thus inflicted that the gentle wife set herself to
heal, when she possibly could. It was amidst the explosions of friendships, formed in flattery, and broken off
by treachery—amidst the wrath of every kind and degree evoked by her husband, or under his permission,
that her modest dignity and her cheerful kindliness com-

[III]

*The literary
offences of
Croker and
Lockhart.*

2*

[III]

manded admiration, and **won love from those who** would never **more meet the reckless editor, who** quizzed the emotions **he had excited.** His success was all-sufficient, in his own estimate. The transcendent literary merits of the *Review* placed it **high** above failure ; and he did not care for censure. It was his own callousness which made the sensitiveness of others **so** highly amusing to him. Yet there are passages **even in** his later writings which make one wonder what **he did,** in an ordinary way, with feelings which seem to have dwelt in him— to judge by their occasional manifestation. For instance, there is something remarkable in his selection, from among all Scott's writings, of the passage of most marked spiritual beauty—that passage of his preface to "Ivanhoe" in which he accounts for not having made Rebecca's lot "end happily." Such a choice seems to show that Lockhart should properly have won something more than admiration of his accomplishments as a writer and converser, and fear of him as a satirist. It seems as if there might have been, but for his own waywardness, some of that personal respect and con- fidence, and free and constant friendship, which he never enjoyed nor appeared to desire. It appears as if there was truth in the remark made by Allan Cunning- ham, that there was "heart in Lockhart when one got through the crust."

Lockhart's callousness.

A saying of Allan Cunning- ham.

The good-will which he did not seek in his happy days, was won for him by the deep and manifold sorrows of his latter years. The extraordinary sweep made by death in his wife's family is a world-wide wonder and sorrow. Lady Scott went first ; and the beloved child—Lockhart's intelligent boy, so well known under the name **of** Hugh Littlejohn—died when the

Heavy griefs.

[III]

grandfather's mind was dim and clouded. Soon after Scott's death, his younger daughter and worn-out nurse followed him; and in four years more, Mrs. Lockhart. The young Sir Walter died childless in India, and his brother Charles, unmarried, in Persia. Lockhart was left with a son and a daughter. As years and griefs began to press heavily upon him, new sorrow arose in his narrow domestic circle. His son was never any comfort to him, and died in early manhood. The only remaining descendant of Scott, Lockhart's daughter, was married, and became so fervent and obedient a Catholic, as to render all intimate intercourse between the forlorn father and his only child impossible. He was now opulent. An estate had descended to him through an elder brother; and he held an office—that of Auditor of the Duchy of Cornwall—which yielded him 300*l.* a year. He had given up the labor of editing the *Quarterly :* but what were opulence and leisure to him now? Those who saw him in his daily walk in London, his handsome countenance—always with a lowering and sardonic expression—now darkened with sadness, and the thin lips compressed more than ever, as by pain of mind, forgave, in respectful compassion for one so visited, all causes of quarrel, however just, and threw themselves, as it were, into his mind, seeing again the early pranks with "Christopher North," the dinings by the brook at Chiefswood, the glories of the Abbotsford sporting parties, the travels with Scott in Ireland, and the home in Regent's Park, with the gentle Sophia presiding. Comparing these scenes with the actual forlornness of his last years, there was no heart that could not pity and forgive, and carefully award him his due, as a writer who has afforded much pleasure in his day, and

The forlornness of his last years.

[III] left a precious bequest to posterity in his Life of the great Novelist, purged, as we hope it will be, of whatever is untrue and unkind, and rendered as safe as it is beautiful.

Mr. Lockhart travelled abroad in 1853, under continually failing health. He has left a name which will live in literature, both on his own account, and through his family and literary connections.

IV.

MARY RUSSELL MITFORD.

DIED JANUARY 10TH, 1855.

Miss Mitford was old, having been born in December, 1786. Her decline was so protracted that there could be no surprise or shock mingled with the sorrow which the English public could not but feel on the occasion of her death. After a fall from her pony-chaise in the autumn of 1852, her life was understood to be very precarious. The interest which was taken in her state might appear to be disproportionate to her abilities and her achievements; but if so, there must be a reason for it, and the reason is that she was so genial and so cheerful as to command the affection of multitudes who would have given no heed to a much higher order of genius invested with less of moral charm. There is nothing so popular as cheerfulness; and when the cheerfulness is of the unfailing sort which arises from amiability and interior content, it deserves such love as attended Mary Russell Mitford to her grave. Her ability was very considerable. Her power of description was unique. She had a charming humor, and her style was delightful. Yet were her stories read with a relish which exceeded even so fair a justification as this—with a relish which the judgment could hardly account for; and this pleasant, compelled

Her unfailing cheerfulness.

enjoyment was no doubt ascribable to the glow of good spirits and kindliness which lighted up and warmed everything that her mind produced. She may be considered as the representative of household cheerfulness in the humbler range of the literature of fiction.

Her tendencies showed themselves early. She took up the pen almost in childhood, and was an avowed poet, in print, before she was four-and-twenty. However hard was her filial duty when she was herself growing old, she had all her own way in her early years ; and her way seems to have been to write an immense quantity of verse as the pleasantest thing she could find to do.

She was born at Alresford, in Hampshire. Her father was a physician, one of the Northumberland family of Mitfords. Her mother was the child of the old age of a Hampshire clergyman, who had seen Pope, and been intimate with Fielding. Her father was, as it is understood, disliked and disapproved, if not despised, by everybody but his devoted daughter, whose infatuation it was to think him something very great and good ; whereas there seems to be really nothing to remember him by but his singular and unaccountable extravagance in money matters, and the selfishness with which he went on to the last, obtaining, by hook and by crook, costly indulgences, which nobody else in his line of life, however independent of creditors, thought of wishing for. Dr. Mitford ran through half-a-dozen fortunes, shifted about to half-a-dozen grand residences, and passed the last quarter of a century of his life in a cottage, where, humble as seemed his mode of living, he could not keep out of debt, or the shame of perpetual begging from the friends whom his daughter had won. His only child was carried about, before she was old enough for school,

Dr.
Mitford.

from Alresford to Reading ; from Reading to Lyme, and
thence to London, where, when she was ten years old,
her father was making up his mind to retrench and do
something at last—a resolution which went the way of all
the former ones. It was at that time the well-known incident happened which Miss Mitford related with so much
spirit half a century afterward.

The little girl chose for a birthday present a lottery
ticket of a particular number, to which she stuck, in
spite of much persuasion to change it, and which turned
up a prize of 20,000*l.* This money soon disappeared,
like some 40,000*l.*, which had vanished before. Her
father put her to school in London, and there she spent
five years, while he was amusing himself with building a
very large house, four miles from Reading, to which she
returned at the age of fifteen, to write poetry, and dream
of becoming an authoress. After 1810 she put forth a
volume almost every year. This was all done for pleasure ; but she was meanwhile giving up to her selfish
father one legacy after another, left to herself by the
opulent families on both sides, after her mother's handsome fortune was exhausted ; and hence at length arose
the necessity of her writing for the sake of the money she
could earn.

In their poverty they went to lodge for a summer at a
cottage in the village of Three Mile Cross, near Reading, and there they held on for the rest of Dr. Mitford's
long life. The poetess looked round her, and described
in prose what she saw, sending the papers which, collected, form the celebrated "Our Village," to Campbell
for the *New Monthly Magazine.* Campbell made the
mistake of rejecting them—an error in which he was
followed by a great number and variety of other editors.

[IV]

A prize in a lottery.

Becomes an authoress.

"Our Village."

[IV]

It was in *The Lady's Magazine*, of all places, that articles destined to make a literary reputation of no mean order first appeared. They were published in a collected form in 1823 ; and from that time forward Miss Mitford was sure of the guineas whenever she chose to draw for them in the form of pleasant stores under her well-known and welcome signature. Few of her many readers, however, knew at what cost these pleasant stories were produced. They seem to flow easily enough ; and their sportive style suggests anything but the toil and anxiety amidst which they were spun out. It is observable that each story is as complete and rounded as a sonnet, and provided with a plot which would serve for a novel if expanded. Each has a catastrophe—generally a surprise, elaborately wrought out in concealment. It was for stories of this kind that Miss Mitford exchanged the earlier and easier sketches from the Nature around her which we find in "Our Village ;" and the exchange increased immensely the call upon her energies. But the money must be had, and the Annuals paid handsomely ; and thus, therefore, the devoted daughter em-

Father and daughter.

ployed her talents, spoiling her father, and wearing herself out, but delighting an enormous number of readers. After frittering away the whole day, incessantly on foot, or otherwise fatiguing herself, at his beck and call, and receiving his friends, and reading him to sleep in the afternoons till she had no voice left, the hour came when she might put him to bed. But her own day's work still remained to be done. It was not a sort of work which could be done by powers, jaded like hers, without some stimulus or relief ; and hence the necessity of doses of laudanum to carry her through her task. When the necessity ceased by the death of her father,

her practice of taking laudanum ceased; but her health had become radically impaired, and her nervous system was rendered unfit to meet any such shock as that which overthrew it at last. Miss Mitford so toiling by candlelight, while the hard master who had made her his servant all day was asleep in the next room, is as painful an instance of the struggles of human life as the melancholy of a buffoon, or the heart-break—that "secret known to all"—of a boasting Emperor of All the Russias.

While this was her course of life, however, she was undergoing something of an intellectual training, together with her moral discipline. All this reading to her father, and the impossibility of commanding her time for any other employment than reading by snatches (except gardening), brought her into acquaintance with a wide field of English literature; and some of it of an uncommon kind. The fruits are seen in one of her latest works—her "Notes of a Literary Life;" and in her indomitable inclination to write Tragedies for immediate representation. Several of her plays were acted; and she herself was wont to declare that she should be immortalized by them, if at all; moreover, there are critics who agree with her: yet her case certainly appears to us to be one of that numerous class in which the pursuit of dramatic fame is a delusion and a snare. In no other act or attempt of her life did Miss Mitford manifest any of those qualities of mind which are essential to success in this the highest walk of literature. It does not appear that she had any insight into passion, any conception of the depths of human character, or the scope of human experience. Ability of a certain sort there is in her plays; but no depth, and no compass. Four tragedies and an opera of hers were acted at our first theatres;

Miss Mitford's Plays.

[IV]

[IV]

and we hear no more of *Julian, Foscari, Rienzi,* or *Charles I.* At first the difficulties were imputed to dramatic censors, and the great actors, and injudicious or lukewarm friends ; but all that was over long ago. The tragedies were acted, and we hear no more of them. It is true Mr. Colman did refuse his sanction to *Charles I.*

" Charles I." and " Cromwell."

when it bore the name *Cromwell* (an amusing incident to have happened in the reign of poor William IV., whose simple head was very safe on his shoulders) ; and it is true that Young and Macready wrangled so long about the principal characters in her first acted play, that the tantalized authoress began to wonder whether it would ever appear : but the plays have all appeared ; and they do not keep the stage, though Miss Mitford's friends were able and willing to do all that interest, literary and dramatic, can do in such a case. All the evidence of her career seems to show that her true line was that in which she obtained an early, decisive, and permanent success—much humbler than the Dramatic, but that in which she has given a great deal of pleasure to a multitude of readers. Her descriptions of scenery, brutes, and human beings have such singular merit that she may be regarded as the founder of a new style ; and if the freshness wore off with time, there was much more than a compensation in the fine spirit and resignation of cheerfulness which breathed through everything she wrote, and endeared her as a suffering friend to thousands who formerly regarded her only as a most entertaining stranger.

A subscription and a pension.

Dr. Mitford died in 1842, leaving his affairs in such a state, that relief for his daughter had to be obtained by a subscription among her friends and admirers, which was soon followed by a pension from the Crown. The daughter inherited or contracted some of her father's extremely easy feelings about money, and its sources and uses; but the temptation to that sort of laxity was removed or infinitely lessened when she was left alone with a very sufficient provision. She removed to a cottage at Swallowfield, near Reading, in 1851; and there, with her pony-chaise, her kind neighbors, her distant admirers, and the amusement of bringing out a succession of volumes, the materials of which were under her hand, she found resources enough to make her days cheerful, even after the accident which rendered her a suffering prisoner for the last two years of her life. She remained to the end the most sympathizing and indulgent friend of the young, and the most good-humored of comrades to people of all ages and conditions. However helpless, she was still bright: and her vitality of mind and heart was never more striking or more genial than when she was visibly dying by inches, and alluding with a smile to the deep and still bed which she should occupy among the sunshine and flickering shadows of the village churchyard. Finally, the long exhaustion ended in an easy and quiet death.

Though not gifted with lofty genius, or commanding powers of any sort, Miss Mitford has been sufficiently conspicuous in the literary history of her time to claim an expression of respect and regret on her leaving us. Her talents and her character were essentially womanly; and she was fortunate in living in an age when womanly ability in the department of Letters obtains respect and observance, as sincerely and readily as womanly character commands reverence and affection in every age.

[IV]

Her life at Swallowfield.

V.

CHARLOTTE BRONTË [1]

("CURRER BELL").

DIED MARCH 31st, 1855.

"CURRER BELL" is dead! The early death of the large family of whom she was the sole survivor, prepared all who knew the circumstances to expect the loss of this gifted creature at any time ; but not the less deep will be the grief of society that her genius will yield us nothing more. We have three works from her, which will hold their place in the literature of our century ; and but for her frail health, there might have been three times three, for she was under forty, and her genius was not of an exhaustible kind. If it had been exhaustible, it would have been exhausted some time since. She had every inducement that could have availed with one less high-minded to publish two or three novels a year. Fame waited upon all she did ; and she might have enriched herself by very slight exertion ; but her steady conviction was that the publication of a

Her conscientiousness.

[1] In signing her letters, and giving her address, Charlotte spelt her name Brontë. But on the monumental stone in the church where they worshipped, where the successive deaths of the whole family are recorded, the name stands as Brontë ; and this must be considered the established spelling.

book is a solemn act of conscience; in the case of a novel as much as any other kind of book. She was not fond of speaking of herself and her conscience; but she now and then uttered to her very few friends things which may, alas! be told now, without fear of hurting her sensitive nature,—things which ought to be told in her honor. Among these sayings was one which explains the long interval between her works. She said *The long interval between her works.* that she thought every serious delineation of life ought to be the product of personal experience and observation, —experience naturally occurring, and observation of a normal, and not of a forced or special kind. "I have not accumulated, since I published 'Shirley,'" she said, " what makes it needful for me to speak again; and, till I do, may God give me grace to be dumb!" She had a conscientiousness which could not be relaxed by praise or even sympathy—dear as sympathy was to her keen affections. She had no vanity which praise could aggravate or censure mortify. She calmly read all adverse reviews of her books for the sake of instruction; and when she could not recognize the aptness of the criticism, she was more puzzled than hurt or angry. The common flatteries which wait upon literary success she quizzed with charming grace; and any occasional severity, such as literary women are favored with at the beginning of their course, she accepted with a humility which was full of dignity and charm. From her feeble constitution of body, her sufferings by the death of her whole family, and the secluded and monotonous life she led, she became morbidly sensitive in some respects; but in her high vocation she had, in addition to the deep intuitions of a gifted woman, the strength of a man, the patience of a hero, and the conscientiousness of a saint.

[V]

[V]

In the points in which women are usually most weak—in regard to opinion, to appreciation, to applause—her moral strength fell not a whit behind the intellectual force manifested in her works. Though passion occupies *Her pictures* too prominent a place in her pictures of Life, though *of life.* women have to complain that she represents Love as the whole and sole concern of their lives, and though governesses especially have reason to remonstrate, and do remonstrate, that their share of human conflict is laid open somewhat rudely and inconsiderately, and with enormous exaggeration, to social observation, it is a true social blessing that we have had a female writer who has discountenanced sentimentalism and feeble egotism with such practical force as is apparent in the works of "Currer Bell." Her heroines love too readily, too vehemently, and sometimes after a fashion which their female readers may resent ; but they do their duty through everything, and are healthy in action, however morbid in passion.

How admirable this strength is—how wonderful this force of integrity—can hardly be understood by any but the few who know the story of this remarkable woman's life. The account of the school in "Jane Eyre" is *Schooldays* only too true. The "Helen" of that tale is—not pre- *and after.* cisely the eldest sister, who died there—but more like her than any other real person. She is that sister, "with a difference." Another sister died at home soon after leaving the school, and in consequence of its hardships ; and "Currer Bell" (Charlotte Brontë) was never free, while there (for a year and a half), from the gnawing sensation, or consequent feebleness, of downright hunger ; and she never grew an inch from that time. She was the smallest of women ; and it was that school which stunted her growth.　As she tells us in "Jane Eyre," the visitation of an epidemic caused a total change and radical reform in the establishment, which was even removed to another site.　But the reform came too late to reverse the destiny of the doomed family of the Brontës.

These wonderful girls were the daughters of a clergyman, who, now[1] very aged and infirm, survives his wife and all his many children.　The name Brontë (an abbreviation of Bronterre) is Irish, and very ancient. The mother died many years ago, and several of her children.　When the reading world began to have an interest in their existence, there were three sisters and a brother living with their father at Haworth, near Keighley, in Yorkshire.　The girls had been out as governesses: Charlotte at Brussels, as is no secret to the readers of "Villette."　They rejoiced to meet again at home—Charlotte, Emily, and Ann ("Currer," "Ellis," and "Acton").　In her obituary notice of her two sisters, "Currer" reveals something of their process of authorship, and their experience of failure and success. How terrible some of their experience of life was, in the midst of the domestic freedom and indulgence afforded them by their studious father, may be seen by the fearful representations of masculine nature and character found in the novels and tales of Emily and Ann.　They considered it their duty, they told us, to present life as they knew it; and they gave us "Wuthering Heights," and "The Tenant of Wildfell Hall." Such an experience as this indicates is really perplexing to English people in general; and all that we have to do with it is to bear it in mind when dis-

[V]

The Brontë family.

---

[1] 1855.

[V]

" *Jane Eyre*" *and Charlotte Brontë.*

posed to pass criticism on the coarseness which to a certain degree pervades the works of all the sisters, and the repulsiveness which makes the tales by Emily and Ann really horrible to people who have not iron nerves.

"Jane Eyre" was naturally and universally supposed to be Charlotte herself; but she always denied it calmly, cheerfully, and with the obvious sincerity which characterized all she said. She declared that there was no more ground for the assertion than this: she once told her sisters that they were wrong—even morally wrong—in making their heroines beautiful, as a matter of course. They replied that it was impossible to make a heroine interesting on other terms. Her answer was: "I will prove to you that you are wrong. I will show to you a heroine as small and as plain as myself, who shall be as interesting as any of yours." "Hence 'Jane Eyre,'" said she, in telling the anecdote: "but she is not myself any further than that." As the work went on, the interest deepened to the writer. When she came to "Thornfield," she could not stop. Being short-sighted to excess, she wrote in little square paper books, held close to her eyes, and (the first copy) in pencil. On she went, writing incessantly for three weeks; by which time she had carried her heroine away from Thornfield, and was herself in a fever, which compelled her to pause. The rest was written with less vehemence, and with more anxious care: the world adds, with less vigor and interest. She could gratify her singular reserve in regard to the publication of this remarkable book. We all remember how long it was before we could learn who wrote it, and any particulars of the writer, when the name was revealed. She was living among the wild

Yorkshire hills, with a father who was too much absorbed in his studies to notice her occupations : in a place where newspapers were never seen (or where she never saw any), and in a house where the servants knew nothing about books, manuscripts, proofs, or the post. When she told her secret to her father, she carried her book in one hand and an adverse review in the other, to save his simple and unworldly mind from rash expectations of a fame and fortune which she was determined should never be the aims of her life. That we have had only two novels since, shows how deeply grounded was this resolve.

"Shirley" was conceived and wrought out in the midst of fearful domestic griefs. Her only brother, a young man of once splendid promise, which was early blighted, and both her remaining sisters, died in one year. There was something inexpressibly affecting in the aspect of the frail little creature who had done such wonderful things, and who was able to bear up, with so bright an eye and so composed a countenance, under not only such a weight of sorrow, but such an prospect of solitude. In her deep mourning dress (neat as a Quaker's), with her beautiful hair, smooth and brown, her fine eyes, and her sensible face indicating a habit of self-control, she seemed a perfect household image—irresistibly recalling Wordsworth's description of that domestic treasure. And she was this. She was as able at the needle as at the pen. The household knew the excellence of her cookery before they heard of that of her books. In so utter a seclusion as she lived in—in those dreary wilds where she was not strong enough to roam over the hills ; in that retreat where her studious father rarely broke the silence—and there was no one else to. do it ; in that forlorn house, planted on the very clay of the churchyard, where the

Domestic griefs.

3

[V]

Her marriage.

graves of her sisters were before her window; in such a living sepulchre, her mind could not but prey upon itself; and how it did suffer, we see in the more painful portions of her last novel, "Villette." She said, with a change in her steady countenance, that she should feel very lonely when her aged father died. But she formed new ties after that. She married; and it is the old father who survives to mourn her. He knows, to his comfort, that it is not for long. Others now mourn her, in a domestic sense; and as for the public, there can be no doubt that a pang will be felt, in the midst of the strongest interests of the day, through the length and breadth of the land, and in the very heart of Germany (where her works are singularly appreciated), France, and America, that the "Currer Bell" who so lately stole as a shadow into the field of contemporary literature has already become a shadow again—vanished from our view, and henceforth haunting only the memory of the multitude whose expectation was fixed upon her.

VI.

SAMUEL ROGERS.

DIED DECEMBER 18TH, 1855.

THE author of "The Pleasures of Memory" has died at his house in St. James's-place, in the ninety-sixth year of his age.

Samuel Rogers has been spoken of, ever since anybody can remember, as "Rogers the Poet." It is less as a poet, however, that his name will live than as a Patron of Literature—probably the last of that class who will in England be called a Mecænas. His life was a remarkable one, from the great age he attained during a critical period of civilization ; and his function was a remarkable one— that of representing the bridge over which Literature has passed from the old condition of patronage to the new one of independence. He heard "the talk of the town" (recorded by Dr. Adams) on Johnson's Letter to Lord Chesterfield ; and he lived to see the improvement of the Copyright law, the removal of most of the Taxes on Knowledge, and so vast an increase of the reading public as has rendered the function of patron of authorship obsolete. No patron could now help an author to fame ; and every author who has anything genuine to say can say it without dreaming of any application to a rich man. Samuel

An English Mecænas.

[VI]

*Contempo-
rary events.*

Rogers lived through the whole period when the publishers were the patrons, and witnessed the complete success of Mr. Dickens's plan of independence of the publishers themselves. He was a youth of fifteen or thereabouts when half "the town" was scandalized at Dr. Johnson's audacity in saying what he did to Lord Chesterfield; and the other half was delighted at the courage of the rebuke. It was not long before that the "Letters of Junius" had burst upon the political world; and Rogers was quite old enough to understand the nature of the triumph when the prosecution of Woodfall failed, and the press preserved its liberty under the assaults of Royal and Ministerial displeasure. His connections in life fixed his attention full on the persecution of Priestley and other vindicators of liberty of speech; while he saw, in curious combination with this phase, that kind of patronage which even the Priestleys of those days accepted as a matter of course:— Dr. Priestley living with Lord Shelburne, without office; and afterward, his being provided with an income by the subscription of friends, to enable him to carry on his philosophical researches. Then came the new aspect of things, when the Byrons, the Moores, Campbells, and Scotts, were the clients of the Murrays, the Longmans, and the Constables—that remarkable but rather short transition stage when, as Moore said, the patrons learned perforce, through interest, the taste which had not been formed by education. Those were the days of bookselling monopoly, when the publisher decided what the reading public should have to read, and at what price. Rogers saw that monopoly virtually destroyed; the greatness of the great houses passing away, or reduced to that of trade eminence simply; and authors and the public brought face to face, or certain to be so presently. His own function, all the while, was a mixed one, in accordance with the changes of the time. He was, in the course of his long life, both client and patron; and for a great part of it he was both at once. His purse was open to the poor author, and his influence with the great publishers was at his service, while he himself sat at great men's tables as a poet and a wit, more even than as a connoisseur in Art; and certainly much more than as a rich banker. The last character he kept out of sight as much as possible. When, some years since, his bank was robbed to so enormous an amount by the pillage of a safe that everybody supposed it must stop payment; and when it did not stop, and all his great friends testified their sympathy first, and then their joy, it was a curious thing to observe the old poet's bearing, and to hear the remarks upon it. He was wonderfully reserved, and passed off the whole with a few quiet jokes, through which was plainly seen his mortification at being recognized as a banker, in a sphere where he hoped he was known as an associate of the great, and the first connoisseur in pictures in England.

His was not a case of early determination of the course of life. In his early youth, his father one evening asked all his boys what they would be. Sam would not tell unless he might write it down, for nobody but his father to see. What he wrote was, "A Unitarian minister." He was destined for business, however; but his love of literature was not thwarted by it. We have seen Moore die in decrepit old age; yet did Moore, in his boyhood (when he was fourteen), delight in Rogers's "Pleasures of Memory"—the poem being then so common as to have found its way into schools in class-books and collections. When young Horner came to

[margin notes:] [VI] *The poet and wit,* *and banker*

[VI]   London to begin his career, he found Rogers a member
of the King of Clubs, the intimate of Mackintosh (who
was his junior), Scarlett, Sharpe, and others—long gone
to the grave as old men—and one, Maltby, who was a
twin wonder with himself as to years. The last evening
that Mackintosh spent in London before his departure
for India was at Rogers's. "Somewhat a melancholy
evening" we are told it was ; and the host, then between
In middle   forty and fifty, must have felt the uncertainty of the party
age.   reassembling, to spend more such evenings as those that
were gone. And some were dead before Mackintosh
returned ; but the host lived to tell, half a century afterward, of the sober sadness of that parting converse. It
was Rogers who "blabbed" about the duel between
Jeffrey and Moore, and was the cause of their folly being
rendered harmless ; and it was he who bailed Moore : it
was he who negotiated a treaty of peace between them ;
and it was at his house that they met and became friends.
Such were his services of one kind to literature—using
his dignity of seniority to keep these young wits in order.
He must have been lively in those days—"the Bachelor,"
as his name was among his friends ; and he never married.
Moore names him as one "of those agreeable rattles
who seem to think life such a treat that they never can
get enough of it." One wonders whether he had had
enough of it fifty years later, when Sydney Smith (one of
"the agreeable rattles") had long laid down his, after
having for some time told his comrades that he thought
life "a very middling affair," and should not be sorry
when he had done with it. There was much to render
life agreeable to a man of Rogers's tastes, it must be
owned. He saw Garrick, and watched the entire career
of every good actor since. All the Kembles fell within

his span. He heard the first remarks on the "Vicar of Wakefield," and read, damp from the press, all the fiction that has appeared since from the Burneys, the Edgeworths, the Scotts, the Dickenses, and the Thackerays. As for the poetry, he was aghast at the rapidity with which the Scotts, Byrons, and Moores poured out their works; and even Campbell was too quick for him,—he, with all his leisure, and being always at it, producing to the amount of two octavo volumes in his whole life. The charge of haste and incompleteness alleged against his "Columbus," in the *Edinburgh Review*, forty years since, was very exasperating to him; and so absurd that one cannot but suspect Sydney Smith of being the author of it, for the sake of contrast with his conversational description of Rogers's method of composition. Somebody asked, one day, whether Rogers had written anything lately. "Only a couplet," was the reply—(the couplet being his celebrated epigram on Lord Dudley). "*Only* a couplet!" exclaimed Sydney Smith. "Why, what would you have? When Rogers produces a couplet, he goes to bed, and the knocker is tied,—and straw is laid down,—and caudle is made,—and the answer to inquiries is, that Mr. Rogers is as well as can be expected." Thus, while he was cogitating his few pages of verse, "daily adding couplets," as Moore said, showing a forthcoming poem in boards, "but still making alterations," he was now and then seeing a whole new world of poetical subject and treatment laid open; and not seldom helping to facilitate the disclosure. Moore always said that he owed to Rogers the idea of "Lalla Rookh." Rogers had lingered so long over his story of the "Foscari," that Byron did it first, to his great distress; but he received the drama with a very good grace. Meantime,

[VI]

His method of composition.

[VI]
His deeds of munificence.
he was always substantially helping poor poets. Besides the innumerable instances, known only to his intimates, of the attention he bestowed, as well as the money, in the case of poetical basket-makers, poetical footmen, and other such hopeless sons of the Muse, his deeds of munificence toward men of genius were too great to be concealed. His aids to Moore have been recently made known by the publication of Moore's Diaries. It was Rogers who secured to Crabbe the 3,000*l.* from Murray, which were in jeopardy before. He advanced 500*l.* to Campbell to purchase a share of the *Metropolitan Magazine*, and refused security. And he gave thought, took trouble, used influence, and adventured advice. This was the conduct and the method of the last of the Patrons of Literature in England.

The draw-backs.
All honor to him for this! But not the less must the drawbacks be brought into the account. In recording the last of any social phase, it is dishonest to present the bright parts without the shadows; and Rogers's remarkable position was due almost as much to his faults as his virtues. He was, plainly speaking, at once a flatterer and a cynic. It was impossible for those who knew him best to say, at any moment, whether he was in earnest or covert jest. Whether he ever was in earnest, there is no sort of evidence but his acts; and the consequence was that his flattery went for nothing, except with novices, while his causticity bit as deep as he intended. He would begin with a series of outrageous compliments, in a measured style which forbade interruption; and, if he was allowed to finish, would go away and boast how much he had made a victim swallow. He would accept a constant seat at a great man's table, flatter his host to the top of his bent, and then, as is upon record, go

away and say that the company there was got up by
conscription—that there were two parties before whom
everybody must appear, his host and the police. Where
it was safe, he would try his sarcasms on the victims
themselves. A multitude of his sayings are rankling in
people's memories which could not possibly have had
any other origin than the love of giving pain. Some
were so atrocious as to suggest the idea that he had a
sort of psychological curiosity to see how people could
bear such inflictions. Those who could bear them, and
especially those who despised them, stood well with him.
In that case, there was something more like reality in the
tone of his subsequent intercourse than in ordinary cases.
The relation which this propensity of his bore to his
position was direct. It placed him at great men's tables
and kept him there, more than any other of his qualifications. His poetry alone would not have done it. His
love and knowledge of Art would not have done it ; and
much less his wealth. His causticity was his pass-key
everywhere. Except the worship paid to the Railway
King for his wealth, we know of nothing in modern
society so extraordinary and humiliating as the deference
paid to Rogers for his ill-nature. It became a sort of
public apprehension, increasing with his years, till it
ceased to be disgraceful in the eyes of the coteries, and
the flatterer was flattered, and the backbiter was pro-
pitiated, almost without disguise or shame, on account of
his bitter wit. "Rogers amusing and sarcastic as usual;"
—this note of Moore's may stand as the general description of him by those who hoped, each for himself,
to propitiate the cynic. As age advanced upon him, the
admixture of the generous and the malignant in him
became more singular. A footman robbed him of a

His ill-nature, and the deference paid to it.

3*

[VI]

A curious human problem.

large quantity of plate; and of a kind which was inestimable to him. He was incensed, and desired never to hear of the fellow more,—the man having absconded. Not many months afterward, Rogers was paying the passage to New York of the man's wife and family— somebody having told him that that family junction might afford a chance of the man's reformation. Such were his deeds at the very time that his tongue was dropping verjuice, and his wit was sneering behind backs at a whole circle of old friends and hospitable entertainers. Such was the curious human problem offered to the analyst of character, and such is the needful explanation of the mixed character of client and patron which Rogers sustained to the last.

His celebrated literary breakfasts will not be forgotten during the generation of those who enjoyed them. They became at last painful when the aged man's memory failed while his causticity remained. His hold on life was very strong. He who was an authority on the incidents of the Hastings' trial, and who was in Fox's room when he was dying,—he who saw George III. a young man, and was growing into manhood when Johnson went to the Hebrides, survived for several years being run over by a cab of the construction of the middle of the nineteenth century. His poetry could scarcely be said to live so long as himself, as it was rather the illustrations with which it was graced than the verse itself that kept the volumes on sale and within view. The elegance and correctness of his verse are beyond question; but the higher and more substantial qualities of true poetry will hardly be recognized there. It should be remembered that there is a piece of prose writing of his of which Mackintosh said that "Hume could not

improve the thoughts nor Addison the language." That
gem is the piece on Assassination, in his "Italy." In it
may be clearly traced the influence of his early noncon-
formist education. When he wrote it, half a lifetime
ago, worldliness had not quite choked the good seed of
early-sown philosophy ; and the natural magnanimity of
the man was not extinguished by the passions—as strong
as any in their way—which spring from the soil of conventionalism. If Rogers is to be judged by his writings,
let it be by such fragments as that little essay : if further,
by his deeds rather than his words. So may the world
retain the fairest remembrance of the last English
Mecænas, and the only man among us perhaps who has
illustrated in his own person the position at once of
patron and of client.

[VI]

VII.

JOHN WILSON CROKER.

Died August 10th, 1857.

Conspicuous in politics and literature.

John Wilson Croker was a conspicuous man during a long course of years in politics and literature. He was widely known as Secretary to the Admiralty—which office he held for one-and-twenty years; as a Member of Parliament for twenty-five years; as an industrious and accomplished author; and, above all, perhaps, as the wickedest of reviewers,—that is, as the author of the foul and false political articles in the *Quarterly Review*, which stand out as the disgrace of the periodical literature of our time. His natural abilities, his capacity and inclination for toil, the mingled violence and causticity of his temper, and his entire unscrupulousness in matters both of feeling and of statement, combined to make him a remarkable, if not a very loveable personage, and a useful though not very honorable member of a political party.

He was the son of the Surveyor-General of Ireland, and was born in that Connaught which was then the "hell" of the empire. "To Hell or Connaught," was still the imprecation of the day when Croker was born; that is, in 1780. He was always called an Irishman; and very properly, as Galway was his native place; but he

was of English descent. As for temperament, we do not
know that either England or Ireland would be very anxious to claim him : and he certainly was *sui generis*—remarkably independent of the influences which largely af-
fect the characters of most men. He was educated at
Trinity College, Dublin, and was called to the bar in 1802.
His first publication, "Familiar Epistles to F. E. Jones,
Esq.," shows that his proneness to sarcasm existed
early ; but the higher qualities which once made him
the hope of the Tory party were then so much more
vigorous than at a later time, that the expectations
excited by the outset of his public life were justifiable.
It was in 1807 that he entered Parliament, as Member
for Downpatrick ; and within two years he was Secretary
to the Admiralty. He had by that time given high proof
of his ability in his celebrated pamphlet on the "Past
and Present State of Ireland." The authorship was for
some time uncertain. Because it was candid and painfully faithful, the *Edinburgh Review*, so early as 1813,
could not believe it to be his ; while, on the other hand,
there was the wonder that the man who so wrote about
Ireland should be so speedily invited to office by the
Government under Perceval. That Irish pamphlet
may be now regarded as perhaps the most honorable
achievement of Mr. Croker's long life of authorship.

Just before this he had joined with Mr. Canning,
Walter Scott, George Ellis, Mr. Morritt, and others, in
setting up the *Quarterly Review*, the first number of
which appeared in the spring of 1809. The *Edinburgh
Review* had then existed seven years ; and while obnox-
ious to the Tory party for its politics, it was not less so
to the general public for the reckless ferocity of some of
its criticism, in those its early days. If the *Quarterly*

[VII]

*His Irish
pamphlet.*

*The
"Quarterly
Review."*

[VII]

Macaulay's character of Croker.

proposed to rebuke this sin by example, it was rather curious that Mr. Croker should be its most extensive and constant contributor for forty years—seeing that he carried the license of anonymous criticism to the last extreme. Before he had done his work in that department, he had earned for himself—purchased by hard facts—the following character, calmly uttered by one of the first men of the time :[1]—"Croker is a man who would go a hundred miles through sleet and snow, on the top of a coach, in a December night, to search a parish register, for the sake of showing that a man is illegitimate, or a woman older than she says she is." He had actually gone down into the country to find the register of Fanny Burney's baptism, and revelled in the exposure of a misstatement of her age; and the other half of the charge was understood to have been earned in the same way. He did not begin his *Quarterly* reviewing with the same virulence which he manifested in his later years. That malignant ulcer of the mind, engendered by political disappointment, at length absorbed his better qualities. It is necessary to speak thus frankly of the temper of the man, because his statements must in justice be discredited; and because justice requires that the due discrimination be made between the honorable and generous-minded men who ennoble the function of criticism by the spirit they throw into it, and one who, like Croker, employed it at last for the gratification of his own morbid inclination to inflict pain. The propensity was so strong in Croker's case, that we find him unable to resist it even in regard to his old and affectionate friend Walter Scott, and at a time when that old friend was sinking in adversity and disease. He

[1] Macaulay.

reviewed in the *London Courier* Scott's "Malagrowther Letters," in 1826, in a way which called forth the delicate and touching rebuke contained in Scott's letter to him, dated March 19th of that year,—a rebuke remembered long after the trespass that occasioned it was disregarded as a peice of "Croker's malignity." The latest instance of this sort of controversy called forth by Mr. Croker's public vituperation of his oldest and dearest friends, was the series of letters that passed between him and Lord John Russell, after the publication of Moore's "Diaries and Correspondence." Up to the last his victims refused to believe, till compelled, that the articles had proceeded from his pen—well as they knew his spirit of reviewing. When he had been staying at Drayton Manor, not long before Sir Robert Peel's death, had been not only hospitably entertained but kindly ministered to under his infirmities of deafness and bad health, and went home to cut up his host in a political article for the forthcoming *Quarterly* —his fellow-guests at Drayton refused as long as possible to believe the article to be his ; and in the same way, as Lord John Russell informed him, Mrs. Moore would not for a long time credit the fact that the review of the poet's *Life* was his, saying she had always understood Mr. Croker to be her husband's friend. It was in the *Quarterly* that the disappointed politician vented his embittered feelings, as indeed he himself avowed. He declared, when Lord Grey came into office, that he did not consider his pension worth three months' purchase ; that he should therefore lay it by while he had it, and make his income by "tomahawking" liberal authors in the *Quarterly*. He did it, not only by writing articles upon them, but by interpolating other people's articles with his own sarcasms and slanders, so as to compel the real reviewers, in repeated instances, to de-

Vituperation of his oldest friends.

mand the republication of their articles in a genuine state and a separate form.

When he entered Parliament, he was an admirable debater—ready, acute, bold, well furnished with information, and not yet so dangerously reckless as to make him feared by his own party. It is rather strange now to find his name foremost in the list of parliamentary orators in the books of foreigners visiting England after the Peace. He was listened to by the House as an inferior kind of Disraeli, for the amusement afforded by his sarcasm ; and foreigners mistook this manifestation of the old English bull-baiting spirit for an evidence of the parliamentary weight of the satirist ; and a House of Commons that enjoys that sort of sport deserves the French commentary—the imputation of being led by a Croker. There were occasions, however, on which he appeared to advantage on other grounds than his sarcastic wit. It should be remembered that it was he who, in 1821, before Catholic Emancipation could be supposed near at hand, proposed to enable the Crown to make a suitable provision for the Catholic clergy. Lord Castlereagh opposed the motion, which was necessarily withdrawn ; but Mr. Croker declared that he considered the principle safe, and should bring forward the measure till it should be adopted. He was steady to the object, and in 1825 actually obtained a majority upon it in the Commons ; and there is no question of his earnestness in desiring a measure of considerable relief to the consciences and liberties of the Catholic body.

He held his ground with the chiefs of his own party by other qualities than his official ability. His command of detail was remarkable ; and so were his industry and his sagacity within a small range. His zeal for party interests was also great—a zeal shown in his eagerness to fill up places

In Parliament.

with party adherents, from the laureateship (which he pro- [VII]
cured for **Southey**) to the lowest office that could be filled
by an electioneering agent ; but he was also a most acceptable political gossip. It was this which made him a frequent guest at rhe Regent's table, and an inimitable
acquaintance at critical seasons of ministerial change,
when such men as he revel in the incidents of the day,
and in the manifestation of such human vices and weaknesses as come out, together with noble virtues, in the
conflict of personal interests. The congenial spirit of the
Beacon newspaper, which made such a noise in 1822,
made him the proper recipient of Scott's confidence on
the matter ; and to him therefore Scott addressed his
painful explanations, as they stand in the *Life.* It is *Croker and*
probable that the intercourse between him and Scott, *Scott.*
though not without an occasional ruffle, was about the
most cordial that the survivor ever enjoyed. Scott's real
geniality and politic obtuseness to offence enabled him to
bear more than most men would : and, in their literary
relations, he contrived to show himself the debtor. He
avowed that his "Tales of a Grandfather" were suggested
and modelled by Croker's "Stories from the History of
England ;" and he was aided in his "Life of Napoleon"
by Croker's loans of masses of papers. He met Cabinet
Ministers, by the half-dozen at a time, at the Secretary's
table ; and received from him reports of handsome sayings
of the Regent about him. The cordiality could not, on
Croker's side, withstand the temptation to insult a friend
through the press, as he showed at the very time by his
remarks on *Malagrowther ;* but on Scott's side it was
hearty. When the political changes of 1827 were going
forward, his first thought seems to have been for Croker.
"I fear Croker will shake," he wrote, "and heartily sorry

[VII]

The Reform Bill.

Retiring from public life.

I should feel for that." The shaking, however, only shook Croker more firmly into his place and function. In 1828 he became a Privy Councillor; and he retained his Admiralty office till 1830. It was the Reform Bill that destroyed him politically. It need not have done so. There was no more reason for it in his case than in that of any of his comrades; but he willed political suicide. He declared that he would never sit in a reformed House of Commons; and he never did. He expected revolution; and he thought it prudent to retire while he could yet save life and fortune. His view is shown by his mournful account in the House of the spectacle of a Montmorenci rising in the French Constituent Assembly, to propose the extinction of feudal rights and dignities, such as his ancestors had earned and been ennobled by; and he let fall no word to show that he recognized any grandeur in the act. He thought that pitiable which to others appears the crown of the nobleness of the Montmorencis. He proposed to grant nothing to any popular demand, because something might at length be demanded which it would be impossible to grant; and before the shadows of the possible evils which he conjured up, he retired from public life, leaving its actual difficulties to be dealt with by men of a higher courage and a more disinterested patriotism. His Political action, for the rest of his life, consisted merely in the articles he put forth in the *Quarterly Review,*—articles which (to say nothing of their temper) show such feebleness of insight, such a total incapacity to comprehend the spirit and needs of the time, and such utter recklessness about truth of both statement and principle, that elderly readers are puzzled to account for the expectations they once had of the writer. It was the

heart element that was amiss. A good heart has wonderful efficacy in making moderate talent available.
Where heart is absent, the most brilliant abilities fail,
as is said in such cases, "unaccountably." Where
heart is not absent, but is not good, the consequences
are yet more obvious; the faculties waste and decline,
and the life sinks to nothing before death comes to close
the scene. It is impossible to avoid such reflections as
these, while contrasting the strength and goodness of
Croker's early work on Ireland with his latest judgments
on public affairs in the *Quarterly Review*, and his correspondence with Lord John Russell on the business of the
"Moore's Diaries." It may be observed, by the way,
how such a spirit as his stirs up the dregs of other
people's tempers. Lord John Russell's note, in allusion *Lord John*
to Mr. Croker, in "Moore's Life," appears to be unneces- *Russell's*
allusion in
sary; he was moved to it by seeing Mrs. Moore stung *Moore's*
by the review; and he met speedy retribution. Pain *Life.*
was inflicted all round; and Croker was the cause of
it all.

He was the author, editor, and translator of various
works, the chief of which is his edition of "Boswell's
Johnson," a book on which he spent much labor, and
which was regarded with high and trustful favor till
Mr. Macaulay overthrew its reputation for accuracy by
an exposure of a singular series of mistakes, attributable
to indolence, carelessness, or ignorance. That review
(which is republished among Macaulay's "Essays")
destroyed such reputation for scholarship as Mr. Croker *Croker's*
had previously enjoyed, and a good deal impaired that *works of*
of his industry. His other works of bulk are the *bulk.*
"Suffolk Papers," the "Military Events of the French
Revolution of 1830," a translation of "Bassompierre's

[VII]

[VII]

Embassy to England," the "Letters of Lady Hervey,"
and "Lord Hervey's Memoirs of the Reign of George II."
Mr. Croker was an intimate of the late Lord Hertford ;
and his social footing was not improved by the choice
of such friendships, and the revelations made on the
trial of Lord Hertford's valet. In brief, his best place
was his desk at the Admiralty ; his best action was
in his office ; and the most painful part of his life was
the latter part, amidst an ignoble social reputation, and
the political odium attached to him by Mr. Disraeli's
delineation of him in "Coningsby." The virulent reviewer found in his old age the truth of the Eastern
proverb—"Curses are like chickens ; they always come
home to roost." He tried to send them abroad again—
tried his utmost severity in attacks in the *Quarterly* on

*The delinea-
tion in
'Coningsby.'*

Disraeli's Budget. But it was too late : and the painter
of the portrait of Rigby remained master of that field in
which the completest victory is the least enviable.

Looking round for something pleasanter on which to
rest the eye in the career of the unhappy old man who
has just departed, we may dwell on the good-will with
which he was regarded by such personal friends as never
were, and never could be, implicated with public affairs,
never tickled his passions, never vexed his prejudices,
and could honestly feel and express gratitude and respect
toward him. There are some who believe him to have
been an "amiable man in private life ;" and there must
have been substantial ground for an estimate so opposite
that which generally prevailed. Again, we may point out
that his name stands honorably on our new maps and
globes. He was Secretary to the Admiralty during the
earlier of the Polar Expeditions of this century ; and it is
understood that the most active and efficient assistance

was always given by him in the work of Polar discovery.
Long after political unscrupulousness and rancor are
forgotten, those higher landmarks of his voyage of life
will remain, and tell a future generation, to whom he
will be otherwise unknown, that there was one of his
name to whom our great Navigators felt grateful for assistance in the noble service they rendered to their country
and all future time.

[VII]

VIII.

MRS. MARCET.

DIED JUNE 28TH, 1858.

As the instructress of an elder generation, Mrs. Marcet may have dropped out of the view of the busiest part of society as it now exists; but it is not fitting that she should go to her grave without some grateful notice. The intimation of her death, in her 90th year, reminds us of more than her own good services to Society : it reminds us of the progress that Society has made since she began to work for it; and at a dark season like the present, when men are everywhere feeling after an organic state of political and social life, it is cheering and animating to note the advance made in other departments —in Science on the one hand, and Education on the other—toward something better than the loose, uncritical state they were in when our aged friend (for she was the friend of the entire elder generation) began her labors for the promotion of intelligence in the middle classes of England.

In her 90th year.

It appears wonderful that our instructress, who seemed always so up to the time and so like ourselves, should actually have been born in the year when Ganganelli was made Pope, and when Hyder Alee was ravaging the Carnatic, and Paoli flying from Corsica, and Wilkes's

Middlesex election was convulsing Parliament and people at home; but so it was. She was born in 1769; and she was thus a witness to the whole course of existence of the American Republic. She might very well remember the Declaration of Independence, and the birth of Political Economy, in the form of Adam Smith's work, at the same date, she being seven years old at the time; and greatly astonished might she and her friends have been, if they could have foreknown that before her death her works would be text-books in many hundreds of schools, and her pupils be tens of thousands of young republicans, learning from her the principles of Political Economy in a State peopled by nearly thirty millions of inhabitants. Her alert and eager mind was always picking up knowledge, and entertaining itself with the interests of scientific society, long years before she thought of imparting her amusements to the public. Ancient as her earliest works now appear to the oldest of us, they were not produced in early life. She was, we believe, between forty and fifty when she began to write for the public. Dr. Marcet's high repute as a physician and a chemist placed her in the midst of scientific and literary society; while a constitutional restlessness which always troubled her existence, and became at last an insuperable malady, indicated the employment from which she derived the greatest solace and relief the case admitted of. It was under her husband's counsel and guidance that she applied herself to authorship; and he witnessed her first successes before his death in 1822.

When she began to write.

[VIII]

On the death of her father—Mr. Haldimand, an opulent merchant, Swiss by birth, but settled in London, who left a considerable fortune to this only daughter— Dr. Marcet relinquished his appointment in Guy's Hos-

[VIII]

*The " Con-
versa-
tions on
Chemistry."*

pital, and the **medical profession altogether, and devoted**
himself exclusively to **experimental Chemistry. His wife's**
"Conversations on Chemistry" presently opened an entirely fresh region of ideas to the mind of the rising generation of that day, to whom the very nature of chemical
science was a revelation. We may smile now at the sort
of science offered by that book—the dogmas, the hy-
potheses, the glib way of accounting for everything by
terms which are a mere name for ignorance ; but it was
a valuable book in its day ; and there was nobody else
to give it to us. Mrs. Marcet never made any false
pretensions. She never overrated her own books, nor,
consciously, her own knowledge. She sought information from learned persons, believed she understood what
she was told, and generally did so ; wrote down in a
clear, cheerful, serviceable style what she had to tell ; submitted it to criticism, accepted criticism gayly, and always
protested against being ranked with authors of original
quality, whether discoverers in science or thinkers in
literature. She simply desired to be useful ; and she
was eminently so.

*Her
" Political
Economy."*

Her other works of the same class were almost as
widely diffused as the Chemistry. In 1817 her "Conversations on Political Economy" appeared ; and a second edition was called for before the writer had time
to collect criticisms for its improvement. She purposely
omitted some leading questions altogether, as deeper
reasoners than herself were irresolute or at variance upon
them ; but she administered to young minds large supplies of the wisdom of Adam Smith, in a form almost
as entertaining as the "Wealth of Nations" is to grown
readers. Her intimate acquaintance with Say, Malthus,
and other chiefs of that department of knowledge, helped

to enrich her work with some modern developments, which prevented its becoming so soon antiquated as her volumes on Natural Science ; and it is perhaps the book by which she is best known to the present generation, though her "Conversations on Natural Philosophy" and on "Vegetable Physiology" came after it.

[VIII]

The grandmammas of our time, however, declare with warmth, as do many mothers and governesses, that Mrs. Marcet's very best books are her "Stories for Very Little Children ;" and certainly, judging by observation of many little children, those small volumes do appear to be unique in their suitableness to the minds they were addressed to. Mrs. Barbauld's "Early Lessons" were good ; Miss Edgeworth's were better ; but Mrs. Marcet's are transcendent, as far as they go. The capital common sense which little children are obstinate in requiring in the midst of the widest circuits of imagination ; the simplicity, the apt language, the absence of all condescension, and the avoidance of lecturing, on the one hand, and of enhancement of the child's importance on the other, are high virtues, and bring the little reader at once face to face with his subject. Mrs. Marcet was never herself offended at any prominence given to her humblest books ; and we doubt not the willingness of those who have charge of her memory to accept acknowledgments graduated in the same manner. Her pleasure in this kind of intercourse with childlike minds somewhat impaired the quality of her later works, "Mary's Grammar" and "Land and Water," which are not only in what the *Quarterly Review* calls "the garrulous form," but too much of the garrulous order. Her humbler applications of political economy in "John Hopkins's Notions," and in other small pieces, were

As an authoress for children

4

less successful than her earlier efforts. The fact was, Mrs. Marcet hardly considered herself an author at all. Full of vivacity, easily and strongly impressed, simple under the strongest conventional influences, and essentially humble under an appearance of self-confidence, she was precisely fitted to work under incitement from her friends, and to be at their command as to the way of doing it. Flattery set her to work, but did her no real harm ; for she was too genuine to be seriously befooled. Criticisms set her to work to mend mistakes, and render her books as useful as she could make them. Whig partisans set her to work out of good-natured zeal for her friends. Philanthropists set her to work by mere representations of the evils caused by bad political economy anywhere within reach of the press. It may be confidently said that vanity never set her to work, nor love of money, nor jealousy, nor any unworthy motive whatever. There were not wanting persons who did their utmost to spoil her ; and the tractableness with which she lent herself to their purposes caused many a smile ; but she was never spoiled. Her nature was above it. This does not exactly mean that the conventional life she led produced no effect upon her. She suffered from it in forming her estimate of life and of persons. Her good sense was apt to be occasionally submerged in the spirit of clique, and the prejudices of party, and the atmosphere of complacency and mutual flattery, and bookish gossip, and somewhat insolent worldliness in which the Whig literary society which surrounded her revelled during her most social years. But almost any other woman of ability and celebrity would have suffered more than she did. She let herself slide into other people's management too much ; but yet she was always her own

Mrs. Marcet's good sense and high motives.

honest self, humble at heart and generous in spirit, even when appearing most conventional in her views, and prejudiced in her impressions.

[VIII]

No fine speeches from great men could spoil her as a companion for children ; and the longest course of breathing the atmosphere of Whig insolence never starved out her sympathies with the sufferers of society. She did not forget John Hopkins and little Willy in the society of foreign ambassadors and ex-chancellors.

For some years she had been lost sight of, her nervous malady having grievously prostrated her, it was understood, in her extreme old age. We must hope that she was more or less aware of the prodigious start forward that Society had made since she first became its instructress. In what a host of discoveries have her chemical doctrines long been merged! What a new face has Natural Philosophy assumed! And how antique seem already some of the abuses shown up in her Political Economy! The irreversible establishment of Free Trade in England was a blessing which she deserved to witness ; for she had unquestionably some share in bringing it on. She hailed our deliverance from the "gangrene" of the old Poor-law ; and she lived to see the decline, and almost the extinction, of Strikes in the cotton and woollen districts. She witnessed the timely relief afforded by the gold discoveries. She enjoyed the full and free introduction of the subject of popular Education into Parliament and general discussion, after having witnessed in her middle age the abortive efforts of Mr. Whitbread and other friends of education early in the century. If she was aware of a later demonstration still—the Oxford and Cambridge Middle-class Examinations—she must have cordially rejoiced at such a sign of the times.

The progress of Society since she first became its instructress.

[VIII] She saw Ireland raised from the dead, as it were : and if she saw her beloved France—or Paris rather—consigned to political death, her cheerful confidence would assure her that there would be a resurrection there too. Most of her life was spent in London ; but a good deal of it also at or near Geneva—the birthplace of her husband and herself, and the residence of several of her relatives. The travelled English well knew the hospitable abode of her brother, Mr. Haldimand, on Lake Leman. One of her own children also lived there ; but her usual abode was with her son-in-law and daughter, Mr. and Mrs. Edward Romilly, at whose house in London she died. Though we may not regret her death, under her burden of years and infirmity, we may well be thankful for her life **and** services.

IX.

HENRY HALLAM.

DIED JANUARY 21ST, 1859.

By the death of Mr. Hallam we have lost an eminent representative of a class of men, few in number, but inestimable in value at present—the scholar-author—the Working Man of Letters. The influences of our time are not favorable to the training and encouragement of that sort of mind; and it will stand on record as one of the social blessings of the last half-century in England that we had Henry Hallam among us. He was so constituted intellectually that he could not but delight himself perpetually with literature; and he was so constituted morally that he could not but communicate his delight. A singular disposition to intellectual combativeness joined with a childlike earnestness, combined with these tastes to make him the most admirable of critics; while his vivacious temperament kept him from idleness under the name of study. The reader of his weighty (not heavy) works, impressed with the judicial character of the style both of thought and expression, imagined him a solemn, pale student, and might almost expect to see him in a Judge's wig; whereas, the stranger would find him the most rapid talker in company, quick in his movements, genial

An admirable critic.

in his feelings, earnest in narrative, rather full of dissent from what everybody said, innocently surprised when he found himself agreeing with anybody, and pretty sure to blurt out something awkward before the day was done— but never giving offence, because his talk was always the fresh growth of the topic, and, it may be added, his manners were those of a thoroughbred gentleman. He was an admirable subject for his friend Sydney Smith's description. In a capital sketch of a dinner-party to which Sydney Smith went late, Hallam was one of the figures : " And there was Hallam, with his mouth full of cabbage and contradiction ;" a sentence in which we see at once the rapid speech and action, and the constitutional habit of mind. Better still was the wit's account of Hallam in the influenza, not only unable to rest, but throwing up the window at every transit of the watchman, to "question" whether it *was* "past one o'clock," and again whether it *was* "a starlight morning." Such were the vivacious tendencies of the most accomplished critic, the most impartial historian, and the most patient, laborious, and comprehensive student of Letters of our time. The indomitable character of his energies and spirits, and the strength of the vitality of his mind, were proved by his endurance of a singular series of domestic bereavements. He is, perhaps, almost as well known as the father of Arthur Hallam, celebrated by Tennyson in his "In Memoriam," as by his own literary fame. Apparently heartbroken at the time of each bereavement, he rallied wonderfully soon, and resumed his habits of life ; and it was only by the nervous vigilance with which he watched the health of the children who were left that it was revealed how he suffered by the loss of those who were gone.

Mr. Hallam was the only son of Dr. Hallam, afterward

Sydney Smith's description of him.

Domestic bereavements.

Dean of Bristol; and he was born, we believe, in 1778. [IX]
He went to Eton; and what he did there remains an
honorable record in the pages of the "*Musæ Etonenses*,"
in which his name is found connected with some of the
last of those very good and beautiful compositions. His
was exactly the mind to benefit most by sound classical
training; and we reap the fruits of it in our enjoyment
of his admirable style. He went to Oxford, where we
find he was known by the name of "the Doctor"—in
what sense of the word we know not. He next entered
on the study of the Law in chambers at Lincoln's Inn. *Law and*
Probably the first mention of him in connection with *literature.*
literature, after his schoolboy days, is in a letter, in 1805,
from Horner to Jeffrey, in which he says that Hallam
will review "Ranken's History" for the young *Edinburgh;*
adding, "He is a very able man, full of literature and
historical knowledge; but I do not know how he will
write." Horner soon found how his friend could write,
and enjoyed the discovery not a little. It is a characteristic trait that when the question of the Peninsular war
became pressing, and there was bitter political strife
between Hallam's Whig companions and those who would
have left the Spaniards to their fate, he was found studying
Spanish literature—turning his political sympathies, as he
did all his life, into the channel of literature. He lived
in political society from his youth to his death; and the
single effect seemed to be to qualify him for his historical
works, and his Survey of the Literature of all Europe.

He was rich, and able to follow his inclinations in
regard to his mode of life; and his choice was, not Law,
but Literature. He married the eldest daughter of Sir
Abraham Elton, a Somersetshire baronet, by whom he
had a large family of children, of whom only one, a

[IX]

*His
" Europe
during the
Middle
Ages" and
" Consti-
tutional
History."*

daughter, survived him.   Most or all of them, and also
their mother, died instantaneously ; and few men could
have borne the repeated shock as he did.   In 1818 he
brought out the work which first gave him his great fame
—his " View of the State of Europe during the Middle
Ages."   In the preface to that work, and in that of his
" Constitutional History," he tells us that he found his
subject open to his view, and grow upon his hands so as
to impress him with a sense of presumption in what he
had undertaken.   He speaks of it as "a scheme projected early in life with very inadequate views of its
magnitude ;" and he desisted from the undertaking of
continuing his subject—happily excepting his review of
the Constitutional History of England, from the reign of
Henry VII. to that of George III.   It is rather interesting, in a somewhat melancholy way, to look back now
on the reception of this valuable book, the " Constitutional
History," by the *Quarterly Review,* and to contrast the
article of 1828 with the subsequent reviews of him, when
his political opinions had become better known.   Mr.
Hallam associated with the leading Whigs of the time—
was the intimate friend of Lords Lansdowne and Holland,
and a very constant member in their social meetings.
He used to complain pathetically of the sameness of
luxury at London dinner-tables, and say how necessary
it was now and then to dine at home on a plain joint to
keep up his appetite at all ; and it was at the table of
Whig politicians that he was usually to be found.   Judging
from this, and not knowing the man well enough to be
aware that his opinions would be, if not certainly opposite to those of his habitual companions, very particularly
independent of them, the *Quarterly* Reviewer assailed
that highly Conservative History with a virulence of abuse

truly ludicrous in comparison with the tone of subsequent articles written after the mistake was discovered. Mr. Hallam had in 1815 declared himself in favor of the restoration of the Bourbons; but it was not till he was found in 1831 to be a strong anti-reformer, and to be opposing the Reform Bill at the tables of the authors of the measure, that the *Quarterly* began to discover his merits. After that time it could never sufficiently praise the celebrated chapter on the Feudal System in his first great work, and the impartiality, solidity, and dignity of the second—qualities which indeed deserved all the praise accorded to them there and elsewhere. It makes one smile now, as it probably made him laugh at the time, to read the last sentence of that notorious first review of a man eminent for impartiality, an enthusiastic sense of justice, a comprehensiveness which taught him modesty, and the most genial of spirits. The *Quarterly* said of this man that he had, in his History, "the spirit and feeling of the party to which he has attached himself, its acrimony and arrogance, its injustice and its ill-temper." Hallam attached to a party, unjust, arrogant, and ill-tempered! The sentence is valuable, as showing what the criticism of the time was really worth.

No better illustration of the true character of Mr. Hallam's mind could perhaps be offered than the whole of his conduct and language through life on the strange but important subject of Mesmerism. He used to tell how he and Rogers had, long years before anybody in England had revived the subject, seen in Paris, and carefully tested, phenomena which could not possibly leave them in any doubt of the leading facts of Animal Magnetism. He used to tell that they were so insolently

[IX]

Hallam's politics.

and rudely treated, at friends' tables, on their saying what
they had seen, that there was no course to take, in consideration for the host, but silence ; and then that, as fact
after fact came out, one after another became convinced ;
till, at last, even physicians grew grave and silent.

*Hallam's
opinions on
Mesmerism.*

"Rogers and I," he used to say, "have had the experience which is too rare to be had so often as once in
a century—that of witnessing the gradual reception, by
a metropolis, of a great new fact in Natural Science."
On fair occasions, he told what he had seen and inquired
into, and was at length listened to with respect, while
Rogers jested or was pathetic, according to the company
he was in ; so that no one knew what he thought ;
whereas Hallam's earnestness left no such doubt in regard
to him.   His   conclusion   was   at   the   service   of   all
who asked for it.   His words, often spoken, and written in
at least one letter, were of great importance, as coming
from him.   "It appears to me," he wrote, "probable that
the various phenomena of Mesmerism, together with
others independent of Mesmerism, properly so called,
which have lately been brought to light, are fragments
of some general Law of Nature which we are not yet
able to deduce from them, merely because they are
destitute of visible connection—the links being hitherto
wanting which are to display the entire harmony of
effects proceeding from a single cause."   Thus did he
bear witness to Mesmerism in the presence of doctors,
as he criticised the Reform Bill at Holland House or
Bowood.

It is needless to tell what was the promise of his son
Arthur, whose qualities and honors were the joy and
pride of his life.   The young man was advanced in his
professional studies, was engaged to a sister of Alfred

Tennyson, and had the prospect of the brightest of lives, when he went on the Continent with his father, for a tour of recreation. At a German town he was slightly unwell, with a cold; and Mr. Hallam went alone for his afternoon walk, leaving Arthur on the sofa. Finding him sleeping on his return, he took a book and read for an hour; and then he became impressed with the extreme stillness of the sleeper. The sleeper was cold, and must have been dead from almost the moment when he had last spoken. In like manner died the eldest daughter; and in like manner the cherished wife—an admirable woman. These latter bereavements took place while he was writing his Introduction to the Literature of Europe, the first volume of which was published in 1837, and the last in 1839. There is an affecting allusion to his domestic griefs in the leave-taking of the final Preface, wherein he says that he stands among solemn warnings that he must "bind up his sheaves" while yet he may. There was still a son, Henry, but he died too in opening manhood; and then there was but one daughter, and she married, to cheer his old age. Yet he seemed always cheerful. His social disposition, and his love of literature, and his generosity of spirit, and his kindly sympathies kept him fresh and bright for many a long year after the sunshine of his life seemed to be gone. To those who knew him, and enjoyed his genial qualities as a friend, or even a mere acquaintance, his last great work will always be a great solace on his account. There is something in the "manly amenity" (which the *Quarterly Review* justly ascribes to him) of its tone, in the generous justice to all intellectual claims, and in the subdued moral and poetical enthusiasm of that long piece of criticism, which discloses the consoling truth that he was

[IX]

The sudden death of his son Arthur, his eldest daughter, and his wife.

happy while he wrote it, and that he found honest intellectual labor to be its own "exceeding great reward." The memoir of Lord Webb Seymour, in the Life of Horner, was written during the preparation of that excellent book. It is the last acknowledged piece of authorship of Mr. Hallam's that we have. Whatever he wrote will live; and we trust the memory of the man will live, vivid as himself. He was the representative, in a time of much crudeness, of the old scholar-like race of authors, while keeping up with the foremost men and interests of his time. He was an honorable gentleman, disinterested alike in regard to money and to fame, with a youthful innocence and earnestness unimpaired in old age, and a manly spirit of justice and independence, which made him an object of respect as much in his weakest as in his highest moments. It will not be pretended anywhere that he was not a gossip; but his coterie was the most gossiping perhaps in London; and in Hallam's gossip there was no ill-nature, though sometimes a good deal of imprudence, which came curiously from a man who was always testifying on behalf of prudence. It would be amusing to know what he was as a courtier. He was one of the two or three literary persons who were invited to the Palace in the early days of the reign; and the question was whether that remarkable notice was owing, like the royal notice of Rogers, to Mr. Hallam's knowledge of Art; or to his intimacy with the Queen's earliest and most favored advisers; or to his being a man of large fortune—independent of literature while illustrated by it. However that may be, we know what he was to us—a man who represented a fine phase of the Literary Life, and who was faithful to Literature, its champion, its worshipper, and its ornament, throughout

A representative of the scholar-like race of authors.

a half-century whose peculiar influences justified an apprehension that such a man and mode of life might **appear**
among us no more. His name is thus fraught with associations which will last as long as his books ; and that
they will be long-lived was years ago settled by the
acclamation of the **wise.**

[IX]

X.

MRS. WORDSWORTH.

DIED JANUARY 17TH, 1859.

THE last thing that would have occurred to Mrs. Wordsworth would have been that her departure, or anything about her, would be publicly noticed amidst the events of a stirring time. Those who knew her well, regarded her with as true a homage as they ever rendered to any member of the household, or to any personage of the remarkable group which will be forever traditionally associated with the Lake District; but this reverence, genuine and hearty as it was, would not, in all eyes, be a sufficient reason for recording more than the fact of her death. It is her survivorship of such a group which constitutes an undisputed public interest in her decease. With her closes a remarkable scene in the history of the literature of our century. The well-known cottage, Mount, and garden at Rydal will be regarded with other eyes, when shut up, or transferred to new occupants. With Mrs. Wordsworth, an old world has passed away before the eyes of the inhabitants of the District, and a new one succeeds which may have its own delights, solemnities, honors, and graces, but which can never replace the familiar one that is gone. There was something mournful in the

The sur-vivor of a remark-able group.

lingering of this aged lady—blind, deaf, and bereaved in her latter years; but *she* was not mournful, any more than she was insensible. Age did not blunt her feelings, nor deaden her interest in the events of the day. It seems not so very long ago that she said that the worst of living in such a place (as the Lake District) was its making one unwilling to go. It was too beautiful to let one be ready to leave it. Within a few years, the beloved daughter was gone; and then the aged husband, and then the son-in-law; and then the devoted friend, Mr. Wordsworth's publisher, Mr. Moxon, who paid his duty occasionally by the side of her chair; then she became blind and deaf. Still her cheerfulness was indomitable. No doubt, she would in reality have been "willing to go" whenever called upon, throughout her long life; but she liked life to the end. By her disinterestedness of nature, by her fortitude of spirit, and her constitutional elasticity and activity, she was qualified for the honor of surviving her household—nursing and burying them, and bearing the bereavement which they were vicariously spared. She did it wisely, tenderly, bravely, and cheerfully, and she will be remembered accordingly by all who witnessed the spectacle.

It was by the (accident so to speak) of her early friendship with Wordsworth's sister that her life became involved with the poetic element, which her mind would hardly have sought for itself in another position. She was the incarnation of good sense, as applied to the concerns of the every-day world. In as far as her marriage and course of life tended to infuse a new elevation into her views of things, it was a blessing; and on the other hand, in as far as it infected her with the spirit of exclusiveness which was the grand defect

[X]

A good housewife.

[X]

Strangers in the Lake region.

of the group in its own place, it was hurtful; but that very exclusiveness was less an evil than an amusement, after all. It was a rather serious matter to hear the Poet's denunciations of the railway, and to read his well-known sonnets on the desecration of the Lake region by the unhallowed presence of commonplace strangers; and it was truly painful to observe how the scornful and grudging mood spread among the young, who thought they were agreeing with Wordsworth in claiming the vales and lakes as a natural property for their enlightened selves. But it was so unlike Mrs. Wordsworth, with her kindly, cheery, generous turn, to say that a green field with buttercups would answer all the purposes of Lancashire operatives, and that they did not know what to do with themselves when they came among the mountains, that the innocent insolence could do no harm. It became a fixed sentiment when she alone survived to uphold it; and one demonstration of it amused the whole neighborhood in a good-natured way. "People from Birthwaite" were the bugbear—Birthwaite being the end of the railway. In the summer of 1857, Mrs. Wordsworth's companion told her (she being then blind) that there were some strangers in the garden—two or three boys on the Mount, looking at the view. "Boys from Birthwaite," said the old lady, in the well-known tone which conveyed that nothing good could come from Birthwaite. When the strangers were gone, it appeared that they were the Prince of Wales and his companions. Making allowance for prejudices, neither few nor small, but easily dissolved when reason and kindliness had opportunity to work, she was a truly wise woman, equal to all occasions of action, and supplying other persons' needs and deficiencies.

In the "Memoirs of Wordsworth" it is stated that she was the original of

[X]

"She was a phantom of delight,"

and some things in the next few pages look like it; but for the greater part of the Poet's life it was certainly believed by some who ought to know that that wonderful description related to another, who flitted before his imagination in earlier days than those in which he discovered the aptitude of Mary Hutchinson to his own needs. The last stanza is very like her; and her husband's sonnet to the painter of her portrait in old age discloses to us how the first stanza might be so also, in days beyond the ken of the existing generation. Of her early sorrows, in the loss of two children and a beloved sister who was domesticated with the family, there are probably no living witnesses. It will never be forgotten by any who saw it how the late dreary train of afflictions was met. For many years Wordsworth's sister Dorothy was a melancholy charge. Mrs. Wordsworth was wont to warn any rash enthusiasts for mountain walking by the spectacle before them. The adoring sister would never fail her brother; and she destroyed her health, and then her reason, by exhausting walks, and wrong remedies for the consequences. Forty miles in a day was not a singular feat of Dorothy's. During the long years of this devoted creature's helplessness she was tended with admirable cheerfulness and good sense. Thousands of Lake tourists must remember the locked garden gate when Miss Wordsworth was taking the air, and the garden chair going round and round the terrace, with the emaciated little woman in it, who occasionally called out to strangers, and amused them with her clever

A train of afflictions.

Wordsworth's sister Dorothy.

*Words-
worth in his
old age.*

sayings.   She outlived the beloved Dora, Wordsworth's
only surviving daughter.   After the lingering illness of
that daughter (Mrs. Quillinan), the mother encountered
the dreariest portion, probably, of her life.   Her aged
husband used to spend the long winter evenings in grief
and tears—week after week, month after month.   Neither
of them had eyes for reading.   He could not be com-
forted.   She, who carried as tender a maternal heart as
ever beat, had to bear her own grief and his too.   She
grew whiter and smaller, so as to be greatly changed
in a few months : but this was the only expression of
what she endured, and he did not discover it.   When he
too left her, it was seen how disinterested had been
her trouble.   When his trouble had ceased, she too was
relieved.   She followed his coffin to the sacred corner of
Grasmere churchyard, where lay now all those who had
once made her home.   She joined the household guests
on their return from the funeral, and made tea as usual.
And this was the disinterested spirit which carried her
through the last few years, till she had just reached the
ninetieth.   Even then, she had strength to combat
disease for many days.   Several times she rallied and
relapsed ; and she was full of alacrity of mind and body
as long as exertion of any kind was possible.   There
were many eager to render all duty and love—her two
sons, nieces, and friends, and a whole sympathizing
neighborhood.

*Grasmere
churchyard.*

The question commonly asked by visitors to that
corner of Grasmere churchyard was—where would *she* be
laid when the time came? the space was so completely
filled.   The cluster of stones told of the little children
who died a long lifetime ago ; of the sisters Sarah Hutchinson and Dorothy Wordsworth ; and of Mr. Quillinan,

and his two wives, Dora lying between her husband and father, and seeming to occupy her mother's rightful place. And Hartley Coleridge lies next the family group; and others press closely round. There is room, however. The large gray stone which bears the name of William Wordsworth has ample space left for another inscription; and the grave beneath has ample space also for his faithful life-companion.

Not one is left now of the eminent persons who rendered that cluster of valleys so eminent as it has been. Dr. Arnold went first, in the vigor of his years. Southey died at Keswick, and Hartley Coleridge on the margin of Rydal Lake; and the Quillinans under the shadow of Loughrigg; and Professor Wilson disappeared from Elleray; and the aged Mrs. Fletcher from Lancrigg; and the three venerable Wordsworths from Rydal Mount.

The survivor of all the rest had a heart and a memory for the solemn *last* of everything. She was the one to inquire of about the last eagle in the District, the last pair of ravens in any crest of rocks, the last old dalesman in any improved spot, the last round of the last pedler among hills where the broad white road has succeeded the green bridle-path. She knew the District during the period between its first recognition, through Gray's "Letters," to its complete publicity in the age of railways. She saw, perhaps, the best of it. But she contributed to modernize and improve it, though the idea of doing so probably never occurred to her. There were great people before to give away Christmas bounties, and spoil their neighbors as the established almsgiving of the rich does spoil the laboring class, which ought to be above that kind of aid. Mrs. Wordsworth did infinitely more good in her

The Lake valleys.

[X]

Fruits of her example.

own way, and without being aware of it. An example of comfortable thrift was a greater boon to the people round than money, clothes, meat, or fuel. The oldest residents have long borne witness that the homes of the neighbors have assumed a new character of order and comfort, and wholesome economy, since the Poet's family lived at Rydal Mount. It used to be a pleasant sight when Wordsworth was seen in the middle of a hedge, cutting switches for half-a-dozen children, who were pulling at his cloak, or gathering about his heels: and it will long be pleasant to family friends to hear how the young wives of half a century learned to make home comfortable by the example of the good housewife at the Mount, who was never above letting her thrift be known.

Finally, she who had noted so many last survivors was herself the last of a company more venerable than eagles, or ravens, or old-world yeomen, or antique customs. She would not in any case be the first forgotten. As it is, her honored name will live for generations in the traditions of the valleys round. If she was studied as the Poet's wife, she came out so well from that investigation that she was contemplated for herself; and the image so received is her true monument. It will be better preserved in her old-fashioned neighborhood than many monuments which make a greater show.

XI.

THOMAS DE QUINCEY.

Died December 8th, 1859.

In noticing, on the occasion of his departure from us, the life and character of De Quincey, none of the doubt and hesitation occur which render the task generally embarrassing as to what to communicate to the public and what to suppress. The "English Opium Eater" has *His perpetual self-study.* himself told publicly, throughout a period of between thirty and forty years, whatever is known about him to anybody; and in sketching the events of his life, the recorder has little more to do than to indicate facts which may be found fully expanded in Mr. De Quincey's "Confessions of an Opium Eater," and "Autobiographic Sketches." The business which he has in fact left for others to do is that which, in spite of obvious impossibility, he was incessantly endeavoring to do himself; that of analyzing and forming a representation and judgment of his mind, and of his life as moulded by his mind. The most intense metaphysician of a time remarkable for the predominance of metaphysical modes of thought, he was as completely unaware as smaller men of his mental habits, that in his perpetual self-study and analysis he was never approaching the truth, for the

[XI] simple reason that he was not even within ken of the necessary point of view. "I," he says, "whose disease it was to meditate too much, and to observe too little." And the description was a true one, as far as it went. And the completion of the description was one which he could never have himself arrived at. It must, we think, be concluded of De Quincey, that he was the most remarkable instance in his time of a more than abnormal, of an artificial condition of body and mind,—a characterization which he must necessarily be the last man to conceive of. To understand this, it is necessary to glance at the events of his life. The briefest notice will suffice, as they are within the reach of all, as related in his own books.

Thomas De Quincey was the son of a merchant engaged in foreign commerce, and was born at Manchester *One of eight children.* in 1786. He was one of eight children, of whom no more than six were ever living at once, and several of whom died in infancy. The survivors were reared in a country home, the incidents of which, when of a kind to excite emotion, impressed themselves on this singular child's memory from a very early age. We have known only two instances, in a rather wide experience of life, of persons distinctly remembering so far back as a year and a half old. This was De Quincey's age when three deaths happened in the family, which he remembered, not by tradition, but by his own contemporary emotions. A sister of three and a half died ; and he was perplexed by her disappearance, and terrified by the household whisper that she had been ill-used, just before her death, by a servant. A grandmother died about the same time, leaving little impression, because she had been little seen. The other death was of a beloved kingfisher, by a doleful accident. When the boy was five he lost his playfellow and, as he says, intellectual guide—his sister Elizabeth, eight years old, dying of hydrocephalus, after manifesting an intellectual power which the forlorn brother recalled with admiration and wonder for life. The impression was undoubtedly genuine ; but it is impossible to read the "Autobiographical Sketch" in which the death and funeral of the child are described without perceiving that the writer referred back to the period he was describing with emotions and reflex sensations which arose in him, and fell from the pen, at the moment. His father meantime was residing abroad, year after year, as a condition of his living at all ; and he died of pulmonary consumption before Thomas was seven years old. The elder brother, then twelve, was obviously too eccentric for home management, if not for all control ; and, looking no further than these constitutional cases, we are warranted in concluding that the Opium Eater entered life under peculiar and unfavorable conditions.

He passed through a succession of schools, and was distinguished by his eminent knowledge of Greek. At fifteen he was pointed out by his master (himself a ripe scholar) to a stranger in the remarkable words, "That boy could harangue an Athenian mob better than you or I could address an English one." And it was not only the Greek, we imagine, but the eloquence too that was included in this praise. In this, as in the subtlety of the analytical power (so strangely mistaken for entire intellectual supremacy in our day), De Quincey must have strongly resembled Coleridge. Both were fine Grecians, charming discoursers, eminent opium-takers, magnificent dreamers and seers, large in their promises, and helpless in their failure of performance. De Quincey set his heart upon going to College earlier than his guardians

[XI]

His knowledge of Greek.

[XI]

Runs away from his tutor's house.

Physical sufferings in London.

The resort to opium.

thought proper ; and, on his being disappointed in this matter, he ran away from his tutor's house, and was lost for several months—first in Wales, and afterward in London. He was then sixteen. His whole life presents no more remarkable evidence of his constant absorption in introspection than the fact that while tortured with hunger in the streets of London for many weeks, and sleeping (or rather lying awake with cold and hunger) on the floor of an empty house, it never once occurred to him to earn money. As a classical corrector of the press, and in other ways, he might no doubt have obtained employment ; but it was not till afterward asked why he did not, that the idea ever entered his mind. How he starved, how he would have died but for a glass of spiced wine in the middle of the night on some steps in Soho-square, the Opium Eater told all the world above thirty years since ; and also, of his entering College ; of the love of wine generated by the comfort it had yielded in his days of starvation ; and again, of the disorder of the functions of the stomach which naturally followed, and the resort to opium as a refuge from the pain. It is to be feared that the description given in those extra-ordinary "Confessions" has acted more strongly in tempting young people to seek the eight years' pleasures he derived from laudanum than that of his subsequent torments in deterring them. There was no one to present to them the consideration that the peculiar organization of De Quincey, and his bitter sufferings, might well make a recourse to opium a different thing to him than to anybody else. The quality of his mind, and the exhausted state of his body, enhanced to him the enjoyments which he called "divine ;" whereas there is no doubt of the miserable pain by which men of all consti-

tutions have to expiate an habitual indulgence in opium. [XI]
Others than De Quincey may or may not procure the
pleasures he experienced ; but it is certain that every one
must expiate his offence against the laws of the human
frame. And let it be remembered that De Quincey's
excuse is as singular as his excess. Of the many who
have emulated his enjoyment, there can hardly have been
one whose stomach had been well-nigh destroyed by
months of incessant, cruel hunger.

This event of his life—his resort to opium—absorbed
all the rest. There is little more to tell in the way of
incident. His existence was thenceforth a series of *His exist-*
dreams, undergone in different places—now at College *ence a series*
and now in a Westmoreland cottage, with a gentle suf- *of dreams.*
fering wife by his side, striving to minister to a need
which was beyond the reach of nursing. He could
amuse his predominant faculties by reading metaphysical
philosophy, and analytical reasoning on any subject ;
and by elaborating endless analyses and reasonings of
his own, which he had not energy to embody. Occasionally the torpor encroached even on his predominant
faculties ; and then he roused himself to overcome the
habit—underwent fearful suffering in the weaning—began
to enjoy the vital happiness of temperance and health ;
and then—fell back again. The influence upon the
moral energies of his nature was, as might be supposed,
fatal. Such energy he once had, as his earlier efforts at
endurance amply testify. But as years passed on, he not
only became a more helpless victim to his prominent
vice, but manifested an increasing insensibility to the
most ordinary requisitions of honor and courtesy, to
say nothing of gratitude and sincerity. In his hungry
days in London he would not beg or borrow. Five years

[XI]

later he wrote to Wordsworth, in admiration and sympathy ; received an invitation to his Westmoreland valley ; went, more than once, within a few miles ; and withdrew and returned to Oxford, unable to conquer his painful shyness ;—returned at last to live there, in the very cottage which had been Wordsworth's ; received for himself, his wife, and a growing family of children, an unintermitting series of friendly and neighborly offices ; was necessarily admitted to much household confidence, and favored with substantial aid, which was certainly not given through any strong liking for his manners, conversation, or character. How did he recompense all this exertion and endurance on his behalf? In after years, when living (we believe) at Edinburgh, and pressed by debt, he did for once exert himself to write ; and what he wrote was an exposure, in a disadvantageous light, of everything about the Wordsworths which he knew merely by their kindness. He wrote papers which were eagerly read, and of course duly paid for, in which Wordsworth's personal foibles were malignantly exhibited with ingenious aggravations. The infirmities of one member of the family, the personal blemish of another, and the human weaknesses of all, were displayed ; and all for the purpose of deepening the dislike against Wordsworth himself, which the receiver of his money, the eater of his dinners, and the dreary provoker of his patience strove to excite. Moreover, he perpetrated an act of treachery scarcely paralleled, we hope, in the history of Literature. In the confidence of their most familiar days Wordsworth had communicated portions of his posthumous poem to his guest, who was perfectly well aware that the work was to rest in darkness and silence till after the Poet's death. In these magazine articles De Quincey—using for this

atrocious purpose his fine gift of memory—published a
passage which he informed us was of far higher merit
than anything else we had to expect. And what was
Wordsworth's conduct under this unequalled experience
of bad faith and bad feeling? While so many anecdotes
were going of the Poet's fireside, the following ought to
be added. An old friend was talking with him by that
fireside, and mentioned De Quincey's magazine articles.
Wordsworth begged to be spared any account of them,
saying that the man had long passed away from the
family life and mind; and he did not wish to ruffle himself in a useless way about a misbehavior which could
not be remedied. The friend acquiesced, saying, "Well,
I will tell you only one thing that he says, and then we
will talk of other things. He says your wife is too good
for you." The old Poet's dim eyes lighted up instantly,
and he started from his seat, and flung himself against
the mantelpiece, with his back to the fire, as he cried
with loud enthusiasm—"And that's *true!* *There* he is
right!" and his disgust and contempt for the traitor
were visibly moderated.

During a long course of years De Quincey went on
dreaming always—sometimes scheming works of high
value and great efficacy which were never to exist;
promising largely to booksellers and others, and failing
through a weakness so deep-seated that it should have
prevented his making any promises. When his three
daughters were grown up, and his wife was dead, he
lived in a pleasant cottage at Lasswade, near Edinburgh
—well known by name to those who have never seen its
beauties, as the scene of Scott's early married life and
first great achievements in literature. There, while the
family fortunes were expressly made contingent on his

[XI]

*Words-
worth's
exclamation
at his
fireside.*

[XI]

abstinence from his drug, De Quincey did abstain, or
observe moderation. His flow of conversation was then
the delight of old acquaintance and admiring strangers,
who came to hear the charmer and to receive the impression, which could never be lost, of the singular figure
and countenance and the finely modulated voice, which
were like nothing else in the world. It was a strange
thing to look upon that fragile form, and features which
De Quincey might be those of a dying man, and to hear such
in con- utterances as his : now the strangest comments and in-
versation. significant incidents ; now pregnant remarks on great
subjects ; and then, malignant gossip, virulent and base,
but delivered with an air and a voice of philosophical
calmness and intellectual commentary such as caused the
disgust of the listener to be largely qualified with amusement and surprise. One good thing was, that nobody's
name and fame could be really injured by anything De
Quincey could say. There was such a grotesque air
about the mode of his evil-speaking, and it was so gratuitous and excessive, that the hearer could not help
regarding it as a singular sort of intellectual exercise, or
an effort in the speaker to observe, for once, something
outside of himself, rather than as any token of actual
feeling toward the ostensible object.

Let this strange commentator on individual character
meet with more mercy and a wiser interpretation than he
was himself capable of. He was not made like other
men ; and he did not live, think, or feel like them. A
singular organization was singularly and fatally deranged
in its action before it could show its best quality. Marvellous analytical faculty he had ; but it all oozed out in
barren words. Charming eloquence he had ; but it de-
generated into egotistical garrulity, rendered tempting by

the gilding of his genius. It is questionable whether, if he had never touched opium or wine, his real achievements would have been substantial—for he had no conception of a veritable standpoint of philosophical investigation ; but the actual effect of his intemperance was to aggravate to excess his introspective tendencies, and to remove him incessantly further from the needful discipline of true science. His conditions of body and mind were abnormal, and his study of the one thing he knew anything about—the human mind—was radically imperfect. His powers, noble and charming as they might have been, were at once wasted and weakened through their own partial excess. His moral nature relaxed and sank, as must always be the case where sensibility is stimulated and action paralyzed ; and the man of genius who, forty years before, administered a moral warning to all England, and commanded the sympathy and admiration of a nation, has lived on, to achieve nothing but the delivery of some confidences of questionable value and beauty, and to command from us nothing more than a compassionate sorrow that an intellect so subtle and an eloquence so charming in its pathos, its humor, its insight, and its music, should have left the world in no way the better for such gifts—unless by the warning afforded in "Confessions" first, and then by example, against the curse which neutralized their influence and corrupted its source.

XII.

LORD MACAULAY.

DIED DECEMBER 28TH, 1859.

THE time was when England would have said that in losing Macaulay she would lose the most extraordinary man of his generation in this country, the greatest and most accomplished of her statesmen of the nineteenth century. Such, and no less, was the expectation entertained of Macaulay when he first came forward as orator and poet, and on to the time when he had shown what he could do in Parliament. The expectation has not been fulfilled ; and for many years it has been in course of relinquishment. He was not a great statesman, but *Rhetorician and Essayist.* he was the most brilliant Rhetorician and Essayist of his day and generation, and the most accomplished of that order of Scholars who make their erudition available from moment to moment, for illustration and embellishment, for the benefit of the multitude. He was no statesman, nor philosopher, nor logician, nor lawyer : but he was so accomplished a Man of Letters, and so incomparable a speaker and writer in his own way, that he will be regretfully remembered by his own generation while they live to miss the treat afforded from time to time by his suggestive pages and his enrapturing speeches.

He was the son of that excellent man, Zachary
Macaulay, whose honored name is inseparably connected with the Anti-Slavery movement of the beginning
of the century. Strange as the saying may seem, there
is in our minds no doubt that his parentage was his
grand disadvantage, and the source of the comparative
unfruitfulness of his splendid powers. Zachary Macaulay
sacrificed fortune, health, time, peace and quiet, and
reputation, in behalf of the great philanthropic enterprise
of his time; and, instead of his distinguishing qualities
being perpetuated in his son, the reaction from them was
as marked as often happens in the case of the children
of eminent men. We see the sons of remarkably pious
clergymen grow up to be men of the world; the sons of
metaphysical or spiritual philosophers make a rush to
the laboratory, or wander about the world, hammer in
hand, to chip at its rocks. The sons of mathematicians
turn to Art; and the families of statesmen bury themselves in distant counties, and talk like graziers of
bullocks and breeds of sheep. The child of a philanthropist, Thomas Macaulay wanted heart: this was the
one deficiency which lowered the value of all his other
gifts. He never suspected the deficiency himself; and
he might easily be unaware of it; for he had kindliness,
and for anything we know, a good temper; but of the
life of the heart he knew nothing. He talked about it,
as Dr. Blacklock, the blind poet, wrote descriptions of
scenery—with a complete conviction that he knew all
about it; but the actual experience was absent. From
the eclectic character of his mind it has been said that
Macaulay thought by proxy. This was in the main true;
but it was more remarkably true that he felt by proxy.
However it might be about his consciousness in the first

[XII]

*His
parentage
a dis-
advantage.*

*Want of
heart.*

case, it is certain that in the second he was wholly unaware of the process.   He took for granted that he was made like other people, and that therefore other people were amenable to his judgment.   Thus it happened that his interpretations of History were so partial, his estimate of life and character so little elevated ; and, we may add, his eclecticism so unscrupulous, and his logic so infirm. Very early in life he heard more than boyhood can endure of sentiment and philanthropy ; the sensibilities of the Clapham set of religionists proved too much for "the thinking, thoughtless schoolboy ;" and we have no doubt that it was the reaction from all this that made him a conventionalist in morals, an insolent and inconsistent Whig in politics, a shallow and inaccurate historian, a poet pouring out all light and no warmth, and, for an able man, the most unsound reasoner of his time. Heart is as indispensable to logic as to philosophy, art, or philanthropy itself.   It is the vitality which binds together and substantiates all other elements ; without it, they are forever desultory, and radically unsubstantial —like the great gifts of the brilliant Macaulay.

Honors at Cambridge.   He was born in 1800.   The first of his long series of distinctions and honors were those he won at Trinity College, Cambridge, where he took his Bachelor's degree in 1822.   Very high were those early honors ;   and thenceforth many eyes were upon him, to watch the next turn of a career which could not but be a marked one. He obtained a fellowship at Cambridge, went to Lincoln's Inn to study Law, and was called to the Bar in 1826.   His first recorded speech was made in 1824, at an Anti-Slavery meeting, where the tone he had caught up from the associates of his life thus far, expressed itself in a violence and bitterness which, being exceedingly eloquent at the same time, brought on him the laudation of the *Edinburgh Review* and the scoldings of the *Quarterly*—the former being the organ of the Abolitionists, and the latter of the West India interest—at that time very fierce from excess of fear. The *Edinburgh Review* placed the speech of this promising young man above all that had been offered to Parliament, and reported Mr. Wilberforce's heartsome saying, that his friend Zachary would no doubt joyfully bear all that his apostleship brought upon him "for the gratification of hearing one so dear to him plead such a cause in such a manner." This was, however, the last occasion, or nearly so, of the young orator appearing as one of the Abolitionist party. In the same year he presented himself as a poet, in *Knight's Quarterly Magazine*; and not long after obtained high credit even from the *Quarterly Review*, for his fine translation of Filicaia's "Ode on the Deliverance of Venice from the Turks." The versification was pronounced to be loftily harmonious, and worthy of Milman. Thus had he already taken ground as an orator and a poet; and in 1826 he reaped his first fame as an essayist, in his article on Milton, in the *Edinburgh Review*. Whatever he might think at the time of the party puffery of that article, he showed on occasion of its compelled republication long afterward, that he valued the youthful effort at no more than its deserts. There was promise enough in it, however, to add his qualification of essayist to his other claims to high expectation. Parliament was to be his next field; and to Parliament he was returned in the first days of Reform, becoming member for Calne in 1832, and for Leeds in 1834. He was rendered independent in the first instance by his office of Com-

*[XII]
Macaulay's
first re-
corded
speech.*

*The essay
on Milton
in the
"Edin-
burgh
Review."*

*Returned to
Parliament.*

[XII]

missioner of Bankrupts, given him by the Grey Government ; and then by being Secretary to the India Board.

In Parliament, his success at first did not answer to ministerial expectation, though it was a vast gain to the Administration, when their unpopularity began to be a difficulty, to have Macaulay for their occasional spokesman and constant apologist. The drawback was his *His early parliamentary speaking.* want of accuracy, and especially in the important matter of historical interpretation. If he ventured to illustrate his topic in his own way, by historical analogy, he was immediately checked by some clever antagonist, who, three times out of four, showed that he had misread his authorities, or more frequently had left out some essential element, whose omission vitiated the whole statement or question. It was this fault which afterward spoiled the pleasure of reading his essays in the form of reviews. Very few could singly follow him in his erudite gatherings of materials ; but the thing could be done by the united knowledge of several minds ; and those several minds found that, as far as each could go *Want of accuracy.* along with him, he was incessantly felt to be unsound, by the omission or misstatement of some essential part of the case. When this was exhibited in regard to his early parliamentary speaking, the defence made was that he was yet young ; and he was still spoken of by the Whigs as a rising young man, and full of promise, till the question was asked very widely, when the "promise" of a man above thirty was to become fruition. It was not for want of pains that his success was at first partial. Those who met him in the Strand or Lincoln's Inn in those days saw him threading his way unconsciously, looking at the pavement, and moving his lips as in repetition or soliloquy. "Macaulay is going to give us a speech to-night," the observer would report to the next friend he met; and so it usually turned out. The radical inaccuracy of his habit of thought was decisively evidenced by his next act in the drama of life. In 1834 he resigned his office and his seat in Parliament to go to India as member of the Supreme Council of Calcutta, to frame a Code of Law for India. It was understood that his main object, favored by the Whig Ministry, was to make his fortune, in order to be able to pursue a career of statesmanship for the rest of his life. Ten years were talked of as the term of his absence; but he came back in three, with his health considerably impaired, his Code in his hand, and a handsome competence in his pocket. The story of that unhappy Code is well known. It is usually spoken of by Whig leaders as merely shelved, and ready for reproduction at some time of leisure; but the fact is, that there is scarcely a definition that will stand the examination of lawyer or layman for an instant; and scarcely a description or provision through which a coach and horses may not be driven. All hope of Macaulay as a lawyer, and also as a philosopher, was over for any who had seen his Code.

After his return in 1838 he was elected by Edinburgh, on his making the extraordinary avowal that he was converted to the advocacy of the Ballot, Household Suffrage, and short Parliaments. For a moment, the genuine reformers believed that they had gained the most eloquent man in Parliament to their cause; but it was not for long. They soon found how thoroughly deficient he was in moral earnestness, and how impressible when the interest or impulse of the hour set any particular view, or even principle, brightly before him. He did not become a Radical any more than Peel or

[XII]

Spends three years in India.

Elected by Edinburgh.

[XII]　Melbourne.　When appointed Secretary at War, the year after, he turned out rather more than less aristocratic than other reformers to whom fate affords the opportunity of dating their letters from Windsor Castle, when sent for to attend a Council.

This was the time of his greatest brilliancy in private life.　As a talker, his powers were perhaps unrivalled. It was there that he showed what he could do without the preparation which might, if it did not, insure the splendor of his essays and his oratory.　At the dinner-table he poured out his marvellous eloquence with a rapidity equalled only by that of his friend Hallam's utterance.　He talked much, if at all ; and thus it was found that it did not answer very well to invite him with Jeffrey and Sydney Smith.　Jeffrey could sit silent for a moderate time with serenity.　Sydney Smith could not without annoyance.　Both had had three years of full liberty (for they did not interfere with each other) during Macaulay's absence ; but he eclipsed both on his return.　After some years, when his health and spirits were declining, and his expectations began to merge in consciousness of failure, he sometimes sat quiet on such occasions, listening or lost in thought, as might happen. It was then that Sydney Smith uttered his celebrated saying, about his conversational rival :—"Macaulay is improved ! Yes, Macaulay is improved ! I have observed in him of late flashes—of silence." Meantime, he was the saving genius of the *Edinburgh Review*, then otherwise likely to sink prone after the retirement of Jeffrey, and during the unpopularity of the Whig Government, all of whose acts it set itself indiscriminately to uphold.　Brougham, with his brother William, Senior, and Macaulay, with some underlings, wrote up every

Macaulay as a talker.

Whig act and design, and made a virtue and success of every fault and failure ; but it would not all have done if Macaulay's magnificent articles, in a long and rich series, had not carried the *Review* everywhere, and infused some life into what was clearly an expiring organization. The splendid historical, biographical, and critical dissertations of Macaulay were the most popular literature of the day ; and they raised to the highest pitch the popular expectation from his History. A History of England by Macaulay was anticipated as the richest conceivable treat ; though some thoughtful, or experienced, or hostile person here and there threw out the remark that as his oratory was literature, and his literature oratory, his history would probably be something else than history—most likely epigrammatic criticism. There was some further preparation for his failure as well as success as an historian after his article on Bacon in the *Edinburgh.* That Essay disabused the wisest who expected services of the first order from Macaulay. In that article he not only betrayed his incapacity for philosophy, and his radical ignorance of the subject he undertook to treat, but laid himself open to the charge of helping himself to the very materials he was disparaging, and giving as his own large excerpts from Mr. Montagu, while loading him with contempt and rebuke. But those who were best aware of Macaulay's faults were carried away by the delight of reading him. As an artist, we are under deep obligations to him ; and in his own walk of Art—fresh, and open to the multitude—he was supreme. The mere style, forceful and antithetical, becomes fatiguing from its want of repose, as well as its mannerism ; but his cumulative method of illustration is unrivalled. It has been, is, and will

[XII]

Saves the Whig "Review."

His method of illustration unique.

[XII] be, abundantly imitated, but quite unsuccessfully ; for this reason—that it requires Macaulay's erudition to support Macaulay's cumulative method ; and men of Macaulay's erudition are not likely to have his eclectic turn ; and, if they had, would make their own path, instead of following at his heels. In 1842 he published his "Lays of Ancient Rome," very charming, but eclectic with a vengeance. He was no poet it was clear, though he had given us a book delightful to the unlearned. In 1847 he was excluded from Parliament by his rejection

Rejected at Edinburgh. at Edinburgh—on account merely of a theological quarrel of the time. The citizens compensated this slight, as far as they could, by promoting his election to such Scotch honors as could be conferred upon him —such as being chosen Lord Rector of Glasgow University, and, on the death of Professor Wilson in 1854, President of the Edinburgh Philosophical Institution.

Absence from Parliament and satisfaction at his return. He was sorely missed in the House, though his speaking had become infrequent. When at length he returned with new literary honors accumulated on him, the eagerness to hear him showed what the privation had been. From the Courts, the refreshment-rooms, the Committee-rooms—from every corner to which the news could spread that Macaulay was "up," the rush was as if for a matter of life or death.

Meantime, while he was in this parliamentary and official abeyance, he brought out what were called the first volumes of his History ; neither he nor any one else having any doubt that the rest, up to the reign of George III., would follow regularly and speedily. The beauty of the book exceeded expectation ; and its popularity was such as no book had met with since the days of the Waverley novels ; and with regard to some characteristics and some portions of the book, the first enthusiastic judgment will stand. His portrait of William III., and the portions which may be called the historical romance of the work, will be read with delight by successive generations. But the sober decision already awarded by Time is that the work is not a History; and that it ought never to have been so called, while the characters of real men were treated with so little regard to truth. Of praise and profit Macaulay had his fill, immediately and tumultuously; and openly and heartily he enjoyed it. But the critical impeachments which followed must have keenly annoyed him, as they would any man who cared for his honor, as a relater of facts, and a reporter and judge of the characters of dead and defenceless men. Failing health added its dissuasion to industry. He became subject to bronchitis to a degree which rendered his achievements and his movements uncertain. He was once more elected for Edinburgh in his absence; and it was on this return to the House that the rush to hear him was so remarkable a spectacle. He spoke seldom; and men felt that their opportunities would henceforth be few. Before his retirement from the House of Commons in 1856, he was the mere wreck of his former self. His eye was deep-sunk and often dim, his full face was wrinkled and haggard; his fatigue in utterance was obviously very great; and the tremulousness of limb and feature melancholy to behold. In 1857 he was raised to the Peerage; a graceful compliment to literature.

Macaulay's was mainly an intellectual life, brilliant and stimulating, but cold and barren as regards the highest part of human nature. As in his History there

[XII]
The "History of England."

Raised to the Peerage.

[XII] is but one touch of tenderness—Henrietta Wentworth's name carved upon the tree—so in his brilliant and varied display of power in his life, the one thing wanting is heart. Probably the single touch of sensibility was in him, and we should find some bleeding gashes, or some scars in the stiff bark if we were at liberty to search ; but hard and rugged it was, while throwing out its profusion of dancing foliage and many-tinted blossoms. It was a magnificent growth ; and we may accept its beauty very thankfully, though we know it is only fit for ornament, and not to yield sweet solace for present, or perennial use. If we cannot have in him the man of soul, heroic or other, nor the man of genius as statesman or poet, let us take him as the eloquent scholar, and be thankful.

XIII.

MRS. JAMESON.

DIED MARCH 17TH, 1860.

MRS. JAMESON's name and works have been so long
before the world that there is a prevalent impression
that she was one of the marked generation who could
describe to us the early operation of the *Edinburgh* and
Quarterly Reviews, the first days of the Regency, and
the panics on account of the French Invasion. It was
not exactly.so ; nor, on the other hand, did Anna Murphy
rush into print, or into fame, while yet in her teens. She
was born in the last century ; but it must have been very
near the end of it ; for there is a strong character of
youth and inexperience about her first work, though it
was known by her married name as soon as any name at
all was affixed to it. Her father, the artist Murphy,
Painter in Ordinary to the Princess Charlotte, was in the
habit of taking up his abode for a few months at a time
in some provincial town where the inhabitants were disposed to sit for their portraits. In one of those cities
(Norwich) he was living temporarily, when the "Diary of
an Ennuyée" came out, and was immediately in all the
book-clubs. At a party made for Mr. Murphy, the half-
hour before dinner was beguiled by lively criticism on
the book, in which more or fewer faults were found by

The "Diary of an Ennuyée.

every person present. At length, Mr. Murphy was asked whether he could give any information about the author. Had he ever met her? Was he acquainted with her? *How* well acquainted?—for some uneasiness began to prevail. "She is my daughter," was the reply, which plunged the whole company in dismay. Mrs. Jameson was not a little troubled at the consequences of her mistake in that case, of mixing up a real journal with a sentimental fiction, in order to disguise the authorship. This mistake of mere inexperience exposed her to charges of bad faith in regard to her travelling companions, and to ridicule on account of the pathos of her own fictitious death. She was anxious to have it understood that there had been a want of co-operation between herself and her publishers; and she wisely withdrew the book in its first form, revised the best parts of it, and republished it with various welcome additions, as "Visits and Sketches at Home and Abroad." In its first form the work appeared in 1826 : in the second, in 1834. One incident of the case ought, perhaps, to be considered; that her object in putting this journal to press was understood to be to afford immediate pecuniary aid to Mr. Jameson under some difficulty of the moment. And here it is best to say the little that should be said about the mar-

riage of the parties. Mr. Jameson was a man of considerable ability and legal accomplishment, filling with honor the posts of Speaker of the House of Assembly of Upper Canada, and the Attorney-General of the Colony; and he is spoken of with respect by his personal friends in England; but the marriage was a mistake on both sides. The husband and wife separated almost immediately, and for many years. In 1836, Mrs. Jameson joined her husband at Toronto; but it was for

a very short time; and they never met again. This is [XIII]
all that the world has any business with; and the chief
interest to the world, even that far, arises from the effect
produced on Mrs. Jameson's views of life and love, of
persons and their experience, by her irksome and unfortunate position during a desolate wedded life of nearly
thirty years. Mr. Jameson died in 1854.

The energy of Mrs. Jameson's mind became immediately manifest by the courage with which she returned
to the press after the disheartening first failure; and she
had, we believe, no more failures to bear. She became *Becomes a*
a very popular writer; and to the end of her life she *popular*
proved that her power was genuine by the effect of *writer.*
appreciation upon the exercise of it. She did not dete-
riorate as a writer, but improved as far as the quality of
her mind permitted. She had the great merit of diligence, as well as activity in intellectual labor. She
worked much and well, putting her talents to their full
use—and all the more strenuously the more favor they
found. Another great merit, shown from first to last,
was that she never mistook her function; never overrated the kind of work she applied herself to; never
undervalued the philosophy to which she could not
pretend, nor supposed that she had written immortal
works in pouring out her emotions and fancies for her
personal solace and enjoyment. Perhaps her own account *Her account*
of her own authorship may be cited as the fairest that *of her*
could be given. *authorship*

In the introduction to her "Characteristics of Shakspere's Women," she says: "Not now nor ever have I
written to flatter any prevailing fashion of the day, for
the sake of profit, though this is done by many who have
less excuse for coining their brains. This little book

[XIII]

was undertaken without a thought of fame or money. Out of the fulness of my own heart and soul have I written it. In the pleasure it gave me—in the new and varied forms of human nature it has opened to me—in the beautiful and soothing images it has placed before me—in the exercise and improvement of my own faculties—I have already been repaid." She could honestly have said this of each work in its turn, we doubt not.

The "Characteristics of Women."

This book, the "Characteristics of Women," was apparently the most popular of her works ; and it is perhaps the one which best illustrates her quality of mind. It appeared in 1832, having been preceded by "The Loves of the Poets," and "Lives of Celebrated Female Sovereigns." The "Characteristics" appeared a great advance on the three earlier works ; and it was, at first sight, a very winning book. Wherever the reader opened, the picture was charming ; and the analysis seemed to be acute, delicate, and almost philosophical. After a second portrait the impression was somewhat less enthusiastic ; and when, at the end of four or five, it was found difficult to bring away any clear conception of any, and to tell one from another, it was evident that there was no philosophy in all this, but only fancy and feeling. The notorious mistake in regard to Lady Macbeth, to whom Mrs. Jameson attributes an intellect loftier than that of her husband, indicates the true level of a work which is yet full of charm from its suggestiveness, and frequent truth of sentiment. Mrs. Jameson's world-wide reputation dates from the publication of this book.

Enthusiastic reception of the authoress in America.

It secured her an enthusiastic reception in the United States, when she went there on her way to Canada, in 1836. There could hardly be a more "beautiful fit" than that of Mrs. Jameson and the literary society of the great American cities, where the characteristics of women are perpetually in all people's thoughts and on all people's tongues ; where chivalric honor to woman is a matter of national pride ; and sentiment flourishes as it does in all youthful societies. Mrs. Jameson—pouring out, with her Irish vehemence, a great accumulation of emotions and imaginations, about Ireland and O'Connell, about Shakspere and the Kembles, about German sentiment and Art, Italian paintings, the London stage, and all the ill-usage that women with hearts had received from men who had none—must have been in a state of high enjoyment, and the cause of high enjoyment to others.

Fron the genial welcomes of New York and New England she rushed into a wild Indian life, which she has presented admirably in the work which followed her return—"Winter Studies and Summer Rambles in Canada." In that book appeared with painful distinctness the blemishes which marred much of her writing *The work following her return.* and her conversation, as well as her views of life, from the date of that trip to Canada—a tendency to confide her trouble to the public, or all from whom she could hope to win sympathy—and a morbid construction of the facts and evidences of social life in England. The courage with which she has frequently spoken for benevolent purposes on topics of great difficulty and disgust is honorable to her ; and she has said much that is awakening and stimulating on subjects of deep practical concern ; but her influences would have been of a higher order if she had not been prepossessed by personal griefs, and rendered liable to dwell on the scenery of human passions in one direction till it became magnified beyond all reason. But for this drawback, and that of her unsettled life, which was a perpetual flitting

[XIII]

[XIII]

from place to place, for purposes of Art-study chiefly, perhaps, but in no small degree from restlessness, and craving for society and its luxuries, she might have done more for the security and elevation of her sex than perhaps any other person of her generation. She did a great deal by the pen, by discourse, and by the warm sympathy she gave to the actively great women of the age. She spread the fame of the chief Sisters of Charity of our day; she worked hard to get Schools of Design opened to women; and she published in 1855 an excellent Lecture on "Sisters of Charity Abroad and at Home." The drawback was in the incessant recurrence *A drawback to her usefulness.* to considerations of sex, whatever the topic, and the constant conclusion that the same point of view was taken by everybody else.

In three very different departments Mrs. Jameson was an active worker: in literature, as we have seen; in ameliorating the condition of women in England, by exposing the disabilities and injuries in the field of industry and the chance medley of education; and, again, in the diffusion of the knowledge of Art. Time will probably decide that in this last department her labors have been most effective. Her early readiness to assume the function of Art-critic gave way in time, in some measure, to the more fitting pretention of making Handbooks of Art Collections, and some valuable keys *Her Art Handbooks.* to Art-types, supplied in an historical form. In regard to pictures, as to life and men, her point of view was at first intensely subjective; and her interpretations were liable to error in proportion; so that her knowledge of Art, was denied by the highest authorities. But she studied long, and familiarized herself with so extensive a range of Art, that her metaphysical tendencies were to a considerable extent corrected, and she popularized a great deal of knowledge which would not otherwise have been brought within reach of the very large class of readers of her later works. Her "Handbook" to our public galleries, her "Companion" to our private galleries (in and near London), are works of real utility; and there is much that is instructive as well as charming in her "Legends" of the Monastic Orders, and of the Madonna. After issuing these works between 1848 and 1852, she returned to her favorite habit of authorship — collecting "Thoughts, Memoirs, and Fancies" from her "Common-place Book," and shedding them into the world, under the two divisions which describe the contemplations of her life—"Ethics and Character," and "Literature and Art." The impression left is uniform with that of all her works,— that of a warm-hearted and courageous woman, of indomitable sociability of nature, large liberalities, and deep prejudices.

[XIII] *Popularizing knowledge.*

Her works have been received as happy accidents; and, long after they have ceased to be sought and regularly read, some touch of nature in them, some trait of insight, or ingenuity of solution will come up in fireside conversation, or in literary intercourse, and remind a future generation that in ours there was a restless, expatiating, fervent, unreasoning, generous, accomplished Mrs. Jameson among the lights of the time, by no means hiding her lustre under a bushel, or being too closely shut up at home; a great benefit to her time from her zeal for her sex and for Art; but likely to have been a greater if she could have carried less of herself and her experiences into her pictures and her interpretations of life.

Her rôle in history.

[XIII]   There is not much to say of the mode of living of one who lived in pictures and in speech—whose existence was a pilgrimage in search, or in honor, of the Arts of Expression.   Her circumstances were made easy, after Mr. Jameson's death, by a tribute from her friends and admirers, invested for that purpose.   She enjoyed life, whatever had been its troubles and mortifications ; and the pleasures of the imagination, and the stimulus of society, were as animating to her as they were necessary, as disease advanced and strength wasted away.

XIV.

WALTER SAVAGE LANDOR.

DIED SEPTEMBER 17TH, 1864.

THE great age to which Mr. Landor attained affords[*]
some sort of presumption that certain attributes of his
by which he was best known to the multitude were
qualities of style rather than of soul—we do not mean
of literary style only, but style of expression by life and
act, as well as by the pen. Contempt and bitterness are
not conducive to long life. As the ancients said, they
dry up the vital juices. As we moderns say, they fret
the brain and nerves, and intercept the complacent
enjoyment of good-humor and benevolence, which
eminently promotes length of days. As Walter Savage
Landor was born in 1775, and has only now departed,
it seems that, after all, he had not any fatal proportion
of contempt or bitterness deep down in his nature; and
the question remains how he came to be so markedly
known by as much as he had. The truth is, he had in *Para-*
him a strong faculty of admiration; and a deep, pure, *doxical*
fresh current of tenderness and sweetness ran under the *in his*
film of gall which Nature unhappily shed over his *character.*
existence at the fountain. This was one of the contradictions of which this paradoxical being was made
up; and it is, with the rest, worthy of some contem-

6

[XIV]

plation ; not because paradoxical persons or the paradoxes they produce are choice objects of study in a
striving and practical age like ours, but because Landor
achieved some things that were great, and many that
were beautiful, in spite of the paradoxical elements of
his life and character.

Experience of the youthful scholar in the perusal of Landor's writings.

The young of thirty years ago, to·whom Literature
was an important pursuit and pleasure, were often seen
in a transport of admiration, amazement, and anger,
when rising from Landor's books. They were quite
sure that nothing so noble, nothing so tender, nothing
so musical was to be found in our language as the "Imaginary Conversations" between Pericles and Sophocles,
between Demosthenes and Eubulides, between Ascham
and Lady Jane Grey, and plenty more. The patriotism,
the magnanimity, and the sweet heroism of the sentiments call up the flush or the tear ; and the familiarity
with the ancients, in their habit of mind and speech,
enraptures the youthful scholar. After a time, he
relaxes in his reading of Landor—still declares, when
he is talked of, that his is a grand and beautiful fragmentary mind ; but he no longer reads his later volumes ;
and at last grows so weary of his Jacobin doctrines, his
obtrusive spirit, and sententious style, that when the
well-known name in large letters appears in the newspaper, at the foot of a denunciatory letter, or a curse in
stanzas, it is a signal to turn the leaf. The standard
criticism of the country seems to have undergone something of the same process as the individual student.
The *Quarterly Review* once despised everybody who
could stop to notice Landor's faults, and eloquently
described the process of the elevation of his fame, till
it should become transcendent among the worthies of

England; but it may be questioned now whether the
Quarterly Review has any more expectation than the
Edinburgh that the writings of Landor will survive,
except as curiosities in literature. The fact seems to
be that, with some of the attributes of genius, Landor
fell just short of it. He had not the large spirit and
generous temper of genius. His egotism was extreme;
but it was not that of genius. He has been called a
prose Byron; and certainly he complained abundantly
of Man and Life, and abhorred tyrants, and lived long
in Italy, and fought for liberty abroad; and especially,
he was at once a Jacobin or democrat in literature, and
a man of family and fortune; but there the resemblance
stops. Where Byron moaned, Landor scolded. Landor
had no patience with Royalty, or any rule but the
popular, because it stood between men and their
happiness; whereas Byron looked upon tyranny as a
mere symptom of human corruptness and misery, and
saw no happiness on the other side of it. Byron was
an embodiment of the growing spirit of his time, which
uttered itself through him because his lips had been
touched with fire; but Landor's utterances were almost
entirely personal and constitutional—expressed no prevalent sentiment or need—not being even the utterance
of a party in politics or literature, but the presentment
of an unchanging egotism, under majestic or graceful
disguises furnished from the stores of his learning or
the resources of his imagination. It is one of the
paradoxes about Landor, not that he should have but
one style—for that might be expected; but that that
style should have been dramatic. Well as he succeeded in hitting the mode of thought of many of his
discoursing personages, it was by means of his learning,

[XIV]

*Falls short
of genius.*

*Byron and
Landor.*

[XIV]

*Landor
speaking
in the
"Imaginary
Conversa-
tions."*

and not of his sympathies, that he did so. They were
all raised from the dead in their habits as they lived;
but it was in order to be possessed by Landor in every
case—his spirit speaking through their brains, perhaps,
as well as through their lips—but always his spirit and
no other.   Hence his failures in the case of Milton, and
partly, even in that of Cromwell; though there he might
have been expected to succeed pre-eminently.   Yet more
modern English personages fail more and more conspicuously, in comparison with old Greeks, and mediæval
Italians, and far-away Spaniards; for the obvious reason
that the former, living amidst modern associations, and
represented by a writer who is too much of an egotist
and a mannerist to have genuine dramatic power, must
be simply Landor himself, cramped and debilitated by
the restraints of his disguise.   These are the tokens and
proofs of his falling short of true genius.   Yet there
is so genuine a force of Liberalism in his writings,
so constant a vigilance against the encroachments of
tyranny, as may neutralize a large admixture of self-love
and self-will; and it really is so rare to see the claims of
the democracy so presented, amidst the music and the
lights reverberated and reflected from the classic ages,
that the man who has done that service may be fairly
considered an original of high mark, even if he be too
paradoxical, and too measured an egotist, to be entitled
to high honors of genius.

But paradox carries away others than the inventors
and utterers; and we have been commenting on the
mind of the vigorous old man who is gone from us,
before we have glanced at his life, which was, from first
to last, as characteristic as his writings; as characteristic
as his face and form, and everything pertaining to him.

We may be called paradoxical ourselves if we say (but it is true), that never was anything more of a piece than the mind and life, the surroundings, the utterances and the acts of this wonderfully sane yet thoroughly inconsistent being. His tall, broad, muscular, active frame was characteristic ; and so was his head, with the strange elevation of the eyebrows, which expresses self-will as strongly in some cases as astonishment in others. Those eyebrows, mounting up till they comprehend a good portion of the forehead, have been observed in many more paradoxical persons than one. Then there was the retreating but broad forehead, showing the deficiency of reasoning and speculative power, with the preponderance of imagination, and a huge passion for destruction. The massive self-love and self-will carried up his head to something more than a dignified bearing —even to one of arrogance. His vivid and quick eye, and the thoughtful mouth, were fine, and his whole air was that of a man distinguished in his own eyes certainly, but also in those of others. Tradition reports that he was handsome in his youth. In age he was more. The first question about him usually was why, with his frame, and his courage, and his politics, and his social position, he was not in the army. One reply might be, that he could neither obey nor co-operate ; another was, that his godfather, General Powell, wished it ; and Landor therefore preferred something else. As for that something else—his father offered him 400*l.* a year to study Law, and reside in the Temple for that purpose, whereas he would give him only 150*l.* if he would not ; and of course, he took the 150*l.*, and went as far as he well could from the Temple—that is, to Swansea. Warwick was his native place. He was born in the best house

[XIV]

His form and features.

Born at Warwick.

in the city, where the fine old garden, with its noble elms and horse-chestnuts, might have influenced his imagination, so as to have something to do possibly with his subsequent abode in Italy. His mother was of the ancient family of Savage; and hereditary estates lay about him in Staffordshire and Warwickshire, which had been in the possession of the family for nearly seven centuries.

Sells hereditary estates.

These he sold, to shift himself to Wales; and nowhere did his spirit of destructive waywardness break out more painfully than in the sale of those old estates, and his treatment of the new. He employed many scores of laborers on his Welsh estates, made roads and planted, and built a house which cost him 8,000*l.* He set his heart upon game-preserving (of all pursuits for a democratic republican), and had at times twenty keepers out upon the hills at night, watching his grouse; but, with 12,000 acres of land, he never saw a grouse on his table. His tenants cheated him, he declared, and destroyed his plantations; and, though he got rid of them, he left, not only Wales but Great Britain, in wrath. Then, the steward in charge of his house cheated him, when he not only got rid of the steward, but had his splendid new house pulled down—out of consideration, he declared, for his son's future ease and convenience, in being rid of so vexatious a property. His flatterers called this an act of characteristic indignation. To others it appeared that his republican and self-governing doctrines came rather strangely from one who could not rule his own affairs and his own people; and who, finding his failure, could do nothing better than lay waste the whole scene.

He had obtained some of his scholarship at Rugby, and somewhat more at Oxford—where, however, his stay

was short. Having fired a gun in the quadrangle of his [XIV]
college, he was rusticated ; and, instead of returning,
published a volume of poems, when he was only eighteen.
While at Swansea, he studied, and wrote "Gebir." On
the invasion of Spain, he determined to be a soldier on *Aids the*
his own account, raised a small troop at his own expense, *Spaniards*
and was the first Englishman who landed in aid of the *as a soldier.*
Spaniards. He was rewarded for this aid, and for a gift
of money, by the thanks of the Supreme Junta, and
by the rank of Colonel on his return to England ; but
he sent back his commission and the record of thanks
when Ferdinand set aside the Constitution. Among
many good political acts, perhaps none was better than
this. At thirty-six years of age he married a French *Marries a*
lady of good family ; and a few years after, in 1818, *French lady*
fixed his residence in Italy,—first in the Palazzo Medici, *and resides*
in Florence, and when obliged to leave it, in a charming *in Italy.*
villa two miles off. That Villa Gherardesca was built
by Michel Angelo. Few British travellers in Italy fail
to go and see Fiesole ; and while Landor lived there
he was the prey of lion-hunters,—as he vehemently
complained on occasion of the feud between him and
N. P. Willis, the American, who lost a MS. confided to
him for his opinion. Such a subordination of the full,
ripe scholar and discourser to the shallow, flippant
sketcher by the wayside, might seem to deserve such
a result ; but it did not tend to reconcile Landor to
lion-hunters. While in Italy, he sent to English newspapers, and especially to the *Examiner*, frequent comments on passing events in the political world, in the
form of letters or of verse. He was collecting pictures
all the while ; and when he returned to England to pass
the rest of his days, as he supposed, he left the bulk

[XIV]

of his collection in his villa, for his son's benefit, bringing
only a few gems wherewith to adorn such a modest
residence as he now intended to have in his own country.
That residence was in St. James's-square, Bath, where he

*Becomes an
octogena-
rian at
Bath.*

became an octogenarian living for a while in peace and
quiet—still commenting on men and measures through
the Liberal papers, and putting forth, in his eightieth year,
the little volume called "Last Fruit from an Old Tree."
The spectacle of a vigorous, vivid, undaunted old age,
true to the aims and convictions of youth, is always
a fine one; and it was warmly felt to be so in Landor's
case.   His prejudices mattered less, when human affairs
went on maturing themselves in spite of them; and many
of his complaints were silenced in the best possible way
—by the reform of the abuses which he, with some
unnecessary violence, denounced.   He, for his part,

*His pre-
judices and
his opinions.*

talked less about killing kings; and his steady assertion
of the claims of the humble fell in better with the spirit
of the time, after years had inaugurated the works of
peace.   About many matters of political principle and
practice he was right, while yet the majority of society
were wrong; and it would be too much to require that
he should be wholly right in doctrine and fact, or very
angelic in his way of enforcing his convictions.   Nature
did not make him a logician, and if we were ever disappointed at not finding him one, the fault was our own.
She make him brave, though wayward; an egotist in his
method, but with the good of mankind for his aim.   He
was passionate and prejudiced, but usually in some great
cause, and on the right side of it; though there was a
deplorable exception to that general rule in the particular instance of defamation which broke up the
repose and dignity of his latter days, and caused his

self-exile from England for the remnant of his life. This brief notice of the painful fact is enough for truth and justice. As for the rest, he was of aristocratic birth, fortune, and education, with democracy for his political aim, and poverty and helplessness for his clients. All this would have made Walter Savage Landor a remarkable man in his generation, apart from his services to Literature ; but when we recall some of his works—such pictures as that of the English officer shot at the Pyramids—such criticism as in his Pentameron—and discourses so elevating and so heart-moving as some which he has put into the mouths of heroes, sages, scholarly and noble women, and saintly and knightly men, we feel that our cumulative obligations to him are very great, and that his death is a prominent incident of the time.

[XIY]
His self-exile from England in his latter days.

6*

II.

SCIENTIFIC.

I.

GEORGE COMBE.

DIED AUGUST 14TH, 1858.

A MAN must be called a conspicuous member of society who writes a book approaching in circulation to the three ubiquitous books in our language—the Bible, "Pilgrim's Progress," and "Robinson Crusoe." George Combe's "Constitution of Man" is declared to rank next to these three in point of circulation; and the author of a work so widely diffused cannot but be the object of much interest during his life, and of special notice after death. It seems as if Nature were as capricious as fortune in appointing the destinies of Man. George Combe's wide influence over society arose out of natural causes; but, as in many similar instances, there was nothing in the man to account for the eminence of his position. He was a good man, and in certain directions a wise one; but he was not a thinker, nor a poet, nor an orator, nor an enthusiast, nor a quack. He did not owe his social influence to any of the ordinary sources of that kind of influence, from the loftiest to the meanest. Of course the solution of the marvel must be looked for in circumstances chiefly external to the man; and there, in fact, the solution is easily found.

Ubiquitous book.

[I]

*His parents
and early
training.*

The Combes—a family of seventeen, of whom George and Andrew were the two conspicuous members—were descended on both sides of the house from respectable tenant-farmers.   Their father was a tall, robust, stanch Presbyterian, of whom his phrenological sons report that he could never find a hat that he could get his head into, and was obliged to have a block to himself. Their mother was energetic and conscientious, as indeed the mother of seventeen children had need to be.   Neither parent had much education ; and both seem to have been excessively strict in the religious discipline of their family.   The want of knowledge and the asceticism of the well-intentioned parents caused the death of several of their children, and radically injured the health of the rest.   Such is the testimony of the two brothers, in their reminiscences of the low, damp situation of their father's dwelling, at the brewery of Livingston's-yards, near Edinburgh, and of its crowded and ill-aired rooms, and of the dreary Sundays and dismal sectarian instruction, which was all that their parents attempted to give them in person.   No doubt this experience tended to turn the attention of the brothers to the subject of the conditions of health, and to deepen their convictions to the utmost that their nature admitted.   They have done great things for their own and future generations in spreading practices of cleanliness, and a demand for fresh air, through a vast proportion of society ; and if they had been men of genius, or capable of enthusiasm, they would have had "a mission" and have ranked among the apostles of the race.   The influence of ignorance in degrading and deteriorating the human body cut out such a mission as that of restoring its claims long ago ; and the Combes might have been the apostles of that mission if nature had given them genius instead of an order of faculties which doomed them to triteness in the conception and expression of their most earnest convictions.

George Combe (nine years older than Andrew) was born in 1788. He was bred to the Law, became a Writer to the Signet in 1812, and took a house in Bank-street, Edinburgh, to which a sister removed as housekeeper, and Andrew, for health's sake, and to pursue his studies in greater quiet than in the over-crowded old home. In no house in Edinburgh or elsewhere could Dugald Stewart have then found more devoted disciples—more ardent admirers of his so-called Philosophy of Mind. The matter-of-fact George seems to have been lifted nearer to poetry by his attendance on Dugald Stewart's lectures than at any subsequent period of his life. His conscience was kept quiet by the lecturer's assurance that his Philosophy was founded on the inductive method; and as long as George believed this he was satisfied, though at times surprised to find that this Philosophy did not seem to be applicable to any purpose but delighting hearers and readers. The lecturer was for ever promising magnificent results; and George fully anticipating these, tried to obtain them by operating upon Andrew's mind; a process which he afterward described as that of the blind leading the blind. Such was the state of affairs in Bank-street when, in 1815, Dr. John Gordon of Edinburgh, an esteemed lecturer on anatomy and physiology, furnished Jeffrey with an article for his Review, which was intended to demolish, and was for a time supposed to have de-molished, "the Physiognomical System of Gall and Spurzheim," as the title of that system stands in the

[I]

Attends the lectures of Dugald Stewart.

Gall and Spurzheim's System.

[I]

books of the time. No one laughed more heartily than George Combe (as we learn from himself) at the "thorough quackery," the "impudence," and what not of "the Germans" who dared to offer us anything but Werther sentimentalism. The Review represented Gall as "bitter," and Spurzheim as "splenetic," and both as vulgar quacks—a piece of bad policy as well as a mistake.[1] It was too late in 1815 to extinguish Gall's discovery as quackery; for it had been fairly before the world five years, and accepted by eminent scientific men abroad. Metternich, who should have been a Natural Philosopher, had taken care of that. In 1802, the Government at *Gall and* Vienna had suppressed Gall's work on the "Functions *Metternich.* of the Brain;" but Metternich saw its value, and guaranteed the expenses of its publication in 1810, when he was Austrian Ambassador at Paris. It soon became on the continent what it has now long been in England, the source of new views of the Structure and Functions of the Brain. As for the "bitterness" and "spleen" of the German philosophers, the appearance of Spurzheim in Edinburgh presently disposed of the imputation. Spurzheim was found to be a modest, amiable, intelligent man, and quite as good a logician as an observer. He was not a discoverer, but he was a good teacher. He made some way at once, even as Dr. Gordon's antagonist on his own ground; and he did more for the establishment of his doctrine by a course of popular lectures, where he was listened to by a small body of earnest young men. The Combes

[1] It is understood that Dr. Gordon was not responsible for this injurious language; and that he indignantly protested against the editor's conduct in interpolating the article with expressions as revolting to the writer's sense of justice as to his taste.

were among the scoffers outside. They never saw the
Lecturer ; and much less would they have cared to hear
him. One day, however, a brother lawyer met George
in the street, and invited him to his house to see Spurzheim dissect a human brain. What he saw there satisfied
him that the human brain is something very unlike
what it seemed to dissectors, who sliced it through and
looked no further. He attended the Lecturer's second
course, and reached a conviction, which determined
the character of his mind and life. He himself tells us
that he was not "led away by enthusiasm," but won by
the evidence that the doctrine was "eminently practical."

Great was the misfortune to the young man himself,
and yet greater to the world, of his passion for "the
practical." He did not understand the very terms of
true science ; and his mind had no scientific quality
which could give him insight into the bearings of theory
and practice, hypothesis, discovery, and explanation.
In this one bit of science, which he supposed himself
to have acquired, he recognized a practical value in an
application which a schoolboy of the present time would
be above making. He, and Andrew also, thought it
was "practical" to say that such and such a faculty was
too strong for some other—(as if it required phrenology
to say that) ; and that they considered that they had
"explained" a case when they had stated that No. 16
was out of proportion to No. 6 ; and that No. 20 had
no chance under the predominance of No. 5. They
supposed that they thus "accounted for" the character
of people's minds ; and to the end of their lives neither
of them had the remotest conception that the only
meaning of the act of "explaining" (in a philosophical
sense) is referring some particular fact to a general law.

[I]

Spurzheim's lectures.

Combe's passion for " the practical."

[I]   Thus, in their published letters, there is something as
painful as ludicrous in the perseverance and unremitting
complacency with which the brothers write of one another's faculties, and their own and other people's ; of
Andrew's "wit" (Heaven help it!) and George's fluency,
and the superior individuality of the one and causality
of the other ; and so on.   If this had been the first
excess of an early enthusiasm, it would have mattered
little ; but the men never got an inch beyond it ; and
hence the misfortune to themselves and to the world.
It was not only that they helped to originate a new and
pernicious pedantry ;   a greater mischief was that they
retarded, as far as in them lay, the development of a
genuine scientific discovery.   No power on earth could
stop it.   Jeffrey, and other Edinburgh worthies, who
The opposi-   had hastily committed themselves, raised a periodical
tion to   scoff and outcry against it.   The Editor of the "Encyclo-
phrenology.   pædia Britannica" refused the subject of "Phrenology"
(for the revised edition of that work) to a phrenologist,
and gave it to Dr. Roget to treat (which is like setting
a Romanist to give an account of Protestantism, or a
Hindoo to report of Mohammedanism) ; but in spite of
all opposition, the truthful part of the modern physiology
of the brain has become established.   But the Combes,
and especially George, had from the outset probably
done more to damage it in one way than to aid it in
another.   George took it up as Spurzheim gave it him
in his young days ; he received it as something compact
and finished ;   and he never practically admitted that
there could be anything more in new discoveries than
the Jeffreys and the Rogers recognized in those which
he held ; or even so much, for they, with all the rest of
Edinburgh, at length admitted Gall's anatomy of the

brain, while rejecting his physiology of the mind. To
George's "practical" eye, the human brain and mind
appeared as in a map of a completely surveyed country:
whereas he should have seen that only the latitude and
longitude, and vertebral heights and broken coast-lines,
were ascertained, and that wide regions remained un-
explored, and deep recesses unentered. It mattered
nothing to him that a vast proportion of brain was
assigned to a single faculty, while there were faculties
which no numbered organ or mutual action of organs
could account for. It mattered nothing to him that
evidence was offered of the one supposed organ being
a group of many. It mattered nothing to him that
proved developments were made which Gall himself
would have received with rapture. George Combe
looked on unmoved and immovable in his complacency.
He piqued himself greatly on his liberality; which was
indeed perfect in one direction. He saw that opinions
(in the strict sense of the word) are not voluntary; and
he thoroughly and consistently accepted the correlative
duty of absolute liberality to dissentients. He cordially
and practically admitted every mans' right to his own
views, and he never meddled with other people's opinions,
while carefully impressing his own protest against them.
But he stopped there. He never examined other people's
opinions, nor opened his mind to what they had to say
about them. He never sought other persons' point of
view, nor showed any sympathy in their researches, nor
respect for their attainments, unless they were offered to
him in confirmation of his own "philosophy." This
unprogressive character of mind, in a professed apostle of
a progressive science, was a misfortune, great under any
circumstances, and especially in a case where the social

[1]

*George
Combe's
complacency.*

influence was so extraordinary as in the case of George Combe.

In 1825, the Society for the Diffusion of Useful Knowledge was instituted—chiefly for the purpose of supplying good and cheap books to Mechanics' Institutes, where the want of books, as supplementary to lectures, was severely felt. Political troubles caused delay; but the scheme was resumed in 1826; and in March, 1827, the issue of the Society's tracts began. Lord Brougham and his coadjutors had promised means of political, social, and what may be called personal knowledge. Theological teaching was wholly excluded; and morality had no chance. Now, the thirst of mankind for moral philosophy is unquenchable; and the refusal or neglect of the Diffusion Society to give it merely turned the mechanics of the country loose, to find what they wanted for themselves. Six weeks before the appearance of the first of the Society's tracts, George Combe had read to the Phrenological Society of Edinburgh the first part of a work "On the Harmony between the Mental and Moral Constitution of Man and the Laws of Physical Nature." This was the first form of his celebrated "Constitution of Man in relation to External Objects," which was published in 1828, and read with unexampled eagerness by almost the entire reading classes of the nation. A benevolent gentleman, named Henderson, left a sum of money to be spent in rendering the book as cheap as possible; and extremely cheap it was made, so that multitudes possessed it who never owned any other book. Its circulation had long ago amounted to 100,000 in Great Britain and Ireland; and it is in almost every house in the United States, besides having been translated into various continental languages. The good

effects of this book, on the whole, are the best counter-
balance that its author afforded for the damage he inflicted on the "science" to which he believed his life to
be devoted. It was a prodigious boon to the multitude,
high and low, to be led to the contemplation of their
frame in relation to the external world; to obtain the
first glimpse (as it was to them) of Man's position in the
universe as a constituent part of it, subject to its laws
precisely like every other part. Much else there is in
the book which fell in remarkably with the needs and
desires of the time; and there can be no doubt that the
effect of the work, as a whole, on the health, morality,
and intellectual cultivation of the people, has been something truly memorable. It is the great work and the
great event of the life of George Combe. He wrote other
works; but he is known by his "Constitution of Man."
In 1819 he published his "Essays on Phrenology," and
afterward his "Elements," "Outlines," and "System"
of the same subject; and a volume of "Moral Philosophy," and "Lectures on Popular Education," "Notes"
of his travels in America, and a Life of his brother
Andrew; and, we regret to add, his views on Art after
his visits to Germany and Italy in pursuit of health. The
slightest appreciation of the qualities of his intellect
must show the absurdity of his attempting criticism in
Art; and it is a curious illustration of the small range of
a professed "practical" judgment that George Combe,
who prided himself on such a judgment, should have
supposed himself a judge of pictures, statues, and architecture, and have believed that he "explained" anything
in the department of art by his applications of what he
called his Philosophy. Perhaps the most useful thing he
did was translating a part of Gall's writings; and there

[I]

*The useful-
ness of the
work.*

*His other
publications.*

[I] can be little doubt that he would have made the very best use of his time and such talents as he had, if he had given us a condensed version of these writings, instead of lucubrations of his own which have disguised more than they have propagated Gall's discoveries. In his great work, the "Constitution of Man," he was preceded by Spurzheim, whose "Natural Laws" effected for its readers what Combe's works did for the working classes. If he had given us the teachings of the Masters themselves, we should have been in a better position than by seeing them represented in the person of a special pleader who assumes to be their comrade.

His perti-
nacity in
maintain-
ing the
rights of
Opinion.

The merit of Combe was great in pertinaciously and effectively sustaining the rights of Opinion, and some facts of science, in the *Phrenological Journal*, against an opposition unsurpassed in violence and dishonesty. For this he was well fitted by nature and training. His remarkable self-esteem ; his self-consciousness, rendering him very faintly impressionable ; his good-nature and real benevolence ; his shrewdness and caution ; the absence of all keen sensibility, and the presence of a constant sense of justice,—all fitted him to hold any given ground well against unscrupulous and passionate adversaries. No romance of duty dazzled him ; no idolatry of the ideal intoxicated him ; no sympathy with human passion or devout aspiration put him off his guard. Standing above the perils of gross selfishness and dishonesty; and below those which attend high intellectual and spiritual gifts, he was the man to hold a certain ground, and he held it steadily, cheerfully, and well. It would not be honest, however, to pass over without notice the snare into which he fell, and into which he led some of his followers, through his deficiency in the high qualities just referred to. It was not necessary to have his personal acquaintance to become aware, in the latter part of his career, that, with all his appearance of frankness toward the public, he was not in the habit of really opening his mind on matters of opinion of the deepest importance. It was all very well for Mr. Huskisson, as an Administrative Reformer, to open his hand, as he said, by one finger at a time, because the people or their rulers could not receive a whole handful of the truth about Free Trade. This is excusable, if not wise, in a matter of fiscal doctrine ; and Mr. Huskisson, while waiting his time, never conformed to the sayings and doings of the Protectionists. But George Combe went to work, in regard to religion and morals, as Mr. Huskisson did, so far as letting out only by the little finger ; and he did even this by conforming to established notions and forms of expressions which, it came out at last, were in his opinion false. A collocation of the evidence afforded by himself in a course of years shows that he accommodated himself to the popular view and language on theological and moral subjects, where there was no real sympathy of opinion. Now and then, when Popular Education, or some other cause that he really had at heart, was in question, he came out boldly against intolerance ; but otherwise, there is a coaxing quality in his teachings, a forced character in his sympathy, and a measured and patronizing tone in his intercourses with thinkers which point to the truth, that this teacher (believing himself a philosopher) took the old philosopher's license, to which he had no sort of right in his place and time, of having an esoteric and an exoteric doctrine, and organizing a sect on that ground. The ground proved infirm, of course. The Phrenologists are no longer a mere sect,

[I]

His reticence and apparent conformity to established notions.

and they never could be organized as a sect holding secrets. The result of the attempt was to shake everybody's confidence in George Combe, from the time when it became clear that he was appearing to entertain one set of opinions while holding another. This is, amidst some foibles, the one serious fault chargeable on George Combe, in his assumed character of Philosopher and Teacher. Great virtues attended on that function all the while; benevolence, a genial cheerfulness and kindliness; a large power of liberality in himself, and a virtuous persistence in requiring the same from others in behalf of everybody. We do not, indeed, see how the honors of genius, or of philosophical achievement, or of original thought, can be awarded to him; but he was the agent, if not the author, of a great revolution in popular views, and in sanitary practices. If he did not advance his own department of science, but rather hindered its development by his own philosophical incapacity, he prepared for its future expansion by opening the minds of millions to its conception. The world owes him much, however disappointed it may be that it does not owe him more.

His one serious fault.

In 1833 George Combe married Miss Cecilia Siddons. Four or five years after, he quitted the practice of his profession, and in 1838 went, accompanied by Mrs. Combe, to the United States, where he remained, lecturing and preparing his journal, till 1840. Dr. Spurzheim had visited the United States in 1832, and died there in a few months; and the disciples he had obtained, wishing for another master, invited George Combe to go and lecture to them. The years after his return were varied by continental journeys, too often rendered necessary by failing health. The latter period of his life was one of

His marriage,

and visit to the United States.

very infirm health—the result, as he believed, of the early adverse influences which turned his own and his brother's attention so strongly to sanitary subjects. After more and more shutting up for the winters, and less and less ability to enjoy the business and pleasures of life and society within his own home, he died at his friend Dr. Lane's hydropathic establishment, at Moor Park, just as he had completed his threescore years and ten.

[I]

7

II.

ALEXANDER VON HUMBOLDT.

DIED MAY 6TH, 1859.

THE remarkable brothers William and Alexander von Humboldt were descendants of a Pomeranian family. William made himself a memorable name in Germany, and Alexander in the whole civilized world. William, the elder by rather more than two years, was a philosopher in the realms of Literature and Art, while Alexander devoted himself, not to the study of the human mind or its productions, but to the medium or environment in which it lives. William was frankly told by his friend Schiller that his mind was of too ratiocinative and critical a cast to permit him to produce works of art, in literature or otherwise ; and his highest achievements were, accordingly, in the department of philology. However great these might have been, they could never have won the heartfelt love with which William von Humboldt was regarded by some of the best men of his age. It was his political action which won him that love. He was ever found asserting the principles of liberty—earnestly, wisely, and unflinchingly ; and hence it was certain, as he very well knew, that he would never be a great man in the Berlin Court sense of greatness, when once he had been called upon to declare an opinion

William von Humboldt.

which differed from that of the Monarch who pretended
to ask his counsel. He filled a succession of diplomatic
and administrative offices for above nineteen years; but
when it became necessary to remind his Sovereign, in
opposition to Von Hardenberg, of the promise of a constitution made in 1813, the King declined to keep his
promise and his faithful councillor, and preferred losing
his honor and his good Minister in order to retain
power (in the sense in which he understood it), and the
Minister who flattered his love of it. William von
Humboldt had still fifteen years to live. He passed
them in philological and literary studies, and died,
honored and beloved, without doubt or drawback, in
the sixty-ninth year of his age, in 1835. He had signed
the Treaty of Chatillon, and attended the Vienna Congress as the representative of his country. His brother
attended the Congress of Verona in the King's suite.
The elder incurred the royal displeasure by his Liberal
tendencies; but the younger enjoyed grace and distinction
at Court to the end; patronage being showered upon
him, without too close an inquiry on the one hand, or
too frank an explanation on the other, in regard to the
principles and practice of government. As William retired to explore the roots and genealogies of language,
and to write the hundred sonnets which were found after
his death, Alexander was displaying more stars on his
coat, and receiving more honors on his head. There
could never be any rational objection to the brothers
taking different lines, as their natural preparation might
indicate. The noticeable point was the descent of Court
honors on the Naturalist, while disgrace fell on the
Statesman; and a smile went round the circles, both of
philosophy and politics, when Alexander, in laying out

*Treatment
of the
brothers by
the Court.*

[II] the scheme of his "Kosmos," proposed to omit the whole subject of Mental Philosophy. The idea of presenting a delineation of the universe, not in mere external form but as moved by its forces, and omitting the most marvellous of all manifestations and forces, seemed to his readers more remarkable for caution than for philosophical wisdom.

William was born at Potsdam in 1767; and Alexander —or, as his name stands at full length, Frederick Henry Alexander von Humboldt—was born at Berlin in 1769, on the 14th of September. Their father died when they were twelve and ten years old; but their mother, a cousin of the Princess Blucher, was a woman of fine capacity and cultivation; and the family fortunes were good; so that the boys had every educational advantage. Alexander received his academic training at Göttingen and Frankfort on the Oder, and a part of his scientific instruction at the Mining School of Freiburg. Nothing could be more marked than his early determination toward Natural Science, and toward travel in pursuit of his researches. The more he was thwarted and hemmed in by the obstructions of war, the intenser grew his desire to explore the heights, depths, and expanses of the earth, in order to extort the secrets of Nature. Geology did not yet exist; and for want of the generalizations with which he, more than any other man, has since furnished us, Natural Science was fragmentary and confused to a degree scarcely conceivable to students now entering on that vast field. We complain at present of the desultory condition of Natural Science from the speciality of pursuit which is the great disadvantage of our existing stage; and from which we must be relieved ere long by the formation of a new class of philosophers,

Early bent of Alexander's genius.

whose business it will be to establish the mutual relations
of all the sciences, and all the departments of each
science ; but when Humboldt was a youth, even the
stage of speciality was scarcely reached.   The ardent
mind of the boy seems to have contemplated—as other
boyish minds have done—the exhibition of those relations,
after a due exploration of the details, and generalization
of the results in the various departments.   Many are the
youths who have formed this conception, and resolved
upon the work ; but, since Aristotle, Humboldt is the
most remarkable—some might say the only—example of
an approach to the achievement of such a scheme.   Our
own opinion is, that others have approached as nearly—
the disadvantages of their times being considered ; and
that Humboldt's achievements, prodigious as they are,
fall short precisely in the points in regard to which his
own expectations were highest.   His investigations and
arrangement of details was perfectly marvellous from its
scope and equality of treatment ; his generalization were
so splendid, and so fruitful beyond all estimate, that it is
a reluctant judgment which ranks them below his more
concrete studies, in regard to quality ; but there can be
no difference of opinion about his failure in his highest
effort, as exhibited in his " Kosmos."   We have every
reason to believe it impossible, practically speaking, for
the same mind to effect what Humboldt did and what he
failed to do.   Whenever (if ever) we have a " Kosmos,"
it will be given us by a man who can immediately and
thoroughly adopt the results of other men's labors as
material for his peculiar faculty of ascertaining relations
between vastnesses and aggregates which are to him
manageable single portions of the great whole.   The
discoverer of a Solar System could not possibly be the

His achieve- ments in Natural Science.

[II]

man who should resolve first to understand the Natural
History of all the constituents of the globe ; but rather
the man who takes up our globe as a planet, and carries
it as a unit into his scheme of planetary study. It is
therefore no wonder that Humboldt is found to halt,
waver, and diverge in his presentment of the great
Scheme of the Universe. Sometimes he quits his own
definition or description ; sometimes he loses the precision of his great idea in a cloud of words which look
philosophical, but will not bear a plain rendering ; and
often he rambles away from his central point of view
into wide fields of facts, extremely interesting, and marvellously rich, but not directly related to the object they
were cited to illustrate.

*His
deficiencies.*

Thus much of failure is ascribable to the mere fact
of the limitation and inequality of human faculty. The
other great cause of failure in the most ambitious of
Humboldt's works is of a moral nature. He declines
to speak out on some essential points which, in a scheme
like his, cannot be slighted. His ambition and his
caution are irreconcilable. On the essential topics,
for instance, of Creation, of Spontaneous Generation,
and of the basis and scope of Mental Philosophy, with
some other such ticklish subjects, he either keeps back
his views, or permits them to be discoverable only by
a process of inference of which none but the highly
qualified are capable. In this matter, however, it is
necessary to state that he should not be judged by the
English translations of "Kosmos ;" even the best, and
that sanctioned by himself. The word "creation" used
repeatedly for the universe, is misleading, or at least
perplexing to readers who have duly attended to some
preceding passages ; and if they turn to the original

they find that Humboldt spoke of the frame of things, the universe, the collective phenomena of nature, or the like. But the omission of some prominent philosophical bases, whether through caution or anything else, renders the "Kosmos" of Humboldt a hybrid production between poetry and science which is not the philosophy it pretends to be. It is wealthy in its facts, and splendid in its generalizations ; but it is not Kosmos.

Humboldt's preparation for this, which he considered his crowning work, may be said to have begun when he became the pupil of Werner, the first Geologist, at Freiburg, when he was two-and-twenty. He had already travelled in Holland and England, and even published a scientific book—on the Basalts of the Rhine. He was employed as a Director on the Government Mines ; and, in the course of his travels to explore the mineral districts of various countries, he lighted upon Galvani in Italy, and became devoted for a time to the study of Animal Electricity, and to the observation of some of the phenomena of the animal frame which were supremely interesting to him in his latest days. In 1849 he verified, to his own entire satisfaction, and that of his philosophical coadjutors, the fact of the deflection of the needle as a result of human volition, through the medium of muscular contraction. "The fact," he said, in his letter to Arago, the next year, "is established beyond all question of doubt." "Occupied myself for more than half a century in this class of physiological researches, the discovery which I have announced has for me a vital interest. It is a phenomenon of Life, rendered sensible by a physical instrument." Thus were his earliest and latest scientific

[II]

His preparation for the production of the Kosmos.

His discovery of the deflection of the needle.

interests linked by the discoveries of the remarkable age in which he lived; but what an experience had he undergone in the mean time! He had stood on higher ground than human foot had till then attained. He climbed Chimborazo to the height of 19,300 feet; an elevation since then surpassed, but never attained till that June day of 1802. He went down into the deepest mines, in pursuit of his geological researches. He not only visited three of the four quarters of the world, but explored parts of them which were then completely savage in the eyes of the civilized world. It was through no remissness of his own that he did not travel in Africa. He was at Marseilles, on his way to Algiers and to the top of Atlas, whence he meant to go to Egypt, when the war, which seemed to stop him at every outlet, turned him back. While chafing under his confinement to Europe, he did the best he could within that prison. When the war raged in Italy, he travelled with Von Bach in Styria, examining the mountains and their productions. When London was inaccessible, he went to Paris, where he made the acquaintance of his future comrade, Bonpland. When the war came to Germany, he was off to Spain; and there, at last, he met his opportunity. He obtained a passage to South America, and narrowly escaped imposing upon us the honor or disgrace, whichever it might be, of having Alexander Humboldt for our prisoner of war. He has told in his works of his ascent of the Peak of Teneriffe (which just enabled him to deny not having taken Africa in his course of travel), and of what he saw and felt among the vast rolling rivers, and grassy plains, and tropical forests, and overwhelming mountains of South America. He explored Mexico, landing on

its Pacific side, after having crossed the Andes; and
then, by way of Cuba, visited the United States, and
lived two months in Philadelphia, in 1804. The world
had never seen such scientific wealth as Humboldt
brought to Havre, in his collections in every branch
of Natural History, illustrated by such a commentary
as he was now qualified to give. He planned an encyclopædic work which should convey in detail all his
discoveries and classified knowledge; and the issue
of this work was one of the mistakes of his life which
cost him most uneasiness. After twelve years of constant
labor he had issued only four-fifths of this prodigious
series of works; and it has never been completed,
though portions have dropped out even within a few
years. Before those twelve years were over—that is,
before 1817—he had been overtaken in research, and
forestalled in publication, by men whom he had himself,
by his example, inspired and trained. In the next
year he broke off from this slavery, and visited Italy.
He was in England in 1826. He was then regarded
as an elderly man—being fifty-seven years old—and
notorious for a quarter of a century. But he was just
about to make trial of a new mode of life; and there
were, after that, extensive travels before him.

His plan of an encyclopædic work.

He fixed his abode at Berlin, and immediately became
a royal favorite, and, consequently, a politician. He
was made a Councillor of State, and tried his hand at
diplomacy. But those are not the things by which he
will be remembered; and nobody cares to dwell on that
part of his life, except those who would fain have
Englishmen see that the foreign method of rewarding
scientific or literary service by political office seems
never to answer well in practice. In most cases the

Becomes a politician.

[II]

practice is simply the spoiling of two things by mixing them ; in Humboldt's case, we merely forget the political part of his career, which was the artificial portion of his life, as it was the natural portion of his brother's. When Alexander came to England with the King of Prussia, on occasion of the baptism of the Prince of Wales, his appearance in the royal suite gave a sort of jar to English associations about the dignity of science. It was felt that that splendid brow wore the true crown ; and many a cheek flushed when the sage played the courtier, and had to consult the royal pleasure about his engagements with our scientific men, as a lacquey asks leave to go out. It is certain, however, that Humboldt took kindly to that sort of necessity. He was a courtier all over. We see it in his over-praise of all *savans* whom he names, and by his dexterous omission of such names as the Court or learned classes of Berlin did not wish to hear of. We see it in his cumbrous style, which is more like network to catch suffrages than a natural expression of what the writer was thinking about. And we see it in those nebulous or deficient portions of his "Kosmos," of which we have spoken above. Those who knew him in his last days saw it in the contrast between his written and spoken comments on his contemporaries. After hearing one of his dramatic descriptions of sittings in the Scientific Academies of the European capitals, with satirical presentments of the great men there, his elaborate compliments to the same persons, incessantly issued in one form or another, have been found very curious reading. There was no envy or jealousy in this—only an irresistible provocation to amuse himself and others, through his insight into human nature. He was

In the Royal suite.

thoroughly generous in the recognition and aid of ability; or rather, as he was high above all competition, regarding Science as his home, he looked upon all within that enclosure as his children. It was with a true paternal earnestness and indulgence that he strove for their welfare. Almost every man of science in Germany who has found his place has been conducted to it by Humboldt; and this, not only by a good use of his influence at Court, but by business-like endeavor in other directions. Napoleon and Wellington were born in the same year with him. Wellington never showed more studious skill in the arrangement of his forces, nor Napoleon a more efficient will in the distribution of the sceptres of European empires, than Humboldt, to the very last, in disposing his forces, and conferring crowns in the interests of the kingdoms of the higher realm of Nature. He gloried in so long outliving the achievements of those great contemporaries: and truly it was a noble sight to see, so many years after the Great Captain had done his wars, and the Great Despot had expiated his trespasses, the Monarch of Science still urging his conquests, and winning his victories, in a career which cost no tears to others, and left no place for repentance for himself.

The hindrance imposed on his scientific researches by his political position was very evident on occasion of his last long journey. By the express desire of the Czar, he travelled to Siberia, in company with Ehrenberg and Gustav Rose, in 1829, and explored Central Asia to the very frontier of China. Yet this journey, which, if he had set out from Paris, he would have thought worthy to absorb some years, was hurried over in nine months, as he happened to set forth from the Court of Berlin. He did great things for the time—instituting observatories, improving the Russian methods of mining, kindling intelligence wherever he went, and bringing home knowledge, more great and various than perhaps any living man but himself has gained in so short a time. After his return he spent the rest of his life, with intervals of travel, in maturing the generalizations by which he has done his chief service of all—that of indicating the laws of the Distribution of the forms of existence, and especially of Biological existence. He also compiled his "Kosmos" from the substance of sixty-one lectures which he delivered in Berlin in 1827-8. His frame wore wonderfully; and there was no sign of decay of external sense or interior faculty while younger men were dropping into the grave, completely worn out. He was the last of the contemporaries of Göthe; and as the tidings came of the death of each—philosopher, poet, statesman, or soldier—Humboldt raised his head higher, seemed to feel younger, and, as it were, proud of having outlived so many. If silent, he was kindly and gentle. If talkative, he would startle his hearers with a story or scene from a Siberian steppe or a Peruvian river-side—fresh and accurate as if witnessed last year. He forgot no names or dates, any more than facts of a more interesting kind. In the street, he was known to every resident of Berlin and Potsdam, and was pointed out to all strangers, as he walked, slowly and firmly, with his massive head bent a little forward, and his hand at his back holding a pamphlet. He was fond of the society of young men to the last, and was often found present at their scientific processes and meetings for experiment, and nobody present was more unpretending and gay. He has been charged with putting down all talk but his own; but this was the natural mistake of the empty-

His old age.

minded, who were not qualified either to listen or talk in his presence. There was no better listener than Humboldt in the presence of one who had anything worth hearing to say on any subject whatever. Though he liked praise, he could run the risk of blame on serious occasions. Though he probably did not say at Court what he said to his intimates elsewhere, "I am a democrat of 1789," he used his position and influence to utter things in high places which would hardly have been otherwise heard there. It was the impression among his friends that he was as hearty an anti-Russian amidst the political complications of 1854 as any man in Berlin. Whether the king was equally aware of it there was no knowing. If he was, Humboldt's position was too well secured to permit any manfestation of royal annoyance.

His liberal tendencies.

It is a great thing for Germany that, at the period when the national intellect seemed in danger of evaporating in dreams and vapors of metaphysics, Humboldt arose to connect the abstract faculty of that national mind with the material on which it ought to be employed. The rise of so great a Naturalist and initiator of Physical Philosophy at the very crisis of the intellectual fortunes of Germany is a blessing of yet unappreciated value ; unappreciated because it is only the completion of any revolution which can reveal the whole prior need of it. If Alexander Humboldt suffered, more or less, from the infection of the national uncertainty of thought and obscurity of expression, he conferred infinitely more than he lost by giving a grasp of reality to the finest minds of his country, and opening a broad new avenue into the realm of Nature to be trodden by all peoples of all times.

His influence on German thought.

[II]

III.

PROFESSIONAL.

I.

DR. BLOMFIELD.

RESIGNED THE BISHOPRIC OF LONDON IN SEPTEMBER, 1856.
DIED AUGUST 5TH, 1857.

THOUGH he had laid down his episcopal title and dignity some months before his death, Dr. Blomfield will be known in history as the Bishop of London. Of all the incumbents of the Metropolitan See since the Reformation, scarcely any one has held the office in a more remarkable and critical time for the Church than Charles James Blomfield. His episcopate was a very long one: and the period almost exactly comprehended the term of crisis—as far as that crisis has yet proceeded—in Church principles and government. If the character and destiny of any Church are exhibited more or less in the mind and conduct of its chief dignitaries, the life of Bishop Blomfield must have an interest, not only for our own generation, but for others to come. *Critical period of his episcopate.*

He was the son of C. Blomfield, Esq. ; and he was educated at Cambridge, where he obtained, when a Middle Bachelor, a classical prize in 1809. He was a Fellow of Trinity College, and in orders in 1810, and highly distinguished among scholars for his edition of Æschylus and the controversies which it occasioned. He was permitted by his College to use Porson's notes ; *His edition of Æschylus.*

[I]

and the opponents of the Porsonian school castigated him and his work accordingly. His rival, Mr. Butler, oddly enough as it seems to us now, accused him in a pamphlet of being the Reviewer of Butler's "Æschylus" in the *Edingburgh Review ;* and Hermann, in his notice of Blomfield's edition (in the *Weimar Annual,*) says that it is remarkable for "a great arbitrariness of proceeding, and much boldness of innovation, guided by no sure principle." Adding to this the consideration of vast and willing toil bestowed upon the work, we have already, so early as 1810, a disclosure of the mind and character of the man. In those days, a divine rose in the Church in one of two ways—by his classical reputation, or by aristocratic connection. Mr. Blomfield was a fine scholar, *His liberal views in early life.* but he was, in early life, a Liberal in politics, and a friend to religious liberty in the form of Catholic and every other Emancipation. His views changed, as he himself professed, after he became tutor in the family of some near relatives of the Minister of the day ; and he was soon after in the enjoyment of a living of 4,000*l.* a year *Consecrated Bishop of Chester.* in London, and was next made Bishop of Chester (in 1824), and Clerk of the Closet to George IV., retaining the emoluments of all these offices at once. He was as zealous in his opposition to Catholic claims as he had been, not long before, in advocating them ; and *Hansard* can exhibit in his case one of the most curious states of *Opposes Catholic Emancipation.* mind conceivable. He grounded his frequent deprecation of Catholic Emancipation on the sins and errors of Popery, which were quite as well known to him before, but which he had formerly thought, very properly, not to be the question in dispute, but rather whether the errors of any faith ought to exclude men from civil rights. His natural impetuosity led him into inaccuracies of statement which were made the most of by the Liberals of the time ; their strictures induced him to declare himself a martyr ; his complaints of his severe trials endeared him to the Duke of York, who was at that time fierce in his Anti-Catholic politics ; and all the world predicted the highest honors of the Church for Bishop Blomfield whenever the Duke of York should succeed to the throne. He became Bishop of London, however, in 1828, before the death of George IV., Bishop Horsley going to Canterbury. In the true spirit of a Churchman of the olden time, he was always insisting, up to the moment of Catholic Emancipation, that the proper remedy for Irish discontent was the granting, not of rights of conscience, but bounties on linen and flax, appropriations for public works, and penalties on absenteeism. His confirmation as Bishop of London took place at Bow Church on the 16th of August, 1828.

Appointed to the See of London.

While the Bishops were engrossed with political interests, that disturbance in the interior of the Church had begun which has gone on increasing to this day ; and it was the total silence of the Bishops, on the first occasion of the subject being brought before Parliament, which fixed the attention of the public on their position in the House of Lords ; and which, when contrasted, some years afterward, with their remarkable act of throwing out the Reform Bill, raised the temporary cry, and confirmed the conception of their "release," as it was called, "from their duties in Parliament." It was in the year before Dr. Blomfield became Bishop of Chester that the first symptom occurred of the awakening of the High Church spirit of domination over faith which has since roused the clergy—some to an exemplary discharge of their duties, and others to insubordination. In the

Conduct of the Bishops in Parliament.

[I]

[I]   Session of 1821, the celebrated Peterborough Questions
—the eighty-seven Questions imposed upon candidates
for orders by Dr. Herbert Marsh, Bishop of Peterborough
—were appealed against in the only place where an
appeal could lodge—in the House of Lords. The
Archbishop of Canterbury had refused to entertain the
subject. The Lords also refused to entertain the subject,
both then and on occasion of another petition the next
year. On both occasions the prominent subject of
remark was the silence of the Bishops on a matter
which vitally concerned the constitution and interests
of their Church. They were taunted with it in the
House, and by Lord Carnarvon especially. But they
were in fact unprepared. The subject of Liberty of
Opinion was coming up before they were aware ; and it
was certainly very plain that they were no more fit to
open their lips upon it than any other set of men in
England.

   Just at that time, Dr. Blomfield took his seat among
the Bishops ; and, unaware that his life would be occupied
with the strifes of opinion and the conflicts on the
question of religious liberty, he rushed into politics, and
committed himself early on the wrong and losing side of

*The Trac-
tarian Con-
troversy.*
the Catholic Question. The uncertainty and obscurity
of his conduct and his views on the great Tractarian
controversy of the time was a singular spectacle to those
who best knew his love of decision, his love of power,
his love of whatever was strong and substantial. We
believe that to the last it was uncertain to everybody
what his Church views really were. While the Oxford
party were advocating Art as auxiliary to religion, the
Bishop of London refused all countenance to the Westminster Abbey Festival in 1834, though the Archbishops

of Canterbury, York, and Armagh were in attendance on
the King and Queen at the performances. The Oxford
party advocated popular amusements, and on Sundays,
after service, as much as other days ; and the Bishop of
London proclaimed in the Lords the number of boats
that went under Putney-bridge on Sundays. This was
never forgotten or forgiven ; and the image of the Prelate,
in his purple, sitting in his palace at Fulham, counting
the people who came for fresh air on their only day of
the seven, was often brought forward years after the
Bishop himself was suspected of Tractarianism. The
suspicion arose in the very midst of apparent Low-Church
scruples. When Tractarian practices crept into London
churches, and he was appealed to on their account, his
Charges were looked for with extreme eagerness ; but it
was difficult to learn more from them than that he was
at a loss what to say. His hair-splitting on rubrical
subjects is well remembered ; and his nice distinctions
are on record—his so-called decisions, which decide
nothing, about candles lighted and unlighted, gown and
surplice, bowings, &c., &c. He strove evidently to take
a middle course on a subject which does not admit of it ;
and he had no principle to assign. In one so fond of
power, so haughty to his working clergy, so prone to
decision and arbitrariness, so impetuous and apt to be
possessed by an idea, such weakness was very remarkable,
and not a little interesting as showing what the difficulty
of Church government must at the moment be. The
truth is, Bishop Blomfield was not adequate to his charge
in such a time of crisis, though his really great and good
qualities fitted him for the same position in an organic
period of the Church.

If he was not strong enough in his best days, much

[I]

His nice distinctions.

less had he any chance of being an ecclesiastical hero—
like the Seven Bishops, to whom he compared himself
in the days of the Catholic Question—when his health
failed, and his spirits were borne down by pressure of
business, and perplexity and irresolution of mind.   There
was a time when, of all the prelates on the Bench,
Dr. Blomfield would have been selected, from his
activity, his self-confidence, his devotion to business, and
his habits of authority, to contend with the schism in the
Church, and to take care that, in his own province at
least, all should be orthodox and unquestionable : but
that time was over long ago ; and if the historian of the
struggle were required to point out which of all the

Unequal to his position. Bishops most disappointed expectation on this one
ground, he would indicate the Bishop of London.   Not
the less credit, but perhaps the more, should he have for
his best qualities and his most useful work and example.
Of his conscientiousness no doubt, we believe, was ever
raised.   The reputation of his head gave way to that
of his heart on all doubtful occasions.   He had what
Sydney Smith called "an ungovernable passion for business," and devoted eight hours a day to the administration of his diocese.   He aided in the construction of
the new Poor-law, and manifested as much sagacity and
sound principle as industry in that difficult matter.   He
was the author and chief component part of the
Ecclesiastical Commission.   He was told that he was
destroying the Church, and that no good Churchman
would join him : he replied that the Church could by
no other means be saved ; and he was *not* left alone.   The
reproach was a remarkable one to be addressed to him
who considered himself and the Church so completely
identified, that, according to Sydney Smith's joke, the

form of his dinner invitations was, "The Church of England and Mrs. Blomfield request the pleasure," &c.

[I]

But his labors would have been more respected and more effectual if he could so far have thrown off Church influences as to divest himself of some of his wealth and patronage. There were reductions in the Bishop's incomes; but these incomes were still preposterous, while he was incessantly and pathetically lamenting the case of hungry sheep scantily tended. The wealth of bishops and poverty of curates came to be called "the sheep and shepherd principle" of Church government; and the Church gained no credit by it. Provincial Dean of Canterbury, Dean of the Chapels Royal, and holding nearly one hundred livings in his gift, he was not so respectfully treated in regard to his reforms as his conscientiousness really deserved.

His Church patronage.

As in so many other cases, the evil was in the system more than in the man. Devoted to his business, and what he conceived to be his duty, charitable (though highly arbitrary) in his acts, amiable in domestic life, and agreeable in his social manners, he was regarded with much affection by those who were once attached to him. Society wonders what has become of the power from which the world, and himself especially, anticipated so much; and, on the whole, his must be regarded as a vocation *manqué*. He "came in like a lion and went out like a lamb." His power was not only less than all supposed, but it was unsuited to the time; and there can be no doubt that, in the midst of his purple and gold, and his palaces, and his large domestic circle, he must have endured many a painful hour, under difficulties that he could not cope with, and perplexities that he could not solve. His virtues, his deficiencies, and the prero-

The system and the man.

[I]   gatives and troubles of his lot, alike furnish the lesson to those who hold the power of appointment to bishoprics. that Greek scholarship is of little consequence in these days, in comparison with clear and honest convictions, ripened judgment in ecclesiastical matters, liberal views, inflexible courage and decision, and unquestionable disinterestedness. Whatever may be the zeal and piety of any number of individual members of a Church, that Church cannot stand as an Ecclesiastical Establishment which shows, like ours at this day, large variations in the views of its prelates, without any combined action or consistent administration.

II

ARCHBISHOP WHATELY.

DIED OCTOBER 8TH, 1863.

WE live in days when the fortunes of Church dignitaries —in other words, the qualities which raise Churchmen to dignities—are a pregnant sign of the times. Of this class of phenomena, none has been more striking to our generation than the presence of Richard Whately on the bench of bishops ; and his elevation to the Archbishopric of Dublin was scarcely more astonishing to Ireland than it was to the rest of the United Kingdom,—to say nothing of foreign countries, from Rome to the farthest West where the Irish immigrant rears his shanty on the prairie. To those who remember 1830, and knew any- *How his elevation was received.* thing of the dismay of the then young Tractarian party at Oxford, and of the exultation of the Church Reform party, of whom Dr. Arnold may be considered a repre- sentative, when the announcement was made that the Annotator on Archbishop King's Discourse on Predesti- nation, the Bampton Lecturer, the author of "Elements of Logic," the audacious thinker, the outspoken Richard Whately, was to be the new Archbishop of Dublin, our words will not appear extravagant. The discontent on the Liberal side was that the elevation was not sufficiently great and effective. "But alas !" wrote Dr. Arnold, "for

[II]

your being at Dublin, instead of at Canterbury." In Ireland, however, where Catholic equality was yet new and raw, and the two Churches were rapidly exchanging converts, even Dr. Arnold saw that there was much for a Liberal prelate to do.   " It does grieve me most deeply," he wrote, "to hear people speak of him as a dangerous and latitudinarian character, because in him the intellectual part of his nature keeps pace with the spiritual—instead of being left, as the Evangelicals leave it, a fallow field for all unsightly creeds to flourish in.   He is a truly great man, in the highest sense of the word ; and if the safety and welfare of the Protestant Church in Ireland depend in any degree on human instruments, none could be found, I verily believe, in the whole empire, so likely to maintain it."   It is no new thing for the event to rebuke the discontents and exultations which wait on portents, or what seem such.   The excitement about this Whig appointment soon subsided ; and the Church is very much where it would have been if Whately had devoted his days to logic and political economy in some country parsonage, or the lecture hall at Oxford.   A certain interest, however, hangs about the personal history from the early achievements of the man, and the high expectations he awakened ; and his disappearance from the Church and the world awakens thoughts and feelings worthy of heed and of record.

Dr. Arnold's opinion o Whately.

His birth, 1786.

Richard Whately was born in 1786, his father being a clergyman, who lived at Nonsuch Park, Surrey.   Oriel College was made eminent at that period by the names of some of its Fellows, and by its being the last refuge of the study of Logic, and the one school of Speculative Philosophy in England.   Thus it was regarded at the time ; and strange it is to remember this now, after all

that has happened since. Whately's comrades there were
Coplestone, Davison, Keble, Hawkins, and Hampden,
soon joined in their fellowships by Newman and Pusey.
In 1819 Whately became a Fellow, and in 1822 Principal
of St. Alban's Hall. Of his earliest work (or that which
usually stands first in the list), "Historic Doubts," little
seems now to be remembered, beyond its giving assurance to the world of an independent thinker among the
rising clergy. His Notes to Archbishop King's Sermon
on Predestination appeared in 1821, and proved him to
have that sort of English inclination (as foreigners call
it) which seeks "a craggy subject to break one's mind
on." The impression at the time was that Archbishop
King's editor failed in logic, though no one could
seriously demand that logic should avail in bringing the
thinker to the desired conclusion. Mr. Whately (as he
was then) was respectfully treated by his theological
critics ; but the weak point in him was declared to be
his logic. Yet had his work on Logic been maturing in
his mind for a dozen years at that very time. Before it
appeared, however, he had become further known to the
Church and the public by "Two Discourses on Obe-
dience to Civil Government," and by his "Bampton
Lectures," delivered in 1822. He published his eight
lectures under the title, "The Use and Abuse of Party-
feeling in Matters of Religion considered." Looking
back upon them now, under the light of the author's
after-life, we smile to see the politico-economical doctrines which were already his study applied in a spiritual
sense to theological affairs—the advantages of party-
feeling being exhibited in division of employments and
co-operation in Church matters ; and then we meet with
what compels a sigh. Most rationally, most unanswer-

[II]

*His con-
temporaries
at Oxford.*

*His early
publications*

[II] ably, he set forth the policy, as well as the beauty, of candor, gentleness, and modesty in collisions of opinion. It would have been well if he had always kept his own lessons in mind.

His thoughts on logic. He declared in 1827 that for fourteen years his mind had brooded over the leading points of his work on Logic ; and during all that time the desire had grown stronger to remedy the state of things by which (to use his own words) "a very small proportion, even of distinguished students, ever become good logicians ; and by far the greater part pass through the University without knowing anything at all of it." He attributed the deficiency to Logic having never been ennobled by being made a condition of academical honors. Other people believed that this was but one of various causes of the neglect of Logic ; and some were far from desiring to see the study so eagerly and generally pursued as to cause a demand for popular teaching, and to open the most sacred study next to theology to the deterioration which theology had undergone in Germany, from competitive lecturing, suited to the popular demand for excitement. Logic extolled beyond its true scope, or lowered to purposes of popular entertainment, has its dangers, serious and formidable ; but these perils form no case for neglect of it—for such neglect as Whately took to heart, and did much to remedy. It had become useless to compel the study of Logic at Oxford ; and the students hailed with joy the proposal to leave the study altogether to the option of candidates for honors. The very name and pursuit seemed doomed to lapse, like some other studies which the classics and theology had *Publishes his "Elements."* driven out, when Dr. Whately, then Principal of St. Alban's Hall, published his "Elements of Logic," and commanded, by his station and reputation, an opposition and an advocacy which rescued his favorite science (so called) from oblivion, and did more for its interests than Oxford could show for above a century. During the next ten years, more books on Logic came out than Oxford had sent forth during the preceding hundred and thirty. The merits of the work are another question. They have been abundantly discussed elsewhere. Perhaps the permanent conclusion has been for some time reached that the work, and Whately's powers in that direction, were, as was natural, overrated at the time. Deficiencies could hardly be avoided under the circumstances of the case ; but the positive errors charged upon the work by contemporary and later writers lowered Dr. Whately's reputation more and more with time. His career has for some years past shown his warmest admirers that they were mistaken in their estimate of the logical part of his construction. He at once perpetually exaggerated the functions of logic, and occasionally misplaced its principles and misapplied its art; and long before his death he had lost the reputation, once almost undisputed, of being an irrefragable reasoner. It is not the less true that to him we owe the rescue of Logic from extinction in our universities.

Between the publication of his "Elements" and his being made Archbishop of Dublin, he became Professor of Political Economy, and published the introductory lectures of his course. In 1830 he issued his volume, "The Errors of Romanism traced to their Origin in Human Nature ;" and we do not know that any of his works more effectually exhibits the characteristics of his mind. It has the spirit and air of originality which attend upon sublime good sense ; and the freshness thus

[II]

Appointed Professor of Political Economy.

[II]

cast around a subject supposed to be worn out is a
sample of the vigor which in those days animated
everything he said and did.   Its fault was the fault of
its author's life—its want of thoroughness.   Its reasonings
and illustrations stop short at the point where their application to his own Church would be inconvenient ; and
thus the work was eagerly seized on by the Dissenters,
and its omissions supplied.   It is remarkable that the
logician who was believed by his friends, and by a large
portion of the public, to be the most irrefragable reasoner
of his time, should have been subject throughout his
public life to refutation on each special occasion by the

*His
career of
intellectual
activity.*

one party most concerned in the argument.   But so it
was ; and the result was seen in the virtual closing of
his career twenty years before his death.   His constitutional activity was irrepressible ; and no apprehensions
and anxieties during his years of vigor, nor any infirmities of his latter days, deadened his inquisitiveness
into the smallest fragments of knowledge, or checked
his discursiveness of mind and conversation : but his
fame stood still from the time when he assumed his
great responsibilities, and he did nothing afterward to
revive it.   Not many months after he became Archbishop of Dublin, he one day plucked at his sleeve,
saying, as if in soliloquy, "I don't know how it is ; but
after we once get these things on, we never do anything
more."   It was a severe distress to the friends of his
early manhood that after he had got on his lawn sleeves,
he never did anything more—in the way at least of such
service as was expected from him.   They accounted for
the fact in various ways ; but they did not dispute it.
"Where," wrote Dr. Arnold, in 1836, "is the knowledge,
where the wisdom, and where the goodness, which com-

bine to form the great man? I know of no man who approaches to this character except Whately; and he is taken away from the place where he was wanted, and sent where the highest greatness would struggle in vain against the overpowering disadvantages of his position." Dr. Arnold would have said, if his generous affections had not been in the way, that "the highest greatness" makes its own position of usefulness; and again, that the headship of the English Church in Ireland is a position of singular advantage for a true and courageous Church reformer.

Two causes were concerned in the failure in this case. Dr. Whately lay under the suspicion of heterodoxy; and the knowledge of this fact disheartened him. He was not a man of the highest moral courage, though his strong self-will drove him into occasional recklessness. The story of his connection with Blanco White, from first to last, is a complete illustration of his character of mind. A friendship grew up between him and Blanco White while the latter was, in belief and practice, a clergyman, and the comrade of the rising clergy of Oxford. In their passion for logic, and their blindness to the insufficiency of logic, these two able men thoroughly sympathized; and it is probable that Whately suffered from nothing more in his whole life than the spectacle of the failure and wretchedness of the existence of the best logician he knew, as well as perhaps the most virtuous man, in purity of heart and conscientiousness. Blanco White totally lacked imagination, and was destitute of science; so that, on the one hand, he regarded theological dogmas in a logical light, ending of course in the surrender of them all; while, on the other hand, he was not qualified to

His friend-ship with Blanco White.

[II] ascertain **any other** standpoint; and **his** heart, **his** conscience, **and his** reason were forever craving a **resting-place** which they could not find. His published Memoirs are, we believe, considered by those who know them the **most melancholy book** they ever read. If it is mischievous, **in one direction, by its** disheartening exhibition **of the pains and penalties** incurred by an avowal of heresy, it ought to be instructive in another, by **its** clear admonitions against Blanco White's method **of seeking truth,** and reliance upon a narrow and barren exercise **of the** reasoning power, without regard to its true scope **and** sufficiency of material. This deeply suffering man was united in a close friendship with Dr. Whately by their similarity of logical power, **and** yet more by their pure goodness **of heart,** and a liberality in theology and politics rare **among** clergymen at that time. Whately went so **far with his friend in the** direction of heterodoxy that **his letters, for some time** after their separation, **are** as curious as **anything he** ever wrote. All the resources of his hair-splitting ingenuity were used **(and** all were insufficient) to justify his being an archbishop and his friend an outcast, while it **was so** exceedingly difficult to point out where their opinions differed. This was, of course, before Blanco White had relinquished his hold on Christianity as a revelation, though after he had, with due delicacy, resigned his office of chaplain and home in the Archbishop's family. His friend's unhappiness, as well as his integrity, was a perpetual pain and eyesore to Whately; and the pain at length proved too much for his temper, while it impaired

Suspected of heterodoxy. his usefulness. He carried about with him the consciousness of being under suspicion of heterodoxy; and he had not courage or temper to sustain such a trial well.

The imputations on his orthodoxy made him sore, and everything chafed his mind. He became irritable and more overbearing than ever, till his suffering exploded in a burst of anger and calumny on occasion of the publication of his friend's Memoirs. He asserted widely, positively, and in black and white, that physicians had declared his old friend to be insane; and the assertion was met by abundant medical testimony that this was not true. He asserted that the biographer of Blanco White had made use of private letters of his and his family's against prohibition and legal warning, and for the sordid purpose of turning the penny; and this was again met by positive proof that the letters in question, so far from being published, or prepared for publication, were placed at the Archbishop's disposal, and returned to him on his first request. As for the imputed sordidness, it was a prominent statement in the book that the biographer's labor was altogether gratuitous, Blanco White's will having assigned the entire profits of the work to his son. These injurious assertions were at first regarded as an ebullition of temper, and as such would have been presently forgotten; but unhappily, the Archbishop, never accessible to explanation, and always unable to own himself wrong, renewed his statements after the disproof had been supplied to him, and to the particular public whom he had misled. His liberality to his friend in regard to his personal comforts, and the benevolence of the whole family in this and in all cases in which they could assist the suffering, were signal; but in the department of Opinion, fear and pride bore down all before them.

In this chapter of his life we find an epitome of his conduct and experience in his ecclesiastical relations.

8*

[II]

The hopes of the Liberal Government, and of the reforming section of the Church, were disappointed ; and if no High Church or Low Church scandal ensued from his being placed at Dublin, neither was there any approach to a solution of the difficulty of the English Establishment in Ireland. Dr. Whately had voted for Peel, at Oxford, in the critical election of 1829 ; yet he *Antagonism* inclined more and more to direct antagonism with the *with the* Catholics from the time he went to Ireland ; and we saw *Catholics.* him in 1852 presiding over the Society for protecting the Rights of Conscience in Ireland, in defiance of his long-preached conclusions in political economy, and his understood neutrality toward the Catholics. The atmosphere of the country, and, it is believed, domestic influences, drew him in to preside over an Association for providing employment for the people of one way of thinking who were out of favor with people of another faith. A similar difficulty occurred in the department of the Schools, in which he long rendered inestimable service. The ladies of his family had a school at their country-seat, near Dublin ; and one of their classes was composed of Catholic children for the purpose of having the Protestant Bible read and expounded to them. The local priest remonstrated, then threatened to withdraw the children, and finally appealed to the Board, on whose interference the practice was discontinued. This was not the kind of action anticipated when a Whately was sent to Ireland.

The His great service, and that by which he will be hon- *National* orably remembered, was his support of the National *School* School system. The Liberal reputation with which he *system.* went to Ireland indicated his place at once, at the head of the enterprise ; and he worked long, strenuously, effectively, and with a patience truly wonderful in him, to keep the doors of the National Schools wide open, and to provide an education of a high order within. For more than twenty years he devoted himself to this great branch of service; and when at last he gave way and resigned, on occasion of the dispute about the Scripture Lessons, the feebleness of age was creeping over him, and he could not have done much more if no such trouble had arisen.

Another of his great services was his unanswerable advocacy of the admission of Jews to Parliament. The same clear vigor in defence of the liberties of the Jews which so sorely distressed Dr. Arnold when Whately's opinions were to find expression in Paliament, was at the command of the injured sect as often as it was the Archbishop's season of attendance in the House of Lords; and the years when he was present were considered by the Jews the most favorable to their cause. If their case had been determinable by reason and principle, they would long ago have owed their admission to full political rights to Archbishop Whately.

He rendered other secular services of high value. He was as largely concerned as the Bishop of London in the reform of the Poor Laws; and he did more than perhaps any other man, unless it were Sir Wm. Molesworth, to abolish penal Transportation. His letter to Earl Grey on Secondary Punishments, published in 1833, contributed mainly to our change of system. At a later time, just after the Irish famine, the Statistical Society of Dublin was formed under his encouragement; and he filled the chair and delivered the Inaugural Address. He fulfilled the same function for the Society for promoting Scientific Inquiries into Social Questions, which

[II]

His secular labors.

[I]   was founded in 1852. It would be difficult to overrate
the promise of benefit to Ireland from these associations,
by which the science of the first Economists of the
country is brought to bear on practical questions, and
itself improved by the consultations and co-operation of
the members. For some years past no sensible person
would think of describing or legislating for Ireland
without having studied, as his best material, the papers
issued by these Societies. The name of Archbishop
Whately will be honorably connected with them, as
long as they are heard of. His lively interest in fresh
knowledge of every kind never flagged. Up to the
last, when he was too feeble and infirm to go about
unsupported, the best-informed young people said that
nothing gave them so keen a sense of their own ignorance as the presence of the Archbishop, whose inquisitiveness left nothing unobserved, or exempt from
being reasoned on. In matters of Science and Natural
History he had the good sense and courage which failed
him in the department of theology and its profession.
In secular matters he did justice to his own admirable
precept— "It is not enough to believe what you maintain. You must maintain what you believe, and
maintain it because you believe it."

Whately and the Tractarian party.   The reaction against the Tractarian movement, which
set in after 1840, could not pass without notice from a
prelate in his position and of his particular reputation.
In 1841 he published two Essays on Christ and His
Church, in which his faculty of dealing with the claims
of Evidence, and exposing false pretensions of Tradition,
had full play. In 1843, when several Bishops took
courage to charge against the High Church heresy, and
to publish their Charges, Dr. Whately was one of the

number. He went so far as to demand a Convocation, [II]
in view of scandalous tamperings with the formulas, and
mutual recriminations within the Church, and the ruinous
aspect of the institution to those outside the pale. His
demand was not seconded by the Irish Bishops who
spoke their minds at the time ; and it is remarkable that
Whately, who knew better than most men the powers
and shortcomings of authority in matters of faith, and
the small chance of harmony in affairs of administration,
to be found in clerical Councils, should have been the
man to desire a Convocation when the divisions in the
Church had reached their height. As far as we are
aware, his more recent opposition to Puseyism has been
in the form of ridicule of its pretensions, in the pulpit
and in private ; and not in further propositions through
the press. His latest work was a Charge delivered in *His latest*
the last year of his life. It is directed against the dan- *work.*
gers peculiar to the times, inculcating reverence for the
Scriptures, and opposing a spirit of finality in ecclesiastical affairs. A few weeks ago it was announced that
the Archbishop was ill, and not likely to recover. His
sufferings, borne with exemplary meekness and fortitude,
were terminated by death on the 8th of October.

III.

THE MARQUIS OF LONDONDERRY.

DIED MARCH 1ST, 1854.

As a remarkable man in his way, Lord Londonderry ought not to pass to his grave without some exercise of our judgment on his career.

According to Conservative authorities, he was not remarkable in Statesmanship and Diplomacy. In the eyes of Liberals he was very remarkable in those departments —but not in a favorable sense. Now that he is gone, we had rather look at other parts of his character and action, some of which men of all parties can regard with cordial respect, and others with an amiable amusement. The world of politics and fashion owes a great deal of amusement to the departed nobleman; and those who smiled oftenest felt a real kindness and regard for him.

Charles Stewart Vane, Marquis of Londonderry, was brother to the more eminent or notorious Lord Castlereagh and Londonderry of the beginning of the century. Re-

Compared with his brother Lord Castlereagh.
garding them with the differences of their professions as Statesman and Soldier, there was a strong family likeness between them. There was the same high courage; the same prodigious self-esteem, joined to genial kindness; the same utter insensibility to popular claims, and inability to conceive in the remotest manner of popular

liberties; the same delusion about their own greatness, which gave a taint of vulgarity to their minds and manners (especially when among the really great); and the same extraordinary use of the English language, and other tokens of a defective education. There was a likeness, too, in their personal accomplishments. Lord Castlereagh attracted all eyes as he rode in the parks; and Charles Stewart is still remembered by old soldiers as a fine spectacle to troops and civilians when, on his charger, he led his hussars into the Escurial nearly fifty years ago. He did fine service in the dark days when Napoleon himself was pressing Sir John Moore into the northwest provinces of Spain. Charles Stewart crossed the Tormes, engaged and defeated the Imperial Guard, and so covered the retreat of the British. He saw almost the last man embarked at Corunna before he left the beach; and at most of the great battles in Spain he was among the bravest and heartiest. He was busy in the politics of warfare, too, keeping Bernadotte faithful to the allies when he was destined to occupy Berlin, before the battle of Leipsic, but was known to be wavering between the old master to whom he owed his crown, and the English who had clothed and armed his troops. Charles Stewart went and came, and was busy among the camps of the allies; but what good he did was by strong will and courage. His proper place was the battle-field, and not the council-board. His best days were, therefore, over when the war came to an end, though he remained as our representative at Vienna till 1823.

From that time he was great in Irish politics, spouting his remarkable English in county Down, taking for granted that he was to have his own way about members of Parliament, tenants, Catholics and Protestants there,

[III]

His services in the Peninsula.

[III]

as about coals and colliers, and the representation in the county of Durham, where his other estates lay. He had an unlimited capacity of astonishment, as appeared whenever he could not get his own way. He called the world's attention to the phenomenon when anybody refused to vote for his member, or to work for his wages, or to accept his terms for farms, or to receive his visits (as sometimes happened abroad). If the sun did not shine when he meant to go up a mountain, he thought it very extraordinary; and if the roads made his carriage jolt, he said it was too bad. He became a great traveller, and published his travels: and very amusing they are, showing how confidently he supposed himself acceptable everywhere, and how this was not always the case; and how very unmannerly it was of certain Princes not to be as glad to see him as he would have been to see them at Holdernesse House or Wynyard. By his travels we learn too how modest, and how unambitious and peace-loving, Nicholas, the Emperor of all the Russias, is; and how astonishingly he has been ill-treated by "his rebellious subjects," the Poles. This cordiality of Lord Londonderry toward the Czar marked him out for the embassy to Russia, when the Peel-Wellington administration of 1835 wanted to send a representative there. The nation, however, thought the appointment, to use the Marquis's favorite description, "too bad;" and Parliament let him and the Government know so unmistakably the popular opinion of him as a diplomatist, and of his attachment to the Czar, Don Carlos, Dom Miguel, and such gentry, that he immediately resigned his appointment—with his usual astonishment—and, indeed, with rather more than usual, because the affairs of Turkey were then very pressing, and it would have

Peculiarities of character.

Appointed ambassador to Russia;

but resigns on account of its unpopularity.

been so delightful that the British Minister should be of [III]
precisely the same opinions as the Emperor he was to
consult with. By a challenge of his own to the Foreign
Secretary of the day, Lord Dudley, the fact came out
that he had been importunate for a pension, in consideration of diplomatic services ; and that the calm and
moderate Lord Liverpool had written on the back of the
letter of application, "This is too bad." The Marquis
himself got the story made known; and he was not
a whit ashamed of it, because, in his view, the people
and their purses were created for the benefit of the
aristocracy. Sir Robert Peel would have maintained the
appointment; but the Marquis ingenuously declared at
once that he saw he could do no good at St. Petersburg
while disowned as a representative by any large number
of the people of England. Those who admired his
manliness only regretted that he could not be made
Russian Minister at the court of London—which post
would have suited him exactly.

All that was nearly twenty years ago. In the interval, *His conduct*
the old soldier has been very busy. His electioneering *toward his*
correspondence, and his letters to his tenantry, must be *tenantry.*
fresh in all minds. He treated his tenants according to
the old methods of managing fractious or well-behaved
children : now he declared himself ashamed of them,
and now he patted their heads. He had . the notion
and habit of command of a mediæval baron, without the
dignity and composure of aristocratic bearing; but he
was always ingenuous, always brave, and meaning to be
kind. He bore admirably the destruction by fire of his
noble seat, Wynyard ; and one of our latest recollections
of him is one of the pleasantest—his persevering inter-
cession with the French Emperor for the release of

[III]

*His inter-
cession for
Abd-el-
Kader's
liberation.*

Abd-el-Kader. There will be mourning at Broussa when the tidings of his death arrive there. There will be regret in many quarters, in the remembrance of his large hospitalities, and his genuine good-will toward his serfs on the one hand, his imperial friends on the other, and all between who would take him as he was. No doubt, his last view of the world was a stare of astonishment that his country could go to war with his Russian idol. He has escaped the yet greater amazement of finding his idol vulnerable. One who knew him well remarked, on finishing his book of travel, that " his heaven is paved with malachite." It is well that the notion was not

*His Russian
idol.*

cruelly broken up in an old man's mind ; but the Czar has lost in him his one English admirer and champion. As for us, we feel some regret in parting with one of our last Peninsular heroes, and one who, with all his foibles, intellectual and social, was never wanting in the frankness and manliness which give its best nobleness to nobility itself.

IV.

LORD RAGLAN.

Seven Months before his Death.

The elevation of Lord Raglan to the rank of Field-Marshal interests us all, through his past career as well as his present position. He has earned the distinction by hard work in the field and the closet. There is perhaps no incident of social progression more interesting and more agreeable than the preference manifested by men of rank, in their own case, to personal merit over distinction of birth. In all aristocracies, at all times, there have been individuals whose constitutional energy has instigated them to social service as arduous as if they were winning a station in life for themselves and their posterity; but the spectacle of almost a whole generation of noblemen working like middle-class men in the public service, and taking their chance of success among middle-class men, is certainly modern; and surely it is full of significance. We doubt whether there is a more remarkable example of this characteristic of our times than Lord Raglan—a descendant of the proud Somersets, and himself one of the most quiet and modest of the true working men of England. A prouder lineage few men could be conscious of than the Somersets and Seymours, who were of the same stock; and a

Personal merit and distinction of birth.

prouder man was never seen in England than the Duke of Somerset of two centuries ago—who had the highways cleared before him, that he might not be looked on by vulgar eyes, and who rebuked his second wife for tapping his shoulder with her fan, saying, "Madam, my first wife was a Percy, and *she* never took such a liberty." For that matter—of pride—we may go back at once to Cardinal Beaufort, who was of the first generation of the family, apart from royalty—he being the natural son of John of Gaunt. There is a better ground of pride in the family, however, than either royalty or antiquity. Among the proud Somersets was he who, in early life, commanded a little army, raised by his father for the service of Charles I., and who in after years invented the steam-engine. It was the author of the "Century of Inventions" who first applied the condensation of steam to a practical purpose : though his invention was used only for raising water, he saw that this method of creating a vacuum might be extensively applied ; and therefore is it admitted to be fair to call this Edward Somerset, Marquis of Worcester, the real inventor of the steam-engine. He was the last noble who held out in his castle against Cromwell ; and the stronghold was the Raglan Castle which gave his title to the Field-Marshal now commanding our army in Turkey. There was so far a resemblance between that Marquis of Worcester and this gallant soldier that they united valor in the field with strenuous work in the closet. The difference was that the closet work of the one was the gratification of an irresistible taste for the pursuit of Natural Philosophy and Mechanics ; while that of the other was, if less exalted, more modest, and strongly impressed with the character of humble duty,—a characteristic

which, full of charm always, is eminently so when the
working man is of high birth and of unqualified Toryism
in politics. For the greater part of forty years, Lord
Raglan labored like a clerk at the military organization
of the country ; and we owe to him something more than
the perfect carrying out of the Duke of Wellington's
principles and methods in providing for the Defence of
the country, and for a future safety and glory which
would probably bring him no commensurate fame.

[IV]

*His length
of service at
the Horse
Guards.*

This does not mean that his services, even in that
department, began with the peace. Though he was
then only seven-and-twenty, he had been extemely
useful for some years in the Duke's cabinet, while distinguishing himself also in action. The youngest son
of the fifth Duke of Beaufort, he was born in September,
1788, and christened Fitzroy James Henry Somerset.
He was a cornet in the 4th Light Dragoons at sixteen,
and rose in military rank, as the boyish sons of dukes
do rise, over the heads of their seniors. He was a
captain at twenty—a thing which we believe and trust
could not happen now, after the sound reforms which he
himself has instituted. He went with the troops to
Portugal, and fought in the first great battle, that of
Talavera, in which the French and English armies fairly
and singly tried their strength against each other. Lord
Fitzroy Somerset was then under one-and-twenty, and
it was not the first conflict he had seen since he landed
in the Peninsula. He learned much of his military
science within the lines of Torres Vedras, and was
severely wounded at the battle of Busaco. By this time
the young soldier had won the notice and strong regard
of Wellington, who made him first his Aide-de-camp
and then his Military Secretary—a singular honor for a

*His first
battles.*

[IV]

man under two-and-twenty. The duties of his various functions kept him diligently occupied during the whole of the Peninsular war, and no doubt trained him in that habit of industry and aptitude for business which has distinguished his whole life, and made him, in regard to the military executive, a sort of double of the Duke of Wellington. He was present and active in every one of the great Peninsular battles; and was, in the intervals, the medium of all the Duke's commands and arrange-

The Duke of Wellington's opinion.

ments. The Duke's avowed opinion was that the successes of that Seven Years' War were due, next to himself, to his Military Secretary; and that, but for Lord Fitzroy Somerset, they would not have been obtained. He became Major in 1811, and Lieutenant-Colonel the year after. He returned to England after Bonaparte's abdication in 1814, and met with the honor due to his intrepidity in the field from those who could not be aware of his yet more important services in perfecting the organization and discipline of the Army, which went out a mass of raw material, or something not much better, and returned, as Wellington declared, "a perfect

Marries a niece of Wellington's.

machine." Lord Fitzroy Somerset married in the August of that year the second daughter of Lord Mornington, and thus became the nephew by marriage of the Duke of Wellington. None then dreamed what misfortune awaited the young bridegroom within the first year of his marriage. On Napoleon's return from Elba, the Secretary went out with the Commander-in-Chief; and as his Aide, he was on the field during the three days of June which ended the war. The Duke was wont to offer to bear the responsibility of an omission in the battle of Waterloo—the neglecting to break an entrance in the back wall of the farmstead, La Haye Sainte—

whereby the British occupants might have been re-en-
forced and supplied with ammunition. It was the want
of ammunition which gave the French temporary possession of the place; and that temporary possession cost
many lives, and Lord Fitzroy Somerset his right arm.
He came home to his bride, thus maimed, before he was
seven-and-twenty, but with whatever compensation an
abundance of honor could afford. In his despatch,
Wellington said of him, "I was likewise much indebted
to the assistance of Lieutenant-Colonel Lord Fitzroy
Somerset, who was severely wounded." He was immediately made full Colonel, an extra Aide-de-camp
of the Prince Regent, and Knight Commander of the
Bath.

For nearly forty years afterward it was supposed by
himself and the world that his wars were ended; and he
devoted himself to official service at home. He entered
Parliament for the borough of Truro in 1818, and was a
very silent member, voting invariably with the Tories,
and seldom or never addressing the House. He was
always in request for secretaryships at the Ordnance and
to the Commander-in-Chief. He rose in military rank
at intervals, and became a Lieutenant-General in 1838.
When the Duke of Wellington died, and Lord Hardinge
was made Commander-in-Chief, Lord Fitzroy Somerset
became Master-General of the Ordnance, and was raised
to the peerage by the title of Baron Raglan. But many
good and true soldiers audibly complained that the supple
courtier had been preferred to the man who had the true
interest of the army at heart. It presently appeared that
his wars were not over. During the long interval he had
sent out his eldest son in the service of his country, and
lost him on the field at Ferozeshah in 1845. Nine years

[IV]

His services at Waterloo.

Enters Parliament, 1818.

Made Master-General of the Ordnance.

[IV]

*Appointed
Com-
mander-in-
Chief of
the Army
in the
Crimea.*

after this bereavement the stricken father went out himself once more ; and this time in full command. When
war with Russia was determined on, there could be no
doubt as to who should be chosen to conduct the English
share of it. With Lord Raglan dwelt the traditions of
his master ; and no one was so thoroughly versed in the
wisdom which had for seven long and hard years won
the successes of the Peninsular war. No one so well
knew the army and its administration ; and no one else
so effectually combined the military and practical official
characters :—a combination which, if always necessary
to make a good general, is most emphatically so in the
country which is the scene of the present war. To
Turkey therefore he went—in much the same temper,
and with much of the same demeanor, as his great
master. He just showed himself enough in London and
Paris, on festal occasions, to prove that he could be
dégagé, as a brave man always can ; but he permitted
no "nonsense." He declined noisy honors where he
could, held serious and rapid counsel with his coadjutors
at Paris and Constantinople, and lost no time. If there
were delays, they were not his. Here again, then, he
stands, in his sixty-seventh year, on the battle-field, first
in command on the part of England, and charged
with the function of carrying forward the old spirit
into the new war, and keeping green the laurels won
by his great master and the nation he represented forty
years before.

V.

THE NAPIERS.

LIEUTENANT-GENERAL SIR WILLIAM NAPIER,
K.C.B.

DIED FEBRUARY 12TH, 1860.

Two generations of Englishmen have rejoiced in the felt and lively presence of a family who seemed born to perpetuate the associations of a heroic age, and to elevate the national sentiment at least to the point reached in the best part of the Military Period of our civilization, while our mere talkers were bemoaning the material tendencies and the sordid temper of our people in our own century. The noble old type of the British knight, *Types of the ancient British knight* lofty in valor and in patriotism, was felt to exist in its full virtue while we had the Napiers in our front, conspicuous in the eyes of an observing world. We have every reason to hope that the type will not be lost, whatever may be the destiny of Europe as to war or peace: but the Napiers must pass away, like other virtues and powers; and now we have lost the last of the knightly brothers, and nearly the last of the family group, by the death of Lieutenant-General Sir William Francis Patrick Napier, K.C.B.

The family have a remarkable ancestry. It seems a *Remarkable ancestry.* strange jumble of names and characters. Henry IV. of

9

[V]

France, Charles II. of England, the Dukes of Richmond, Charles James Fox, and Lord Edward Fitzgerald are among the relatives on the one side of the house, and the great Montrose and John Napier, the inventor of logarithms, were among the forefathers on the other.

The Hon. George Napier.

The Hon. George Napier, the father of this band of brothers, was a man of remarkable qualifications in every way; and it was a mystery to his children that he did not attain a higher position in the world than theirs. Two of his sons inherited his noble personal presence, and all the five early gave evidence of the force of character which they believed had marred their father's fortunes, by exciting jealousy among the public men of his time. However that may be, Colonel Napier's want of distinguished success in life gave his children the great advantage of being reared in what they call "poverty." It was an advantage to them, because it was a stimulus, and not an oppression. Their pride in their father and his name kept them in good heart; their love for their widowed mother cheered them in their efforts; and their own individual force bore them up against all obstacles.

The mother, and her betrothal to George III.

From their mother they inherited the sensibility which is as conspicuous as force in them all. Her mother, the wife of the second Duke of Richmond, died of heart-break within the first year of her widowhood; and what the strength and vivacity of Lady Sarah Napier's feelings were we see by the letters of her son Charles to her and about her, as they are given in his "Memoirs." She was beautiful in youth, and indeed throughout her long life, and venerable in age; and she was an object of public interest early and late—first as the beloved and betrothed of George III., and finally as the mother of

"Wellington's colonels." The early story is well known
—the rejection of the King's addresses by a girl of seventeen, her subsequent acceptance of them on sufficient proof of the sincerity of his attachment, the inevitable breaking-off of the match for political reasons,
and the long lingering of the affection on one side at
least. It seems rather far-fetched to suppose that the
family of Colonel Napier were neglected and discouraged
by the sons of George III., on account of the attachment between the respective parents ; but it is understood that the royal lover was watched with solicitude
for years after all intercourse with Lady Sarah Lennox
was broken off. She became the second wife of Colonel
Napier. To young readers it must appear as if there
must be a mistake in the narrative here—as if a generation had been dropped out of view. Is it possible that
the man whom we have now lost—whom we all know by
sight—could have heard his mother tell of her engagement to George III.? Even so ; but there was remarkable longevity all round. Lady Sarah was born in 1746.
Her eldest son was born in 1782, and William in 1785,
and he has died in a good old age. One sister of Lady
Sarah was the mother of Lord Edward Fitzgerald, and another of Charles James Fox.

Longevity in the family.

The three eldest sons of Colonel and Lady Sarah
Napier were soldiers. Charles, the hero of Scinde, and
of many another scene, was the eldest. George was
the next. He was the well-remembered Governor at
the Cape, where he showed an administrative genius
almost as remarkable as his elder brother's in Scinde.
He was as eminent a soldier, too, and bore a no less
astonishing amount of wounds. Wellington's letter to
Lady Sarah on the occasion of George's loss of an arm

The three eldest brothers in the Army.

[V]

[V]

at the storming of Ciudad Rodrigo, is one of the best remembered of his private despatches. All the three brothers suffered from their wounds to the end of their lives ; all won high military rank ; all were K. C. B.'s ; all were Governors of dependencies—for William was Lieutenant-Governor of Guernsey, Alderney, and Sark, while George was ruling at the Cape, and Charles in

The fourth in the Navy.

Scinde. The fourth brother, Henry, was in the Navy. He was like his brothers, in the union of literary ability with the qualities most eminent in active service. His voluminous " History of Florence" will be of great historical value to a future generation. He was even a greater sufferer than his brothers from the constitutional sensibility of the family. The early loss of an adored wife at Florence, broke the spring of his life. He became subject to cruel suffering from neuralgic disease during long years, which left their record on his Florentine history ; and he survived his brother Charles only a few weeks. George died in 1855 ; and then only two re-

The youngest in the legal profession.

mained—the subject of this notice, and Richard, the accomplished youngest brother, admitted to the bar, but preferring study to the exercise of his profession.[1]

One quality in common.

Strong as was the family likeness among the five brothers in all the salient points of intellectual and moral character, the one quality which chiefly marked them all, and separated them from the rest of the world, was their absolute fearlessness of nature. In our age of caution this characteristic could not but glorify them, and at the same time fill their lives with strife, unless they also possessed that repose of nature which ought to accompany fearlessness. This, as all the world knows, they had not. They would have been demigods indeed,

[1] Died in 1867.

if, with all their strength and tenderness, all their genius [V] and their humanity, their power and their graces, they had also manifested that serenity which is the true sign of the godlike. Their "utterances of passion" went for more than they ever intended ; their wrath was usually on be- half of the wronged and helpless ; their clamor, when indignant for one another's sake, bore no relation to any self-regards or low objects ; but still they did clamor and vex the world sometimes with their "passion." It was a pity : but men are not perfect ; and few are the men, of any age or race, who, bearing about so strong a nature, have so little sin of intemperance to answer for. The world saw little of their nobler nature in the pugnacity which exhibited itself through the press. In private life, the gentleness and courtesy of those men, the faithful tenderness with which they bore with and alleviated one another's infirmities, their close, mutual friendship to the end of their lives, their ardent domestic attachments, and the lofty and pure sentiment which graced and refined their existence, made the external quarrels appear to observers like a troubled dream. It was not a dream, however, but too truly a weakness and a fault. Great excuse may be pleaded ; and there is no difficulty in allowing for it ; but the fact remains that they lived in storm, instead of above the clouds. Superior as they were to the world of their day in in- sight, foresight, sense, principle—in short, power—it would have been wiser, and would have marked a yet higher order of men, if they had quarrelled less bitterly with the world for its inferiority in each particular in- stance. This kind of remark applies to Charles and William, as the best known brothers, and the virtual representatives of the family. It is the Napier genius

Their com- bativeness.

[V]

which we have been speaking of, and not the weaknesses of every one of the brotherhood.   On the contrary, the piece of controversy by which Richard is known—his Defence of Charles against the well-known accusations of Outram—is distinguished by calmness of temper and statement.   The long and short of the matter is, as regards the warrior trio, that they are of the hero stamp, and not the sage ; while yet they have so many of the qualities of the sage that we find ourselves unreasonably disappointed when the combative character comes uppermost, and wisdom gives place to valor before the eyes of the multitude.

William Napier.

William, the third of the warrior brothers, was born on the 17th of December, 1785, at his father's residence, ten miles from Dublin.   One strange risk which he happily escaped, was that of being reared at Court as a page. As no Napier was likely to repay any amount of Court discipline, the result of such an experiment would probably have been disgrace of a kind to nourish, rather than mortify pride.   He did much better in entering the army at the age of thirteen, when he joined a regiment of Irish artillery.   He served afterward in the Cavalry and the Infantry, and was also on the Staff.   He was present at the siege of Copenhagen with the 43d Regiment ; and at the time there was a story enacted which brought out the character of the young captain of two-and-twenty.   His company was sorely tempted, by the incitements and direct calls of a Hanoverian general officer, to plunder.   One man obeyed the call, but was ordered back by the young captain, who gave the Hanoverian his opinion of the matter in the open street, evidently in genuine Napier fashion, and declared his resolution to lead his company back to the regiment.

Four hundred prisoners were put under his charge, to be marched to headquarters—more than three-fourths of them being women and decrepit men. For three days they traversed the flats of Zealand; and whenever a prisoner pointed to a church on a rising gronud as his or her village church, leave was given to go home, till the party was reduced to sixty able-bodied men, who were presented at headquarters. This is the first glimpse we have of William's military life.

[V]

At the battle of the Coa, in July, 1810, he was wounded in the hip, and suffered severely for two months. On the 14th of March in the next year Charles was making the best of his way, bandaged for his own terrible wound in the face, received at Busaco, when he met a litter of branches, covered with a blanket, and borne by soldiers. It was his brother George, with a broken limb. Presently he met another litter. It was William, declared to be mortally hurt. Charles looked at the spectacle which met him at the end of a ninety miles' ride, and rode on into the fight. Wellington might well relish talking of "my Colonels" the Napiers. Nearly thirty years afterward we find Charles snatching time from his anxious business of keeping the Chartists quiet to explain to William a medical opinion of the causes of the terrible suffering William was enduring :— "He said it was the ball pressing upon some large nerve, or upon the backbone," &c. For three years William commanded the 43d in the Peninsula, where he was wounded four times, and for which he received seven decorations, and was made K.C.B. He had done and borne a good deal as a soldier ; but the distinctive work of his life was not begun, nor as yet dreamed of.

Meeting of the three wounded brothers.

Wellington's colonels.

In 1819 he retired on half-pay, and soon settled down

The "History of the Peninsular. War."

into the literary life by which he has rendered his highest service—and an immortal service—to the British nation. It is not because his "History of the Peninsular War" is the finest military history ever produced that his labors should be so spoken of, but because the act of writing that narrative was a political service of incalculable importance. When he entered on his work Wellington was unwilling that the melancholy facts of the early part of the struggle should become known to the world ; and if he, the conqueror, was unwilling, it may be imagined what was felt by the obstructive officials who had done their utmost to crush the commander and his enterprise. Well as we understand it now, nobody knew at the close of the war that Wellington's greatest difficulties lay within the Cabinet and the War Office at home. Whether we ever should have learned the truth without Napier's help there is no saying ; but we know that to him we owe the full and clear understanding that we have of the true scheme and character of the Peninsular War, of the ability, temper, and conduct of the Ministry of the time, and of the merits of our great General.

Its effects.

That History has therefore modified our national policy, and our views, plans, spirit, and conduct as a people. There are few books on record which have effected such a work as this. It is this view of it which explains the wrath it excited. The raging vindictiveness of the Tory Government party is faithfully expressed in the *Quarterly* reviews (in two successive numbers) of the History. The political and literary distrust combined found a mouthpiece in Southey, whose own History of the same war was naturally annihilated by its military rival. Lord Wellesley's indignant remonstrances on behalf of his brother in the House of Lords had been sneered at by

Ministers and slighted by everybody else, as explosions of family vanity or natural partiality; and it was not till Napier's History appeared that Englishmen were at all generally aware what a war they had passed through, and how bad a Government, and how transcendent a General, had been transacting their affairs. Apart from the literary merits of the work, it is, and ever will be, remarkable as a disclosure of the real history of England during a period otherwise shrouded in thick darkness. This we understand to be the great and distinctive service of Sir William Napier's life.

Of the literary quality of the book it is needless to say more here than that it fired the spirit of our army in the Crimea. Passages from it were the luxury of the nights in the trenches, and the weary days in hospital. After all the fault that can be found by critics, military and literary, everybody loves and admires the book as much as ever. Some may pick holes in the narrative, and some impugn the judgments, and others show that the style has a dozen faults; but it all makes no difference: we read just as eagerly the third time as the first; and some of us are haunted by whole passages which pursue us like strains of music. Such involuntary judgments thrust all ordinary criticism aside, at least while the author is lying dead; and we think of the book as one of the weapons and the honors which should lie on his coffin with his sword and his spurs, his symbols and decorations.

Eighteen years were diligently employed over the History. His wife was his main helper. She was a niece of Charles James Fox; and it may possibly be attributable to her influence and that of Holland House, that the estimate of Napoleon in the History is so unlike

[V]

The admiration which the "History" elicits.

His wife a coadjutor.

9*

[V] what now appears to us reasonable. The view of the Spanish, as allies and patriots, which was denounced by the Government and the *Quarterly Review* of the time, has turned out only too correct ; but, making the most of all modifications introduced from place to place, the appreciation of Napoleon is certainly essentially false. If the Fox connection is more or less answerable for this misfortune, it did great things for the work in other ways. It gave the historian the wife who was his amanuensis during that long labor, and who disclosed the contents of French documents of great importance, transmitted in cipher, which baffled the penetration of everybody else. The labor was mere child's play compared with the anxieties entailed by the work on the devoted wife. Whether any man was ever so often challenged within a certain number of months may be a question. What to do in such a case was a serious embarrassment. We will not go into the details. The work abides, the quarrels have gone by, and the author survived to a great age, amidst increasing honor and admiration.

His other literary labors

His other literary works were review articles on military subjects—as Jomini's "Art of War," and the "Life of Sir John Moore," in the *Edinburgh Review*, and the "Wellington Despatches," in the *London and Westminster Review*, of January, 1838 ; a few political pamphlets ; his Histories of the "Conquest of Scinde," and of "Sir Charles Napier's Administration of Scinde," partly written in Guernsey, where he repaired as Governor after concluding his "History of the Peninsular War ;" and the "Life and Opinions" of his brother Charles, in four volumes, published in 1857. The political pamphlets are perhaps a fair representation of the political side of the man, and of his brothers, or some of them. Sir

Charles Napier's letters and journals while in command [V] of the northern districts of England, in troublesome times, are a good family exposition in the same way. The most commonplace people found it most difficult to understand the Napier politics. From their connections *The Napier* and their towering pride they might be expected to be *politics.* particularly aristocratic, yet they were exactly the reverse. They were as Conservative as Wellington in some lights, and as Radical as Cobbett in others. That they had quarrels with Tories, Whigs, and Radicals in turn, was, unhappily, not very wonderful; but what were their principles? Sir W. Napier's pamphlets on the Poor Law and on the repeal of the Corn Laws explain a good deal; but the best key to their social principles was seeing the *The daily* action of their daily lives. The servants, all made friends *life of the* of, and living on and on, as in a natural home; the *Napiers.* laboring class, treated with respect and courtesy as long as they were just and kind in their own walk, but encountered as an enemy when guilty of oppression,—these were evidences of the genuine democratic spirit which dwelt in those proud hearts, those sincere and just minds. Sir William's friends can bear witness to the vigilance of that spirit in him. He never let pass, among his intimates, such expressions as "the lower orders," "common soldiers," and the like. He was pacified by the explanation that "order" in this sense did not mean difference of species, as in natural history, but the primitive sense of "ranges," in which some must naturally find a higher and some a lower place; but the other expression he never would endure. There *is* no such thing as a common soldier in England, he declared; ours are not "common soldiers," though they may be "privates." He had to defend himself, some years ago, in a characteristic cause.

[V]

*Curious
trial for
assault.*

An action for assault was brought against him by a man whom he had thrashed for persistent cruelty to a horse. The trial is deeply impressed on the minds of all present by the peculiarity that the only witnesses for the defence were two deaf-and-dumb youths—Sir W. Napier's only son and a comrade of his. It was a strange and pretty sight—the pantomime, the clear account rendered by the finger-speech, and the father's spirit which shone out in the youth debarred from the father's eloquence. Everywhere tyrants, small and great, were, in one way or another, thrashed by the Napiers after obstinate refusal to desist from oppression. This was the one clear point about their politics. As for the rest, Sir W. Napier objected to the principle of our Poor Law, and protested against its application. He approved of Free Trade in corn, but protested against the application of the principle in so factitious a state of society, and under the burden of such a debt, as ours. Happily he lived to see how well the true principle worked, and how needless had been his forebodings.

*The family
of Sir. W.
Napier.*

He had, as we have said, one son. Nine daughters were born to him, five of whom survive him. His life was happy in old age. His utterly fearless nature saved him from the suffering which most of us would undergo in provoking and sustaining hostile controversies. His wife, some unmarried daughters, many grandchildren, and all whom his benign domestic temper had attached to him, ministered to his ease, and to his intellect as well ; so that his decline was gentle. Till a late stage of his life his accomplishments as an artist were a precious resource to him. Others besides his immediate friends will remember his statue—the Death of Alcibiades—in virtue of which he was made an honorary member of

*His accomplishments
as an artist.*

the Royal Academy. His paintings are no common-
place amateur daubs, but both explain and are explained
by the splendid picture-gallery of his great historical
work.

V

For many years he was a neighbor of the poet Moore,
at Sloperton ; and the two Irishmen, opposite in almost
every respect but nationality, much enjoyed one another's
society. Napier, the giant, with a head like Jupiter
Tonans (as he appears in the frontispiece of the second
volume of the "Life of Sir C. Napier"), and half-soldier
and half-demigod, contrasted wonderfully with the dapper
little chamber songster. The wine-cup was associated
with love and war in Moore's imagination : while in
Napier's war was associated with famine, torture, and
seas of blood ; but both were Irishmen, both patriots in
their several ways, both lovers of literature ; and they
were good neighbors. Latterly, Sir W. Napier lived at
Clapham, at Scinde House (called by cabmen *Shindy
Hall*). Thence to the last he studied every turn of
human affairs, watching over his brother's fame as vigi-
lantly as if he were still writing his Life. When the
Indian revolt broke out he pointed out his brother's clear
foresight of the calamity, and of the mode of it. When
the revolt was put down, and reorganization of the
Indian administration began, he made the world observe
how his brother's institutions—despised and destroyed in
a day of presumption—were revived under a better spirit
of government ; the Scinde Police, for one, extended
now from State to State ; and the Camel-corps, which
means life or death under circumstances of Indian warfare ; and again, the Barracks. With pride the faithful
dying brother told his friends that the soldiers in India
would not call their new airy wholesome barracks by

*Sir W.
Napier and
Thomas
Moore.*

*Watchful
over his
brother's
fame.*

[V] their proper names in diffcrent places, but called them all "Napier barracks."

He has left those behind who will guard his memory no less well, if indeed any other guardianship is needed than the national feeling toward the gallant brotherhood of knights, and the historian of the Peninsular War in particular. They are gone. We have many gallant men left, as we always have had, and always shall have ; but there never have been any, and there never can be any, *A theme for* like the Napiers. They were a group raised from among *Tradition.* the mediæval dead, and set in the midst of us, clothed in a temperament which admitted all the ameliorating influences of our period of civilization. They were a great and never-to-be-forgotten sight to our generation ; and our posterity will see them in the mirror of tradition for ages to come. We are wont to say that Tradition is old, and has left off work ; but it is not often now that Tradition has such a theme as the Napiers. It will not willingly be let die till Tradition itself is dead.

VI.

REAR-ADMIRAL SIR FRANCIS BEAUFORT, K.C.B.

DIED DECEMBER 17TH, 1857.

No pressure of national interests or calamity should preclude any one of the honors due to the memory of such a man as Admiral Sir Francis Beaufort, who was not only a priceless treasure to his country, but a bene-factor to the world. There are perhaps not many, beyond the bounds of the scientific class and of his own pro-fession, who are aware of his claims to such a description ; for his great age obscured his early services from the existing generation ; and his later achievements were of a kind which it takes time to make known to society at large. The popular benefits of scientific developments always bring about a grateful recognition of the originator, sooner or later ; but such tardy honor is not enough. Those who understand what society has possessed and lost in the life and by the death of Francis Beaufort should say what they know of him, that he may be mourned as he deserves, and that future generations may not inquire in vain how so great a citizen lived and died.

A bene-factor to the world.

And not only future generations, but distant nations in our own time. Wherever science is cultivated, there Francis Beaufort is honored. The contemporary of a

[VI]

great band of philosophers, in a scientific age, he held a prominent place among them, and was revered by them all, be they who they might. He lingered so long behind them, that they could not show the world how to value his memory; but in every civilized country there are heirs of their labors and their tastes, who will be grateful for any information as to the career and the immortal claims of the man whose name they have never heard mentioned but with praise. To his friends he was venerable as "the best man they had ever known." It is pleasant to the aged to think of how many men they have heard this said in the course of their lives;

His labors in practical science.

but it is rarely said so often in the case of one man as it is in Francis Beaufort's. His professional career is a sort of favorite romance in the navy; but his labors in practical science form that link between his life and that of society at large which justifies the title of benefactor to the world. He has been called so by hundreds of firesides, and wherever scientific men meet together, in the few weeks which have elapsed since his death. We have no doubt that the title will be ratified by all who may become acquainted with the history of his life.

His French extraction.

He was born in 1774, and was an Irishman of French extraction, as his name testifies. His father, the Rev. Daniel Augustus Beaufort, was Vicar of Collon, in the county of Louth, and was directly descended from an ancient and noble French family. Francis was the second son, and the heir of some of his father's talents and tastes,—the best map of Ireland previous to the Ordnance Survey, and an able memoir on Ireland, being among the good deeds of the Collon vicar.

Though only thirteen when he went to sea, Francis had already many of the requisites of an able officer.

On his first voyage, which was with Captain Lestock
Wilson, in the *Vansittart*, East Indiaman, as a "guinea-
pig,"—that is, in virtue of the payment of a hundred
guineas,—he was remarkable for his skill in observation,
and the amount of his nautical knowledge; so that he
afforded valuable assistance to his commander in surveying the Straits of Gaspard, in the sea of Java. His
perilous adventures began thus early. The survey was
just completed when the *Vansittart* struck upon a rock
off the island of Banca, close by the spot where the
Transit lately went down. A hole was stove, through
which daylight and sea poured in alternately. An
effort was made to keep the ship afloat till the flat
Shore of Sumatra could be reached; but even the hope
of a landing on Banca was presently given up; and she
was run aground on an island seven miles from Banca.
The crew escaped in the boats, and, with the loss of six
lives and one boat, reached two English ships after five
days' rowing, with great suffering, in the open sea, close
to the line. This adventure happened in August, 1789.

The young Beaufort's name had already been for two
years on the books of H.M.S. *Colossus;* but on his return
from the East he joined H.M.S. *Latona*, Captain Albe-
marle Bertie; and afterward H.M.S. *Aquilon*, in which
he was engaged in the memorable action off Brest, of
the 1st of June, 1794, in which ten of the enemy's ships
were dismasted; seven were taken; three only joined
their Admiral; and Lord Howe brought into Portsmouth
six French ships of the line, which the King and Royal
Family came to inspect, at the end of the month. They
went on board the *Aquilon*, to sail round the fleet; and
thus young Beaufort made, probably, his first acquaintance with Royalty. He was for some years the sole

[IV]

surviving officer of that great battle. He followed his
Captain, the Hon. Robert Stopford, to H.M.S. *Phaeton*,
in which ship he was serving when Vice-Admiral Corn-
wallis made his celebrated retreat from the French
fleet, on the 17th of June, 1795. In this ship, afterward commanded by Captain James Nicholl Morris,
he assisted at the capture and destruction of many of
the enemy's ships, and of nine privateers and other
vessels. It was in May, 1796, that he obtained his rank
of Lieutenant. It was in October, 1800, that his first
great opportunity of distinguishing himself occurred.

*Captures
the " San
Josef."*

While cruising off the coast of Malaga, his commander
observed that a Spanish polacca, the *San Josef*, and a
French privateer brig, had taken refuge under the fortress
of Fuengirola ; and at night the young Lieutenant was
sent, in command of the *Phaeton's* boats, to board the
San Josef. The French brig intercepted the launch ;
but the other crews did their work without its aid. The
resistance they encountered was desperate ; but they
obtained their prize, with the loss of one man to thirteen
of the enemy—Beaufort, however, receiving no less than
nineteen wounds. This made him a Commander, with
a small pension.

*The estab-
lishment of
a line of
telegraphs.*

The next two years were spent on shore amidst hard
work, like all the years of his long life. Miss Edgeworth
tells us that they were "devoted, with unremitting zealous
exertion," to establishing a line of telegraphs from Dublin
to Galway ; an object of great importance as long as
the west of Ireland was perpetually liable to invasion
from continental enemies. He received the thanks of
Government for his efforts, declining any other acknowledgment.

Once more at sea, he was heard of from the East first,

and then the West. As commander of the *Woolwich*, 44, he convoyed from India sixteen Indiamen in 1806. In 1807 he was surveying the La Plata; and he afterward went to the Cape and the Mediterranean. In 1809 he was hovering about the enemy's merchantmen on the coast of Spain and at Quebec, being in command of the sloop-of-war *Blossom*. In 1810 he obtained his post rank, and the command of the *Fredericksteen* frigate : but before he joined he was employed in protecting the outward-bound trade to Portugal, Cadiz, and Gibraltar; in accompanying two Spanish line-of-battle ships to Minorca; and in acting for some months as captain to the *Ville de Paris*, a first-rate, in the fleet off Toulon, commanded by Sir Edward Pellew.

A remarkable incident in his life.

It does not appear to be on record in which year of his life it was that he so nearly perished by drowning, and underwent the remarkable experience of the intellectual condition under such a crisis, which he afterward recorded in a letter, at the request of Dr. Wollaston. He described himself as "a youngster, at Portsmouth, in one of the King's ships." He was not himself impressed as others were by the remarkable character of his sensations; but he saw the importance of every such record, and made it accordingly. Interesting in itself, the story is extremely valuable as coming from one as singularly truthful in recording experience as skilled in detailing it. One of his most striking accomplishments was his power of saying what he meant. The effect of this power was seen wherever he went in the harmony he seemed to establish by the clearness of his ideas, and the transparency of their presentment. All the little chafings and perplexities which follow, like yelping curs, at the heels of men of confused mind and speech, were ex-

[VI]

[VI]
tinguished by Beaufort's mere presence. He at once put his neighbors in possession of their own and each other's views and objects, leaving no foggy spaces in which they could run foul of one another. Such a power, turned in the direction of philosophical observation and record, is inestimable ; and the deep interest with which all manner of persons have read the letter to Wollaston, when they could lay hands on it, is not to be wondered at. The letter is published in Sir John Barrow's "Auto-biography," which our readers may not, for the most part, have seen. As both the incident and the record are important features in the life of Beaufort, it is our business to cite the most essential passages of the narrative.

It relates that he capsized a very small boat by stepping on the gunwale, in an endeavor to fasten her alongside the ship to one of the scuttle-rings ; that, unable to swim, he could not reach either the boat or the floating oars ; that he had drifted to some distance astern before he was observed ; that two of his comrades jumped overboard to his assistance, and a third followed in a boat ; that, in his violent shouting, he had swallowed a great deal of water ; and that, before aid reached him, he had sunk below the surface, and given up all hope of life. The narrative proceeds :

Description of his sensations while drowning.

"So far these facts were either partially remembered after my recovery, or supplied by those who had latterly witnessed the scene ; for during an interval of such agitation, a drowning person is too much occupied in catching at every passing straw, or too much absorbed by alternate hope and despair, to mark the succession of events very accurately. Not so, however, with the facts which immediately ensued ; my mind had then undergone the sudden revolution which appeared to you so remarkable, and all the circumstances of which are now as vividly fresh in my memory as if they had occurred but yesterday. From the moment that all exertion had ceased—which I imagine was the immediate consequence of complete suffocation—a calm feeling of the most perfect tranquillity superseded the previous tumultuous sensations—it might be called apathy, certainly not resignation, for drowning no longer appeared to be an evil—I no longer thought of being rescued, nor was I in any bodily pain. On the contrary, my sensations were now of rather a pleasurable cast, partaking of that dull but contented sort of feeling which precedes the sleep produced by fatigue. Though the senses were thus deadened, not so the mind; its activity seemed to be invigorated, in a ratio which defies all description, for thought rose above thought with a rapidity of succession that is not only indescribable, but probably inconceivable by any one who has not himself been in a similar situation. The course of those thoughts I can even now in a great measure retrace—the event which had just taken place—the awkwardness that had produced it— the bustle it must have occasioned (for I had observed two persons jump from the chains)—the effect it would have on a most affectionate father—the manner in which he would disclose it to the rest of the family—and a thousand other circumstances minutely associated with home, were the first series of reflections that occurred. They took then a wider range—our last cruise—a former voyage, and shipwreck—my school—the progress I had made there, and the time I had misspent—and even all my boyish pursuits and adventures. Thus travelling backward, every past incident of my life seemed to

[VI] glance across my recollection in retrograde succession; not, however, in mere outline, as here stated, but the picture filled up with every minute and collateral feature. In short, the whole period of my existence seemed to be placed before me in a kind of panoramic review, and each act of it seemed to be accompanied by a consciousness of right or wrong, or by some reflection on its cause or its consequences; indeed, many trifling events which had been long forgotten then crowded into my imagination, and with the character of recent familiarity.

"May not all this be some indication of the almost infinite power of memory with which we may awaken in another world, and thus be compelled to contemplate our past lives? Or might it not in some degree warrant the inference that death is only a change or modification of our existence, in which there is no real pause or interruption? But, however that may be, one circumstance was highly remarkable—that the innumerable ideas which flashed into my mind were all retrospective: yet I had been religiously brought up; my hopes and fears of the next world had lost nothing of their early strength: and at any other period, intense interest and awful anxiety would have been excited by the mere probability that I was floating on the threshold of eternity; yet, at that inexplicable moment, when I had a full conviction that I had already crossed that threshold, not a single thought wandered into the future: I was wrapt entirely in the past.

"The length of time that was occupied by this deluge of ideas, or rather the shortness of time into which they were condensed, I cannot now state with precision; yet certainly two minutes could not have elapsed from the moment of suffocation to that of my being hauled up.

"The strength of the flood-tide made it expedient to pull the boat at once to another ship, where I underwent the usual vulgar process of emptying the water by letting my head hang downward, then bleeding, chafing, and even administering gin ; but my submersion had been really so brief, according to the account of lookers-on, I was very quickly restored to animation.

"My feelings, while life was returning, were the reverse in every point of those which have been described above. One single but confused idea—a miserable belief that I was drowning—dwelt upon my mind, instead of the multitude of clear and definite ideas which had recently rushed through it ; a helpless anxiety, a kind of continuous nightmare seemed to press heavily on every sense, and to prevent the formation of any one distinct thought, and it was with difficulty that I became convinced that I was really alive. Again, instead of being absolutely free from all bodily pain, as in my drowning state, I was now tortured by pain all over me ; and though I have been since wounded in several places, and have often submitted to severe surgical discipline, yet my sufferings were at that time far greater, at least in general distress. On one occasion I was shot in the lungs, and after lying on the deck at night for some hours, bleeding from other wounds, I at length fainted. Now, as I felt sure that the wound in the lungs was mortal, it will appear obvious that the overwhelming sensation which accompanies fainting must have produced a perfect conviction that I was then in the act of dying. Yet nothing in the least resembling the operations of my mind when drowning then took place ; and when I began to recover, I returned to a clear conception of my real state."

[VI]

[VI]

His work "Kara-mania."

When he took the command of the *Fredericksteen*, in 1811, he was on the road to fame in authorship. Sir J. Barrow tells us that Beaufort was selected out of the whole Mediterranean fleet to survey an unknown portion of the coast of Syria. The result of this errand was, not only a capital survey, but an historical review of the country, as illustrated by its remains of antiquity. Beaufort's "Karamania" was the great book of travels of its day—sound, substantial, and learned (thanks to the good classical education his father had given him), and full of interest at once for the man of science and the scholar. It was this book, with its discoveries and verifications of ancient sites, which sent Fellows, and Spratt, and Forbes, and more recently Charles Newton, to Asia Minor, to tell us of the works of art which are extant there, and to bring over the Halicarnassian Marbles to the British Museum.

Seriously wounded in Syria.

After much hazardous service against the pirates in the Greek waters, Captain Beaufort went to work on the survey of Syria, in the course of which he underwent extreme danger. In June, 1812, his party were surrounded by armed Turks, led by a crazy dervish; and he was wounded in the hip-joint so seriously that the wonder was that he ever walked again. It was a severe struggle for life itself; and when his ship was paid off, in the next October, he was still undergoing much pain from the exfoliation of the bone. He solaced his enforced

His Admiralty Charts.

leisure by work, preparing for the Admiralty such a set of charts of the coasts of Asia Minor, the Archipelago, the Black Sea, and Africa, as had never before been seen at the Admiralty. They were so drawn, finished, and arranged as to be fit for transference to the copper without any aid from the hydrographer or his assistants.

Such is the testimony of Sir John Barrow. Sir John Barrow naturally recommended him to Lord Melville for the post of Hydrographer, declaring that Captain Beaufort had no equal in that line, and very few in most other branches of science.

[VI]

This was in 1829. In 1823 Captain Hurd had died; and Captain Parry was requested by Lord Melville to fill the post temporarily; which he did twice, if not three times. After the resignation of the Duke of Clarence as Lord High Admiral, Lord Melville again became First Lord; and one of his objects was to fill the office of Hydrographer with the best man that could be found, who should hold it permanently. There were many applicants; but by 1829 two names only remained for a choice—and one of them, at least, was not an applicant —Captains Beaufort and Peter Heywood. Lord Melville declined the responsibility of deciding between them, and requested Sir John Barrow and Mr. Croker to advise him. Sir John Barrow had, as we have seen, selected Beaufort out of the whole Mediterranean fleet for the survey in Asia Minor; and that survey having issued as it did, he could but desire to see the office of Hydrographer filled by the accomplished officer who had thus distinguished himself. For twenty-six years Beaufort was at the Admiralty as Hydrographer; and very early in that period he had made his office the model on which Paris, Copenhagen, and St. Petersburg constructed theirs. Everywhere Hydrography took a new form and existence through the life which he put into his work. There is not a geographical discoverer, nor a zealous professional student in any naval service in the civilized world, who does not feel under direct obligation to Beaufort for his scientific assistance, given through his

Appointed Hydrographer to the Admiralty.

[VI]   works, or more special encouragement, by his personal
aid and counsel.   Those who remember the enthusiasm
with which Commander Wilkes, of the United States
Exploring Expedition (the unfortunate assailant of the
Trent at the beginning of the late American war), used
to speak of the effectual friendship of Captain Beaufort,
in preparing for that important enterprise, have witnessed

Apprecia-
tion of his
world-wide
labors.

a specimen of the appreciation in which he was held by
his professional brethren of all nations.   It has been no
small benefit to the world that the most accomplished
Hydrographer of his own or any time was at our Admiralty for six-and-twenty years, always awake to chances
of increasing the general knowledge, always indefatigable
in furthering such chances, and genial and generous in
assisting every man of any nation who devoted himself
to geographical discovery or the verification of glimpses
already obtained.   His name is attached to several
stations in newly discovered lands and seas : for instance,
it will be uttered in all future times by voyagers passing
up either the eastern or western shores of the American
continent to the Polar Sea.   But not the less is his name
really though invisibly connected with almost every other
modern enterprise of geographical discovery ; for he gave
a helping hand to every scientific adventurer who applied
to him,—and no one thought of instituting scientific
adventure without applying to him.

Changes
at the
Admiralty.

When he entered the Admiralty, nearly thirty years
ago, he found his own department a mere map-office.
His friends well remember what a place it was—small,
cheerless, out of the way, altogether unfit and inadequate.
The fact is, nobody but the *élite* of the naval profession
had any conception of the importance—one might almost
say of the nature—of the function of Hydrographer.

Maritime surveying on an extended scale was only beginning. We were not yet in possession of the full
results of the labors of Flinders, Smyth, King, and
Owen ; and Sir Edward Parry's view of his office was,
that it made him the Director of a Chart-Depôt for the
Admiralty, and the supporter, rather than the guide or
originator, of maritime surveys. Becoming conscious
that the times were requiring something more than he
could give, he wisely resigned. The manner in which
Captain Beaufort was appointed, without solicitation on
his own part, and simply because the best judges considered him the fittest man, encouraged him to lay large
plans, and to indulge high hopes. He began a great
series of works, in which he intended to comprise,
gradually and systematically, all the maritime surveys
of the world—our own coasts, still shamefully obscure,
being destined for a thorough exploration in the first
place. He designed and began what Lieutenant Maury
has since achieved. His instructions to surveying officers
show how extensive were his purposes as to deep-sea
soundings so long ago as 1831 ; and the object was never
lost sight of, though he was baffled in the pursuit of it.
Whatever depended on his own energy was done,
throughout his whole term of office ; but he had to
endure the affliction which breaks the heart of every
highly qualified servant of the Government—the destruction of his aims by failure of sympathy in those who hold
the power and the purse, manifested either in opposition
to useful projects or in parsimony in providing for them.
After Beaufort had so shown what his office might be as
to stimulate every other Government in Europe, he was
compelled to see them all outstrip his own, through the
senseless and needless parsimony of the authorities above

[VI].

His plans.

[VI]

him. The Whigs, on their accession to power, felt themselves pledged to economy, and were so pledged ; but they did great injustice to the people of England, in supposing that they grudge money for the support of national objects and genuine public service.   It is quite right, and will always be inevitable, that every Administration, of any politics, will be called to account for reckless experiments in shipbuilding, and such dockyard waste as is witnessed from one ten years to another : but there is not a member of the Legislature, nor an intelligent elector in the kingdom, who would not, on the least word of explanation, have voted whatever funds were necessary to the due prosecution of all the Maritime Surveys desired by such an authority as our late Hydrographer.   But he had to suffer under the evil of the political tenure of Admiralty office. His establishment was diminished when it should have been enlarged :

False economy.

foreign surveys were restricted from year to year ; and at length the exploration of our own shores was reduced to something wholly inadequate to the need.   It is no small mortification to compare our Hydrographical Establishment with that at Paris, where the Dépôt de la Marine might be taken for the office of the greatest Maritime Power in Europe; or with those at St. Petersburg, Copenhagen, Utrecht, and Washington : but the annual summary of shipwrecks, and the detail of lives lost through want of that knowledge which Beaufort would have established a quarter of a century ago, is a severer grief.   It weighed heavily on his heart ; and it was probably the most painful experience of his life. Scientific men bitterly feel the truth of the words uttered from the Chair of the Royal Society : "The natural tendency of men is to undervalue what they cannot understand ;" but

the censure should in this case rest on the right parties; [VI]
and those are not the people of England. Scientific
pursuit is the prevailing popular taste in our time; and
there are no bounds to the popular support which would
be afforded to it, on any fair appeal; but the misfortune
is, that the supplies voted for such an object as the
Hydrographical Department are lumped together with
others which are justly open to objection—the abortive
shipbuilding, and other mismanagement by which, after
an enormous expenditure, we find ourselves ill supplied
for maritime purposes, while parading the most marvellous
marine that any empire ever possessed.

Captain Beaufort had a remarkable power of discerning *His dis-*
and appropriating ability to its right object, whenever it *cernment.*
came in his way; and at every turn of his life he was
using this power on behalf of others; yet he could not
avail himself of it on his own. He was so restricted in
his office, that he had no subordinate who could be a
comrade in his labors; and all that he had at heart
must be done by his own hand. Disappointed in his
hopes, baffled in his aims, pinched in his official expenditure, he turned the full forces of his strong will on
making the best of the hard circumstances of the case.
He now proved himself as true a patriot as when he was
receiving his nineteen wounds in boarding the *San Josef,*
while the wounds of his hopes were more painful than
those of the body, and there was no praise to be won.
It was not his doing that the virtue was ever known.
His industry, of constitutional origin, and sustained by
principle, appeared something miraculous under this
stress. Day by day, for a quarter of a century, he might
be seen entering the Admiralty as the clock struck; and
for eight hours he worked in a way which few men even

[VI]

understand. A man who carried his own letter-paper and pens to the Admiralty for his private correspondence, was not one to occupy his official hours with other than official business ; and the labors that Captain Beaufort undertook for benevolent objects were carried on at home. For many years he rose at five, and worked for *His benevolence.* three hours before his official day began. The anecdote of his connection with the maps of the Diffusion Society has recently gone the round of the newspapers ; and all the world knows that, in order to get these maps sold at sixpence instead of a shilling, he offered to superintend their preparation. As if he had not enough to do in his own function, he gave the world that set of maps,—so valuable as charts that no ship in the United States Navy is allowed to sail without them ; and it is his doing that they are in a thousand houses which they would never have entered but for their cheapness.

This is one of his innumerable charities. There was no sort of charity in which he was not just as liberal and as wise. There was no pedantry in his industry any more than in his knowledge. He never seemed in a hurry. While too seriously engaged for gossip, he had minutes or hours to bestow where they could really do good : he had conscientious thought to spare for other people's affairs, and modest sympathy in their interests, and intrepid advice when it was asked, and honest rebuke when it was deserved and might be effectual. His unobtrusiveness was, perhaps, the most striking quality of his manner to observers who knew what was in him. His piety, reverent and heartfelt, was silent, as he pre- *His home.* ferred that that of others should be. His domestic affections were unconcealable ; but spoken sentiment was quite out of his way. His happy marriage (with the daughter of his first commander, Captain Lestock Wilson) ended in a mingling of pain and privilege which touched the hearts of all witnesses. Never was so much understood with so little said. She died of a lingering and most painful disease, making light of it to others as long as possible, though the full truth was known to both; she kept her young children about her, with their mirth wholly unchecked, to the latest possible day; and the few who looked in on that sacred scene saw that it was indeed true that, as she said, she had never been happier than during that painful decline. As for him, there was not the slightest remission of outside duty while the domestic vigilance was that which so marvellously smoothed the passage to the grave. Now that both are gone, it is right to present this feature in the character of the man so long before known as hero and as *savant.* He came out from the long trial so much changed that it seemed doubtful whether he would ever regain his health and buoyant cheerfulness. He lived, however, to see his children fulfilling their own career of labor and honor: one son in the Church, another Legal Remembrancer (Attorney-General) in Calcutta, and a third a judge in Bengal. His second marriage, with a sister of Maria Edgeworth, secured a friend to himself and his daughters for many of the latter years of his life.

Among his public labors were those of the successive offices of Commissioner of Pilotage, entered upon in 1835, and of Member of the Committee of the Tidal Harbors and Ports of Refuge in the United Kingdom in 1845. In 1846 he became Rear-Admiral on the retired list, rather than surrender his office: but he never liked his "yellow flag;" and the mortification of his retirement was but slightly solaced by the honor of the

VI

His sons.

[VI]   Knighthood of the Bath, conferred in 1848. The sudden expansion of railway projects so increased his work that his health began to fail ; but not till he had reached an age at which few men think of work at all. Early in 1855 he was obliged to give up, and go home to a sick-bed for such time as might be left by a painful and incurable disease. He was the same man to the last, active and clear in mind, benevolent and affectionate at heart, and benign in manners. His activity never inter-fered with his profound quietude and peace ; and his quietude and peace deepened as his mind brightened.

His personal appearance.   He must have been personally known, more or less, to many readers of this record. They will not forget his countenance. He was short in stature, but his coun-tenance could nowhere pass without notice. Its astute intelligence, shining honesty, and génial kindliness re-vealed the man so truly that, though he never spoke of himself, few were so correctly understood. It now occurs to us that we never heard a fault attributed to him ; and we cannot say that we ever observed one in him. To record this is simple truth. He was attended in his last hours by his adoring children, and died in the midst of them on the 17th of December, 1857. They and society should be thankful together that such a man was spared to them so long.

VII.

SIR JOHN RICHARDSON.

DIED JUNE 6TH, 1865.

ANOTHER of our naval heroes—another of the band of [*]
Polar Discoverers, is gone, the mere news of whose
departure revives in some of their own generation the
enthusiasm of early days on behalf of the heroism
which finds its exercise in enterprises of peace more
arduous than those of war. The elders of our time have
not all forgotten the first occasion on which they heard
the name of John Richardson; it was in 1819, when
Lieutenant Parry was already exploring among the ice,
and when it seemed probable, as the Admiralty said,
that Parry's object might be promoted by the despatch
of a second expedition to ascertain where the Coppermine River fell into the sea, and to trace the shore of
the Polar Sea eastward from it. This second charge
was devolved upon Lieutenant Franklin, with whom *Associated with Franklin.*
was associated Dr. Richardson, a naval surgeon, de-
scribed as well skilled in Natural History. Partners in
that enterprise, they were friends for life; and, as none
of us can have forgotten, devoted in death. It would
have been strange to them, ready as they were for the
same fate, to have foreknown how differently they would
end their lives. One died behind the veil, as it were—

nobody knowing where he was, and how it fared with him—far away among the ice, with the sun circling round the sky, permitting no night till the night of death fell on him—amidst damp and dreariness; discomfort, if not hunger; obstruction and discouragement, if not hopelessness; with only the glare of the sunshine on the snow, and the blue ice, and the glittering stretches of the sea. The other died in a happy old age, in the same month of the year—in so different a scene, and under such different conditions! Amidst the richest of summer verdure, in a still valley near Grasmere, whither he had just returned from gay intercourse with old friends, and surrounded by his family, he passed away in the night without pain. There was but a year of difference in the age of the two friends; there was a wonderful likeness in the most prominent of their experiences; but a singular contrast in their way of leaving life.

Sir John Richardson was a native of Dumfries, and was educated at the Grammar School there. At Edinburgh he qualified himself for the medical profession, and entered the Navy at twenty, as Assistant Surgeon. He saw something of war; for he was at the siege of Copenhagen, and served afterward on the coasts of the Peninsula. Before he was thirty he took his degree of M. D. at Edinburgh, and at thirty-one he married the first of his three wives. It was in the next year that he became an object of interest to the public, by his association with Parry and Franklin's explorations. From May, 1819, till the next January, he and Franklin remained together; and then the latter, with Lieutenant (now Sir George) Back, proceeded on a sort of preparatory trip of several hundred miles to the western end of Lake Athabasca, while Dr. Richardson was to stay in winter-quarters at Cumberland House, with Lieutenant Hood, till the opening of spring should enable them to advance to the Coppermine River. The physician explored the vegetation and animal life of the neighborhood, while the lieutenant made acquaintance with the Indians, sketching them, and joining their hunting parties.

Spring arrived; the friends joined forces and proceeded northward, but everything went wrong. The winter caught them in August, midway; no supplies overtook them, and they had to winter while food and ammunition were diminishing alarmingly. Lieutenant Back started southward for supplies, and returned; but there were new difficulties at every step; some of the worst being caused by jealousies which induced officials of the North-West Company to detach their servants from the British officers, so as to leave them helpless in the wilds. When the party was next heard of in England, their story moved universal pity and admiration. They had navigated the Coppermine, and the sea and coast for some distance east and west; they had discovered lead, copper, and coal; they had seen their canoes destroyed by the fault of the Canadians who had charge of them; and Dr. Richardson had all but perished in the heroic attempt to swim the icy waters of the Coppermine River. He was drawn out apparently dead, and was revived with great difficulty—to risk his life again and again in recovering the poor fellows who had dropped by the way, or overtaking those who had gone astray in their frenzy of terror and misery. All this was fearful enough; but it was worse that their quarters were found empty; no supplies, no re-enforcements, no token of aid was there; but the only prospect of living on a

[VII]

The expedition to the Coppermine River.

[VII]

His fearful suferings.

diet of old shoes and unwholesome moss till they could live no longer. Then there was the murder of poor Hood by an attendant, who so clearly intended to destroy the two remaining Englishmen, Dr. Richardson and the seaman Hepburn, that Dr. Richardson very properly shot the wretch on the first opportunity. The sufferings of that fearful time, and especially the necessary homicide, left their traces for life on the countenance of the fearless and devoted explorer. The frequent remark of strangers, to the end of his life, was that his face had the expression of a man who had suffered to excess. The relief sent to them by Lieutenant Back reached the survivors just in time; and the kindness of the Indians who brought it, aided their recovery. When the dreary story was told in England, the news came with it that Dr. Richardson had brought away some scientific facts and observations of his own and poor Hood's, as well as their brave chief's; and these appeared in the Appendix to Franklin's Narrative.

Fresh explorations.

Three years had been consumed in this Expedition; and any man might have been excused from encountering the risk of such sufferings a second time; but in 1825 the two friends started again for the same dreary region. They explored the Mackenzie River—the one the western line of its delta, and the other the eastern, Dr. Richardson succeeding in coasting along to the mouth of the Coppermine River, which he ascended as far as it was navigable. The friends returned in two years, and published in partnership their narratives of their explorations. In 1829, and at intervals till 1836, Dr. Richardson published the work on the Zoology of the North British American regions which gave him his fame as a naturalist.

He seemed now to be settled at home, in a repose which was not likely to be disturbed. In 1838, being made physician to the fleet, he went to live at Haslar; and two years later he became an Inspector of Naval Hospitals. But there had been domestic changes. The death of his first wife, from whom his duties had separated him for six years of their union, was followed by a second marriage in 1833, which was ended by death in 1845. It was in his grief under this bereavement that he committed himself once more to the work of Polar Discovery. Under the loosening of his ties to home and life, he spontaneously promised Sir John Franklin, when the latter sailed on his final voyage, that if the expedition did not reappear by the close of 1847, he would go and try for a meeting on the part of the Polar coast they had explored in common. In the interval he married again; and the pledge to Sir John Franklin must have weighed heavily upon him. One sign that it did so was that he and his household steadily insisted on the certainty of Sir John Franklin's return in the coming February. They refused to admit any doubt of this happy issue, when all the rest of the world was disheartened and almost despairing. January passed without news; but then, January was not the month for that news. It would be in February, they had always said, and not before. February came without news; but there might be news in February till February was gone. At last February was gone; and there could be no more resistance to the necessity. He must go; and he went with the courageous cheerfulness of a brave and devoted man. He looked to the bright side—was confident he should soon find Franklin—did not contemplate a long absence, called on his friends to admire his

[VII]

Appointed an Inspector of Naval Hospitals.

His promise to Franklin.

[VII]

*Sets out in
search of
Franklin.*

provision of furs and eider-down, carried his Shakspere
and his Wordsworth to pass the evenings and dreary
days in the wilds, and, after writing from the last practicable point, disappeared as completely as if he was
dead. By August, he and his comrade, Mr. Rae, were
on the Polar shore, searching for traces of the Expedition everywhere between the Mackenzie and Coppermine
rivers. Two other Expeditions were searching west and
east of him ; and it did not appear that he could do
anything more by remaining. He therefore returned
in 1849, leaving Mr. Rae to prosecute inquiries which in
two years more had no result. He returned, to wander
no more, but to live a home-life, partly active and partly
studious, partly professional and partly scientific, while
hearing now of the completion of the discovery of a
Northwest Passage, and now again of the ascertainment
of the fate of Franklin and the doomed Expedition.
Franklin had been dead before his friend started on the
last journey ; and there, it seemed, ended Polar Exploration—at least in our time. They little knew the effect
of their own example, and the influence of such narratives of adventure and glorious suffering as theirs.
Possibly Captain Sherard Osborne's new project, so zeal-
ously supported and admiringly hailed, may have
disclosed to the aged explorer now departed something
more of the effect of such a life as his than he had
hitherto imagined.

For some years more he remained at Haslar, superintending the Museum, and publishing the narrative of his
latest travels, and various communications to scientific
journals, besides discharging his duties as Inspector.

*Retires from
public life.*

When he drew near the age of seventy he resigned his
post, and retired to the Lake District, where he lived ten

more years in the repose suitable to his time of life. A healthy activity remained to the end ; he was known all round the neighborhood, from Windermere to Grasmere, by his exertions of one kind or another. As, on the shores of the Polar Sea, in a hut of drift-wood, caulked with moss, with the sullen waters moaning outside, he delivered lectures to the hunters and boatmen of the Expedition on the soils they were to observe and report on, and the specimens they were to collect, so in the green valleys, and under the slated roofs of Westmoreland, he lectured to the country people on natural productions, and on the pursuit of knowledge. He was happy in his home, proud of his sons, and among his neighbors, if grave and still, as if by nature or the discipline of suffering, still genial at heart, and more so in demeanor, as time passed on. He was never seen more cheerful, and even gay, than on the last day of his life, when he went among the tradespeople, and was visiting friends to within eight hours of his death. He appeared in perfect health, and was reading late. A stroke of apoplexy carried him off before the early summer dawn. After all the risks to which he subjected his life, and the condition to which he was repeatedly reduced by cold, prolonged hunger, and other hardships, he lived into his seventy-eighth year.

[VII]

His useful life.

VIII.

LORD DENMAN.

DIED SEPTEMBER 22D, 1854.

THE death of Lord Denman is an impressive event for other reasons than the universal reverence and affection in which he was held, and the rank he obtained in his profession. There were a few points in his life and action which will connect him in history with some of the marked events of his time, and the news of his decease vividly calls up in many minds the most memorable scenes they have witnessed in our London streets, our country villages, and our Houses of Parliament. During the exciting summer of 1820 his name was, with *His early association with Brougham.* his "brother Brougham's," in every mouth. For long years after he was a sort of popular saint, through the virtuous sympathy that our people have the happiness of being subject to with those whom they clearly understand to have sacrificed worldly objects for something higher. In the conflict between the claims of law and Parliamentary Privilege, from 1836 to 1841, he was the central figure; and with these salient points of the history of our time the name of Thomas Denman will ever be associated.

His family. His father, one of the Court physicians in the time of George III., was the son of a tradesman or farmer at

Bakewell, in Derbyshire; a locality to which the family [VIII]
for successive generations has been so attached that the
line of descendants is likely to perpetuate the residence.
Dr. Denman was fond of his farm at Stoney Middleton,
near Bakewell; and Lord Denman improved the farm-
house into a delightful residence. Dr. Denman had
three children, Thomas, and two daughters, one of whom
was married to Dr. Baillie, and the other to the unhappy
Sir Richard Croft, who attended the princess Charlotte
in her confinement, and, being unable to get over the
shock of her death, committed suicide. It is probably
because he was surrounded by physicians in his family
relations that Lord Denman has been reported to have
been originally intended for the medical profession. This
was not the case, his destination and choice having
always been the bar. He was born in 1779: and,
not being obliged, like most young barristers, to defer
marriage to middle life, or to plunge their wives into
poverty, he indulged himself with a home at an early
age. He married, in 1804, Theodosia Ann Vevers, *His*
eldest daughter of a clergyman of Saxby, and grand- *marriage*
and
daughter of a Lincolnshire baronet. Fifteen children *numerous*
were the offspring of this marriage, of whom eleven *offspring.*
survived, five sons and six married daughters, when Lady
Denman died in 1852.

Mr. Denman's position at the bar became early a very
honorable one; and his name was connected especially
with causes and trials in which the liberty of the press
was concerned. He appears on almost every occasion
in the records of the prosecutions for political libels, *At the bar.*
blasphemy, and sedition, so frequent during the Tory
Administrations of the early part of the century; and
so late as 1841, when a London publisher was prose-

[VIII] cuted for the publication of Shelley's "Queen Mab" in
the collected works of the poet, Lord Denman, as Chief
Justice, repeated the conviction which he had been
wont to avow as a young barrister. In summing up, he
remarked that it was better to subvert objectionable
opinions and sentiments by reason and argument than
to suppress them by persecution of the promulgators.
The circumstances of this latest trial showed him, in a
way which must have been highly agreeable to his liberal
mind, the progress that society had made since his early
days. The prosecution was instigated by a Free-thinker
who had undergone the penalties of an earlier time, to
prove the absurdity of the consequences of carrying out
the law.

Returned as M.P. for Wareham. Mr. Denman was introduced into Parliament in 1818,
by Mr. Calcraft, who had him returned for the borough
of Wareham. He immediately distinguished himself
by his earnest advocacy of popular freedom—side by
side with Brougham and Lambton—on all the many
occasions furnished by the troubled years of 1819 and
1820. In those times of a Manchester massacre, a
Cato-street conspiracy, Burdett letters, and prosecution
of authors and printers, Mr. Denman was always found
vigilant and eloquent in opposing Seizures of Arms Bills,
Seditious Meetings Bills, Blasphemous and Seditious
Libels Bills, and doing his best to spoil the whole
machinery of moral torture and intellectual restriction
His popularity. framed by the Eldons, Sidmouths, and Castlereaghs of
those unhappy days. His popularity was already great
when his advocacy of the cause of Queen Caroline, on
her return to England in 1820, made him the idol of
more than "the populace," with whose admiration he
was taunted so scornfully. He accepted the office of

Solicitor-General to the Queen—at a sacrifice, he well knew and everybody knew, of his fair professional prospects. From the hour that, as one of her Commissioners (Mr. Brougham being the other), he met the Duke of Wellington and Lord Castlereagh as the King's Commissioners, it was felt that he had ruined himself, if professional advancement was the object of his life. Not only were all the high offices of the law closed to him during the reign of the King, who was not yet crowned ; but the royal brothers, who were in the course of nature to succeed him, were almost as virulent as the King against all aiders and abettors of the Queen's claims. Mr. Denman suffered, as he knew he must, a long abeyance of professional advancement; but the English nation were not likely to allow this to last forever; and Thomas Denman was their Chief Justice at last. No one could wonder at the strength of the popular feeling in his favor who heard, or even saw, his pleading on behalf of his injured client. His noble features and majestic form were all alive with emotion ; his utterance was as natural as that of any kindly citizen who was pitying the Queen by his own fireside : and the strength of his feelings roused his intellect and warmed his eloquence to a manifestation of power greater than appeared before or after. All England was in tears at that pathetic saying of his about the omission of the Queen's name in the Liturgy,—that if she was prayed for at all, it was in the prayer "for all that are desolate and afflicted." All England exulted when he drove home the charge of the prosecution against the Royal Husband himself in the felicitous quotation from "Paradise Lost :"

Out of favor at Court.

His defence of Queen Caroline.

A felicitous quotation.

[VIII]

"The other Shape—
If shape it might be called that shape had none;
Or substance might be called that shadow seemed;
For each seemed either: . . . *what seemed his head
The likeness of a kingly crown had on.*"

Before the case was decided, and during an interval of adjournment, Mr. Denman went to Cheltenham, to obtain some repose after the excessive fatigues of the summer—the hottest of summers. His reception there was a fair indication of the feeling of the country toward him. The clergyman had refused permission to have the bells rung on his arrival. The inhabitants drew his carriage to his lodgings, and when he had retired from the window, whence he briefly thanked them, they demolished the clergyman's windows, broke open the church, and rang a merry peal till late into the night. The Corporation of London chose him their Common Sergeant; and whatever dignity could be conferred, outside the political and professional pale which he had declined to enter unworthily, was awarded him by popular reverence and gratitude. One of the finest of his productions was the discourse at the opening of the Aldersgate-street Mechanics' Institute, in 1828, when such associations had existed only five years. In the concluding passage of that address he urged the view of applying literary enlightenment to the pursuit of social duty, and the wise and conscientious discharge of political obligation; and he who had himself so turned his enlightenment to account had a right to the enthusiasm with which his hearers received his exhortation to a virtuous use of the suffrage.

The period of exclusion was now, however, drawing to an end. When the Grey Ministry was formed in

His reception at Cheltenham.

Common Sergeant of London.

1830 he was made Attorney-General, and knighted for the office, according to custom. The Nottingham people returned him to Parliament with high pride and delight. The Duke of Clarence, who had joined in the persecution of the Queen, had now laid aside old controversies ; and he made the Liberal Attorney-General a peer in 1834, and Chief Justice of the King's Bench. In two more years, Lord Denman pronounced the decision that brought on the perilous quarrel between the Law Courts and Parliament. The history of the controversy need not be given here, as it may be found in the chronicles of the time, and seen to involve much more than Lord Denman's share in the business. It was he who brought on the struggle by his decision, in November 1836, that the authority of Parliament could not justify the publication of a libel ; whereas the House of Commons could not surrender their claim to publish what they thought proper, in entire independence of the Law Courts. The Hansards were bandied about between law and privilege ; the Sheriffs of London were imprisoned, quizzed, pitied, and caricatured ; but thoughtful men felt that the occasion was one of extreme seriousness ; and Lord Denman had to bear the responsibility of having perilously overstrained one of the indispensable compromises of the Constitution. He was confident throughout that he was right, and patriotically employed in vindicating the liberty of the subject from oppression by Parliament : and Parliament was equally convinced that the national liberties depended on their repudiating the control of the Law Courts. A more difficult question can never occur under a Constitutional Government ; and it is sure to come up, from time to time, like that of State Rights in America, when some earnest

[VIII]
*Attorney-
General*

*and Chief
Justice.*

*The
struggle
between
Parliament
and the
Law Courts.*

[VIII] man sees his own side to be right without being able to perceive that the other may not necessarily be wrong. In the controversy opened and conducted by Lord Denman, the respective claims were left unsettled ; and nothing was done but doubtfully providing for the single case of the publication of Parliamentary Reports. Lord Denman's service in the case was depositing in the armory of the Law Courts a quiverful of arguments for the use of successive combatants, whenever the battle shall be renewed. Perhaps the only good result of the whole affair was a lesson of caution to others than the narrow-minded and superficial how they stir the great questions which, while they are the roots of our growing and flourishing Constitution, are incapable of definition and circumscription. They are not a matter of ordinary party politics ; for aristocratic and democratic institutions are alike troubled with them ; as indeed it might be said, in a large way, that all methods of human association in fact are.

It was Lord Denman's business to preside in the House of Peers, as its Lord High Steward, on occasion of the absurd trial of the troublesome and quarrelsome Lord Cardigan in 1841, for a "felonious attempt" to fight a duel. The Earl was acquitted through a mistake, accidental or otherwise, in the name of the person challenged. The waste of time, money, and solemnity on such a farce was vexatious enough ; but the treat of the occasion was the noble-looking Judge. To the last day of his sitting in his own Court, strangers thronged in to gaze on that majestic and benevolent countenance. It was in 1850 that his intimate friend, Lord Campbell (who made his way through life very easy by calling everybody he had to do with his "friend"), discovered

His noble appearance.

that Lord Denman was too old for his office,—though [VIII]
two years younger than Lord Campbell himself. Lord
Campbell urged so forcibly upon everybody the decline *Lord*
in his friend's powers, that people who had not perceived *Campbell's*
it before began to think it must be so. Lord Denman *suggestion.*
declared himself perfectly up to his work ; and his affectionate friend shook his head, and stirred up other people
to appeal to Lord Denman's patriotism to retire before
his function should suffer further from his weight of years.
Hurt, displeased, and reluctant, Lord Denman resigned *Retirement*
his office, and his brisk senior nimbly stepped into it, *from office.*
and enlivened with jokes the tribunal which had been
graced by his predecessor's sweetness and majesty.
Whether Lord Denman's powers were failing, men were
not agreed ; but there was no dispute about whether
Lord Campbell was the proper person to effect his
removal. The tributes of respect and affection offered
by the bar and the public to the retiring judge were
truly consolatory to his ruffled feelings, and as richly
deserved as any honors ever offered to an aged public
servant.

In his retirement he was tenderly cheered, and in due
course nursed by his affectionate children, and especially
by his eldest son, who was his Judge's Associate when
he was on the bench. He interested himself much in *His views*
the Slave Trade question, in favor of the maintenance *on the Slave*
of our squadron of cruisers off the African coast, in *Trade.*
which service his second son, Captain Denman, distinguished himself. As long as he could attend Parliament
Lord Denman spoke annually on the subject ; and then
he wrote upon it. His feelings were considered to be
better than his reasonings in the case : but it was cheering to see that while the gloom of age and infirmity was

gathering round him, the beacon light of human rights, which had guided his whole course, still shone for him and fixed his earnest gaze. The best part of him lasted longest and wore well. While well qualified as a lawyer, he was not made for eminence by that qualification, if *The patriot and the man.* unsupported by others. He was of a higher order as a patriot; and highest as a man and a neighbor. So, when he had retired from his professional career, he commanded respect for his unimpaired solicitude for the public weal, and a tender reverence for his personal virtues and graces. He leaves so numerous a posterity that his name will be a source of domestic pride in many homes, for generations to come; and, however long the tradition may run, the record of History will run parallel with it. In no relation is there any fear that the name of Thomas Denman should be forgotten.

IX.

LORD CHANCELLOR CAMPBELL.

DIED JUNE 23D, 1861.

SUCH was the dignity arrived at by the skilful man who [*] delighted in telling us, with the half-innocent, half-facetious face that he put on as he spoke the often-repeated words, that he was only "Plain John Campbell," the humble son of a humble Scotch minister, while all his hearers knew all the while that there was not such a man for getting on in the three kingdoms. The public heard less, and his own friends heard less, in the latter part of his life, about his plainness and humility, and the paternal manse ; but he had exhibited these things so often in his electioneering speeches and official addresses that he was best known as Plain John Campbell to the last. *His self-dubbed cognomen.*

The paternal manse was in Fifeshire ; and there John was born in 1781. He was educated at St. Andrews, where he took the degree of M.A. He repaired to London to pursue his legal studies, poor in purse, but with a source of income in his pocket in the shape of a letter to Mr. Perry, of the *Morning Chronicle*, who employed him both as theatrical critic and as a parliamentary reporter. His industry was extraordinary ; and he studied law as effectually in the mornings as if he had not been at work half the night. His jocose humor lightened all the labors of his life to himself and his comrades. *At St. Andrews.* *Employed as a reporter.*

11

He was called to the bar in 1806, after completing his studies under Mr. Tidd, the author of the celebrated "Tidd's Practice." His first employment was reporting Lord Ellenborough's judgments at Nisi Prius,—a very high service, as is known to all who are aware of the use made of those judgments as authorities ; and their value is enhanced by the notes of the reporter. Mr. Campbell rose rapidly through the drudging stages of his profession, became leader on the Oxford Circuit and at Nisi Prius, and in 1821 married the daughter of Mr. Scarlett, afterward Lord Abinger. His professional income, already large, became enormous ; and the best care was taken of it. In 1827 he was made King's Counsel, and in 1832 Solicitor-General. In 1834 he was Attorney-General, and in that capacity obtained great professional triumphs, in the two cases of the Melbourne and Stockdale trials.

In the Melbourne case, no doubt, his feelings were really and deeply interested, and his conviction of the mistake involved in the prosecution was entire. In the Stockdale case he enjoyed his work, from the perplexity and ludicrous features of the affair. He argued on behalf of Parliament against his friend Denman and the Court of Queen's Bench, and quizzed the poor innocent reluctant Sheriffs in their quizzical imprisonment, with keen relish. He was, moreover, not at all sorry to turn public notice away from a political false step of his own, which he found, in the autumn of 1839, to be no joke, though he tried to make it one. Chartism was rife, as we all remember, toward the close of 1838. The Ministry and Parliament were willing to be merciful, in consideration of much recent popular suffering ; and it does not appear that their indulgence was misapplied, except in the case of Frost, about whose official position and doings there

was some of that mistake of fact which characterized the
inexperienced Whig rule of those days. The Attorney-
General was naturally and excusably complacent about
the wisdom of the Government in abiding by the ordinary
law, when the Conservatives were crying out for coercion ;
but he let his complacency get the better of his prudence ;
and at a public breakfast given in his honor at Edinburgh, after the riots of the summer of 1839, boasted
that Chartism was extinct. He, as the first Law Officer
of the Crown, had misled the Ministers by similar as-
surances ; and he had also encouraged the Chartists, by
showing them that Government was off its guard. On
the 3d of November occurred the Newport insurrection ;
and Sir John Campbell (as he had become by that time)
had to bear something more than raillery on his not
having the second-sight of his country, nor even the use
of common eyes.

The Chartist riots in 1839

His next promotion was not effected under kindly and
graceful influences. Just before the Whig Government
went out in 1841, and when the event was clearly foreseen by everybody, while struggled against by the holders
of power, a Bill was brought in, and urged forward with
extreme haste, to provide two new Judgeships in the
Court of Chancery ; it being universally understood that
Sir John Campbell was to step into one of them when
obliged to resign the Attorney-Generalship. Remon-
strance was made against the intention to put a Common
Law practitioner, however eminent, into an Equity
Judgeship ; and on other accounts also the measure was
found impracticable ; and it was thrown up. The Chancellor of Ireland, Lord Plunket, was then written to, in
'the same week, to request him to resign the seal to
Sir John Campbell. Lord Plunket indignantly refused.

Chancellor of Ireland.

[IX]

The ministerial newspapers then presented paragraphs about his age and infirmities, and his long-felt wish to retire.   He openly contradicted this news, declared himself quite well, and denied having ever said a word about retiring.   He was pressed more urgently by his ministerial correspondents, and reminded of the Bishopric of Tuam having been recently given to his son, and of other patronage of which he had obtained the fruits ; and he obeyed at last, avowing in his farewell address the facts of the case.   He carried with him his title to a retiring pension of 4,000*l.* a year ; and Plain John, stepping into his seat, anticipated the same.   But the delays had put the matter off rather too long.   Lord Campbell sat as Chancellor of Ireland for only a single day, after having received his peerage for the purpose.   His wife had been a peeress for some years, owing to the curious fact that his services in the Commons could not be dispensed with by the Whig ministry.   His wife was therefore made Lady Stratheden, with descent to her son ; and Sir John was promised a peerage at a future time ; that time arriving when he filled his alienated friend's seat for one day.

Chancellor of the Dncuy of Lancaster.

On leaving Ireland, and giving up his claim for a retiring pension, Lord Campbell became a Cabinet Minister as Chancellor of the Duchy of Lancaster. His energy now devoted itself to literature ; and he began to bring out his "Lives of the Chancellors."   In that work he has described himself better than any one else could describe him.   The style is entertaining, the facts anything that he chose to make them, and the spirit depreciatory to the last degree.   The late Sir Harris Nicolas, the highest possible authority in antiquarian memoirs, accidentally examined some old MSS., which expressly contradicted Lord Campbell's painful account of Sir Christopher Hatton ; and was so struck by the easy style of statement in Lord Campbell's Life of that Chancellor that he made further investigations among State papers, and established and published a case of malversation of materials which will not easily be forgotten. The same process was afterward carried on, with the same result, by the *Westminster Review,* which entirely overthrew the value of the work as History or Biography, while stamping upon it the imputation of libel on the reputation of personages long gone where the voice of praise or censure cannot reach them. Lord Campbell certainly saw Sir H. Nicolas's exposures ; for he omitted a few statements, qualified others, and inserted "it is said" in yet other instances ; leaving, however, a considerable number uncorrected, to pass through successive editions, and become History if no vigilant curator of the fame of the dead does not take measures to preclude an evil so serious.

Literature was not, however, sufficient to occupy the energies of this industrious lawyer ; nor his office to satisfy his ambition. As might easily have been anticipated, he found another judge who might be persuaded that he was too old and infirm for office, and had better resign in his favor. His old friend, Lord Denman, two years younger than Lord Campbell, was pronounced in 1849 so infirm that he ought to resign the Chief Justiceship. Lord Denman protested, as Lord Plunket had done, that he was perfectly well able to go through his duties : but Lord Campbell thought otherwise ; and immediately the newspapers began to bewail Lord Denman's weight of years, and to predict that his sprightly senior would soon be in his seat ; and early in 1850 the

[XI]

His " Lives of the Lord Chancellors,"and its misstatements.

Lord Denman and "Plain John."

[IX]

event took place accordingly. When the spectators who saw him take his seat for the first time remarked on the "green old age" of the vivacious Judge, they asked one another, with mirth like his own, who would ever be able to persuade *him* that he was too old for office. Would he meet with a successor who would take no denial on that point, as he had taken none from the two old friends whom he had superseded? If he had overheard the whisper, he would have laughed with the speculators. His drollery was as patent as ever. Ever since he had entered the Lords he had joined with Lord

Lord Brougham and Lord Campbell in the Lords.

Brougham in enacting perpetual scenes for the amusement of the peers and readers of the debates. The sparring of the two Law Lords was the severest ever known to pass between persons who persisted in calling one another "friend." The noble and learned "friends" said the most astonishing things of and to each other, without ever coming to blows. There was no danger of that ; for Lord Campbell could bear anything, and did not care enough to lose his temper seriously. The same facetiousness manifested itself on the Bench, without being aggravated by the same opposition. Of all the Chief Justices whose lives he in course of time wrote, no one probably could surpass him in the amusement he afforded to the bar, the witnesses, the culprit, and the audience ; sometimes at moments when tears would have come, unless driven back by one of the Judge's puns.

Appointed Lord Chancellor.

In 1859 he attained the highest honors of his profession in the Lord Chancellorship.

In his judicial office in the House of Lords he was extremely diligent, and eminently serviceable. As a lawyer, his abundant reading and unfailing assiduity justified the success which his indomitable determination to get on would probably have obtained at all events. He was not a scholar; nor were his countenance and voice prepossessing, nor his manners good. He was pleasant and good-humored in Court and in the drawing-room; and the consideration he obtained thus, and by his wealth (understood but not manifested), and by his rank, and especially by his success, was enough for him. Heartfelt respect and intimate friendship were not necessary to him; and he would probably have been quite content with the knowledge that, after his death, he would be held up as an example of the social success obtainable in our fortunate country by energy and assiduity, steadily reaching forward to the prizes of ambition.

[IX]

His character and career.

He was not called on to endure the weaknesses of age which he was so acute in recognizing in men younger than himself. In full possession of his powers, he attended a Cabinet Council the day before his death, and afterward entertained a large party at dinner, retiring to rest after midnight, without any tone of fatigue in his "good-night." In the morning he was found dead in his chair. As his life had been gay and fortunate, his death was quiet and easy. Such welfare as he had, need not be grudged to him. Much of it he earned for himself; and some of it was a poor substitute for blessings and enjoyments relished with even a greater keenness than his by poorer, more modest, refined, and honored men.

X.

DAVID ROBERTS, R. A.

DIED NOV. 25TH, 1864.

THE death of Mr. Roberts will excite interest and regret over a wider area than the loss of perhaps any other Artist of the present generation in our country; for no other is familiarly known in so many countries of Europe, and beyond it. He spent his cheerful life in travelling *His travels.* through them, with a keen and studious eye and a busy hand, and in imparting to the world, with eminent fidelity, what he had seen. He published his impressions in so many ways, gave out so many of them, in so various and in such accessible forms, that the people of many countries know what his services have been to their own architectural monuments, their picturesque towns, their characteristic scenery, and the aspect and ways of their inhabitants. His pictures have been engraved for works of a wide range of character and circulation at home and abroad, from the superb folio illustrating the Holy Lands of the East in 246 subjects, to the pretty little Annuals in their early days. The impression he produced was probably very much the same in all the countries and all the societies in which *His speciality.* he was known through his works. His speciality is always assumed to be architectural delineation; and in

this he will long be regarded as supreme among us, [X]
because his genius opened his eyes to the noblest
aspects of noble edifices, subordinating, but not neglecting, the minor characteristics, and so infallibly perceiving the distinctive splendor and beauty of each of
many cathedrals, temples, Eastern pyramids and bazaars,
and old Western towns, with their castles and municipal
buildings, as to show to the residents more in the
edifices before their eyes than they had ever seen
for themselves. It is, doubtless, as a painter of architecture that he will be spoken of in the many lands in
which he will be regretted ; but yet it is difficult to show
that his landscapes are not as true and distinctive, as
broadly viewed and as faithfully presented, as the edifices
which they surround. An equal excellence may, for the
most part, be recognized in the figures which animate
either the one or the other. Such a variety of lines of *His*
practice, and such industry and facility, are rare in *versatility.*
themselves, and very rarely recognized by such a multitude of admirers as in Mr. Roberts's case ; and the
sorrow for his death will be in proportion to the influence of his life and works. The best appreciation of
his truth is to be found among persons who know the
scenes, either as residents or as travellers. His pictures
may be seen to be very variously estimated by a succession of visitors in the same day and the same hour ;
but the difference lies in the knowledge or ignorance of
the scene or its main conditions, on the part of the
gazers. One of his pictures of an Egyptian temple may
bring out from an untravelled observer a remark on the
opaque color, and the wildly unnatural hues of mountain, sand, river, and sky : and at the same moment a
Nile voyager may be feeling, at the first glance, and

11*

[X] more and more as he gazes, a thrill such as he has not felt since he first saw a sunset in the desert. The coloring is true, except in as far as it is necessarily subdued to meet the requirements of Art, as it is understood in England; and the opacity is, to the travelled eye, the special transparency of such climates as that of Egypt, where the clearness of the atmosphere confounds space and distance, and concentrates color in a way incomprehensible to the inhabitants of misty countries. That Mr. Roberts should have conveyed these peculiarities of Egyptian and Arabian scenery, and the characteristics of his own dear Scotland, and of Moorish Spain, and of half-Eastern Austria, and of bright France, and of dim London, manifests a versatility which, in combination with his steadiness of purpose, must be recognized as genius.

This is not the less true for his owing some of his facility to a very unusual early training. He served his apprenticeship to a house-painter, which might not have much to do with it; but he was afterward a scene-painter; and if he escaped the dangers of such a mode of early practice, he was sure to derive advantage from it. In the humbler occupation he had for a comrade Hay, who became a true artist in the province of house-decoration; and his fellow scene-painter at Drury Lane was Stanfield.

A native of Edinburgh. David Roberts was a native of Edinburgh. He was born on the 24th of October, 1796, and was therefore sixty-eight at the time of his death. While still an apprentice to the house-painter, he was admitted to the Trustees' Academy, where Wilkie, Allan, and others began to learn their art. Roberts, however, attended only once, when he made a study of a hand. The first clear view now to be had of him is in his twenty-seventh year, when he was working, with Stanfield as a comrade, for the Drury Lane stage. Two years later, he and an illustrious company of brother artists instituted the Society of British Artists ; and Roberts was Vice-President of this Society for some time. He exhibited in it the first pictures that we hear of ; one of Dryburgh, and two of Melrose Abbey. Thus he began with architectural painting, which was the great object of his life and art to the end. *One of the founders of the Society of British Artists.*

In 1825 he had evidently been beginning his travels ; for he showed to the world what he had seen at Dieppe and Rouen. In the following year he exhibited for the first time at the Royal Academy. He seems, however, to have been happier with the Society, for he exhibited regularly there, while appearing only once for eight years at the Academy. He was travelling and painting during the interval, and the most noticeable work of the period was the picture which he painted for Lord Northwick, and which is now in Sir Robert Peel's collection, "The Departure of the Israelites from Egypt." He had not yet been in Egypt; but neither had he been in India, and we find him painting the Ellora Cave. He worked from a sketch by Captain Grindlay. *Exhibits at the Royal Academy.*

For some years the variety of his subjects seems now as wonderful as his industry. We find in the list Scotch, Dutch, English, and Rhenish towns, from studies of his own. There is a Portuguese one; but that is from a sketch of Charles Landseer's. He was in Spain, however, in 1834 ; and thence he sent the "Geralda at Seville," painted on the spot, and the work which fixed his rank as a great painter—"The Cathedral at Burgos." It may be seen in the National collection, as Mr. Vernon *The multiplicity of his subjects.*

[X]

[X]

immediately purchased it. Mr. Sheepshanks afterward secured the two others which appear in the National Gallery—"The Crypt at Rosslyn Chapel," and the "Spanish Scene on the Davro, at Grenada."

His contributions to the Annuals.

For four years at this time he contributed largely to the Annuals which were the fashion of the period ; and to these, perhaps, he owed his first celebrity beyond his own island ; for, by the illustrated publications of the day the continental people learned to know the scenery of their own and one another's countries. The foreign engravings from his views in the *Landscape Annual*, and in illustration of "The Pilgrims of the Rhine," and his lithographed "Spanish Sketches," were a complete novelty to half the Continent. The grand achievement, however, was the "Sketches in the Holy Land," and in neighboring countries—one of the largest illustrative works in existence, and no less eminent for its fidelity and its character of vitality than for its splendor. It was while he was studying these scenes on the spot that he was made an Associate of the Royal Academy in 1839. In 1841, he became an Academician ; and in the following year the great folio work began to appear— Louis Haghe being the engraver, and Dr. Croly the contributor of the letterpress. The whole required the labor of eight years on the part of the artist and the engraver.

His "Sketches in the Holy Land."

That is above twenty years ago ; and the production of his wealth of that sort has never ceased—scarcely paused—from that time to this. We look back with wonder on such a production of works of such quality— the "Baalbec," the "Jerusalem from the Mount of Olives," "The Temple of the Sun at Baalbec," which our readers will remember at the International Exhibi-

tion of 1862; "The Destruction of Jerusalem;" the
picture painted by royal command of "The Opening
of the Exhibition of 1851;" and the great panoramic
picture of Rome, presented by Mr. Roberts to his
native city. Edinburgh had before given him the freedom of the city; and she was not left unrepresented
amidst the old capitals which he illustrated in long
succession. Rome, Venice, Vienna, and many more,
and finally London, were so painted by him as to secure
to future generations a clear conception of what the great
cities of Europe looked like (as regards their most prominent features) in our century.

Pictures of London from the Thames.

Those pictures of London, as seen from the Thames,
are the latest memorials we have of David Roberts.
He was employed on two of them at the time of his
death. It was nevertheless an old scheme. Turner
once told him that he had thought of painting London
from points of view on the Thames; but he decided that
the scheme was too wide for him. When he relinquished
it, David Roberts seems to have taken it up; and he
accumulated a mass of materials for it which it is mournful to think of, now that he is gone. Our readers must
have a vivid remembrance of the fine rendering of St.
Paul's, as presented in the pictures in the Academy Exhibition. The series was painted for Mr. Charles Lucas,
who has hung them together. One of the unfinished
pictures is a view of St. Paul's from Ludgate Hill; the
other, nearly finished, is the Palace of Westminster seen
from the river.

He leaves a rich legacy of professional treasures, besides these incomplete pictures. He parted with very
few of his water-color sketches and drawings made in the
countries he travelled through. He rarely parted with

an original sketch ; and we may all conceive what a number there must be of them. There is also a complete series of an interesting order of memoranda. It was his habit to make a pen-and-ink etching of every picture he painted, with notes recording the size and other conditions of the work. This is not only a precious legacy to his descendants, but a valuable record for the world of Art.

His geniality.

He was a very cheerful man. This must have been evident to all who had any acquaintance with him ; for his genial temper manifested itself in his face, and his voice, and the mirth of his conversation. He had the enjoyment which belongs to the inclination and habit of industry, without the drawback of the stiffness, and narrowness, and restlessness which too often attend it. In the last autumn of his life, when he was absent from his regular work, and staying at Bonchurch with his daughter and son-in-law and their family, he occupied himself with cleaning and renovating his old sketches, conversing gayly all the while. His health was good ; his fame was rising, as appeared by the constantly increasing prices given for his works ; he was blessed in family affection, and rich in friends. He was passing into old age thus happily when he was struck down by a death which spared him the suffering of illness, infirmity, and decline. On the 25th November he went out from his own house in apparent health, and cheerful as usual. He staggered and fell in the street ; and died at seven the same evening.

All the world knew of his energy and industry. All his acquaintance were aware of his liberality of views and of temper on all the great subjects which usually divide men by their very interest in them. No man was

the worse with David Roberts for any opinions con- [X]
scientiously formed and honestly held ; and he asked
no leave for holding his own convictions. Some, but
not many, knew what his munificence was to the needy *His*
members of any department of Art, and how generous *benevolence.*
his support of all good schemes for the benefit of artists.
His eye, and heart, and hand were open to discern, and
sympathize with, and foster ability in his own line of
life, or in any other. David Roberts, the Royal Academician, will be regretted far and near, and his death
recorded as one of the grave losses of a grave period ;
but as the generous patron, the hearty friend, and the
beloved father and grandfather, he is mourned as deeply
as any man who never ran any risk of being spoiled by
fame, or filled with the pride of his conquest over the
disadvantages of his early life, and his achievement of
such a position as he held. He had made himself a
man of mark ; and he was one of few who, having
energy for such a feat, have preserved heart, and
simplicity, and gentleness enough not to be the less
happy for it.

IV.
SOCIAL.

I.

MISS BERRY.

Born March 16th, 1763.   Died Nov. 20th, 1852.

An event has occurred which makes us ask ourselves *A link with the last century.* whether we have really passed the middle of our century. In the course of Saturday night, November 20, one died who could and did tell so much of what happened early in the reign of George III., that her hearers felt as if they were in personal relations with the men of that time.   Miss Berry was remarkable enough in herself to have excited a good deal of emotion by dying any time within the last seventy years.   Dying now, she leaves as strong as ever the impression of her admirable faculties, her generous and affectionate nature, and her high accomplishments, while awakening us to a retrospect of the changes and fashions of our English intellect, as expressed by literature.   She was not only the Woman of Letters of the last century, carried far forward into our own—she was not only the Woman of Fashion who was familiar with the gayeties of life before the fair daughters of George III. were seen abroad, and who had her own will and way with society up to last Saturday night : she was the repository of the whole literary history of fourscore years ; and when she was pleased to throw open the folding-doors of her memory, they were found to be

[1]   mirrors: and in them was seen the whole procession of literature, from the mournful Cowper to Tennyson the Laureate.

It was a curious sight—visible till recently, though now all are gone—the chatting of three ladies on the same sofa—the two Miss Berrys and their intimate friend, Lady Charlotte Lindsay. Lady Charlotte Lindsay was *The Miss Berrys and Horace Walpole.* the daughter of Lord North; and the Miss Berrys had both received, as was never any secret, the offer of the hand of Horace Walpole. It is true he was old, and knew himself to be declining, and made this offer as an act of friendship and gratitude; but still, the fact remains that she who died last Saturday night might have been the wife of him who had the poet Gray for his tutor. These ladies brought into our time a good deal of the manners, the conversation, and the dress of the last century; but not at all in a way to cast any restraint on the youngest of their visitors, or to check the inclination to inquire into the thoughts and ways of men long dead, and the influence of modes long passed away. It was said that Miss Berry's parties were rather *blue*, and perhaps they were so; but she was not aware of it; and all thought of contemporary pedantry dissolved under her stories of how she once found on the table, on her return from a ball, a volume of "Plays on the Passions," and how she kneeled on a chair at the table to see what the book was like, and was found there—feathers and satin shoes and all—by the servant who came to let in the winter morning light; or of how the world of literature was perplexed and distressed—as a swarm of bees that have lost their queen—when Dr. Johnson died; or of how Charles Fox used to wonder that people could make such a fuss about that dullest of new books—Adam

Smith's "Wealth of Nations." He was an Eton boy,
just promised a trip to Paris by his father, when Miss
Berry was born ; and Pitt was a child in the nursery,
probably applauded by his maid for his success in learning to speak plain.   Burns was then toddling in and out,
over the threshold of his father's cottage.   Just when she
was entering on the novel-reading age, "Evelina" came
out ; and Fanny Burney's series of novels were to that
generation of young people what Scott's were to the next
but one.   If the youths and maidens of that time had
bad fiction, they had good history ; for the learned Mr.
Gibbon gave them volume after volume which made them
proud of their age.   They talked about their poets ; and,
no doubt, each had an idol in that day as in ours and
everybody's.   The earnestness, sense, feeling, and point
of Cowper delighted some ; and they reverently told of
the sorrows of his secluded life, as glimpses were caught
of him in his walks with Mrs. Unwin.   Others stood on
tiptoe to peep into Dr. Darwin's "chaise" as he went his
professional round, writing and polishing his verses as he
went ; and his admirers insisted that nothing so brilliant
had ever been written before.   Miss Berry must have
well remembered the first exhibition of this brilliancy
before the careless eyes of the world ; and she must
have remembered the strangeness of the contrast when
Crabbe tried his homely pathos, encouraged to do so by
Burke.   And then came something which it is scarcely
credible that the world should have received during
the period of Johnson's old age, and the maturity of
Gibbon, and Sir Wm. Jones, and Burns—the wretched
rhyming of the Batheaston set of sentimental pedants.
In rebuke of them, the now mature woman saw the theory
of Wordsworth rise ; and in rebuke of him she saw the

[1]

young and confident Jeffrey and his comrades arise;
and in rebuke of them saw the *Quarterly Review* arise,
when she was beginning to be elderly. She saw Joanna
Baillie's great fame rise and decline, without either the
rise or decline changing in the least the countenance or
the mood of the happy being whose sunshine came from
What she saw of literature, quite another luminary than fame. She saw the rise of
Wordsworth's fame, growing as it did out of the reaction
against the pomps and vanities of the Johnsonian and
Darwinian schools; and she lived to see its decline when
the great purpose was fulfilled, of inducing poets to say
what they mean, in words which will answer that purpose.
She saw the beginning and the end of Moore's popularity; and the rise and establishment of Campbell's.
The short career of Byron passed before her eyes like a
summer storm; and that of Scott constituted a great
interest of her life for many years. What an experience
—to have studied the period of horrors, represented by
Monk Lewis—of conventionalism in Fanny Burney—of
metaphysical fiction in Godwin—of historical romance
in Scott—and of a new order of fiction in Dickens,
which it is yet too soon to characterize by a phrase.

We might go on for hours, and not exhaust the history
of what she saw on the side of Literature alone. If we
attempted to number the scientific men who have crossed
her threshold—the foreigners who found within her doors
the best of London and the cream of society, we should
and of political changes. never have done. And of Political changes, she saw
the continental wars, the establishment of American
Independence, the long series of French Revolutions:
and again, the career of Washington, of Napoleon, of
Nelson, of Wellington, with that of all the Statesmen
from Lord Chatham to Peel—from Franklin to Webster.

But it is too much. It is bewildering to us, though it
never overpowered her. She seemed to forget nothing,
and to notice everything, and to be able to bear so long
a life in such times ; but she might well be glad to sink
to sleep after so long-drawn a pageant of the world's
pomps and vanities, and transient idolatries, and eternal
passions.

Reviewing the spectacle, it appears to us, as it probably
did to her, that there is no prevalent taste, at least in
literature, without a counteraction on the spot, preparing
society for a reaction. Miss Berry used to say that she
published the later volumes of Walpole's Correspondence to prove that the world was wrong in thinking him
heartless ; she believing the appearance of heartlessness
in him to be ascribable to the influences of his time. She
did not succeed in changing the world's judgment of her
friend ; and this was partly because the influences of the
time did not prevent other men from showing heart.
Charles James Fox had a heart ; and so had Burke and
a good many more. While Johnson and then Darwin
were corrupting men's taste in diction, Cowper was
keeping it pure enough to enjoy the three rising poets,
alike only in their plainness of speech—Crabbe, Burns,
and Wordsworth. Before Miss Burney had exhausted
our patience, the practical Maria Edgeworth was growing up. While Godwin would have engaged us wholly
with the interior scenery of Man's nature, Scott was
fitting up his theatre for his mighty procession of cos-
tumes, with men in them to set them moving ; and Jane
Austen, whose name and works will outlive many that were
supposed immortal, was stealthily putting forth her un-
matched delineations of domestic life in the middle classes
of our over-living England. And against the somewhat

*Her opinion
of Horace
Walpole.*

[I] feeble elegance of Sir William Jones's learning there was the safeguard of Gibbon's marvellous combination of strength and richness in his erudition.   The vigor of Campbell's lyrics was a set-off against the prettiness of Moore's.   The subtlety of Coleridge meets its match, and a good deal more, in the development of Science ; and the morose complainings of Byron are less and less echoed now that the peace has opened the world to gentry whose energies would be self-corroding if they were under blockade at home, through a universal continental war.   Byron is read at sea now, on the way to the North Pole, or to California, or to Borneo ; and in that way his woes can do no harm.   "To everything there is a season ;" and to every fashion of a season there is an antagonism preparing.   Thus all things have their turn ; all human faculties have their stimulus, sooner or later, supposing them to be put in the way of the influences of social life.

The close of her ninety years.   It was eminently so in the case of the aged lady who is gone from us ; and well did her mind respond to the discipline offered by her long and favorable life of ninety years.   One would like to know how she herself summed up such an experience as hers—the spectacle of so many everlasting things dissolved—so many engrossing things forgotten—so many settled things set afloat again, and floated out of sight.   Perhaps those true words wandered once more into her mind as her eyes were closing :

> "We are such stuff
> As dreams are made of; and our little life
> Is rounded with a sleep."

II.

FATHER MATHEW.

DIED DECEMBER 8TH, 1856.

A FEW years ago the death of Father Mathew would
have caused a sensation as deep, as wide, and as pathetic
as the death of any man of his generation. As it is, he
slips away quietly, his departure awakening some interesting reflections, but causing no such agitation as
would have attended it twenty years since. Ours is an
age when personal qualities are much less concerned in
the influence and popularity of public men than they
were in a prior stage of civilization ; and ours is a
country in which men of mark become so, generally
speaking, as representatives of some social principle or
phase, rather than through their idiosyncrasy. One Wellington in a generation or a century may keep alive the
old sentiment of heroism and enthusiasm for personal
greatness, while ten men to that unit may create a greater
rage for the hour, and be followed by a larger multitude.
An O'Connell and a Father Mathew may appear for a
time greater than the greatest man of their age ; but it is
because they ride the surging wave of some popular
sentiment during a single tide of social destiny ; and
when the ebb comes they are stranded, or at best carried
back to the level whence they arose. Theobald Mathew
was a benevolent, earnest, well-deserving man in his way ;

Twenty years ago.

[II]   but his prodigious temporary influence was wholly due to the time and circumstances into which he was cast. Another man would have done much the same work if Father Mathew had been living in Spain or Italy instead of Ireland ; and he would himself have passed through life without notice if he had been born half a century earlier or later, or if his parentage had been of another nation. From the large space which, however, he actually occupied in the panorama of the time, he will not pass to his grave without more or less notice and regret from the whole existing generation of his countrymen.

Theobald Mathew was descended from a good old Roman Catholic family in Ireland, and was born at Thomastown in 1790. Becoming an orphan very early, he was adopted by an aunt, who gave him the best education she knew of—first at the lay Academy at Kilkenny, and then, on his showing an inclination for the priesthood, at Maynooth. He appears not to have manifested any quality, intellectual or moral, that was remarkable, except benevolence. He had no enlarged views, no deep moral insight, no great executive power ; but he *His earnest* was earnestly, devoutly, and devotedly benevolent about *benevolence.* any object which was immediately presented to his mind in such a way as that he could grasp it. He could not have originated the Temperance movement, or any other; and he failed utterly under any stress—as, for instance, in the presence of American Slavery, before the difficulties of which his courage, his principle, his reputation, and even his benevolence melted away, like ice, instead of gold in the fiery furnace. This is no matter of censure. He was, in some sort, an apostle at home ; but he was not so made as to be a confessor or martyr abroad, on behalf of those human liberties of which it is absurd to expect any monk but Luther to have any vivid conception.

[II]

Father Mathew, having early taken the vows as a Capuchin, followed the leadings of his heart in ministering among the poor in Cork, when he left Maynooth. His reputation, both as a popular preacher and minister among the city poor, was considerable, and daily rising, when the Temperance movement, begun in the United States, was propagated into Ireland through Belfast. Dr. Edgar, of Belfast, was pondering, in the summer of 1829, the best means of improving the popular morals of the town, when he was visited by Dr. Penny, from America, who reported to him the institution and progress of Temperance Societies in the United States. Dr. Edgar put forth, in August, the first proposal of Temperance Associations on this side the Atlantic ; and during the next year, four travelling agents spread his facts and his tracts all over Ireland. It then became known that six millions a year were spent on proof-spirits in Ireland ; and that four-fifths of the crime brought up for judgment, and three-fourths of the Irish beggary of that day, were directly due to intemperance. Evidence of these facts began to flow in from every kind of authority, medical, judicial, pastoral, and other. Societies were formed here and there ; in New Ross first, by a clergyman of the Establishment, the Rev. George Carr ; and in Cork by some good men who had the wisdom to enlist Father Mathew in the cause. Four citizens, a clergyman, a Quaker, a slater, and a tailor, appealed to the Capuchin Friar (by that time a Superior of the Order), and Father Mathew at once threw his good heart and his inestimable experience into the crusade against the popular vice.

His ministrations in Cork.

The origin of the Temperance societies in Ireland.

Father Mathew's services enlisted.

[II]
*An uncon-
scious agent
of O'Con-
nell.*

The Political Apostle of the day had the sagacity which was not remarkable in the Moral Reformer. O'Connell made Father Mathew his unconscious agent; and hence some of the success, which, to those who did not discern all the springs of the movement, appeared miraculous. O'Connell's aim was to keep up a state of vigilant expectation among the people; and it is certain that the two millions who were presently pledged by Father Mathew believed, generally speaking, that some mighty political event was at hand, for which they must hold themselves ready in a state of soberness. Most of them believed that Dan was to be King of Ireland; many, that the Temperance medal was to be their badge of safety in the day of conflict; and all believed that it was their token of salvation. It was commonly believed that

*Superstition
among the
people.*

Father Mathew could work miracles, and even that he had raised a person from the dead. When inquired of about his action in regard to these superstitions, he wrote a letter containing a few sentences so characteristic, that they almost preclude the necessity of describing his mind. "If I could prevent them," he says of these superstitions, "without impeding the glorious cause, they should not have been permitted; but both are so closely entwined, that the tares cannot be pulled out without plucking up the wheat also. The evil will correct itself; and the good, with the Divine assistance, will remain and be permanent." Such an agitator was the very man for O'Connell. His gatherings trained the people to marching in physical sobriety and moral enthusiasm. With their bands of music and their organization—nearly approaching to the regimental—they were amused for the time, and convinced that some ulterior work was preparing; and an immense revenue

was levied from the sale of the shilling medals—a fund
which was never accounted for. Nobody ever supposed
that Father Mathew pocketed one of those shillings.
He gave many of them to the relief of the poorest of
the crowd ; but he and his relatives became bankrupt by
the movement—his brother by the ruin of his distillery,
and himself by the loans and advances required of him
by the urgency of the movement. Of his perfect disinterestedness there never was any question. He handed
over his life insurance to his creditors ; and the pension
of 300*l.* a year from the Crown was all spent in keeping
up that insurance. While the millions who had rushed
into a condition of temperance under his ministration
were kissing his feet, and making him happy in the
belief that he had been the appointed means of saving
so many souls, the movement was looked upon with
diverse kinds of interest by observers, near and distant.
The political agitators of Ireland saw at their disposal a
mighty army of water-drinkers, as resolute and fanatical
as Cromwell's Ironsides—drilled, trained, looking for the
day of the Lord, wherein their own safety was secured ;
and singularly united by the spirit which breathed
through their brass band harmonies, and their cheers in
the field, when either of their idols was present. More
distant observers, who could form a judgment of the
case, apart from political or moral intoxication, feared
as much as they hoped from the movement. The prodigious power of self-control shown by the breaking off
of a vicious habit by almost an entire nation was a firm
ground of hope for the future destinies of the Irish
people ; but there was a melancholy adulteration of the
good with superstition and other delusion. A check to
vice would no doubt be given by the shutting up of

[II]

*Becomes a
bankrupt by
the move-
ment.*

*Different
views of the
movement.*

[II] distilleries, by the disinfecting of dwellings of the smell of whisky, and by the solemn impression made on the minds of a whole generation of young people. But the habit of self-restraint is too deep and serious a matter to be trusted to any movement either mechanical or impulsive; and the Temperance movement was both. Sober moralists feared failure in the end, and that the last state of many would be worse than the first. Sooner or later, Father Mathew must die; and it was even too probable that his influence would die before him. There must be relapse, to some considerable extent; and relapse in moral conduct is fatal. These misgivings were but too well grounded. O'Connell and the other political agitators are gone, and their schemes have completely evaporated; but the other class of observers now see their anticipations fulfilled, both as to the good and the evil.

His wonderful progress in Ireland. Father Mathew finished his triumphal progress through Ireland, sometimes administering the pledge to 50,000 persons in a day, and pledging between two and three millions altogether during the paroxysm of enthusiasm; and he then came to England. His success would have been called miraculous but for the greater marvel just *His reception in England.* witnessed in Ireland. Here there could not be equal solemnity or enthusiasm; and there was occasionally a manifest levity which must have been painful to the good priest, as it certainly was to some who were neither Catholics nor ascetics. There was too much of patronage exhibited on the hustings by men who revelled in luxury at home, and made jokes in the evening over medals that they had reverently received in public in the morning. The effects of the English crusade were soon effaced when Father Mathew was gone to America.

In America he failed, as abler men have failed, through the mistake, invariably fatal on that soil, of ignoring the monster vice of Negro Slavery while warring with some other. By this, a long series of philanthropists failed before him, and Kossuth after him. Under the notion of propitiating good-will to the Temperance cause, Father Mathew gave himself wholly into the hands of the slave-owners, and lost his object. Of all people, the Americans themselves most vehemently despise such a policy ; and no apostle of any cause has any chance among them who shows want of spirit in this particular form, who proves himself unable to meet this test. What Mitchel and Meagher have lost by recreant speech, Father Mathew lost by recreant silence. By courage and honesty he could but have very partially failed in his own enterprise, while giving great aid to another of yet more solemn importance. As it was, he lost character, destroyed his influence, and incurred simple failure. But he was not the man to meet such a test; and he was also in failing health. It was there, if we remember rightly, that he sustained his first paralytic seizure : and he returned, in 1851, a drooping invalid. He returned to find his enterprise not only drooping, but utterly sunk. The chapel projected for him at Cork is only too faithful a type of the great work of his life. That beautiful chapel stands half finished, broken off before the loftiness of its pillars and the grace of its arches are developed. There are props and coverings ; but they will not make it grow, nor long save it from ruin by wind and weather. It may be said that the good friar's work, like his chapel, was stopped by the famine and the fever. But the truth is, the temperance he taught was enforced by poverty during that crisis ;

[II]

Father Mathew and the slave owners.

His return.

[II]

Wherein he was wanting.

and with the return of prosperity the intemperance has returned. Of this there is no doubt whatever; and it is just what might have been expected. The seed had no root, and the plant has withered away. It will not be a friar who will work moral regeneration in our day; nor will moral reform endure any admixture of superstition. We must look to sound knowledge and the cultivation of the higher parts of Man's nature to cast out the grosser vices. Vows and mechanical association will not do it. Sumptuary and inhibitive laws will not do it. As far as law can go, there is nothing for it but perfect fredom of sale of all that comes under the name of beverage. If our duties on French wines and tea and coffee were removed to-morrow, and our licensing system abolished, we should find once more, what is always true, that men cannot be made virtuous by Act of Parliament. We must give them—what Father Mathew dreaded as much as the whisky—knowledge, and intellectual and moral freedom, by means of education, arming them against, not only the spirit of drink, but the whole legion of devils, by giving every man the entire possession of himself, in all his faculties. Not understanding this, the good friar drooped and sank amidst the ruins of his cause. He suffered under repeated attacks of paralysis, and died.

He did the best he could for his fellow-men. Whatever he knew, he did: whatever he had, he gave. He was devoted and disinterested; and that is much. His memory will be held in sincere though somewhat limited respect; and he will afford to the future historian a curious and instructive study, in his connection with one of the most remarkable social phenomena of his time.

III.

ROBERT OWEN.

Died November 17th, 1858.

With Robert Owen dies out one of the clearest and
most striking signs of our times. He was a man who
would have been remarkable at any period for the
combination that was so strong in him of benevolence
and inclination to ordain and rule; but these natural
dispositions took form under the special pressure of
the time. So entire was the suitability, thus far, of
the man to his age, that lthere can be little doubt that
if he had been gifted with the power in which he was
most deficient—reasoning power—he would have been
among the foremost men of his generation.' As it was, *His
his peculiar faculties so far fell in with the popular need *faculties
and his
that he effected much for the progress of society, and *time.*
has been the cause of many things which will never
go by his name. During his youth and early manhood,
at the end of the last century, ignorance, poverty, and
crime abounded, under the pressure of a long and hard
war; at the same time, the old methods of society had
been brought into question, in a very radical way,
where they were not overthrown, by the French Revolution; and the combined benevolence and administrative power of Robert Owen, applied to social dif-

[III] ficulties, made him a political theorist. As for the result, he could assert dogmatically, and he could prove his convictions, to a considerable extent, by act ; but he could not reason. If he could have reasoned, he might have achieved what he was constantly expecting, and have changed the whole aspect of civilization.

He must have been an extraordinary child, judging by his own amusing account of himself as a teacher in a school from the age of seven. He was under-master at nine. He maintained himself as a shopman for a few years, being always treated with a consideration and liberality which testify to there having been something impressive about him. Arkwright's machinery was then coming into use ; and at the age of eighteen, Robert Owen became a partner in a cotton-mill where forty men were employed. He was prosperous, and rose from one lucrative concern to another, till he became the head of the New Lanark establishment, which included a farm of 150 acres, and supported 2,000 inhabitants. The ordinary notion of Robert Owen among those who have not examined his operations is, that he was that kind of "amiable enthusiast" who is always out at the elbows, and making his friends so ; but nothing could be further from the truth. He was a consummate man of business ; never wrong in concrete matters, however curiously mistaken in his abstract views. He made many fortunes, and enabled others to make them ; and if he had been selfish and worldly, might have died the wealthiest of cotton lords, or a prodigious landed proprietor. No one could go over any of his successive establishments, in Scotland, America, or England, without being convinced, in the first place, of the economy of association, and, in the next, of Mr. Owen's remarkable

The New Lanark establishment.

ability in the ordination and conduct of the machinery of living. His arrangements for the health of an aggregate multitude, for their comfortable feeding, clothing, leisure, and amusement; the methods of cooking, warming, washing, lighting; the management of the mill and the farm, the school and the ball-room, everything requiring the exercise of the economic and administrative faculties, was of a rare quality of excellence under his hand. In ten years, while all the world was expecting his ruin from his new-fangled schemes, he bought out his partners at New Lanark for eighty-four thousand pounds. His new partners and he realized in four years more than one hundred and fifty thousand pounds profit; and he bought them out for one hundred and fourteen thousand pounds. These are facts which ought to be known.

[III]
His administrative ability.

Those New Lanark mills were set up when Owen was a boy, in 1784, by Arkwright, in conjunction with the benevolent David Dale, of Glasgow, whose daughter became Robert Owen's wife. How they were managed by Owen we have seen. In 1816, he found himself at liberty to try his own methods with his work-people; and his social and educational success was so striking that many of the great ones of the earth came to him to learn his method. In spite of his Liberalism, emperors and kings and absolute statesmen went to Lanark, or invited Mr. Owen to their Courts. In spite of his infidelity, prelates and their clergy, and all manner of Dissenting leaders, inspected his schools. In spite of the horror of old bigots and new economists, territories were offered to him in various parts of the world on which to try his schemes on a large scale. Metternich invited him to a succession of interviews, and employed Government

Success of the New Lanark Mills.

Owen and Metternich.

[III] clerks for many days in registering conversations and copying documents; and there was less absurdity than some people supposed in Mr. Owen's sanguine expectation that his "new system of society" would soon be established in Austria. Though he did not see it, there was much in his method of organization which might be turned to excellent purpose by an arbitrary government; and whenever the Prussian system of education, with its fine promises, its sedulous administration, and its heartless results, is brought under our notice, our remembrance travels back to New Lanark, with its dogmas, its discipline, the mild and beneficent solitude which brooded over it, and its dependence for genuine liberty and free individuality on the personal character of the administrator. The discipline in the two cases might be different, and the dogmas opposite; but the educational system had strong resemblances. This ought to be easily conceivable when it is remembered that Metternich was a pupil of Owen's, and the Mexican Government his patron, and Southey his eulogist. In 1828, our own Cabinet sanctioned and furthered his going out to Mexico, to see about a district which was offered him there, 150 miles broad, including the golden California of our day. There must have been something in Mr. Owen's doings to cause such incidents as these. The "amiable enthusiast" himself steadily believed that it was the love of humankind which was the bond between himself and all these potentates; but wise men saw, and the event has proved, that the temptation lay in the opportunity his schemes afforded for training men to a subserviency which he was very far from desiring.

Robert Owen was the founder of Infant Schools.

Many had conceived the idea, but he was the first to
join the conception and the act. De Fellenberg had
instituted education in connection with agricultural industry, but had not particularly contemplated infants
in his scheme. Others had in theirs : but it was not
till Henry Brougham had reported to his parliamentary
and other friends in London what was actually done at
New Lanark, and they had consulted with Mr. Owen,
and borrowed his schoolmaster, that Brougham, Romilly,
Ben Smith, Zachary Macaulay, and Lord Lansdowne
set up an Infant School in Westminster. This was in
1819, when Owen's school had been in operation three
years. As usual in such cases, the immediate benefit
was obvious enough, before the attendant mischiefs
began to show themselves. Robert Owen was extremely
happy in having surrounded these babes with "happy
circumstances," amidst which they could not but grow
up all that he could wish ; and less sanguine men than
he gloried and rejoiced in the prospect of the redemption
of the infant population of our towns. It did not
occur to them that the mortality among the children
might be in proportion to their removal from the natural
influences of the family, and of a home where no two
members of the household are of the same age, or at
the same stage of mind. The disproportionate mortality
from brain disease which has since taken place in Infant Schools was the dark side of the picture which
Owen did not see—the warning given out by the
experiment, which he did not hear. The bright part
of the result was the proof that education could go
on well—and better perhaps than ever before—without rewards and punishments ; or, we may rather say

[III]

*Founder of
Infant
Schools.*

[III]   (as Mr. Owen's benign presence and approbation were a constant reward), without any arbitrary visitation whatever.

And what has come of all the noble promise held out by a man so good, and in many respects so capable, as Robert Owen? He once made nearly 3,000 people an example of comfort, decent conduct, and unusual cultivation, at a time when poverty, crime, and ignorance made all good men's hearts sad. Where are the results? The results lie in the improved views and conduct of a very large number of descendants from Owen's pupils; and yet more in the impulse that he imparted to the Co-operative principle. The Christian Socialists are *Owen's disciples.* his disciples, politically, though not religiously; and the Secularists are his disciples, philosophically, though not as of course politically. He is, and will sooner or later be admitted to be, the father of the great social changes which are preparing, and already going forward, as the evidence of the Economy of Association becomes more clear. But his own special schemes failed—one and all; and if he had lived two centuries, scheming at his own nimble rate, his enterprises would never have succeeded, because they were founded on an imperfect view of the Human Being for whose benefit he lived, and would willingly have died. In 1824 he formed a group of communities in America, having purchased the Harmony Estate, consisting of a village and 30,000 acres of land, from the Rappites, who were emigrating westward. The community, including several thousand persons, improved in mind, manners, and fortunes; *Want of vitality in his schemes.* but there was still the something wanting which was essential to permanence. Duke Bernard of Saxe Weimar stayed there for a week or two, and, amidst all his respect and admiration for Mr. Owen, saw that it would not do ; and in that case the experiment was not a long one. The account given by the Duke of Mr. Owen's expectations is so precisely true, at all periods of his life, that it may stand as a general description of the philanthropist's state of mind for seventy years : "He looks to nothing less than to renovate the world, to extirpate all evil, to banish all punishments, *to create like views and like wants,* and to guard against all conflicts and hostilities." And so he went on to the end. At every moment, his "plans" were going to be tried in some country or other, which would bring over all other countries. Everybody who treated him with respect and interest was assumed to be his disciple ; and those who openly opposed or quizzed him were regarded with a good-natured smile, and spoken of as people who had very good eyes, but who had accidentally got into a wood, where they could not see their way for the trees. He was the same placid happy being into his old age, believing and expecting whatever he wished ; always gentlemanly and courteous in his manners ; always on the most endearing terms with his children, who loved to make him, as they said, "the very happiest old man in the world ;" always a gentle bore in regard to his dogmas and his expectations ; always palpably right in his descriptions of human misery ; always thinking he had proved a thing when he had asserted it, in the force of his own conviction ; and always really meaning something more rational than he had actually expressed. It was said by way of mockery that "he might live in parallelograms, but he argued in circles ;" but this is rather too favorable a description of one who did not argue at all, nor know what argument meant. His

[III]

His aims and "plans."

[III]

His belief in spirit-rapping.

mind never fairly met any other—though at the close of his life he had a strange idea that it did, by means of spirit-rapping.   He published sundry conversations held in that way with Benjamin Franklin and other people ; and in the very same breath in which he insisted on the reality of these conversations, he insisted that the new-found power was "all electricity."

His personal character.

It must be needless to add that, whatever reception his doctrines and plans may deserve or meet with, his life and conduct were virtuous and benign.   No censure attaches to him in his domestic relations, in his personal habits, or in his ordinary social dealings. He was a beloved and faithful husband and father, pure and simple in his way of life, and upright in his transactions.   There was therefore no solid ground for the horror expressed by the *Quarterly Review*, in the name of its constituents, when they heard of Robert Owen from a new place.   When they were expecting, as they declared, to hear of his being in Bedlam, they heard of his being at Court, introduced to the young Queen by her Prime Minister, Lord Melbourne. \ Many have been introduced there who were quite as wide of the mark in speculation, and quite as complacent in their mistakes ; while there can hardly have been many so self-governed, so true to their convictions, so thoroughly superior to the world, so impartial and disinterested, and so devoted to the welfare of the people, individually and collectively.   As long as the name of Robert Owen continues to be heard of, there

Both truth and error in his speculations.

will be some to laugh at it, but there will be more to love and cherish it. The probability seems to be that time will make his prodigious errors more palpable and unquestionable ; but that it will at least in equal

proportion exalt his name and fame, on account of
some great intuitive truths which are at present about
equally involved with his wildest mistakes and his
noblest virtues.

He died where he was born, at Newtown, in Wales.
He had gone on a visit; but death overtook him there,
in the eighty-ninth year of his age.

[III]

IV.

LADY NOEL BYRON.

She was born in 1792; married in January, 1814; returned
to her father's house in 1816; and died on the 16th of
May, 1860.

WHEN the only child of Sir Ralph and Lady Milbank
was born, it would have been considered a strange
prophecy if any seer had told how that infant should
be in character simply a good and true woman, without
genius or any remarkable intellectual qualities, without
ambition or vanity, and that yet she should twice
become an object of deep interest to the English
Her un- people—her name on the tongues of millions, and her
foreseen lot. merits discussed, once with party heat, and again, after
a lapse of more than forty years, with the warmth of
well-grounded popular gratitude. Such, however, has
been the lot of that quiet, beneficent, true-hearted
Englishwoman, Lady Noel Byron. Her life began with
sunshine; then it was shaken by a fearful storm, which
clouded the rest of her life; but she, sitting in the shade,
sent a multitude into the sunshine, and patiently wore
away the last two-thirds of her life in making others
happier than she could be herself.

While everybody assumes to know Lady Byron's history, none but her intimate friends seem to have any
notion of her character. The chief reason of this is

that Lord Byron gave forth two irreconcilable accounts of it; one when he first lost her, and another when it suited him to set up a case of incompatibility of temper. The long tract of time over which she has passed since his death would have settled the matter in all minds if Lady Byron had desired that it should. But she desired only quiet; and it is by her benefactions that the chief part of her life has been recognized and will be remembered.

Her childhood was spent for the most part at Seaham, in Durham, where Sir Ralph Milbank's estate was situated. She preserved such love for the place, up to her latest years, that a pebble from its beach was an acceptable present to her. She was carefully reared, and, for the time in which she lived, well educated. *The representations of Moore and Lord Byron.* Mr. Moore and Lord Byron could have known but little of the education of girls at the opening of the century, and must have been bad judges of the minds and manners of sensible women, if they were sincere in their representations of Miss Milbank, as a "blue," as a "mathematical prude," and so forth. Moore, who had no vigorous intellectual tastes, might have been sincere; and he no doubt was so in the plainness of his avowal that he "never liked her." Lord Byron knew better than he pretended. He knew that she was impulsive, affectionate, natural in her feelings and manners when he first offered to her; and none knew so well as he what she proved herself to be capable of under trial—how passionately she loved him, and how devoted she would have been, through good and evil report, if he had made her companionship possible. *Refuses Byron's first offer.* When he first offered to her, she was, in her girlishness, evidently taken by surprise. She refused him, but

[IV]

The second proposal.

Parental neglect.

desired not to lose him as a friend. When he offered himself again she knew nothing (how should she?) of the profligate spirit in which the deed was done. Moore's account, in his "Life of Byron," of the way in which the second proposal was brought about, and the circumstances under which the letter was dispatched, was the first that most people knew about it. When that book came out, every one saw how wise and how good was the silence which the injured woman had preserved. Her enemies were then convicted on their own confession. To say nothing of what the women of England felt, there was not a man with an honest heart in his breast who did not burn with indignation over the shameless narrative of how the trusting, admiring, and innocent girl, whom the poet had wooed before, was now made sport of among profligate jesters, and deliberately proposed as a sacrifice to the bare chances of the libertine's self-restraint.

What her father was about, to permit his child to enter into such a marriage, seems never to have been explained. The less his child knew of Byron's moral entanglements, the more vigilant should her father have been over her chances of domestic peace; and the more generous she was sure to be about the poverty of her lover, the more should her parents have taken care that she should not leave them for a home which was to be broken into by nine or ten executions in the first year. Never was a young creature led to the altar more truly as a sacrifice. She was rash, no doubt; but she loved him, and who was not, in the whole business, more rash than she? At the altar she did not know that she was a sacrifice: but

before sunset of that winter day she knew it, if a
judgment may be formed from her face and attitude
of despair when she alighted from the carriage on the
afternoon of her marriage-day. It was not the traces
of tears which won the sympathy of the old butler
who stood at the open door. The bridegroom jumped
out of the carriage and walked away. The bride alighted,
and came up the steps alone, with a countenance and
frame agonized and listless with evident horror and
despair. The old servant longed to offer his arm to
the young, lonely creature, as an assurance of sympathy
and protection. From this shock she certainly rallied,
and soon. The pecuniary difficulties of her new home
were exactly what a devoted spirit like hers was fitted
to encounter. Her husband bore testimony, after the
catastrophe, that a brighter being, a more sympathizing
and agreeable companion, never blessed any man's
home. When he afterward called her cold and mathematical, and over-pious, and so forth, it was when public
opinion had gone against him, and when he had discovered that her fidelity and mercy, her silence and
magnanimity, might be relied on, so that he was at full
liberty to make his part good, as far as she was
concerned.

Silent she was, even to her own parents, whose feelings she magnanimously spared. She did not act rashly
in leaving him, though she had been most rash in
marrying him. As long as others called him insane,
she was glad to do so too ; and when she left him for
her father's house, she regarded him as mad. When
Dr. Baillie and other physicians whose opinions were
asked (not by her) declared him sane, she still abstained
from acting on her own impulses or judgment. As the

[IV]

*Her treat-
ment on the
wedding-
day.*

*Her reason
for leaving
Byron.*

[IV]

published correspondence made known, the case was submitted, in an anonymous form, to Dr. Lushington and Sir Samuel Romilly; and the unhesitating decision of these two great lawyers and good men was that the wife—whoever she might be—must never see her husband again. When they knew whose case it was, they did not swerve from their first judgment, but declared that they would never aid or countenance Lady Byron's return to her husband. Under the circumstances, the general sympathy was with the wife, to whose wifely merits the husband had borne such strong testimony at his most trustworthy moment, and who had herself

Her noble silence.

preserved so complete a silence under the insult and contempt with which he afterward endeavored to overwhelm her. If her attachment to him had been more superficial, or if she had been vain or egotistical, or weak, or timid, she would have said something— something which would have let the public into the privacy of her griefs, and have broken down, more or less, the sacred domestic enclosure. All that was said, however, was said by him; and there were always just and generous people enough to remember that they had only Byron's story; and that Byron's stories were not

Campbell's unauthor- ized defence

apt to be over and above true. Great was the disappointment of such people when there appeared, in 1836, in the *New Monthly Magazine*, a sort of disclosure, offered in the name of Lady Byron. The first obvious remark was that there was no real disclosure; and the whole affair had the appearance of a desire on the part of Lady Byron to exculpate herself, while yet no adequate information was given. Many who had regarded her with favor till then, gave her up, so far as to believe that feminine weakness had prevailed at last.

But she, on this occasion, gave another proof of her strength. The whole transaction was one of poor Campbell's freaks. He excused himself by saying it was a mistake of his—that he did not know what he was about when he published the paper, and so forth. Lady Byron's friends knew, all the while, that she had no concern whatever in the transaction. The world did not know it; for she refused to recognize the world's interference in her affairs. She had made no explanations hitherto; and she made none now. She suffered, perhaps, as a weaker woman would have done; but she did not complain. Many years after she wrote to a friend who had been no less unjustifiably betrayed— *Her letter to a friend.* "I am grieved for you, as regards the actual position. But it will come right. I was myself made to *appear* responsible for a publication by Campbell most unfairly, some years ago; so that if I had not imagination enough to enter into your case, experience would have taught me to do so." We are not disposed to countenance the cant of the time about ours being an age of materialism in comparison with others; but if any one case could bring us to such a conclusion, it would be this. All can honor the women, of any age, who have borne the racking of the limbs rather than speak the word which would release them: but few have fitly honored this long endurance, through forty years, of the racking of the tenderest feelings, rather than gain absolution by the simplest disclosure. The source of this strength was undoubtedly her love for her husband. She loved him to the last with a love which it was not *Her love for Byron.* in his own power to destroy. She gloried in his fame; and she would not interfere between him and the public who adored him, any more than she would

[IV]

admit the public to judge between him and her.
As we have said, her love endured to the last. It was
her fortune which gave him the means of pursuing his
mode of life abroad. He spent the utmost shilling of
her property that the law gave him while he lived ; and
he left away from her every shilling that he could
deprive her of by his will ; and what the course of
life was which he thus supported, he himself has left on
record. Yet, after all this, the interview which she had
with his servant after his death, shows what a depth of
passion lay concealed under the calm surface of her
reserve. It will be remembered that when Byron knew
himself to be dying he called to his man Fletcher and
desired him to "go to Lady Byron, and—". . . . Here
his utterance became unintelligible, till he said, "You
will tell her this ;" and Fletcher was obliged to reply,
"I have not heard one syllable that you have been
saying." "Good God !" exclaimed the dying man ; but
it was too late for more. Fletcher did "go to Lady
Byron ;" but, during the whole interview, she walked up
and down the room, striving to stifle her sobs, and
obtain power to ask the questions which were surging in
her heart. She could not speak ; and he was obliged to
leave her.

Since that time there have been many who have
believed and said that no one person in England was
doing so much good as Lady Byron. It was not done,
as her husband gave out, by attending charity balls,
or dispensing soups, and blankets, and maudlin sentiment. Among the multitude of ways in which she did
good, the chief and the best was by instituting and
encouraging popular education. We hear at present
(and glad we all are to hear it), much about the teaching

*Lord
Byron's
death.*

*Her
practical
philan-
throphy.*

of· "common things;" but years before such a process
was publicly discussed, Lady Byron's schools were
turning the children of the poorest into agriculturists,
artisans, seamstresses, and good poor men's wives.
She spent her income (such as her husband left of it),
in fostering every sound educational scheme, and every
germ of noble science and useful art, as well as in
easing solitary hearts, and making many a desert place
cheerful with the secret streams of her bounty. There *Grace in her beneficence.*
was a singular grace in the way in which she did these
things. For one instance :—A lady, impoverished by
hopeless sickness, preferred poverty with a clear conscience, to a competency under some uncertainty about
the perfect moral soundness of the resource. Lady
Byron, hearing of the case, wrote to an intermediate
person to say that the poor invalid could never be a
subject of pity, as the poverty was voluntary ; but that
it seemed hard that the sufferer's benevolent feelings
should be baulked ; and she had, therefore, ventured to
place at her call in a certain bank, 100*l.* for benevolent
purposes ; and in order to avoid all risk of unpleasant
remarks, she had made the money payable to this intermediate correspondent. This was her way of cheering
the sick-room ; and the same spirit ran through all her
transactions of beneficence.

No one could be more thoroughly liberal toward
other people's persuasions, while duly valuing her own.
No one could be further from pedantry, while eagerly
and industriously inquiring after all new science and
literature,—in order to learn, and by no means to display. When we say, as we truly may, that her life was
devoted, after family claims, to the silent promotion of *devotion of her life.*
public morality (without the slightest mixture of cant or

13

[IV]

dogmatism), of science, of education, of human and especially of domestic happiness, wherever she could confer her blessings, we may ask how a much-tried woman's life could be better spent? and, perhaps, how many women so tried could so have spent their lives? What domestic life might and should have been to her all must feel who saw her devotion to her daughter, not only in youth, but yet more in attendance on the slow dying of that one child; and even more still in her labors and sacrifices for her grandchildren. It might have been said that she lived for them, if she had not at the same time been doing so much for the world beyond. Those who are gifted with insight and with a true heart might also see by other tokens what domestic life might and should have been to her. They might see it in the countenance, so worn, while so calm, steady, and thoughtful. They might see it in the wretched health which made her living from year to year a wonder even to her physicians; and in the restlessness which indisposed her to have a settled home, after the name of home had been spoiled to her; and in the few and small peculiarities which told of strained affections and of irremediable loneliness in life. They might see it, too, in the love which she won and unconsciously commanded; and especially in the solace and the care which surrounded her in her decline, and the love and gratitude which watched by her pillow as her life ebbed away. This one child of a happy home grew up almost unconscious of anything beyond it. In her youth she found herself suddenly the subject of the world's conversation, if not of the interest of all England; and she could not but know, when dying, that, notwithstanding her love of privacy, and the steadfast silence of a long life, she

Her love for her grand- children.

would be mourned from end to end of the kingdom; and that her death would create a sensation wherever our language is spoken, and would be referred to with tenderness in all future time, when popular education, and the power of woman to bless society with all gentle and quiet blessings, engage the attention of lovers of their kind.

[IV]

V.

POLITICIANS.

.

I.

THE MARQUIS OF ANGLESEY.

DIED APRIL 28TH, 1854.

At the moment when we are beginning a new war we have to announce the death of one of the heroes of our last great struggle. Field Marshal the Marquis of Anglesey died on the 28th of April, in his eighty-sixth year.

The Water-loo Banquet.

If any sense of relief mingled with the regrets for the death of Wellington, it was that the Waterloo Banquets came to an end. As more and more of the Waterloo heroes dropped off, the ceremony came to have more of mourning than of cheerfulness in it. The drinking to the memory of those who were gone was done in a more and more solemn silence; and no doubt it sometimes crossed the minds of those present that the Duke himself might possibly be the last survivor. There was some comfort in its not being so. Here is another of the band, now gone, who kept one anniversary of Waterloo in his own mind, and perhaps liked that banquet better than the brilliant one at Apsley House. The issue of the institution (as we may call it) of the Waterloo Banquet reminds one irresistibly of that club of the last century, the members of which (all old friends) pledged themselves to keep their anniversary meeting as

[I]

long as any of them lived. The numbers dwindled till there were four gray old men to play the rubber, and sit round the now small supper-table. Next year there were three, and they played dummy. When there were but two, they refused the cards, and sat talking with their feet on the fender. At last there was but one, and he faithfully fulfilled his pledge—spent the evening alone with his bottle of port, in the old room, listening to the fall of the cinders, which was the only break in the silence. Wellington was not left to this survivorship, which was not much relieved by the presence of un-qualified and younger men; and it is well that his imposing club is broken up with him. He left one senior—the old friend who has now followed him. The most interesting personage, perhaps, at the funeral of *The Marquis at Wellington's funeral.* the Duke was the aged Marquis of Anglesey. When, just after daybreak on that November morning, his carriage, surrounded by an escort of the Blues, entered the Park, a manifest thrill pervaded the assembled multitude —every man of whom knew how fiercely and how long he had suffered for his gallantry in the last of England's European battles; and probably every one felt, as he must have himself felt, that he would ere long take his place in the train of funerals which are sanctified by the glories of Waterloo. The gray, shattered, tremulous old comrades who stood looking down into the crypt at St. Paul's were an affecting spectacle, and among them the Marquis of Anglesey was conspicuous, as bearing the Field Marshal's baton of the deceased. It seemed to be his own farewell to the public,—and so it has proved.

The public interest in this most distinguished member of the Paget family began with the battle of Waterloo.

He was a brave soldier before—from his youth up—had
fought in Flanders, and had served under Sir John Moore
in the Peninsula; but it was his brilliant conduct and
effectual aid, during the three days of Waterloo, that
marked him a national hero.   He commanded the
cavalry as lieutenant-general; and on the 17th the
French cavalry followed him while the British army was
changing its ground, and found the consequences serious
enough.   The Earl of Uxbridge—as Lord Anglesey
then was—charged them with the First Life Guards,
and fairly rode over them : "upon which occasion," as
Wellington reported, in his moderate language, "his
Lordship has declared himself to be well satisfied with
that regiment."   On the great 18th he and his cavalry
did gallant things; and they believed the conflict over,
when a ball carried off the general's leg.   "The Earl
of Uxbridge," wrote Wellington again, "after having
successfully got through this arduous day, received a
wound by almost the last shot fired, which will, I am
afraid, deprive his Majesty for some time of his services."
From that day Lord Anglesey was subject to neuralgic
pains, which made his life a long torture, with short
intervals of respite.   That he could live so long under
such a liability was the wonder of all who knew
his sufferings.   As all the world knows, his leg was
buried on the field, and has the honor of a monument.

Like his illustrious friend, he found that political life
had its temptations, when there was no more work to
be done in the field.   When the Duke of Wellington
ceased to be Master-General of the Ordnance, in 1827,
Lord Anglesey succeeded him; and when the Duke
became Premier, to his own amazement and that of the

[1]

*His services
at Waterloo.*

*His political
life*

[1]
*Appointed
Lord-Lieu-
tenant of
Ireland.*

world, at the beginning of 1828, Lord Anglesey became
Lord-Lieutenant of Ireland.   His appointment took
place in February, and he was recalled before the year
was out.   The absurd transaction which occasioned his
recall is an amusing evidence of the soldierly simplicity
of the two gallant statesmen, who were together no
match for O'Connell, and excellent subjects for him to
make a ridiculous spectacle of.   The celebrated Clare
election took place in that summer of 1828, and the
Catholic Association was rampant.   It showed its power
in the absolute extinction, for the moment, of crime in
Ireland, and in its successful repression of Catholic processions, under the extreme provocations offered by the
revived Orange Clubs.   Lord Anglesey and his Government were perfectly quiet till October, when he put
forth a proclamation against such assemblages as had
already yielded to the influence of the Catholic Association.   Presently after, the titular Catholic Primate of
Ireland, Dr. Curtis, who had been an intimate friend
of Wellington's ever since the Peninsular war (when he
held office in the University of Salamanca, and was able
to render good service to the British), wrote a letter to
the Duke on the state of Ireland.   The Duke's reply
found its way to O'Connell and to the Catholic Association, who chose to interpret it as a promise of emancipation.   The Duke was for burying the subject in oblivion
(of all odd proposals), on account of the circumstantial
difficulties which surrounded it.   When the Lord-Lieutenant saw the letter, and Dr. Curtis's reply, his advice
was that agitation should be continued, with the view,
no doubt, of thereby removing the obstacles that embar-
rassed the principle which he supposed the Duke to hold
as well as himself.   It appeared, however, as if he was

acting and speaking in opposition to the head of the
Government; and a stranger thing still was, that he
seemed to know no more than anybody else of the views
or intentions of Government on the greatest question of
the day. "Your letter," he wrote to Dr. Curtis, "gives
me information on a subject of the highest interest. I
did not know the precise sentiments of the Duke of
Wellington on the present state of the Catholic question." Here was a theme for O'Connell! Here was a
fine subject for declamation! Either the Catholic question was a matter of indifference to Government, or the
Viceroy was not in the confidence of the Ministers.
Lord Anglesey added some expressions of regret at finding, from this same letter, that there was no apparent
prospect of emancipation being effected during the
approaching session of Parliament. This letter was
also read to the Catholic Association : and it may be
imagined how it was received, and how its writer was
applauded for "his manliness and political sagacity."
Such attributes were out of place at the moment, however, in a Privy Councillor and Viceroy of Ireland ; and
the next English packet brought his recall. One wonders *His recall.*
what his next meeting with the Duke was like. Both
were pets of the Catholic Association—while the Duke
was recalling the Marquis because the Marquis had involved the Duke in an inextricable difficulty. As it
turned out, the Viceroy was recalled for desiring and
promoting what the Premier was about to do. Catholic
emancipation was the necessary and speedy result of the
strange transaction ; and it was believed that it might
and would have been delayed some time longer but for
the singular simplicity of the Marquis of Anglesey. He
was succeeded by the Duke of Northumberland, but

[I]

[1]

*His re-
appoint-
ment,*

became Viceroy again at the close of 1830, under Lord Grey's Administration.

In 1831, matters went worse than ever. That was the year of the great trial of strength between the Viceroy and O'Connell; the titular ruler of Ireland issuing proclamations against a certain order of public meetings and the virtual ruler disobeying, undergoing trial, pleading guilty, and so getting off harmless as to induce the report and impression, never afterward entirely got rid of, that there was compromise, and even collusion, between the Agitator and the Whig Government. In Moore's Memoirs it appears that the poet thought the Viceroy extremely nervous about the state of Ireland. But in public there was never any appearance of dis-

*and popu-
larity.*

composure. Those who saw him mobbed in Dublin streets, as sometimes happened, can well remember the smiling good-humor, the look of amusement, with which the lame soldier, alone and armed only with his umbrella, used his weapon to rap the knuckles of the noisy Paddies who laid hands on the bridle of his pony. He was very popular, in the midst of his proclamations and coercion. His bearing suited the temper of the Irish; and there really was a good deal of love between them. The Coercion Acts that he called for were, however, fatal to Lord Grey's government. The one he obtained in 1833 was severe. Lord Grey thought it ought to be renewed, with the omission of the provision for martial law. Others thought not; and Lord Grey went out upon it. There was misunderstanding in the cabinet, causing a renewal of the complaint of underhand dealings with O'Connell, while O'Connell declared himself tricked; and Lord Grey's retirement was the consequence. Thus it appears to have been Lord Anglesey's remarkable lot to have

precipitated Catholic emancipation by his first short
tenure of the viceroyalty, and the breaking up of the
Grey cabinet by the second. The pacification of Ireland
since the death of O'Connell must have been an interesting spectacle to Lord Anglesey; and, whatever he
and others thought of his own administration there, with
its legal severity, its private and personal good-humor,
and unbusiness-like misunderstandings—whatever he and
others might think of the subsequent failures of Lords
Wellesley and Normandy, there could be no doubt of
the satisfaction to his kindly heart of seeing Ireland at
length at rest from political agitation, and released
from the worst of her destitution.

Lord Anglesey became Master-General of the Ordnance
on the formation of Lord John Russell's Administration
in 1846; and he held that office till Lord Derby came
into power, in March 1852. He was succeeded by Lord
Hardinge, under that ministry, and Lord Raglan under
the present. His infirmities were for many years so
great, through the pressure of neuralgic pain, that none
but a hero could have courted duty under such a load.
It is well that there was an interval of repose from office
before his last rest.

[marginal note] [1]

Appointed Master-General of the Ordnance.

JOSEPH HUME.

On occasion of the Presentation to MR. HUME of his Portrait,
in recognition of his Public Services, Aug. 5th, 1854.

FOR twenty years past, if the words "veteran reformer"
were caught by any ear, the hearer took for granted that
Joseph Hume was the subject of discourse. His name
has been identified with Reform for nearly forty years ;
and a glance over the facts of his life is, in a manner,
called for by the observances of last week. His father
was the master of a vessel trading from the port of Montrose, where Joseph, who was a younger member of a
large family, was born in 1777. On the death of his
father, which happened in his early childhood, Joseph
Mr. Hume's was placed at a school where the then superior Scotch
education. method and amount of education qualified him for a
professional training. His mother, who supported her
family, apprenticed Joseph to a surgeon at Montrose.
He went through the regular course of study at the
University of Edinburgh, and was admitted a member
of the College of Surgeons there in 1796. Having no
means on which he could sit down and wait for practice
at home, he began his professional career as a naval
surgeon, in the service of the East India Company. If
his politics were not constitutional, his industry was ;

and he rose rapidly by means of his own merits in his own profession. In three years he was on the medical establishment of Bengal; and no sooner was he there than the qualities which made him the reformer *par excellence* began to manifest themselves. He used his opportunity for observing the defects of the Company's management and service, and was particularly struck with the ignorance among those servants of the native languages; and he set to work to study them. In 1803, when he was serving in the Mahratta war (when Joseph Hume was distinguishing himself at the moment that Arthur Wellesley was gaining the battle of Assaye), he found the advantage of his knowledge of the dialects of India, and joined the office of interpreter to that of surgeon; finding time and energy to discharge also the duties of paymaster and postmaster of the troops under Major-General Powell. As he was never known to neglect any duty to which he had pledged himself, this combination of offices shows what his health and habits must have been—that in such a climate he should be able to get through properly the work of three or four men. The secret was, no doubt, that his power of intercourse with the natives gave him a command of assistance which other Englishmen could not make use of. The same facilities enabled him to improve his fortunes by speculation; and he returned to Calcutta, at the end of the war, a wealthy man. He concluded his service in India in 1808, and permitted himself a period of repose and foreign travel before entering upon a new career. He travelled through all the Mediterranean countries on the European side, and visited the Ionian Islands, Malta, and Sicily, accumulating knowledge all the while, according to his wont. It is desirable that

[II]

On the medical establishment of Bengal.

His capacity for work.

His travels.

[II] these facts about the early years of Mr. Hume should be recalled, because it is the practice of his enemies to represent him as a man of no breadth of knowledge—a small-souled Scotchman, who could conceive of nothing beyond the routine of a plodding life like that of his later years; whereas, few men have travelled so much, or learned so much from their travels, as Mr. Hume up to the time when he was five-and-thirty.

Returned to Parliament for Weymouth.

He sat in Parliament first for Weymouth; and it was loyal Weymouth—the bathing-place of the royal family —which found Joseph Hume a seat. During the six subsequent years that he was out of Parliament he was an East India Director, and showed something of his later and best tendencies by the attention and labor he devoted to the promotion of popular education, by the Lancasterian method—which was the first form the movement took. Mr. Whitbread must ever be regarded as the first to treat the subject in a statesmanlike manner: but no one has ever taken it up in a more earnest and disinterested spirit than Joseph Hume. He began with

His services in the cause of education.

aiding the contrivance of children teaching each other; he proceeded with the Wilberforces, Romillys, and Whitbreads of the time to encourage adult schools; and he never relaxed in his efforts, nor ceased to rise in his aims, till he had got the British Museum, Hampton Court, and other places thrown open to the whole public,—adult schools as superior to those of forty years ago as Hume the veteran Reformer was a higher man than Hume at the beginning of his political career.

Returned for Montrose.

When he re-entered Parliament, in 1818, it was as Member for Montrose. The earliest notices that we have of his action in the House indicate the course of the rest of his life. In 1817, the Finance Committee,

which was thoroughly ministerial, had reported in favor
of army reductions; and yet the reductions had not
taken place after a lapse of four years. Mr. Hume
moved an amendment on the Estimates, framing his
motion on the very words of the Finance Committee's
Report. The members of that Committee voted with
the majority against Mr. Hume and their own recom-
mendation, without attempting explanation. They were
silent to a man. The *Edinburgh Review* had by this
time discovered Mr. Hume's value; and we find him
spoken of already as a man whose persevering industry
was above all praise, and who must command the good
will of all but those to whom the preservation of abuses
was dearer than the welfare of their country. Lord
Castlereagh on this occasion instituted the course of
abuse which attended Mr. Hume henceforth, by attempting to caricature him to the House as Harlequin
and Clown. Lord Palmerston and Mr. Huskisson were
against him; and his propositions about saving the
public money, though founded on their own words, were
treated by them as some monstrous quackery, with which
the House had no concern but to be amused at it. It is
instructive and very cheering to contrast this tone of
public men in 1821 with what it was thirty years later,
while Mr. Hume was yet present to enjoy the satisfaction. While observing him during his later years in
Parliament, and seeing the unfeigned and cordial respect
with which the veteran was regarded by leading members
of all sorts of politics, it was an impressive thing to
remember that he was called names by Walter Scott.
Scott might have been glad to feel, as Hume could, that
he had refused office and salary, and spent as much
as would make a good fortune in the service of the

[II]

*His early
labors in
the House.*

*Sir Walter
Scott and
Mr. Hume.*

[II] public, besides all the anxiety and toil of a long life, —receiving as his recompense the abuse and ridicule of men who thought it genteel and refined to live at ease on the national funds. What a commentary does time make on such a judgment!—the critic not saved from debt and poverty even by his large drafts on the public purse, and the man he scorned having spared many thousands of his own earned money to do unrequited public services. While Scott was begging franks for his correspondence with his gossips, or the transmission of his lucrative proof-sheets, Joseph Hume was paying 5*l.* in a day for letters, which it was all toil and no profit to receive or despatch. And he had his share —perhaps no less then Scott—in promoting intellectual recreation and holiday solace. Let any one stand in the British Museum on Easter Monday, and he will see something of what Joseph Hume did for the pleasure of the multitude. If he had been allowed his own way, he—the plodder of Parliament—would have been called the Prince of Holiday-makers in merry England. His advocacy of Canadian interests was thorough, and, on the whole, wise. In the Reform struggle, he poured out his strength and his money like water. He was accused by the Boroughmongers of sending off candidates by coach, properly addressed and forwarded to certain constituencies—half-a-score in a day: which meant that, in the grand difficulty of the time—the finding candidates for liberal constituencies—Mr. Hume was the centre of influence, information, and energy. The Whigs then

Exposing abuses, and advocating cause of the poor. learned the value of the troublesome Radical member, who was always exposing abuses and pleading the poor man's cause: and from that time Mr. Hume's standing in Parliament was one which no one dared to despise, or attempted to underrate. Up to 1830 he sat for Montrose, and again after 1842. In the interval he was once Member for Middlesex, and, for one Parliament, Member for Kilkenny. Since the dissolution of parties consequent on the repeal of the Corn Laws he has been the leader of the more liberal members who would constitute a party. He has refused office; he never dreamed of title; he never spared his purse; and he has really seemed to have no personal desires at all. There has been nothing that anybody could do for him but to further his objects—to improve popular education—to foster the popular health and pleasure—to purify our political institutions and methods—and guard the blessings which have made us the happiest nation upon earth. We do not know that more than this could be said in honor of one who has not pretended to be anything that he was not. We do not know that more could be said of a man who devoted himself, without self-regards, to a life which is usually called a career of ambition. Without ambition, he worked harder than any aspirant of his time. While called "niggard" he has spent his private means without requital. He has *His disin-* worked partly with express benevolent designs, and *terestedness.* partly for the gratification of his own strong and well-directed faculties. What his disinterestedness has been we know by merely opening our eyes upon his career. What his services are, it is for a future generation to appreciate, when they find how far their Joseph Hume introduced virtue into the administration of government; strictness into the routine of business; truth and purity (in theory at least) into our parliamentary representation; the light of intelligence into the mind of the ignorant; and innocent pleasure into the life of the

[II]

[II]

*Posterity
will value
his labors.*

working man. Joseph Hume is not the man of whom studied eulogists prophesy immortality while he pores over his prosaic labors ; but it is not improbable that his name will be familiar and pleasant to men's ears when many a genius idolized by others or by himself shall have gone down into darkness and silence.

P.S. Mr. Hume lived and labored but a few months longer,—dying on the 20th of February, 1855.

LORD MURRAY.

DIED MARCH 7TH, 1859.

LORD MURRAY, the last of the remarkable coterie of Scotch lawyers whose fame has gone forth over all the world, was the John Archibald Murray who was so beloved by Horner, and by a multitude of persons who never saw him, for Horner's sake. Various honors fell to him in the course of his life; but the highest was, unquestionably, the place he fills in Horner's "Memoirs." There may be, and there must be, to the readers of that book, some surprise that the fine promise of the youthful J. A. Murray came to so little as it did in public life; but the image, as there fixed, is a very interesting and a very beautiful one; and the charm hung about his name and fame to the last. He, Horner, and Lord Webb Seymour were bound in the closest friendship in their early youth, and till death parted them. The other two, born in 1778 and 1777, died in 1817 and 1819; and all the many years since has the third lived, not only carrying about a vivid remembrance of his lost comrades, but inspiring the same remembrance in others by his presence. He, too, is gone at last; and the fame of that remarkable set of men is turned over to the tongue of tradition and the pen of history.

The last of a remarkable coterie of lawyers.

His friendship with Horner and Lord Seymour.

[III] John Archibald Murray was the second son of a Judge of the Court of Session, Lord Henderland. His elder brother, William, who never married, remained, in close friendship with his more widely known, but perhaps not abler younger brother, through the whole of their very *His birth.* long lives. John was born in 1780, and was, therefore, two years younger than Francis Horner. By the early letters of the latter we find that Murray was a member of the Literary Society in Edinburgh University at the age of fifteen—that same Literary Society where, at that date, "our friend Brougham" was already making a noise. *His early* Metaphysical disputation was the field for the lads— *tastes.* Dugald Stewart being at the height of his fame ; but they all saw that Brougham meant to do something else than split hairs in metaphysical fashion for the rest of his days ; and eager was the speculation as to what that something would be. At that early time there was not so very much difference between Brougham's, Horner's, and Murray's treatment of their common topics ; and it would have required a keen insight to perceive how the two survivors would diverge—the one into abortive extravagance and inconsistency, and the other into simple mediocrity, while the sound, genuine, fruitful ability was in him who died in his fortieth year.

Our first clear view of the young Murray is during this University season, when Horner was proposing to him that they should "be the Beaumont and Fletcher of metaphysics ;" when they spent their holidays in George-street or at Murrayfield, arguing about Volition, and took long walks in session-time, "describing" the "sensations which constitute the uneasiness of metaphysical perplexity." As they grew older they joined with Jeffrey, Dr. Thomas Brown, Lord W. Seymour, and others in a scheme for translating the political and philosophical writings of Turgot, thus beginning their diversion from metaphysics by political economy; a study which had such charms for them that we find them interposing it as a treat between classics and chemistry, history and poetry. Out of all this naturally grew the *Edinburgh Review*, to which Murray was a copious contributor at the beginning, when he was only twenty-two. Nothing that he ever wrote or did afterward, however, makes anything like the impression caused by his correspondence with Horner. The earnestness without vehemence, the conscientiousness, the effective thoughtfulness, the gentle, quiet fertility of his intellect, together with the constant, vigilant affectionateness of his temper, make up the most charming image of his early manhood, and set the reader speculating on what must have been the confidence, joy, and hope with which a good father must have contemplated such a son. It is truly strange that out of such a company of fellow-students, most of them devoted to political subjects, and pursuing the legal profession, not one good statesman should have been produced. Horner would have been a great statesman, no doubt, if he had lived a few years. But of Brougham's statesmanship nothing need be said; and Jeffrey and Murray failed utterly in political life. We suspect that the metaphysics may be considered answerable for this, in great part; and that the rest is due to the close coterie character of the early association of these remarkable young men, who reached a certain degree of eminence in law and literature, and then stopped short—nobody could well say why. While the Tories were in command of the State, it was supposed that opportunity was wanting; but when the opportunity came, from 1830 onward, there

[III]

A contributor to the Edinburgh Review.

His fellow-students.

[III]

Studies law.

was no one of the coterie surviving who had not his fair trial, and did not disappoint expectation.

Murray studied law, and entered upon the practice of his profession at Edinburgh. At the time of the renewal of the war, in 1803, we find him full of military zeal, like the other young lawyers of the day. Horner went to drill every day; Mackintosh wrote the glorious address of the Merchants and Bankers of London; Brougham put out "weekly incitements to patriotism;" and Murray helped him with something called "The Beacon," now forgotten. They tried to stir up Campbell to produce some lyrics; and Horner wrote to Murray to advise an appeal of the same sort to Walter Scott, whose "border spirit of chivalry" already marked him out for that service. Murray, however, soon subsided into the function which might be called that of his life,—that of furthering Whig elections and other interests, in Scotland first, and elsewhere when he could. In 1806 we find him busy canvassing in favor of Lord Henry Petty's Cambridge election, among the Cambridge graduates who had formerly been at Edinburgh, or the students who were there at that time. Electioneering was a serious business in days when a man like Horner could say to his familiar friend, "Write to me often, my dear Murray: one has no pleasure in dwelling upon any public subjects while the liberties and wealth of England are moldering away, and the institutions of Europe stiffening into barbarism: but the gratifications of private affection are untouched by these revolutions; and though they give a sadder cast to one's conversation, they cannot impair our confidence and freedom." In upholding the Whig interests in Edinburgh, Murray was not only a diligent guardian of those interests, but distinguished, while

His labors for the Whigs.

young, as a light popular orator, in days of fierce contention and of every kind of discouragement to the Liberal side. The chief aberration of the Edinburgh Whigs, their advocacy of Bonaparte, was fully shared by Murray. In their detestation of the reimposition of the Bourbons upon the French they fell back upon Napoleon, as the only alternative, and exalted him to a degree which, as is well known, damaged the influence of their *Review*, and impaired public confidence in them as champions of popular liberty. The readers of Scott's Life are aware how the *Quarterly Review* thence arose ; and also how, when the question was settled by time,— when Napoleon was dead, and it was not foreseen that the Bourbons would be again cast out,—the irate feelings of the politicians of Edinburgh gave way, and they met occasionally like neighbors and friends, in forgetfulness for the hour of the politics of their lives. There is a passage in Scott's Diary about a dinner at Murray's in the winter of 1827, which is interesting now when the host himself is gone. "Went to dine with John Murray, where met his brother (Henderland), Jeffrey, Cockburn, Rutherford, and others of that file. Very pleasant, capital good cheer, and excellent wine : much laughter and fun. I do not know how it is, but when I am out with a party of my Opposition freinds, the day is often merrier then when with our own set. Is it because they are cleverer? Jeffrey and Harry Cockburn are, to be sure, very extraordinary men ; yet it is not owing to that entirely. I believe both parties meet with a feeling of something like novelty. We have not worn out our jests in daily contact. There is also a disposition on such occasions to be courteous, and, of course, to be pleased." Murray's sense and achievement of hospitality

Scott's opinion of the Whig coterie.

14

[III]

Murray's marriage, 1828.

were always remarkable. This capital dinner was given the year before his marriage. In 1828 he married Miss Rigby, the daughter of a Lancashire merchant (then living in Cheshire), and the niece of Sir George Phillips of Manchester. His tea-table at St. Stephen's, when he was Lord Advocate—that remarkable tea-table presided over by Lady (then Mrs.) Murray—is well remembered by those who were weekly guests at it. It was a long table, with an enormous and excessively rich Edinburgh cake in the centre—and such a company round it ! When Sydney Smith was in town he was sure to be there ; and the Jeffreys and Dundases, and all the Scotch, with plenty of English celebrities. The Lord Advocate's chambers were under the same roof with the House of Lords : and in the intervals of the debate, Lords and Commons used to come dropping in for tea, and that unique cake, and chat, till the summons to a division called them away, rushing and scrambling like shoolboys at the last stroke of the bell. As a contrast, there was the Murrays' country-house at Strachur, on Loch Fyne. There, in the depth of Highland seclusion, the guests were expected to make themselves perfectly at home, and be as free as the winds. There were guides always at hand for strangers : there was the lake steamer at command, to carry them up to Inverary. At breakfast, there was every sort of fish yielded by the waters of the region ; and at dinner, everything that could be got from

His hospitality.

mountain or flood—red deer soup, salmon, game pies, grouse, &c. The hospitality of the Murrays was remarkable everywhere ; and their desire to see others happy deepened the concern of their friends at the sorrow which clouded their house. Their only child died early ; and with him their bright enjoyment of life went out.

Mr. Murray's first office was that of Clerk of the Pipe —a sinecure in the Scotch Exchequer, given him when the Whigs came in. The office is now abolished. In 1834 he was made Lord Advocate, and held the appointment for five years, without distinguishing himself, or being able to carry his measures. He was evidently not qualified for political life; and he was removed, as early as practicable, to the Court of Session, where he held a judgeship till his death. As a mark of attention, on account of prior services, he was made a baronet at the same time as a judge, that his wife might be titled also. They spent the remaining years of his long life chiefly in Edinburgh, and at their country-seat; and there were few in the populous parts of Scotland to whom the bland countenance and white hair of the old judge were unknown.

Appointed Lord Advocate.

We may seem to have devoted a disproportionate space to our notice of a man who failed to distinguish himself when his opportunity came, and whose ability seemed really to be in a course of evaporation from early manhood onward. But he was the last of a remarkable set of men who have produced a good deal of effect (though much less than they might have done) on their century. The pall of John Archibald, Lord Murray, covers more than the one last departed. It hides the final glimpse we had of the brilliant period and hopeful company in which this last survivor bore his part, when that life opened before him which disappointed him so strangely. The mighty Edinburgh Whigs who set up the *Review* are now a tradition; and it is natural to linger and gaze to the last as the pall is finally spread over what was so full of vitality and promise, and so ever present to the successive political generations of a period of sixty years.

Last of the Edinburgh Whigs.

LORD HERBERT OF LEA.

Died August 4th, 1861.

When the Empress Catharine of Russia sent her ambassador, Count Woronzoff, to London, neither she nor her ambassador imagined that, though he would live for nearly fifty years, he would scarcely see Russia again. He was not ambassador all the time, but he lived in England as a private gentleman when not in the service of his sovereign. When the Emperor Paul made his crazy friendship with Napoleon, Count Woronzoff resigned his office; but he resumed it on the accession of Alexander. When he died, his grandson, the Lord Herbert of Lea whom we have just lost, was entering upon political life, and exciting expectation beyond his own family that he would become distinguished in the political history of his time. The mother of the young Sidney Herbert, M.P. for South Wilts in 1832, was the only daughter of Count Woronzoff, and the wife of the late Earl of Pembroke, of whom Sidney was the second son.

His relationship to Count Woronzoff.

It is not very unusual for our old families to have some intermixture of foreign marriage in their history; but there is something peculiar in such a connection with Russia. The Woronzoffs were very like English people, certainly. The Count remained here chiefly for the

object of an English education for his children ; but
some singular interests arose from time to time which
must have strongly influenced the minds of his English
descendants. For instance, when Count Michael, Sidney
Herbert's uncle, was appointed Governor of New Russia
and Bessarabia, and from year to year developed the
resources of that country, and opened its grain produce
to the world, the spectacle must have been to his nephew
very unlike what it could have been to any other boy at
Harrow. There were many young men who, at the hero-
worshipping age, were in high admiration of Schamyl,
during his struggle with successive Russian generals and
governors in the Caucasus ; but much keener must have
been Sidney Herbert's interests when his mother's
brother was charged with the subjugation of the Circas-
sians, in conjunction with his government of Southern
Russia. The Count was made prince on the occasion,
supplied with vast forces, and armed with obsolute power.
He did not conquer Schamyl ; but he did everything else
that could be expected of him ; and this Russian Prince-
ruler was an uncle for a young man of any nation to be
proud of. The singularity of the case became most
marked, of course, when the Russian war broke out, and
the nephew was Secretary at War in the country which
was invading his uncle's territory, and his very estates.
No doubt, the scenery of the Crimea, and especially the
region between the wooded heights and the sea, was the
fairyland of the boy's childhood, when nobody knew
more of the Crimea than its dim classical history. He
must have known by description every step in the Woronzoff gardens and palace there, before it had entered anybody's imagination that we should besiege Sebastopol ;
and strange must have been the sensation to the War

[IV]

*Singularity
of events.*

[IV]

Minister in London when, among the camp news, came accounts of excursions made by officers to the Woronzoff estate, with minute descriptions of the walks and steps in the rocks, and the apartments of the mansion which he knew so well by family tradition. There was some natural distrust, for a time, at his holding any office in the Government under the circumstances; and his intercourses with his Russian relations were jealously watched. But Prince Woronzoff was permitted by the Czar to retire into private life during the term of the war, and afterward, for the short remainder of his life; and this obviated all difficulty to his nephew, who was a thorough Englishman, and as completely satisfied of the justice and necessity of the war as any man in the country.

Distrust of him on account of his Russian connections.

On leaving Harrow he had gone to Oxford; and it was simply a matter of course that he should enter Parliament as soon as he was old enough. He was born in 1810; and he took his seat for South Wilts in December 1832. For some months he was regarded as a graceful and accomplished young Tory, an ornament to a party then in disgrace and under chastisement; and any air of pertness which there might be about the young member was far from surprising under the circumstances. His slim figure, and his countenance, bright and amiable, gave to strangers no impression of power; but he was evidently active-minded; and there were rumors about of the considerable expectations of those who knew him well. He was not in any haste to put himself forward, his first speech being in June, 1834. It was the speech of a very young man, though a strong Conservative; and it excites strange emotions to read it now. He seconded Mr. Estcourt's amendment, against the claims of the

Returned as M.P. for South Wilts.

His maiden speech.

Dissenters to admittance to the Universities. Mr. Herbert's apprehension was that the clergy would desert the Universities if the Dissenters entered them; and his proposal was that the Dissenters should have Universities of their own. They would then find that Churchmen would not desire to enter dissenting Universities, and of course, Dissenters would cease to wish to enter the national ones. Such was Sidney Herbert's first essay in the National Council!

For some years he was a constant opponent of the Melbourne policy; but he was chiefly distinguished by his vindication of the Corn Laws. There was an impression that he would be one of the young recruits engaged by the Tories whenever they should come in again; and nobody was surprised when he became Secretary to the Admiralty on Sir R. Peel's return to power in 1841. He did not at first appear to justify the expectations of his party; for he had not yet found the art of giving an animating account of the expenditure of a public department. He was conscientiously minute, and very anxious, and his manner and speech were desultory and hesitating; but the spring of fluency was about to be opened up, and from year to year his speaking awoke more interest; for he was undergoing a change of opinion which he had to account for and to vindicate, and which impelled him to utter himself from his conviction and his heart. He was following Peel in his study of the effects of the Corn Laws. The process was a slow one; for so late as the session of 1845 we find Mr. Herbert announcing to the House that the Government would give a direct negative to Mr. Cobden's proposal of a Select Committee to inquire into the causes of Agricultural distress and into the operation of the Corn Laws. He declared that the

[IV]

Appointed Secretary to the Admiralty.

[IV] farmers had "very susceptible nerves, and would stop business at once if they perceived Mr. Cobden's drift—of 'blowing up the protective system.'" Some years later he deprecated, and very reasonably, the practice, ill suited to our time, of ransacking Hansard for proofs of inconsistency in public men. We are quite of his opinion that consistency (in the sense of immutability of opinion) is not the greatest of virtues in our age of progress ; and we will, therefore, say no more of the contradictions of his utterances at various times. It is enough that they were not referable to greed of any kind ; and that they were converted into continuous progress, after he had made a fair avowal in Parliament of the fact of the change. He was as yet rather saucy, and hasty, and superficial, jeering at Mr. Cobden for a sympathy with the agricultural interest, which he did not understand, and therefore assumed to be a false pretence ; but he learned better afterward, and gave credit for sincerity to others, as he claimed it for himself, in advocating free trade in corn while representing a constituency mainly agricultural.

Advocates the repeal of the Corn Laws.   It was in February, 1846, that he advanced this claim, when he, in his turn, had been jeered by a Protectionist member. It was in the midst of that memorable outburst of party fury which followed upon the contest for power between Peel and Russell, and the pertinacious declaration of the *Times,* repeated amidst clamorous denials, that Sir R. Peel was going to repeal the Corn Laws. Mr. Herbert had become Secretary at War, with a seat in the Cabinet, in 1845 ; and at the beginning of the session of 1846 he was the member of the Government who gave an exposition of the policy of his chief, and vindicated it till they went out of office together, ostensibly on the Irish defeat of the Coercion Bill, but really on account of the repeal of the Corn Laws, the bill for which passed the Lords on the same night that Sir R. Peel's Government received its doom in the Commons. [IV]

During the years of his absence from office Mr. Herbert was as energetic in action as ever. He was remarkably furnished with all appliances and means for doing what he thought proper; and if he had been undistinguished in political life, he would always have been busy in some benevolent scheme. He was wealthy; he had unbounded influence in his own neighborhood and connection; and in 1846 he married a woman of tastes and energy congenial to his own. She was Miss A'Court, a daughter of General A'Court and niece of Lord Heytesbury. The mere mention of her brings up recollections of an extensive emigration of laboring families, and especially of young women, to colonies which suffered most from the inequality of the sexes. Mr. and Mrs. Herbert used all their influence to promote such emigration, superintended the outfit of many hundreds, and went on board the departing ships to start the people cheerily. We heard at the same time, or soon after, of a Model Lodging-house for agricultural laborers, which they had built, and furnished and filled, at Wilton. They have built a church there, which is considered a singularly beautiful specimen of Italian ecclesiastical architecture.

His marriage.

Benevolent efforts for the agricultural poor.

Meantime he ranked with the Peelites in the House— Lord Lincoln (as he was then) and Mr. Gladstone—the three being just of the same age, and all being supposed likely to return to office, though their great *chef* was holding a position higher than office could give. Mr.

[IV] Herbert spoke occasionally—now sketching the state of affairs abroad in 1848 as actual bondage under the appearance of license; and now, in 1849, insisting that no distress had arisen from free trade. In the great Midsummer debate of 1850, on the foreign policy of Lord Palmerston's Government, Mr. Herbert spoke strongly on the Opposition side. It was a question of confidence; and no one more emphatically declared want of confidence than he, in his review of Lord Minto's errand in Italy, and his representation of the unpopularity of England abroad. That debate is consecrated to all parties now by its being the last in which the voice of Peel was heard.

After his death the group of rising statesmen who were distinguished by his name continued in opposition during the remaining Administration of Lord J. Russell, and the short term of Lord Derby, some of them coming in again on Lord Aberdeen's accession to power at the close of 1852. Mr. Herbert was then again Secretary at War.

His conduct as War Secretary during the Crimean War.

Reluctant as Lord Aberdeen was to go to war with Russia, it is probable that his War Secretary was not less so. We may remember the jealous inquiries of the public at that time as to what his Russian relatives were about, and what he and they had to say to each other. He was as thoroughly patriotic on the occasion, however, as any other man in the Ministry; and, as he was incapable of concealment, everybody was presently satisfied of his trustworthiness. This was the great point in his life. He and the Duke of Newcastle, when the functions of the War Office were divided between them, did all they could, and suffered severely. There is no need to describe what the system was which they had to

work at the end of a long peace. It may be doubted
whether the strongest of men could have brought good
results out of a system overgrown with abuses : and
these were not very strong men. They were morally
strong, and altogether devoted ; but they had not
intellectual vigor nor force of will sufficient to create
an adequate organization in the presence of events, or
to bear down the oppositions of aristocratic conceit and
selfishness. They saw our first army perish miserably,
and had to bear the spectacle of the people taking it
into their own hands to save the second, with vast waste,
and by means improvised by their own zeal. They saw
their order thoroughly frightened by the disclosure of
the abuses and lapses of their own department, and were
aware that, in spite of their utmost zeal in remedying
mischiefs, the aristocracy lost a step in the esteem and
the affections of the nation which they could never
regain.

Both were men on whom such a lesson was sure not
to be lost : men honest, devoted, and sincerely patriotic.
The Duke of Newcastle was the special victim of the
national indignation. He lost nothing in regard to
character, but was merely set aside as inadequate to
the working out of his own excellent wishes. Mr. Herbert left the War Office, and undertook the Colonial *Leaves the War Office.*
Secretaryship under Lord Palmerston. He held that
office, however, for only a fortnight, resigning, with
Sir James Graham and Mr. Gladstone, when it appeared
that the Sebastopol Committee was to be proceeded
with, notwithstanding the retirement of Lord Aberdeen.
It was a demonstration of want of confidence which
left Mr. Herbert no choice but to resign. His countenance
and voice, when he made the announcement, on the

[IV] 22d of February, 1855, showed how he had suffered under the painful experience of the preceding year, and the crisis of the winter.   He was manifestly ill; and he retired from his work under a depression as deep perhaps as his nature admitted.

He was, however, incapable of permanent discouragement.   He was too active, too full of resources, and, above all, too disinterested to be subdued by failure or mortification.   While out of office, he was in training, consciously or unconsciously, for the real work and final honors of his political life.   While Lord Panmure and General Peel were administering the affairs of the War Office, Mr. Herbert was preparing himself to become the best friend that the British soldier has ever had.

His reforms in the army. He had already been a great benefactor to the army. The soldier's condition had been cared for in certain respects for some years; and the remission of the lash and institution of the Regimental School had marked a stage in our military history.   Mr. Herbert had promoted whatever was good and contended against what was bad throughout; and he had obtained for the army in the East the attendance of Florence Nightingale and her nurses.   None of us can have forgotten the characteristic letter in which he pressed the scheme upon her.   The letter was furtively copied and published, without the knowledge of writer and receiver; but, except that the treachery brought some undeserved blame upon them, it is difficult to be sorry for the publication.   In acknowledging the blessing he brought upon the country by engaging Miss Nightingale in that particular service, we must bear in mind that her services have never since been intermitted.   When our second army was saved, and it had been proved how high an average of health may be attained in a camp in an enemy's country, Miss Nightingale went on—as she is going on at this day— securing conditions of health of body and mind for the soldier such as the world has never seen before.

When Mr. Herbert returned to the War Office in 1859, he was well furnished for great reforms. It will not be forgotten how strenuously he had labored at the head of the Army Sanitary Commission, and in the Barrack and Hospital Commission, nor what a mass of irresistible evidence he presented us with of the sufferings of our soldiers, and the way to preclude them. We have seen the soldiery already in great part relieved of the curses of bad air, disgusting food, irksome clothing, unhealthy habits, and intolerable *ennui*. We have seen a good beginning made in rescuing our military service from the vagabonds and thieves who long constituted a great pro- portion of its recruits ; and a few years will show what has been done in winning to the service the sort of men most desirable in regard to character and position. We have seen the beginning of a regeneration of the lot of the soldier in India. Our force in China, with its fine health and high spirit, showed us what Mr. Herbert and his coadjutors had been doing for the British and Indian soldier. His own view of the work to be done, and its urgency, appears in an article signed with his initials in the *Westminster Review* of April, 1859—a few weeks before his return to the War Office. That article shows us in part what he had set himself to do ; and the world will have evidences, for many years to come, how he did it. In the province of the treatment of the soldier he has had no equal in the military experience of his country.

[IV]

Appointed War Minister, 1859.

[IV]

In other departments of his office he was not quite so successful. It is true, his deserts are not all apparent yet. He saw the need of a thorough reorganization of the War Office; and he saw how it ought to be done. It is understood that a very comprehensive, sensible, practical scheme has been for many months under the consideration of the Government, for securing the object. If any justice is to be done to his memory, that scheme must be inquired after, and its purposes insisted on, in Parliament and out of it. From it we have yet to learn some of Mr. Herbert's merits in his office. But it is too true that alongside of such merits his characteristic defects have appeared very plainly. He had not strength *His weaknesses.* of will to carry through his own projects; and yet worse, he was incessantly impelled, by his ardent, generous, sanguine spirit, to pledge himself for more than he was sure of accomplishing, and to assume responsibilities belonging to others whom he could not control. There is no need to go into the proof of these weaknesses. They have not, we believe, been denied; and his most devoted friends have always said—not that his defects did not exist, but that in a world where nobody is perfect it is wiser to support a Minister who is not very strong, but who has actually accomplished more for our military system than any other, than to heap difficulty and discredit upon him, so as to make him give way to some man who is pretty sure to have worse faults and fewer virtues. Death has settled this now. He is gone, without redeeming all his pledges about the Purchase System and other matters, and without justifying his chivalrous assumption of the responsibility of appointments, in regard to which it is well known that he was subject to be overruled.

While struggling with obstruction without and weakness within, his health was giving way. It requires prodigious vigor of body and mind to work at the reform of any public department, amidst contempt and apathy from above and defiance from below. But this was an undertaking in addition to the business of his office, rendered overwhelming by absence of all proper organization. For many months he worked on, with unabated spirit; but it became evident last Christmas that he must give up either his office or his attendance in the House of Commons. He would fain have remained in the House. The sacrifice of office was the lesser of the two. But he yielded to the entreaties of some who dreaded any check to the course of reform in the War Office, and accepted a peerage, in order to continue his work as Minister.

His elevation to the peerage.

It was too late, however. He was worn out before he was fifty with excessive toil, and the wear and tear which a spirit like his must go through in a career of political responsibility. He had less to suffer than many Ministers have from hostility and misrepresentation; for he was as winning in manners as he was frank in temper. Everybody felt good-will toward him, more or less; and his personal friends were devoted to him. We may hope and believe that he had many and keen enjoyments in his political career, as he certainly had eminent blessings in his private life. He was made to be a happy man; and we may fully believe that he was so. But yet he suffered enough to break him down prematurely; and to his country he has sacrificed many years of home intercourses, an old age reposing on manly sons and womanly daughters, and a long term of married happiness. His eldest son is only eleven; and one of the happiest

His sacrifices for the public interest.

[IV]

His services a claim on his successors.

homes in England is made desolate by his sacrifice of himself.

Such sacrifices and services must not be in vain. They were a gift to the nation ; and the nation must use them as a claim on his successors, and on every Administration they belong to, for the complete fulfilment of his purposes. We must not wait longer for a thorough War Office reform because Lord Herbert is gone ; and no Minister must reckon on even so much indulgence as he had in regard to the disposal of patronage, and the rectification of the principle of promotion. Any successor must do as much as he did for the army, and the honor of England in connection with it, before he can expect any mercy for even such weaknesses as showed themselves in him. If he did not do all that a Minister of War might be conceived able to do, he did so much as may justify a new criterion of the merits of the Minister, and should render irresistible the popular demand for reforms, which he sanctioned in the proposal, but did not live to achieve.

He was half-brother and presumptive heir of the Earl of Pembroke ; and his title of Lord Herbert of Lea merely lifted him in the interval out of the fatigues of one House of Parliament into the leisure of the other. It is fitting that a new peerage should exhibit in his descendants his claims to honor and national gratitude ; but he will be remembered, politically and privately, as Sidney Herbert ; for under that name he won something better, and far dearer to him, than any peerage.

V.

THE MARQUIS OF LANSDOWNE.

DIED JANUARY 31ST, 1863.

WITH the Marquis of Lansdowne has passed away a political spectacle peculiar to this country,—that of an aristocratic gentleman of moderate abilities, and politics which might be called accidentally liberal, being connected with the entire political history of his time by the force of consistency alone. Consistency is, from the character of the time, not only so out of fashion, but for most people so out of the question, that any one signal instance of it fixes as much attention at the present day as conversion and innovation did in a former one. Lord Lansdowne remained steadfast while the Wellingtons and Peels were changing on the one hand, and the Burdetts and the Broughams on the other; and everybody is interested in seeing how this happened. The first suggestion in the case is, that it could not have happened if he had not been of high and ancient family. It could not have happened if his early course had not been determined in a liberal direction; nor if he had not been of sound reputation; nor if he had been a man of genius, or of any vigorous ability. A brief survey of his career will make the case plain. It cannot be other than one of great interest.

His consistency of character.

[V]
*His
ancestry.*

. The ancestors of Lord Lansdowne figure in Irish history as Barons of Kerry for several hundred years. His father was the celebrated Lord Shelburne, the first Marquis of Lansdowne; and the late Marquis was the son of a second marriage. He was never, nor were his elder brothers, the pupils of Dr. Priestley, as is supposed by many people. Dr. Priestley was never a tutor in the family at all, but resident, nominally as librarian to Lord Shelburne, but really as a friend and a scholarly companion. Lord Shelburne had a dread of public schools, and his two eldest sons were educated at home; but

*His edu-
cation.*

Henry, the subject of this notice, so earnestly desired a public-school education, that he was sent to Westminster. It really appears as if his lifelong solicitude on behalf of education began with his own. From Westminster he went to Edinburgh, and was one of the band of youths, since become statesmen, who debated at the Speculative Society, and worshipped Dugald Stewart. The judgment of his comrades on him was, as Horner tells us, that he was "distinguished by a cool, clear-thinking head, and a plain, firm, manly judgment." One would like to know whether, in the presence of the Speculative Society, he manifested the inaptitude for speculation and the propensity to detail which distinguished his mind in after-life. It was a joke of the season, forty years after, when he and Sydney Smith, with a companion or two, went *incognito* to Deville, the phrenologist in the Strand, to have their characters read from their skulls, and were most perversely interpreted. Lord Lansdowne was pronounced to be so absorbed in generalization as to fail in all practical matters, and Sydney Smith to be a great naturalist—"never so happy as when arranging his birds and his fishes." "Sir," said the divine, with a stare of

comical stupidity, "I don't know a fish from a bird;"
and the Cabinet Minister was conscious that "all the
fiddle-faddle of the Cabinet" was committed to him,
on account of his love of what he called practical
business.

In 1801, when Lord Henry Petty was just of age, he
graduated at Cambridge. After travelling on the Continent with Dumont, he took his seat for Calne, the
family borough, and he sat for two sessions silent, as
he thought became his youth, but diligent in attendance,
and earnest in his study of the chief orators of the time,
—Fox being his great admiration. His maiden speech
was on a politico-economical subject—the effect on
Ireland of the working of the Bank Restriction Act.
The remark at the time was that this young Lord Henry
Petty justified his descent from Sir William Petty, who
had that to say in Cromwell's time which caused him to
be called the father of Political Economy in England.
The first very strong impression made by the young
member was, however, on the 8th of April, 1805, in
the Melville business, when, in addition to the discretion
and good sense which were noted as remarkable in a
man of five-and-twenty, he showed a power which never
reappeared. Fox declared it the best speech that was
made that night. When Parliament was prorogued, he
went to Ireland with Dumont, to explore it politically,
beyond the bounds of the family property. On the
opening of the session of 1806, he was to have moved
the Amendment on the Address—that amendment which
was given up because Pitt was dying. By that time, the
first Marquis was dead, and was succeeded by Lord
Henry's half-brother, who afterward died without issue,
devolving the title and estates on him.

Returned as M.P. for Calne.

On Pitt's death, Lord Henry Petty came in for Cambridge University, over the head of the young Palmerston, who was a grave and modest youth in those days. Fox used to say in private that he looked upon Petty as his political successor; but still, in the notices of the time, it is always the gravity, consistency, and diligence of the young man that we find extolled, and not any power of a higher order. He was made Chancellor of the Exchequer at once, in the Grenville Administration; and he brought forward a financial scheme which was prodigiously admired by his colleagues, who were but too like Fox in their aversion to Adam Smith and the subject of his book; but Lord Henry Petty's financial scheme would not bear examination. His operations ended in a great increase of the assessed taxes and the property tax; and there are caricatures yet in our libraries in which Fox and Petty are seen as bear and dog, taught to dance by Lord Grenville as trainer; and again, as taxgatherers, bearding John Bull. Already we find him busy in doing what he delighted in doing through life, helping people to a position, or fitting people and places to each other. The last entry in Horner's journal bears date June, 1806, and it relates to a negotiation set on foot by Lord Henry Petty for bringing his friend Horner into Parliament under the auspices of Lord Kinnaird. A few months afterward the Grenville Administration went out, letting the Tories into power for nearly a quarter of a century. Cambridge would have no more of the young Liberal; but he indulged himself in a "last act" of patronage, or propitiation of patronage, even at that moment. He got Professor Smyth, the "amiable and accomplished," as his friends called him, appointed to the chair of Modern History. It was, like most of Lord

Appointed Chancellor of the Exchequer.

Lansdowne's appointments, an act of kindness to the [V] individual, but scarcely so to the public. There is no saying what benefit might have accrued to British statesmanship if a man of more vigor, philosophy, and comprehensiveness of mind than Professor Smyth had been appointed to so important a chair.

In 1808 Lord H. Petty married Lady Louisa Emma *His mar-* Strangeways, his cousin,—a woman who had, without *riage.* seeking it, everybody's praise. She was beautiful; and every advantage of natural ability was improved by education, and sanctified and endeared by the finest moral qualities. They lived together to an old age. The year after their marriage, the second Marquis died, and they began, at Bowood, the long series of hospitalities *His hospi-* which made that abode as celebrated in its own way as *tality at* Holland House was in a somewhat different one. The *Bowood.* difference lay in the hostesses; and it was wholly to the advantage of Bowood. It is amusing to see, in Moore's "Diary," an account of consultations between the visitors of the two houses — Rogers, Tierney, Barnes, and Moore—about which of the noblemen was the more aristocratic in his habit of feeling, Lord Holland or *Contrasted* Lord Lansdowne—the impression of those who knew *with Lord* them best being that neither could be more so than the *Holland.* other, while both were blinded to it in themselves, as superficial observers were, by the genuine benevolence which was the prevailing mood of each. As to the ladies—there is no need to describe the hostess of Holland House. Lady Lansdowne had her aristocratic tendencies, as was natural; but they were less than the shyness of her manners led some to suppose; and they were subdued to perfect harmlessness by her personal humility and all-pervading modesty. The hospitalities

[V]

*His labors
in Parlia-
ment.*

of Bowood, so conducted, might well form, as they did, a social feature of the time.

During the quarter century of Tory rule, Lord Lansdowne was steady in his advocacy of the great questions of his youth, and, we may now add, of his old age. He was ranked with Lords Grenville and King as a leader of the Political Economy School. He never let slip an opportunity of advocating popular education; as when, for instance, he said about Scotland, which Lord Liverpool called "the best-conditioned country upon earth," that such welfare as it had was wholly ascribable to its parochial schools, which had counteracted the mischiefs of its political system. He sustained the Catholic claims, quietly and steadily; and he defended coalitions during the whole interval from the first he joined in 1806 to the last in 1852. He declared them to be not only just, but necessary in a free country, as a defence against the encroachments of the Court; and that their principle was the same as that of Party—concession all round, for the sake of combined action. In 1820 he took a noble stand in reprobation of the proceedings against the Queen, and also made a very effective Freetrade speech. In 1821 his friends began to tell him that he was becoming a Parliamentary Reformer: and so he was; but not so fast as his political comrades. When the King took it into his head, at that time, to court the Opposition, and had some of them to dinner at Brighton, the courtesy of Lord Lansdowne's behavior was remarked in contrast with the ill manners of some others—his habitual moderation here standing him in good stead. His advocacy of the independence of the South American Republics prepared some minds for his act, so much disapproved by others, of joining Mr.

Canning in May, 1827. Steady as he had ever been in asserting the virtue of coalition, he was anxious and uneasy in his new position in the Cabinet; declared that he was powerless, was complained of for being too mild with the Opposition when they were hunting Canning to death; and was deeply afflicted by that rancorous and yet most pathetic speech of his friend Lord Grey which is believed to have broken Canning's heart. In October he was Home Secretary in the Goderich Cabinet; but not even the recess enabled the coalition to work; and the Duke of Wellington was Premier in a few weeks. It is rather amusing to find how Lord Lansdowne was beset as the place-procurer during his very short tenure of power, and how he complained in private of the worry of this; while he had really very little patronage—what there was not being at his own disposal. It is clear that now, as later, this sort of business was devolved upon him by his colleagues, under the idea that it suited him better than the larger labors of statesmanship.

[V]

When Lord Grey came into power Lord Lansdowne was President of the Council—an office which suited him and the Council admirably, He continued in office with the Melbourne Ministry—going out when Sir R. Peel was sent for to Rome in November, 1834, and returning on the breaking up of the Peel Administration in the next April. After Lord Grey's retirement he was the leader, when nesessary, of the Opposition in the Lords, and during the Russell Administration, of Government; and it was during that long course of years that his finest qualities appeared—his moderation, his courtesy, his knowledge of, and deference for, parliamentary forms and usages; and better, his sincere

Appointed President of the Council.

[II]

zeal in causes which bore least relation to party warfare. As a Parliamentary Reformer, no one expected much from him ; and he had done his duty long before by questions of liberty of conscience, in the case of the Catholics and the Dissenters. He consistently, but

His labors in the cause of education.

mildly, advocated Free Trade ; but it was in the business of Education that he distinguished himself most. Little that has as yet been done in that cause, that little has been done by Government ; and Government, in this case, meant originally, and always meant chiefly, Lord Lansdowne. After all that can be said, and truly, about the Committee of Council on Education giving him work of detail to do and superintend, and many places to give away, it remains a certainty that here began the work of Popular Education by the State ; that Lord Lansdowne gave his zeal, his interest, and his pains to it ; and that the nation ought to be grateful to him accordingly.

In 1836 he lost his elder son, the Earl of Kerry, who left a widow and one son ; and in 1851 the Marchioness of Lansdowne died. He had a son and a daughter left ; but every one felt, as he did, that his life was drawing toward that closing period which should be one of

Close of his official life.

repose. He took leave of active, and, as he thought, of official life, when Lord John Russell made way for Lord Derby in the spring of 1852. No speech that he ever made won him so many hearts, and so much respectful sympathy, as that in which he declared that, though he should appear in his place in Parliament on occasion, he was then taking his leave of active public life. When the Coalition Ministry under Lord Aberdeen came into power, Lord Lansdowne reluctantly consented to take a seat among them—without office—to afford the Government the benefit of his character of Conservative

Whiggism, of his dignified presence in Parliament, of his urbane and moderating influence in council, and of his experience in the business of statesmanship. This was understood to be only another form of that farewell to public life which he had announced, rather more expressly, on the occasion of the Derby Ministry. [V]

Lord Lansdowne had been gradually declining for some months, when his death was hastened if not actually occasioned by an accident. The venerable nobleman, while walking on the terrace at Bowood, stumbled and fell; and in falling cut his head severely. The shock was too much for his enfeebled frame, and after gradually sinking for some days he expired on the evening of January 31st. *His death.*

15

VI.

LORD LYNDHURST.

Died October 12th, 1863.

His American birth. JOHN SINGLETON COPLEY, Baron Lyndhurst, would have been remarkable, even if he had been a much less able man than he was, as an imported statesman and lawyer; imported, too, from a Democratic Republic. No censure is intended in this statement of a fact. He was no political renegade. He was born before the separation of the American colonies, and never had the least tendency to republicanism in him. He was Tory to the heart's core. His being born so far from the focus of royalty was a mistake of Nature, which she rectified by bringing him at last to be the keeper of the King's con- *His family staunch Royalists.* science in that mother-country to which the family clung with true royalist zeal.

The first revolutionary act, clear and determinate, of the American colonists was throwing a certain notorious cargo of tea into Boston harbor, to prevent the pay- ment of duty on it. The Consignee of the tea would not promise to send it back to England. He was sup- ported by the Governor, of course. The citizens placed a guard over the tea, that it might not be stolen; and when no other means could avail, to prevent its being landed, a band of them, disguised, threw it into the sea.

The tea-merchant in this case was Richard Clarke, the grandfather of Lord Lyndhurst. He was so stanch a royalist that he removed to England on the establishment of American independence. His daughter had married Copley, the artist, in Massachusetts; and when the Copleys also came to England, their son, John, was about nine years old. He was born in or about 1770. His father was not much liked by anybody; but his mother was amiable, generous, and tender-hearted. When John, as a young lawyer, went over to his native country about some land buisness for his father, his townsmen at Boston admired his appearance, his manners, and his talents, and foretold his being a great man; but they pronounced him to be more like his father than his mother in character. He inspired little trust, and was fond of money.

He was destined to get on, both by his better and his worse qualities; by his energy, courage, and resource, as well as by his Tory leanings. It was not at once that he found his place, though perhaps the means he took were the best for bringing him into it. He denounced the Liverpool, Castlereagh, and Sidmouth Ministry so ably and vigorously that he was worth propitiating; in 1818 he entered Parliament for a Government borough, and immediately rendered service on the subject of the Alien Bill, when he answered Romilly, and was answered by Mackintosh. It was a position for an honest politician to be proud of, and for an unsound one to dread. But John Copley dreaded nothing. He was then Mr. Serjeant Copley, with a rich practice. The next year we find him Sir John Copley, Knight, and Solicitor-General. In 1823 he was Attorney-General, and in 1826 Master of the Rolls. In 1827 he appeared as a "Canningite" in the

[VI]

His birth,
1770.

Enters Parliament,
1818.

Appointed
Master of
the Rolls,
1826.

[VI]

short Administration of the dying statesman ; but there was no fear of his being at all better disposed toward the Catholics than his predecessor, Lord Eldon. He was made Baron Lyndhurst, and took his seat on the Woolsack ; but he was one of the three (the two others being Lords Bexley and Anglesey) who were cited as security that the Canning Cabinet would not propose Catholic emancipation. He had very recently declared that if the parliamentary oath which excluded the Catholics was necessary in 1793, it was necessary still. He was looked to for good service in reforming the Court of Chancery, having at first proposed some small reforms, and then accelerated the business there by the appointment of an additional judge, and having again brought in a bill with that object during the short interval of his being Master of the Rolls. The bill was lost by the illness of Lord Liverpool breaking up the Government. He remained on the Woolsack during the various changes of Administration of 1827 and 1828, and descended from it only to yield the seat to Lord Brougham on the advent of the Grey Ministry. It ought to be remembered that Lord Lyndhurst, during this first period of his Chancellorship, set on foot the inquiries out of which grew such reform in the case of Lunatics as we have yet obtained. He issued a circular, which required from all keepers of Lunatic Asylums of every sort an exact return of their patients, and their class and condition in regard to their malady. The replies to this circular first brought in the information which was necessary for further action.

Appointed Lord Chancellor.

Opposes the Reform Bill.

His great deed, that which exhibited at once his courage and his convictions, was throwing out the Reform Bill, by his ingenious motion to postpone the disfranchisement to the enfranchisement proposed by the bill. On this motion he united the Conservatives and the Waverers in the Lords; and thus he obtained a majority of thirty-five. This was on the celebrated 7th of May, 1832; and thereupon the Political Unions assembled at Birmingham, plighted their faith, and sang their hymn. Lord Lyndhurst thus overthrew the Ministry, and showed his determination to consider the House of Lords as "the Citadel of the Constitution," as the *Quarterly Review* was then declaring it, and to preserve it, with all its ancient rights and abuses, or forfeit the Monarchy altogether. Of course, he was immediately the most unpopular man in England. He bore his evil fame with great resolution, aided therein by his profound contempt for popular opinion, as much as by his strong Conservative tendencies. The amazement among his American relations and acquaintances was unspeakable; and the contempt felt by democratic republicans toward one who had gone forth from among them as if on purpose to shut the doors of Parliament against a nation, was quite as strong as the rage of English reformers. Both the rage and contempt were of more weight than they otherwise would have been from the absence of respect for the man, who about this time exposed himself to so much doubt and disrepute that his reception in private society was no more flattering to his feelings than that which he met in the streets. The apparent indifference with which he accepted any diversity of treatment inspired some sort of respect for his courage, in the midst of all the reprobation. The commonest saying about him at that time was, that if ever there was a brow of brass, it was his. Reform, however, was carried in spite of him; and he was not only on

[VI]

His unpopularity resulting therefrom.

[VI] the Woolsack again before the end of 1834, but that extraordinary transaction had taken place which finally overthrew Lord Brougham's political reputation. Lord Brougham, when dismissed from the Chancellorship, wrote to Lord Lyndhurst to offer that they should change places, Lord Lyndhurst having before been Chief Baron of the Exchequer. No answer could be given till Sir R. Peel arrived from Rome; and before that happened Lord Brougham had been made aware, by the public indignation, of his mistake, and had withdrawn his request. From that time, however, his Toryism is usually dated; and his ostentatious, boisterous, and indecorous show of intimacy with Lord Lyndhurst deepened the disrepute of both. When they were amusing themselves with ill-concealed romping in the House of Lords, the popular impression was very strong that Lord Lyndhurst was a second time humoring an infirm brain for his own purposes. In his place both as Lord Chancellor and as *His energy* mere peer, he was diligent and consummately able in *and ability* business. He was the greatest lawyer in the country; *as a lawyer.* and he was capable of vast labor. In Appeal cases he rendered most valuable services; and he was certainly the most formidable enemy the Whigs had in the Lords' House—not even excepting his friend Brougham. The two together were overwhelming. On the dissolution of the Peel Ministry of 1835 the Great Seal was in Commission, till it was given to Lord Cottenham, some months after. The two ex-Chancellors, both men of extraordinary powers of vituperation—both shameless and in close alliance—made the Woolsack their target, and nearly drove the Whig Ministers mad by their speeches and their sarcasms. In August, 1836, Lord Lyndhurst made the speech which is perhaps the best remembered of any he ever made—that in which, reviewing the results of the Session, he exposed the incapacity of the Whigs, and certainly covered them with shame. In 1839, the conjunction of the two critical ex-Chancellors was again too much for the Government. Lord Melbourne had dropped, in his own singular way, an opinion that the legal studies pursued by many of our statesmen had a narrowing effect on their minds. Such an opinion was not a very propitiatory one. Lord Durham's Canada business was at hand for a theme. Lord Durham was personally hated by Lord Brougham. So the friends put forth all their strength, and they succeeded in quelling Lord Melbourne's courage and overpowering his fidelity to an absent colleague; and they broke Lord Durham's heart. There was certainly, as Lord Lyndhurst boasted, no lack of power on the Opposition side of the Lords' House, with these two lawyers to lead the fray, at a time when every question became a fray.

In 1841 he was appointed Chancellor for the third time, and remained so till the breaking up of the Peel Ministry after the repeal of the Corn Laws in 1846. The High Stewardship of Cambridge University had been an object of ambition to him, and he was elected to the office in 1840, having a majority of nearly five hundred votes over his opponent Lord Lyttelton. He was now growing old; and, though he was still the handsomest of Lord Chancellors, infirmity was creeping upon him. After he left office he was blind for a considerable time, from cataract; but his sight was restored; and he came forth again, at nearly eighty years of age, as if he had taken a new lease of life. He enjoyed the opportunity afforded by the Ecclesiastical Titles Bill for opening out once more against the Catholics. He excused his assent

Elected High Steward of Cambridge University.

[VI]

to the Relief Bill of 1829 on the ground that he desired
to see toleration all round ; but he contended that, such
toleration not sufficing Rome, he would go no further.
The true principle of religious liberty which excludes
"toleration," and requires total exemption from all juris-
diction whatever, never, probably, entered his mind at
all—even before his mind was "narrowed," as Lord

*His aristo-
cratic ten-
dencies.*

Melbourne said, by his legal studies. He was too
thoroughly aristocratic by temperament to be capable of
any generous conceptions of human liberty, even though
he came from America. One would think that his clay
had been kneaded from the dust of the old high-born
Governors of the Plantations, and his mind fed on the
obsequious addresses of the colonists to a long series of
Kings and Queens. He was best employed on Law
Reform, in which he took an evident interest, and which
caused less stirring of the Tory spirit in him than politics,
or perhaps any other pursuit.

*His last
labors in
the House of
Peers.*

Two powerful speeches—one on the policy of Prussia
during the Russian war, and one on Earl Clarendon's
policy in 1856—belong to the last era of Lord Lyndhurst's public life. His last great efforts were in defence
of the privileges of the House of Lords, supposed to be
infringed by the creation of Lord Wensleydale's peerage
for life, and the Paper Duty Repeal Bill.

*His personal
charac-
teristics.*

If Lord Lyndhurst had not the peculiar grace and
urbanity which belong to aristocratic birth in an old
country, he had very agreeable manners. With a fine
person, eminent ability, vast information, a cool temper,
much natural energy and cheerfulness, he was a delightful companion to those whom his qualities could satisfy.
When the interest of old age was added, his faults
met with gentle treatment, if not forgetfulness. Still, his

greatest admirers will not deny that their feeling is admiration more than esteem. The Americans would have wished that, if they were to send us a statesman, it should have been one of a different quality; and the Liberal party in England would have preferred one who did not throw the whole force of his genius into the losing cause of middle-age feudalism. But we must take men as they are. Here was an aristocratic self-seeker drifted over to a European shore, where he throve and showed what he could do. On the whole, we are of opinion that Lord Lyndhurst had the best of it in his migration hither. He gained more by making himself an Englishman than the English people can ever feel that they owe to him. He did some of their work very well; but he was not their friend. He will be remembered for the remarkable incidents of his history and his influence; but he is not, and never will be, regretted, except by the partisans of old English Toryism.

VII.

THE EARL OF ELGIN AND KINCARDINE.

DIED DECEMBER 12TH, 1863.

LORD ELGIN has done more in his half century of life —has, as we may say, had and enjoyed more life than most men who die at last of old age : yet it is with keen regret that his country sees his career closed twenty years before its time ; and those who have any knowledge of his personal circumstances cannot but suffer bitter pain in seeing at what sacrifice he has been fulfilling the perilous duty of governing India.

James Bruce, the eldest son of the Scotch Earl of Elgin who gave us the marbles in the British Museum, was born in 1811. Eton was his school, and Christ-church, Oxford, was his college. There must be many men now living who can remember the trio of friends associating at college, so unconscious of any peculiarity in their destiny, but preparing, in fact, to present a re-markable spectacle to the world. Bruce was the elder, a year older than the other two. Ramsay was Scotch, like Bruce ; and both were sons of earls. The third was the son of a commoner, but with reason to be as proud of his name as any other man, for his father was George Canning. No doubt these three youths all had their aspirations, and had already chosen public life for

A trio of friends.

their field of action ; but what would have been their
emotions—with what solemn feelings would they have
gazed on each other, if they could have known that they
were to be the three successive rulers of India during
the transition period of British government there !
Ramsay, as Lord Dalhousie, the last before the Mutiny ;
Canning the overruler of the Mutiny ; and Bruce, as
Lord Elgin, the first who went out as Viceroy after the
Indian Empire was brought under the government of
the Crown.   It is less than a year (11th of February
last) since Lord Elgin himself said, after presiding over
the consecration of the well at Cawnpore, "It is a
singular coincidence that three successive Governors-
General should have stood in this relationship of age
and intimacy."   He said this on occasion of the opening
of the East Indian Railway to Benares, now carried to
within a few miles of Delhi.   At the opening of a former
portion of the line, Lord Canning had proposed the
health of Lord Dalhousie ; and now Lord Elgin was
grieving over the death of his friend Canning ; and we,
in recalling what took place within this present year,
have now to mourn that the survivor of last February
is himself gone, before he had well entered upon his
task of governing India.   They co-operated well for
India, each in his day ; and their names will be remembered together in the history of that empire.   When
Canning arrived at Government House, at Calcutta,
Lord Dalhousie handed him the telegram which told
that all was going right in the newly-annexed territory
of Oude ; and Canning took care of that and all other
bequests of his predecessor, as soon as the subsidence
of the Mutiny gave him power to do so.   For his part,
in the darkest hour of doubt about the issue of the

Mutiny, he too knew what it was to have a friend and old comrade come to Government House with cheer in his face and on his lips. While the Cannings sat, brave and calm, but in utter uncertainty whether every European in India would not have been murdered within a month, Lord Elgin appeared, bringing the regiments which had been given him for his mission in

Lord Elgin's help in the Indian Mutiny.

China. Learning *en route* what was happening in India, and receiving from Lord Canning an appeal for aid, he decided to sacrifice his own object, and to diverge from his instructions, by taking his soldiers to Calcutta. Always and everywhere welcome from his genial spirit and his unfailing cheerfulness, he might well have the warmest welcome from the Cannings when he brought them the first relief in their fearful strait. When he stood, in the sight of the vast multitude, on the well at Cawnpore last winter, he had other mournful thoughts than of the victims who lay below. He and his wife had visited the grave of Lady Canning at Calcutta; and they knew that her husband was now lying in Westminster Abbey—both of them victims to the conditions of their Indian life—its diseases in the one case, and its toils and responsibilities in the other. And now, the survivor has followed—another victim, we must fear, to those toils and responsibilities.

In following out this singular bond which united the three college friends, we have passed far beyond their college days; and we must return. Each followed the path of public life which opened to him. We have here only to do with Lord Elgin's.

His earlier days.

He left Oxford adorned with honors; and a few years later he appeared in Parliament as member for Southampton. This was in 1841. In the next year he

began his long course of colonial rule by going out to
Jamaica—having by this time succeeded to his Scotch
earldom by his father's death.   He carried his young
wife out with him ; they underwent shipwreck ; and his
wife was saved only to die a year later.   The daughter
she left him was one of the bridesmaids of the Princess
of Wales.   Lord Elgin's four years' administration in
Jamaica confirmed the expectations of the Government
which had appointed him, and won the confidence of
that which succeeded it, as appears from a conversation
in the House of Lords which our readers may remember,
in which Lord Derby and Lord Grey contended for
the honor of having first appointed him to office.
It was Lord Grey who did it, while some of the first
official intercourses of the young statesman were with
Lord Derby.

[VII]
*Appointed
Governor of
Jamaica.*

In four years he was wanted to govern Canada ;
and a more arduous charge a Colonial Governor could
hardly have.   The method of responsible government
was new there ; the provinces were still reeking with the
smouldering fires of rebellion ; the repulsion of races
was at its strongest ; the deposed clique who had
virtually ruled the colony were still furious, and the
depressed section suspicious and restive.   It was just at
the time, too, when, between English and American
legislation, the Canadians were suffering from the evils
of Protection and Free-trade at once.   Believing themselves to be made sport of or neglected at home, they
were more strongly tempted to join the United States,
or at least to cross the frontier and become republican
citizens, than they ever were before, or have been since.
Lord Elgin was thoroughly aware what he was undertaking in accepting the government of a society so

*Governor-
General of
Canada.*

disturbed. He was supported in his task by domestic sympathy of a peculiar character. In the autumn of 1846 he married Lady Mary L. Lambton, the eldest surviving daughter of the Earl of Durham. She had lived in Canada during her father's short administration ; she had understood the case enough to have the warmest interest in his policy, its principle, method, and aim. As Lord Elgin's wife, she now saw that policy carried through with vigor, justice, kindliness, and success ; she fulfilled the duties which had been her mother's, as hostess and leader of society ; and she sustained her husband, as she had seen her father sustained, by intelligent sympathy. On occasion there was no little need of fortitude, as when the Parliament Houses at Montreal were burned down, in 1849. The "British party," as they styled themselves, had to yield to the conditions of impartial government, and to go into opposition when their turn came round. To them it naturally seemed as if the world was coming to an end. The Opposition, or "French party," made use of their first opportunity to obtain an indemnity for the losses of such inhabitants of Lower Canada as had suffered in property during the rebellion. The Rebellion Losses Bill passed with the approbation of all dispassionate persons ; and Lord Elgin, in giving it the requisite sanction, finished a transaction which had spread over several years, and employed the anxious care of five commissioners appointed to estimate the damages, and ascertain the innocence of the claimants of all participation in the rebellion. The "British" mob, however, stoned the carriage of the Governor-General as he left the House, and then, while members were yet sitting, broke the windows and burned the building. They met to petition the Queen for the recall of Lord Elgin on the ground that he had been favoring the claims of her Majesty's enemies ; but the better spirit prevailed in the legislature, in which a vote of confidence in the Governor-General, and attachment to the authority he represented, was carried by a large majority. It was in October of the same year that the discomfited malcontents organized an agitation for annexation to the United States, on the ground of their sufferings from the opposite trade policy of the mother country and of their nearest neighbors. Amidst these agitations Lord Elgin pursued a calm and temperate course, industriously applying himself to the development of the country and its resources, by every possible aid that he could afford to all parties. He enjoyed the confidence of each successive Colonial Secretary, as six entered upon the department, and opened correspondence with him ; and he won his way in the colony itself so effectually that his successor found the worst discontents appeased, and the internal perils of Canada at an end. So strong was the impression at home of the dignified character of his neutrality, amidst the conflicts of extreme parties, that some surprise and amusement were caused by his speech at the banquet which was given in his honor, on his return in 1855. Perhaps it was the first time for many years that he had been able to speak as a man speaks at home and among friends ; certainly he was a man of a frank, genial temper ; and, when he spoke at all, he said exactly what he thought. But he was not a rash or intemperate speaker. In his most frank, fluent, and lively utterances he said nothing which he had any reason afterward to regret. This character of his oratory was at once

[VII]

Approval of his administration by the Canadian Legislature.

Effects of his government.

[VII]

Informal manner of his speeches.

appreciated at Calcutta, contrasting as it did with the reserve of his two predecessors. While men there were full of astonishment at the informal and friendly character of the first public address of the new Viceroy, acute observers remarked that there were no indiscreet disclosures in the speech, nothing that need be wished unsaid; and nothing, therefore, that was undignified. In the event, the frankness won confidence and good-will with singular rapidity, both from Europeans and natives, while experience taught them that there were more kinds of dignity than one ; and that to command deference equal to that shown to Lord Dalhousie and Lord Canning, it was not necessary to have their reserve of temper and unbending style of manner.

But between Canada and India were interposed singular scenes of political life. In 1857 Lord Elgin

His embassy to China.

was sent to China, to try what could be done to repair, or to turn to the best account, the mischiefs done by Sir John Bowring's course, and by the patronage of it at home, in the face of the moral reprobation of the people at large. We all remember his success, and the openings which he achieved for the commerce of Europe. With the same energy which determined him to make an opportunity to study the American Republic before he left Canada, he now resolved to learn for himself what he could about China as it is. He went up the

His explo-rations and observations there.

great river to Hankow, studying the country and people as he went, and bringing home narratives and impressions which showed his friends, better than any diplomatic transactions ever can, how true and generous were his sympathies with the simple people of that vast empire, under the perils and sufferings of its decay. He was quick to detect any common ground of instinct or feeling—moral or other—between the people whom we usually treat with ridicule and ourselves. Amidst his keen enjoyment of the fine scenery of the Yang-tse-kiang, some of which warmed his heart by its resemblance to his own Scotch Highlands, his eye and his mind were everywhere, discerning indications of manners, and reflecting on the uses to be made of new opportunities. He learned lessons both by being attacked and by being courted by the imperialist and rebel people along the river. Whenever his ship grounded he was presently exploring on shore, amidst fields or villages, or entering solitary houses wherever a welcome was offered. In the same spirit of activity he went up the hills and followed up the valleys of the island of Formosa, using every hour he could command, wherever he went, in learning everything within reach of the country and people whom he was endeavoring to connect with his own in intercourse and good feeling. What he did in Japan is at this hour the foundation of the hope of many of us who would otherwise give up all idea of any sort of Japanese alliance or reciprocity. Lord Elgin was no visionary. His quick sympathies and cheerful views did not impair his good sense, or dim the impressions of his experience. He was not the man to go and see the Japanese in a fit of glamor, and come home and report of them in a paroxysm of enthusiasm. As he, a man of long-proved good sense, moderation, tact, and vigilant conscience, believed that Britain and Japan might and ought to be a blessing to each other, many of us hold on to the hope, notwithstanding all that has come to pass since he was there. It is true, he may not have supposed possible such an act as the destruction of Kagosima—an act which could

[VII]

His diplomacy in Japan.

[VII]

never have been proposed in his presence, or under his management; but still — considering his acuteness of insight into character, and his practical judgment and experience—it is rational perhaps to believe that, managed as he would have managed it, our intercourse with Japan may yet be what he suggested and believed he foresaw.

What he saw of China and the Chinese on his first visit enabled him to appreciate the extent of what he gained by his negotiation better than anybody at home, outside of the circle of merchant princes, could appreciate it. It could not be expected that the world should believe on the instant that China really was thrown open to the European commerce, or that the value of the change should be at once understood. The merchants

*Acknow-
ledgment of
his services
in the City.*

of London, however, did themselves honor by the thoroughness of their acknowledgment of Lord Elgin's services. Those who were witnesses of the presentation to Lord Elgin of the freedom of the City saw him in one of the happiest hours of his life. He was not a man who required the stimulus of praise, or even sympathy, to keep him to his work. He loved work for its own sake, and of course for its appropriate and special results; and he would have worked on for life, appreciated or overlooked; but he whose sympathies were always ready and warm himself enjoyed being understood and valued: and that welcome in the City was very cheering to him after his long experience of English indifference about Canada and what he had done there.

*Again sent
to China.*

He held the office of Postmaster-General till the hostile acts of the Chinese Government toward the English and French ministers in China rendered it

necessary that Lord Elgin should go out again, and [VII]
accomplish the indispensable object of opening Pekin
to our diplomatists, as ports and rivers had been opened
to our merchants.   To secure this, and to obtain repa-
ration for the recent insult to the European ministers,
was the errand of Lord Elgin and Baron Gros, who
went out together, early in 1860, while forces were
gathering in China, to accompany them up to Pekin.
Lord Elgin had had but too much experience of ship- *Ship-*
wreck before ; and now he had it again, when their ship, *wrecked in*
Galle har-
the *Malabar*, was lost upon a reef in Galle harbor.   In *bor.*
the midst of the terror and confusion on board, and
while the fate of all in the ship was utterly uncertain,
the two ambassadors sat together, tranquil and cheerful ;
their calm courage assisting materially in restoring order
and saving life.   They refused to enter the boats till all
the other passengers were landed ; and a few minutes
after they and their suites left the ship's side she sank.
Not only the decorations and state dresses of the ambassadors, but their credentials went to the bottom,
whence they were fished up by divers.   If this had not
been possible, the whole course of affairs in China might
have been different, through the delay caused by waiting
for fresh credentials, and the consequent loss of the
season in the Chinese seas.   As it was, the plenipotentiaries arrived off the Peiho, ready for their work, in
July.   By November their work was done.   The
convention was signed at Pekin on the 24th of October,
and ratified on the 5th of November.

One of the favoring circumstances of the mission *His*
was the cordial understanding which existed throughout *thorough*
co-operation
between the British and French ambassadors.   If they *with Baron*
had been short of friendly, fatal mischief might have *Gros.*

arisen **out of the dangerous conjunction** of the military forces **of the two countries. We know** something of what **happened about the sack of the** Summer Palace, and **on other** occasions of collision. **But** the two ambassadors prevented all **serious mischief** by their mutual confidence, their united **action, and the** generous **prudence and** silence **with which they treated** passing **vexations.** Lord Elgin was **the very** man for such a **function** of conciliation ; and especially where France is **concerned.** In him were united some of the highest characteristics of both **nations. If in** his unconscious **courage, his steadfastness of** purpose, his idea and habit of domestic life, and the nature of his political ambition, he was altogether **a Briton,** he might have **been** a Frenchman for his **gayety of temper, his incessant** activity, **and his quick and ready tact and** sympathies.

Results of his mission to China.

His mission **required a cultivation of French** good-will, as **much, perhaps, as of Chinese confidence** ; and he **succeeded thoroughly with both. He** returned, as **sensible as ever to the shock of** the failure of his first **expedition, which he had always pointed** out as the **probable consequence of** his being vexatiously prevented from going **up to** Pekin ; but now satisfied that his work was realy and effectually done. Not only was English diplomacy established in Pekin, but a genuine intercourse was carried on with the Government **of China.** Lord Elgin was in no way responsible **for our former** doings in China, **nor for the position in which** they left us. The duty **of raising our relations with** that empire to a higher, firmer, **and more open ground** must be done ; he undertook **it, and there** seems **to be no** question on any hand that he did it well. He **and** his coadjutor, Baron Gros, certainly left a strong impression behind them of their frank wisdom and scrupulous honor, as men and as plenipotentiaries.

[VII]

Appointed Viceroy of India.

Even before his arrival at home early in 1861, he was fixed upon by the public expectation as the successor of Lord Canning in India. It was never without a pang that his wife heard of this; and her dread of that appointment never relaxed. As for him, he prepared for his new work with his characteristic alacrity, and was ready with the personal sacrifices which were a matter of course with him when duty required them. There were four young sons to be left behind; and this was not all. At Christmas, 1846, he had left his bride at home, to spare her the worst cold of Canada; and now he left his wife behind, to spare her the extreme heat of India. Together they visited the Queen at Osborne, in the first weeks of her widowhood—a circumstance which may now be dwelt on with a true though mournful satisfaction: and then the husband and father went on alone. His boys had seen him for the last time. His wife and little daughter went out to him as soon as permitted, in November of last year. Before she reached him he had been ill—from the Calcutta atmosphere, of course. It was soon evident that, if he was to remain at all fit for work, he must (as every new comer must) avoid Calcutta, and "wander about," as carping observers say, or contrive to get meetings of the Council in some central place where Europeans can both live and work. For the summer he went to the Hills, according to custom; and it was at Simla that he received the news of the death of his third son—a fine boy of ten. This was something more than the first break in the happy family circle. It shook all confidence about the rest, during the long years of separation yet to be fulfilled.

[VII]

When the necessity for moving came, the effect of travelling in the hill ranges was salutary. The splendors of nature there were at once rousing and soothing; and it is a satisfaction now to think what his latest pleasures were. It has been suggested that the ascent of the Jilauri pass, 13,000 feet above the plains, may have been fatally injurious to him; but those about him spoke of him as well at a later time. The spectacle of the vast icy range, as seen between the openings of mountains loftier than we ever see, gratified in the highest degree his love of natural beauty; and it is a consolation to think that such was the picture which was last received into his mind, and that it remains in the heart of her whose friendship was the best blessing of his life.

They were on their way to other and very different scenes of grandeur. We know what the great assemblage in the Northwest Provinces was to be, over which he was to preside. We turn away from the thought of it now. His death puts away the whole pageant, and even the serious interests implicated with it, to the furthest horizon of our imagination. We can attend only to what is nearest, and especially to the thought of the enormous sacrifice at which the service of such men is obtained for the nation to which they belong. It cannot be said that, but for his toils, his exposure to many climates, and his overwhelming responsibilities, Lord Elgin might have not lived to the natural period of the life of man. As it is, he is gone at fifty-two. When we think of the young daughters, of the boys deprived of him just when arriving at the need of his care, and of other interests, private and public, we feel as if there must be crime somewhere, that such sacrifices have been repeated so often. It seems scarcely

His premature death.

possible to say more than has been long and often said about the perils of Calcutta. We know that the mere climate of India is not dangerous, but that there is in Calcutta, and in almost every station, an assemblage of every evil condition, which requires only the application of heat to be rendered murderous. The highest functionaries cannot altogether escape these conditions; and they have, besides, their perils of overwork and anxiety. In such a position a man may die without any one of the four or five maladies which carry off thousands of our soldiers and civilians there. Any predisposition may be fatally wrought upon; the weakest part of the frame gives way; and another great man goes down early to his grave.

There rest now the three friends—living so much the same life with such different qualities and powers, charged finally with the same great duty and destiny, and dying the same death. In the noble line of rulers of India they will, in their order, form a group of singular interest, standing on the boundary-line of the old and the new systems of Indian rule. Thus they will always be remembered together, and regarded as apart.

[VII]

Similarity in the career of three Viceroys.

VIII.

THE DUKE OF NEWCASTLE.

Died October 18th, 1864.

His death a political misfortune.

No statesman of our time has won a more universal respect and regard than the Duke of Newcastle ; and few Ministers of any period could be more missed and mourned than he will be by good citizens of all parties and ways of thinking. That such a Minister should be cut off before we began to think of age in connection with him, and when we might have hoped for a dozen or twenty years' more public service from him, is one of the grave political misfortunes which every generation has to bear in its turn. Each generation knows what it is to suffer that sinking and heaviness of the heart which is caused by the news that the admired statesman or the trusted minister is struck down by disease—lost in political or actual death. Living men can recall but too many of such calamities ; and if there was a stronger shock in the case of Canning, and a deeper anguish in that of Peel, there could never have been a sincerer or more general concern throughout England than when the announcement spread that the Duke of Newcastle had sustained an attack which must close his public career, and could not allow him a much longer term of life. Still, hope will linger ; and we were unwilling to acquiesce in having lost him till his death showed us that we ought not to have desired him to live after the usefulness, which was the desire of his life, was at an end.

We need not describe his father. We all remember the Duke of Newcastle who had no doubts about doing what he would with his own. His son was old enough when that was said to be strongly impressed by the sensation it made. To have originated a good proverb is as high an honor as can befall a man ; and in this singular case of having started a saying so monstrous as to have become a proverb, the disgrace could not but be deeply felt by any son and heir of the name. There is no judging how much of the late Minister's characteristic consideration of other men's rights, and modesty about his own, may have been owing to the impressions he early derived from the national reception of his father's claims upon his tenants, in their political capacity.

His father.

The late Duke, Henry Pelham Clinton, Lord Lincoln by courtesy, was born in 1811. His early characteristics seemed to have been the same as those the world now knows so well. At Eton and Christ-church he manifested the sound, substantial, but not brilliant quality of mind which made him for thirty years one of the most useful of public servants. He was a remarkable illustration of the operation of the moral on the intellectual nature. It was his conscientious activity, his moral energy, that set his faculties to work, at all times, and wherever he went ; and it was his personal disinterestedness, his public spirit, his power of subordinating his own feelings to other people's interests which enabled him to keep his faculties at work, in defiance of discouragements which would have daunted many a man of higher original

His early character-istics.

16

[VIII]

Sir Robert Peel's political band.

capacity. It was probably on account of these moral qualities that Sir Robert Peel adopted Lord Lincoln, as he did Sidney Herbert, into his political band. The young man entered upon office at three-and-twenty, on the first opportunity that occurred. He was made a Lord of the Treasury during the short Administration of Sir Robert Peel, from December, 1834, to the next April. He had then been in Parliament two years, sitting for South Nottinghamshire. During the interval till the return of Sir Robert Peel to power in September, 1841, Lord Lincoln won upon the expectation of the House and the notice of the country, so that when his opportunity arrived, he scarcely answered to the idea formed of him. His ability and his reach of political view were as yet in no proportion to his activity and readiness; and that activity and readiness were easily mistaken for self-sufficiency in a man yet so young. He was only First Commissioner of Inland Revenue; and he could hardly show what was in him to any one but his chief and master. Peel understood him rightly, and by his support enabled him to become what we have since seen.

Appointed Chief Secretary for Ireland.

In January, 1846, he seemed to have obtained scope to show what he could do in real statesmanship. He became Chief Secretary for Ireland; but the Ministry went out in July, on the discomfiture of their Coercion Bill for Ireland, which was understood to be an act of vengeance caused by the repeal of the Corn Laws. During the five years more that he remained in the Commons, as member for the Falkirk boroughs, because his father spoiled his chances in his own county of Nottingham, he was one of Sir Robert Peel's most trusted lieutenants, and one of the securities that a Peel party would exist which, however small in numbers, should

compensate by its character for some of the dangers
attending the disintegration of parties which the policy
of its chief had necessarily effected.   From time to
time, Lord Lincoln showed that he was not idle, though
in opposition, and, as all the world knew, unhappy in
the domestic relations in which, of all men, he seemed
the most likely to deserve and obtain happiness.   His
marriage in 1832 had issued in great misery, and he
obtained a divorce in 1850.   His father's treatment of
him was the world's wonder for hardness and absurdity
of wrath, considering that the ground of parental displeasure was merely difference of political opinion.
Lord Lincoln worked away at such work as he could
find or make, keeping silence on his filial injuries—about
which, indeed, the Duke took care that the public should
be sufficiently informed by himself.   One of the ablest
speeches made by Lord Lincoln in this interval was
in 1847, on emigration from Ireland as a means of relief
during and after the famine, and the disorganization of
affairs which it must occasion.   While witnessing such
an emigration as is going on at this day, we ought to
remember how sorely such a relief was needed and
desired when the Irish were far greater in numbers and
far poorer in food and work than now.

At the beginning of 1851 Lord Lincoln succeeded
to the dukedom, and left the House of Parliament in
which he had laid the groundwork of the general expectation of good service from him.   The next year introduced him at last to such office as would show what he
could do.   He became Colonial Secretary under Lord
Aberdeen at the close of 1852, little imagining what
responsibilities and labors he was undertaking.   The
charge and government of half a hundred colonies

[VIII]

*Unhappi-
ness in his
domestic re-
lations.*

*Succeeds to
the duke-
dom.*

*Made
Colonial
Secretary.*

[VIII]

has long been considered an absurdly onerous task for one member of an administration ; but to this was in those days added the virtual management of war in its distant operation.   When war with Russia was declared in March, 1854, the Duke was relieved of his colonial duties, which were undertaken by Sir George Grey ; and

Appointed Secretary for War.

the new Secretaryship for War was filled by the Duke. We all remember but too well what followed—the suffering and mortality among our troops in the East, and the too natural popular impression that the War Ministers must be to blame, and the wrath, and cavil, and ostentatious disparagement with which those two men—the Duke and his friend Sidney Herbert—were

The Crimean War.

treated, while they were working their frames and faculties day and night as few men have worked before, and effecting achievements in the mere neutralizing of other men's blunders and deficiencies, which from another point of view would have excited admiration and gratitude.   It was not their fault that our soldiers suffered and died ; and it was their doing that many more did

His speech on resigning office.

not perish.   No speech of the Duke is probably so well remembered as that which he delivered at the opening of the session of 1855, in which he made a clean breast of it in resigning his office of Minister for War.   He was deeply moved himself, and he moved everybody else.   Nobody after that speech thought of imputing to him indolence, indifference, levity, &c., which had been here and there heard of before ; but still there was something said of incapacity.   This charge he had noticed with the others, saying the only thing that a sensible man can say on that personal charge —that he was the last man who could discuss it, and that the question must be left to time.   He made some brief and modest disclosures of his toil and anxiety, and of the special interest he had in the good conduct of the war, from two sons of his own being in the army and navy. These won him much sympathy; but the interest amounted to enthusiasm when he declared, in his honest way, that the greatest relief and pleasure he could have would be in the better fortune of his successor, whoever he might be, in his official achievements, and his enjoyment of that national confidence and sympathy which he himself had failed to obtain. Now, under the emotion of the hour, his colleagues began to bear testimony to his official merits; but it was too late. The conduct of the war was to be inquired into; and the Duke's continuance in office could not be proposed to him.

[VIII]

The emotion produced by the speech.

As soon as he was at liberty to go abroad, he went to the Crimea and the Black Sea, to examine into many things that can only be taken on credit at home. The proceeding was to himself the most natural thing in the world; but it did him good at home. His mind was wont to dwell on subjects which he had been led or compelled to study. He moved Parliament on Irish Emigration, after having ceased to be Chief Secretary in Ireland; he moved Parliament on Vancouver's Island and the Hudson's Bay Company, after having ceased to be Colonial Secretary; and now, he went to the East, to explore the scenes of the war, after having given up his charge of its concerns. The people at home, however, saw in this something which rebuked their hasty judgment. The late Minister did not keep himself before the public eye, asserting his capacity, and justifying his methods. He quietly went away, to learn what he could, on the very spot where he must be convinced of his

His travels in the East.

own errors, if he had really committed them. Mean-time, Lord Panmure was not slow to do the requisite justice to his predecessor. He lost no opportunity of testifying to the admirable state in which he found the Department, and producing the evidences of wisdom and skill, as well as zeal and devotedness, which he had found there. The faults had taken deep root before the Duke's time ; and any man—even a heaven-born Minis-ter—must have found them insuperable in the first year of a war, after a peace of forty years. It is a testimony due to the Minister for War of ten years ago to say that after all that has been done, there is more still yet to do, from the obstructive and perverse power of the Horse Guards overriding the War Office.

The Duke joined Lord Palmerston's Cabinet in June, 1859, in the midst of the excitement of the Italian war. He was again Colonial Secretary, as he was till his final resignation. It was in this capacity that he was naturally chosen to attend the Prince of Wales in his Canadian travels ; but, apart from that particular fitness, he was the very man to discharge the office of temporary guardian in so responsible a case. There is no need to describe to the existing generation what the guardian's qualities were found to be on a trial so unusual and so stringent. Political wisdom and firmness were requisite, as well as the sense, temper, and manners needed in the guide, friend, and companion of the young heir to the throne. It is enough to mention the Orangemen of Canada to show what this means. As to his manage-ment of his share of the American intercourses, it is not too much to say that the disposition to peace be-tween the two countries may owe as much to the exem-plification the Duke presented of the English gentleman

*Again ap-
pointed
Colonial
Secretary,
and accom-
panies the
Prince of
Wales to
America.*

and statesman as to the genial and hospitable temper
with which the American people welcomed and entertained the Prince and his guardian.

Some of our first thoughts, in losing so untimely such
a statesman and citizen as the Duke of Newcastle, are
with the Prince of Wales. It seems as if he, on reaching
manhood, was fated to lose his best and most needed
personal friends. He has lost his father, and General
Bruce, his Governor ; and now the guardian and companion of his first travels. Perhaps it is thoroughly
true of them all, that they died prematurely from being
worn out. In any position this would probably have
been the fate of the Duke of Newcastle ; and, as he
was a statesman, it was sure to be so. Statesmanship
allows no option—no sanitary security—to earnest and
conscientious men ; and when, as in the present case,
there is a natural tendency to hard work to start from,
there is really no escape from that form of patriotic
martyrdom. This is not one of the pupil's dangers.
He has nothing to beware of in regard to the causes
to which his teachers and guardians have fallen victims.
His part is to feel the nobleness of such self-denial and
devotedness as theirs, and the seriousness of the work
of government, when not only the functions concerned
in it, but the work of training rulers, and carrying on
the unseen business of the Sovereign's home and family,
may call for the sacrifice of valuable lives.

Those who were personally acquainted with the Duke
of Newcastle must ever feel that the impression he made
on them was more peculiar than can be easily accounted
for from his type of character ; and yet those who did
not know him may truly believe that with the mind's
eye they see him very much as he was. Frank, honest

His type of character.

[VIII]

[VIII] unassuming, with a genuine sense of human equality always overriding any consciousness—or rather remembrance—of his rank, hereditary or official, he was easy to know and to understand from afar. Those who were nearest to him were subject to frequent surprises from his simplicity, his unconcealable conscientiousness, and abiding sense of fellowship with all sincere people, whoever they might be. As a nobleman of aristocratic England, he was in this way a great blessing and a singularly useful example. When we think of his candor in his place in Parliament, his diligence, and ever-growing knowledge, and practised sense in his department, and the national confidence he had thus won, we feel that the public loss is irreparable. He never was and never would have been a great political philosopher, or sage, or leader. That was not in his line. But while we need no less a staunch upholder of the natural and honorable welfare of our country, a patriotic promoter of its dignity and lustre, and a devoted servant of the Commonwealth, from the Sovereign on the throne to the poorest adventurer landing in a distant colony, we shall miss and mourn the late Duke of Newcastle, and anxiously watch the rising generations of "the governing classes," to see if we may hope for more like him.

IX.

THE EARL OF CARLISLE.

DIED DECEMBER 5TH, 1864.

THE Earl of Carlisle lies dead at Castle Howard. Such regret as is felt at the departure of this nobleman is something rare in the case of a man who has not rendered himself necessary to his country by his statesmanship, nor commanded homage by his genius, nor established or continued a great family. George William Frederick Howard, who was born in 1802, the *His birth,* eldest of the twelve children of the sixth Earl of Carlisle, *1802.* filled no higher political office than that of Lord Lieutenant of Ireland, was never married, and left no great enduring work behind him to make him known to future generations, or to illustrate his own time ; yet the sorrow, the enthusiasm for the man, the recoil from the thought of his death, which were manifested when he became virtually dead to society, were such as the greatest statesmen, and the heads of the noblest households of sons and daughters, might covet. It was his exquisite moral *His moral* nature, together with the charm of intercourse which *qualities.* grew out of it, which created this warm affection in all who approached him ; and through them the rest of the world received the impression of a man of rare virtue being among them—of singular nobleness of spirit, and

16*

gentleness of temper, and sympathy as modest as it was keen and constant. His function in the world of statesmanship seemed to be to represent and sustain the highest magnanimity, devotedness, and benevolence, properly distinctive of that which is called "the governing class" in this country. He could not overawe by commanding ability, or by power of will; but nothing ungenerous or flippant could be said in his presence; and he saw men and things in a brighter light than others do—less through any optimism of his own than because his own presence raised and refined everybody about him. It is an encouraging thing, we sometimes say, that all of us can tell of somebody that is not only the best person we have ever known, but the best that we can believe to be in the world. This is a pleasing evidence of the commonness of a high order of goodness. Common as it is, we believe that, among those who were personal observers of Lord Carlisle, every one of them would probably say that he was one of the best men they had ever known.

His introduction into public life. His father was himself in public life, and early introduced his son into it. The son of the Lord Privy Seal of that day entered Parliament as member for Morpeth. He had distinguished himself at Eton and Oxford, whence he brought away prizes and honors, and that love of literature which was to the end of his life his refuge and refreshment under the pressure of State cares. He had a near view of official life when his father was in the Cabinet first, and in Ireland just before the passage of the Reform Bill; and he was first heard of *Made Irish Secretary.* in that career when he was Secretary under Lord Ebrington's administration of Ireland. That was the time when a hearty and sustained attempt was made to regenerate Ireland by the very best order of government —by absolute justice and impartiality, together with such considerateness and helpfulness as the dependent quality of the Irish mind required. Lords Ebrington and Normanby (the latter then Lord Mulgrave) each answered to the ideal of a popular Viceroy; and Lord Morpeth was supposed to supply the substance of good government while his chief was engrossing the public eye and haranguing the public ear. In course of time it became understood that it was Mr. Drummond who inspired into the administration of Ireland the vigor which distinguished the period, and which had disposed the English public to see in Lord Morpeth a reserve of future statesmanship for the service of the Imperial government. But though Thomas Drummond was really the great man to whom Ireland owed the best government ever seen there, Lord Morpeth was excellent in his post, and more equal to cope with Orangemen, as Orangemen were then, than anybody had suspected. It was in his time that Mr. Drummond's saying about property having its duties as well as its rights was regarded by Irish landlords as a revolutionary manifesto; and he stoutly supported the new and strange doctrine of his friend. It was Lord Morpeth who signified to Colonel Verner, the representative of the Orangemen in Parliament, his removal from his office of Deputy Lieutenant of Tyrone, for giving the toast of "The Battle of the Diamond" at an election dinner. On such occasions the reasons were given very fully, and the tone was always dignified and courteous; but the rage of the Protestant zealots when they found that not only poor men were dismissed from their humble offices for rampant Orangeism, but that the most powerful leaders of the faction were dealt with

His dealings with Orangemen.

[IX]

in precisely the same manner, exceeded all bounds.
Their hatred to the Government found expression every
day, in all sorts of provoking ways; but they encountered
in the members of the Administration not only good
manners, but a spirit as bold as their own, and much
more manly.   In the short time between 1838 and 1841
Lord Morpeth established such relations between the
Irish people and himself as forecasted his future destination, and theirs, as far as it depended on him.   It was
the Government of which he formed a part which fairly
tried the experiment—regarded at the time as too rash
—of ruling Ireland by the power of the ordinary law,
agitated as was the country from a variety of causes,
and especially by the mortification and wrath of the
Orange faction after the exposure of their designs in
England, on behalf of the Duke of Cumberland, in the
prospect of the female succession which everybody else
supposed to have been settled past dispute.

In 1841 he went out of office, together with the whole
Whig Administration.   One of the imputations on the
outgoing Ministry of Lord Melbourne was its ill-treat-
ment of Lord Plunket at the instigation of Lord
Campbell—then Sir John Campbell, Attorney-General.
The restless, ambitious, intriguing "Plain John Campbell" coveted the Irish Chancellorship; and Lord
Plunket was to be the sacrifice.   The attempt, with other
mistakes, brought down the Ministry, and the Irish col-
The election in 1841. leagues of Lord Plunket among the rest.   None who
can look back to 1841 can have forgotten the sweep
that was made at the election of that summer among
the supporters of the Whig Ministry and its policy.
O'Connell himself was thrown out at Dublin, and Sir
De Lacy Evans at Westminster; but the strongest sen-

sation of dismay on the one side and of triumph on the other was created by the defeat of the present Earl Grey, then Lord Howick, in Northumberland, and of Lord Morpeth and Lord Milton in the West Riding.

[IX]

There are many Yorkshiremen who say at this day that Lord Morpeth's speech after his defeat has never been equalled in the history of elections. Some of us who did not hear the address, but only read the Report of it, are almost disposed, even while reminded of Burke at Bristol, to agree to anything that the actual hearers can say. It was a natural occasion for the magnanimity of the man to appear; and its effect on the election crowd was just what it was every day on those who lived in its presence. The feeling of many hearers was that it was a happier thing to endure a defeat, even of a ministerial policy, in such a spirit of enlightenment and philosophy, than to enjoy the most unexpected triumph, merely as a triumph.

Lord Morpeth's defeat.

Released from office, Lord Morpeth seized his opportunity for travel. He went to the United States and the West Indies; and thus, besides contemplating society generally in those regions, he studied slavery, slaveholders, and abolitionists to great advantage. Antislavery opinions and sentiments were at that time in deep disrepute in the United States: they were "vulgar;" and those who held them were not noticed in society, and were insulted and injured as often as possible by genteeler people and more complaisant republicans. On Lord Morpeth's arrival he saw at once how matters stood, and he acted accordingly. He made no secret of his own anti-slavery opinions; and he formed friendships with the leading abolitionists at least as readily as with anybody else. It happened that the

His travels.

His conduct in America.

(then) annual Anti-slavery assemblage, to hold its Fair, took place, on the part of Massachusetts, while Lord Morpeth was at Boston. To the astonishment of "the *élite* of intellectual Boston," as they called themselves, Lord Morpeth went to that Fair every day, and stayed a long while. In no other way, perhaps, could he have done so much good without doing any harm. Now that the whole people of the North, genteel or otherwise, are anti-slavery, it is remembered that Lord Carlisle, the friend of the North in its struggle for national existence, did what he could twenty years before to warn the citizens of the retribution which they were incurring by their wrong course on the Slavery question. What seemed in him fanaticism or whim at the time, they now see to have been a wisdom which it was not for them to despise.

Again enters the Cabinet. In 1846, Lord Morpeth entered the Cabinet with Lord Russell's Administration. His office was the Woods and Forests; and he presently after succeeded Lord Campbell as Chancellor of the Duchy of Lancaster. In the next year he became Lord Lieutenant of the East Riding of Yorkshire, on his father's resignation of the *Succeeds to the earldom.* office; and in yet another year he succeeded to his father's title and the possession of Castle Howard. He was looked on with some wonder and curiosity by certain of his peers when he entered the Upper House, because he had been a subscriber to the fund of the Anti-Corn Law League. That act had been regarded at the moment as the strongest evidence which had then appeared of the power and security of the movement. Our readers may perhaps remember the efforts that were made to explain away or discredit the fact of Lord Morpeth having joined the League. Some said that the money was in fact for the purchase of votes ; and others scoffed at so paltry a subscription as five pounds. It may be remembered how he, poor in purse, but rich in good-humor, noticed these insults, saying in his speech that if he had been buying favor by his donation, his enemies must at least allow that he had got it cheap. In a little while he had nothing more to do with elections ; but he appeared a dreadful revolutionist to some of the Lords for his share in the repeal of the Corn Laws.

His connection with the Anti-Corn Law League.

In February, 1855, on the change of ministry at the end of the war, he went to Ireland as Lord Lieutenant. It was a time of severe trial to Government. During the Crimean war the gallantry of the Queen's Irish soldiers won honor for themselves, and sweetened the temper of their friends ; and when they returned home, and local festivals were instituted in their honor, it really seemed as if political and religious feuds were forgotten in the patriotic emotions of the hour. But the good understanding did not last long. In September, 1857, the Belfast riots took place, which never ceased to astonish us till those of 1864 eclipsed them. It is remarkable that in 1857 the outbreak was preceded by the erection of a statue of O'Connell in Limerick. As it was the first monumental honor paid to him during the ten years since his death, it excited a strong sensation. The quarrelsomeness of July had also been very lively that year, so that all was ready for an outbreak, even in a prosperous and enlightened place like Belfast, when a few Protestant preachers obstinately refused to leave off preaching in the streets, in the face of the plainest and most fearful risks. The Government placed the town under the Crime and Outrage

Appointed Lord Lieutenant of Ireland.

Unsettled state of the country. .

[IX]

[IX]

Act, and issued a Commission to inquire into the causes of the riots. It was of no great use, as the arms were put where they could be easily got at; and the investigation of the nature of the mischief did nothing toward curing it. The Executive gained no force; and the amount of murder perpetrated in the latter months of that year tried the courage of every member of the

Succeeded by Lord Eglinton.

Government. To such cares Lord Eglinton succeeded in 1858, when the Derby Ministry came in. There was some idea that the office of Lord Lieutenant would be abolished at that time; and the proposal to that effect discussed in Parliament was negatived amidst expressions of belief, on all hands, that Ireland must ere long be governed by a Secretary of State. Lord Carlisle was, however, to be Viceroy again. He used the interval of his being out of office to travel in the East; and on his return he published his "Diary in Greek and Turkish Waters."

Again appointed Viceroy of Ireland.

In the summer of 1859 he resumed the Viceroyalty, with Mr. Cardwell as Chief Secretary, on Lord Palmerston's return to power. Ireland had been prosperous under a series of fine seasons; and there was hope of a diminution of crime—of the crime which recedes or gains ground according to the welfare or suffering of the agricultural population. But there was now a succession of bad agricultural years to be gone through, and the condition of the people was more obviously declining from 1860 to 1863 than at any time since the famine

His labors to develop the resources of the country.

and fever. Lord Carlisle devoted his efforts to improve the agriculture of the country. By exhibitions, by central and local meetings, by every aid that his presence, his eloquence, and his earnest support could give, he tried to give a wise direction to the spirit, and the capital, and industry of the country, during three years of disheartening adversity and decline. When these were over, and fine weather brought good crops to light once more, the small farmers and the better order of laborers were leaving the country as fast as they could. Lord Carlisle stoutly and indefatigably maintained that the emigration, painful as it was to witness, was unavoidable under the relative conditions of the United States and Ireland ; and that it was, under these circumstances, a benefit to those who re- mained behind, as well as to those who went forth. He had the most necessary qualification for a ruler of Ireland in his indomitable hopefulness.

His views on the exodus.

All other Irish interests had his good-will and best assistance, as well as agriculture. He watched over the Queen's Colleges, and the course of the National Schools, and the increase of manufactures, and their introduction into all the provinces. His hospitality, and the genial cheerfulness of his Court and society, were all that the discontented could lay hold of in the way of complaint or ridicule : but in Ireland popularity is a real governing power ; and as long as nothing better is sacri- ficed to it, it is a power in the hands of an accomplished and cheerful-tempered man which he has no right to neglect or despise. Nothing that was done and enjoyed at the Castle impaired the spirit of the Executive in dealing with the rancor of bigots, or the insolence of factious magistrates, or the outrages of agrarian conspi- rators. Lord Carlisle's reign was not signalized—any more than former viceregal terms—by success in extir- pating Ribbon Societies, and in fortifying the loyalty of the rural population to the law : but there were no special causes in the Viceroy or his course of policy or manners to blame for this. He was unable to do what nobody has been able to do yet, and what will probably be done at last by other agencies than that of any one man, or set of men in office. The charge against him was that he governed Ireland by words—by speechification. The question is, how far is it requisite for a good ruler of Ireland to be eloquent; and it may be remarked that after 1829, O'Connell himself did nothing for Ireland but speak, though he had the mind and heart of Ireland thus under his hand.

When the hoped-for change in the fortunes of Ireland set in—when the crops improved, and the farmers began to recover their means, and the emigration showed signs of slackening,—Lord Carlisle's connection with Ireland was dissolving. During the early part of this year speech was becoming difficult to him, through a partial paralysis, which did not show itself otherwise. He had engaged to preside at the Tercentenary Shakspere Festival at Stratford-on-Avon; but when April arrived his physicians remonstrated against his purpose of fulfilling his engagement. It did appear hazardous in the extreme to put to risk his scarcely recovered powers of speech; but the festival seemed to be in danger of failure, several pledged visitors had drawn back, and he was resolved not to fail. There are many who can testify what his address was, in matter and manner. The archbishop by his side—Archbishop Trench—an anxious listener, declared afterward that Lord Carlisle's speech was not only as good, but as finely delivered, as any he had ever heard from him. Others who were unaware how critical was the occasion, were of the same opinion. The effort seemed to have no bad effect. He returned to Dublin better rather than worse. After a time, however, the

Presides at the Ter-centenary Shakspere Festival.

affection returned; and the whole right side became paralyzed. He was in this state when the O'Connell Statue celebration occurred in Dublin, and the consequent faction-fight took place in the form of the Belfast riots. Severe reflections were uttered, in private and in print, about Lord Carlisle's absence at such a time. To be sure it was "for his health," as duly announced; but a man's health should wait on such a crisis as that was. While such things were said Lord Carlisle was at Castle Howard, helpless and dumb; not only speechless, but unable to hold the pen. His public life was closed. He would never speak again, and he would never again be seen in Ireland, or anywhere out of his own home.

[IX]
His serious illness.

His private life, however, had never been more beautiful and beloved than now. Instead of the irritability and depression which usually accompany the disease, even where the intellect remains unaffected, there was in him a serenity, and even cheerfulness, as unmistakable as the clearness of his mind. He was as willing as ever to receive what others said, without manifesting any harassing need to reply. His drives, in the fine autumn days, among the woods at Castle Howard, were a keen pleasure to him as he watched the changing beauty of their foliage. Sad as it was, his decline was so much less grievous and terrible than it must have been in a man of a lower moral nature that it was endurable even to those who loved him best. When it became known that his career was closed, the echoes of his old eloquence must have awakened in many minds;—in the minds of the West Riding electors who had heard his best-remembered speech; of the Leeds mechanics, to whom he had spoken as a lecturer on Pope; and of the Americans and the Irish, to whom he had spoken frankly

His last days at Castle Howard.

[IX]   and affectionately on the interests of their country ; and finally, of the lovers of Shakspere, who heard his last public utterances, and could perceive through them how much poetry had contributed to the happiness of a thoroughly cheerful life. Literature was indeed a solace and delight to him from the opening of his reason, through all the labors and trials of life, and at last in his decline, when all but mental pleasures had become extinct for him.

He will not be remembered as a great statesman ; but the tradition of him will remain as of the best and most beloved man in the company of statesmen of his day and generation.

X.

LORD PALMERSTON.

DIED OCTOBER 18TH, 1865.

HENRY JOHN TEMPLE, known since the age of eighteen as Lord Viscount Palmerston, was born in October, 1784, at the family seat of Broadlands, Hants. The peerage is Irish, and his father was the second viscount. The third, the subject of this notice, was early sent to Harrow, where Dr. Drury was head master. He was among the young men, of all politics, who were attracted to Edinburgh at the opening of the century by the fame of Dugald Stewart ; and he spent three years under him before going to Cambridge. He had just taken his degree at Cambridge, and come of age, when he was brought forward to represent the University. He lost his election to Lord Henry Petty, the Lord Lansdowne of our time. His failure was owing, Wilberforce said, to his modesty and prudence about declaring himself an abolitionist, which he really was, while he was taken to be the opposite. So many of the records of the time agree in ascribing modesty and prudence to the "lad," as his friends called him, that we are bound to suppose that there was a time when Lord Palmerston was the humble, serious, cautious personage who answered to that title fifty years ago. He was clever, and evidently

His birth, 1784.

His defeat in the Cambridge election.

resolved to devote himself to political life; and his opinions were speculated upon with interest, and his first words in Parliament eagerly listened to. He took his seat in the National Council at Christmas, 1806, when affairs were in such a state that no recess could be allowed. It is affecting now to think by whom he was surrounded on his entrance into public life. Canning was in his sauciest vigor. Mr. Grey, become Lord Howick, was beginning to be acknowledged for what he was, through the merits of his speech on the Address. Mr. Perceval, hitherto only known as a violent partisan Attorney-General, was making his first attempt at statesmanship. Romilly, as Solicitor-General, was fixing all eyes and commanding all good hearts, by the nobleness of his principles of legislative justice and mercy. In the group of young men, entering like Palmerston upon their career, were William Lamb, of whom the world was to hear so much as Lord Melbourne; Horner, who was to disappear in a few years; Ward, the able, accomplished, and eccentric Lord Dudley of a later time; and the Henry Petty, who had already put forth pretensions as a financier. Among these sat the young Lord Palmerston, the gravest, the most diffident and cautious of them all. He had not found out his own chief talent— the ingenuity which was to be his distinguishing ability through life; a kind of ability which is perhaps the most unalterable of all—imperishable, but never rising to greatness, obtaining constant admiration, but never commanding the homage due to genius. What a disclosure would have been, at the meeting of that Parliament, the future of its leading members!—the perishing of so many by murder, suicide, madness, disease, and premature death induced by political care, while the grave and prudent youth who came up from Broadlands and Cambridge was to be there half a century afterward, more gay and boyish, more easy and venturesome than the youngest of his comrades whom his seriousness seemed to reprove!

He ranged himself with the Ministerialists, and was made one of the Lords of the Admiralty in 1807, under the Portland Administration. In two years more he was Secretary at War; and in 1811 obtained his desire to represent his University. He was then only seven-and-twenty. When five-and-twenty he actually consulted that very small political gossip, Plumer Ward, as to whether he was likely to prove competent to either of the offices proposed to him—that of Secretary at War, and of Chancellor of the Exchequer; or whether it would be more prudent to take only a seat at the Treasury Board, in preparation for more arduous office. He doubted both his capability in the Cabinet, and his nerve in the House. His friend doubted only the nerve, and went home to pen the patronizing judgment, "Admired the prudence, as I have long done the talents and excellent understanding, as well as the many other good qualities as well as accomplishments, of this very fine young man." Such was Lord Palmerston in 1809, at five-and-twenty. For nineteen years after he made his choice, he filled the office of Secretary at War,—that is, till the breaking up of the Wellington Cabinet in 1828. During the first two Administrations comprised within this period he was a Tory, as a matter of course, under Mr. Perceval and Lord Liverpool. But, holding the same office in all the three Administrations of 1827, his Toryism was clearly giving way. He had always been an advocate for Catholic Emancipation, with Canning;

[X]

Made Secretary at War, 1809.

Plumer Ward's opinion of him in 1809.

[X]
and he was becoming a Free-trader with Huskisson. He stood by Huskisson manfully the next year, when the complication occurred about the East Retford Bill. With the rest of the Canningites—Lord Dudley, Lord Melbourne, and Lord Glenelg—he went out when Huskisson resigned.

His speech in favor of Catholic Emancipation.
He worked well on behalf of the Duke's Administration, in the memorable strife of 1829; and his speech on behalf of the Catholic Relief Bill was pronounced by the *Edinburgh Review* to be worthy of his great ancestor, Temple, in sense, and superior to him in eloquence. That speech was a great act at a time when words were deeds. He felt the admiring sympathy that every man of any sensibility felt for Sir Robert Peel, in his loss of his University seat on that occasion; but the time was near when he had a similar forfeiture to undergo. When he supported Lord J. Russell's Reform Bill, in 1831, Cambridge rejected him, as Oxford had dismissed Sir Robert Peel. He had sat for Cambridge two-and-twenty years; and, no doubt, felt the mortification of his loss; but he got over his mortification better than anybody else; for no one else, perhaps, of genuine ability had so large and ready a self-complacency. He represented in succession, Bletchingley, South Hants, and Tiverton.

Appointed Foreign Secretary, 1830.
In 1830 opened the chief phase of Lord Palmerston's life. He became Foreign Secretary, the capacity in which he will be remembered best at home and wholly abroad. He held the office for eleven years, with the exception of the five months of the Peel Ministry in 1834-5. From 1841 to 1846 he was out of office, and then returned to the Foreign Office for five years. The first great question that occurred after his entrance upon

his function in 1830 was, what should be done with
Holland and Belgium, which had been united by despotic authority fifteen years before, but longed for a
divorce. Politicians who judged by the map thought it
a pity that a union formed on so many conveniences of
boundary, rivers, and so forth—so perfect a *mariage de
convenance*—should be broken up ; but Lord Palmerston
took a profounder and more generous view of the case,
and countenanced the separation. There can be no
doubt that Lord Palmerston greatly increased the importance of the Foreign Office by his administration of
its affairs. He had the ambition to make the influence
of England felt everywhere ; and in a certain sense he
succeeded. Foreign governments positively feared him :
and in the eyes of a large class of his countrymen this
of itself was an achievement to be proud of. But this
feeling was unaccompanied by any growth of confidence
in him on the part of the Liberals of Europe. In his
speech in March, 1830, he developed Canning's idea of
the necessity of increased sympathy on the part of England with the cause of struggling nationality abroad ;
but twenty years afterward he would not have felt
flattered by the judgment which the continental representatives of that cause were everywhere passing on
him. At home the effects of a foreign policy which was
always irritating and unfruitful raised up a strong feeling,
resulting in the parliamentary conflict of 1850 on the
conduct of Lord Palmerston in regard to Greece, which
was condemned by a deliberate vote of the Peers. The
review of his policy by the best men in both Houses,
and especially by Sir Robert Peel in the last speech he
ever made, will not be forgotten either by contemporaries
or in history ; nor the defence, more able and admirable

*His admin-
istration of
foreign
affairs.*

*His policy
condemned
by the Peers,
1850.*

[X]

I 7

[X]
His speech in defence.

His triumph.

The coup d'état in France.

than convincing, of the statesman whose political existence depended on the result. His position was an appeal to parliamentary magnanimity: the vote of the House of Commons was in his favor; and he and his partisans made a triumph of the occasion. But opinions remained much what they were before. The most striking result to observers of the man was that he evinced so much more sensibility—so much more need of sympathy than had been supposed. A great banquet at the Reform Club celebrated what was called his victory; but the feeling still existed that he was standing on his defence. The English Liberals, grieved and indignant at the course of continental reaction in 1849, made use of this occasion for holding meetings which should answer at once the various purposes of manifesting their own sympathies, encouraging the suffering patriots abroad, and attaching Lord Palmerston decisively and irrevocably to the right side. So thought the requisitionists of those meetings; but almost before they were over their expectations were disappointed as regarded Lord Palmerston. He hastened to express to Louis Napoleon his approbation of his *coup d'état;* and such a forfeiture of general expectation precipitated his retirement from the Foreign Office. He resigned the seals in February, 1851. Before long the feeling which had been kindled against him gave place to regret. After all, as Sir Robert Peel said, Englishmen were "all proud of him," and felt an inability to give him up, and a persuasion that if he could not keep despots in awe, nobody could. The public were willing, in spite of long experience, to take the word of the despots for it that he was the worst foe on earth to what they called Order and Paternal Government.

On many questions of domestic policy he pursued a course that was very honorable to him. He did capital service to the right on occasion of the repeal of the Corn Laws. Being appointed Home Secretary in the Aberdeen Ministry in 1852, his prompt and effective action in every part of his charge was a relief and comfort to the whole kingdom. He attended to everything— heard what could be said by well-informed persons on every subject—denounced smoke, damp, fog, cesspools, noisome churchyards, and all manner of nuisances, with effectual vigor as well as extreme relish. The country had just begun to feel that he was in his right place, when it became known that he was in disagreement with his colleagues. That quarrel was made up; and he went on again, and remained until the break-up of the Aberdeen Ministry, in 1855. It was then that a new bond was formed between Lord Palmerston and the nation, and that he took a place in its regard which he never lost. The mistakes, failures, disappointments, and sufferings which had marked the progress of the Crimean war, had sorely tried the heart of England. It was believed that these were traceable partly to defects of administration, and partly to a want of unity and decision in the councils of the Government.

The country felt that it wanted for its leader an energetic statesman of simple, definite aims and firm will. Everybody saw in Lord Palmerston an able administrator, and a statesman who always knew his own mind. He became Premier, an office to which he may be said to have been called by the public voice, and the nation grew calmer as it saw a cheerful, self-possessed, business-like man at the head of its affairs.

[X]

His domestic policy.

Becomes Prime Minister.

[X]

As far as the event depended on the Prime Minister, the war closed with credit. It was believed by many of those who had an insight into the interior movements of the political forces, that if some one else than Lord Palmerston had been at the head of affairs, the war would have continued a short time longer, with a some-what different conclusion. There might have been a more thorough humbling of Russia, a more just distri-bution of the honors of the war between the English and the French, and a treaty of peace more stringently secured from any tampering in the future, if not more effective in its immediate provisions. Lord Palmerston was a good representative of his countrymen in his indifference to the "glory" which is the idol of French-men; and he and they were good-humored together under the sacrifice made to French convenience, self-will, and complacency, under the closing of the conflict at the precise moment when the English forces were sure of carrying all before them, and those of the French were at their lowest point of depression. The peace of 1856 was arranged without obstruction or much remon-strance on the part of the people of England; but the popular distrust of Lord Palmerston's relations with the head of the French Empire was kept alive; and it was again prophesied that mischief would yet arise out of the strange sympathy between a constitutional Minister and the representative at once of the Revolution and absolute rule. In this direction people looked for the Minister's fall, if his fortunes should ever change; but, as far as appeared, he had no misgivings about either his wisdom or his political prospects. His confidence was so far justified as that he issued triumphantly from his appeal to the country against an adverse vote of the

His policy during the Crimean war

and to-ward the French Empire.

House of Commons on the subject of the war with China in 1857. The censure proposed by Mr. Cobden was ratified by the House; but the country, unwilling to lose a Minister so able and so popular, excused him for the fault of going too far in support of the English official in China who created the quarrel. Such a fault, it was said, was an error on the right side; and the consequences in the existing case would be a warning to all ministries to come, to choose their servants better, and keep them in better order. So Lord Palmerston found himself stronger than ever in the new Parliament. But he showed no signs of having gathered wisdom from his recent danger. His temper and manners were less genial and amiable than before; and he suffered by his imprudence in letting it be seen that there were topics and persons before which his serenity and dignity gave way, either in irritation or unseemly arrogance. Thus was he preparing for himself his last and greatest mortification. On occasion of the Conspiracy Bill, Parliament and the country separated themselves from the Minister who was acting more as the tool of the French Emperor and his generals than as the Prime Minister of England, and Lord Palmerston fell. He tried an appeal to the country, and conspicuously failed; and there was some doubt throughout 1858 whether his day was not over.

Every sort of crisis, however, brought the gallant political soldier to the front. In the general alarm about the war in Italy in 1859, everybody remembered what Lord Palmerston had been to us at the time of the latter stage of the Crimean war, and of the Indian Mutiny, and by acclamation Lord Derby's weak Ministry was warned to make way for their abler rivals. From that day Lord Palmerston has conducted the

[X] The China war in 1857

His defeat in the Conspiracy Bill.

Again appointed Prime Minister.

[X]

Review of his char- acter and career.

affairs of the country. Some of us believe that there is much to regret in the fact, and that the consequences will be rued by the next generation, as well as the present. It is admitted by some who consider the admission bold and hard, but required by truth, that he cannot be credited with any great measure, or any substantial, well-defined, wise, or beneficent policy. But the case is graver than this. He never inspired, in any sort of mind, any belief in him, beyond confidence in his ability to avert evil, or to get out of mischief. The more important the principle involved in any affair, the more airy and jocose was he. The effect was not good finally on his own position in the House and before the country; for there were many who had no mind for jesting, and longed for earnestness on serious occasions. This was a small matter, however, compared with the feeling which was growing up against him as the man who, so far from using his popularity to restore and establish the principle and method of government by parties, employed his influence in weakening all political principle, and melting down the whole substance of political conviction, by his treat- ment of all great questions, and his tone in regard to the gravest, as well as the most transient interests which lay under his hand. By his levity he made many things easy; by his industry he accomplished a vast amount of business; by his gay spirits he made a sort of holi- day of the grave course of the national life. But he has done nothing to fit his country, or his party, or even his nearest associates, for a wise conduct of national affairs in the time to come. One reason of the general sorrow for his death is the general misgiving as to what is to come next. We find ourselves adrift, without party, principle, or purpose by [X] which to direct our thought and our action.   Experience, more or less painful, will remedy the evils which our popular Minister has wrought in us, and for us ; but, at the moment, we find ourselves with the most unpromising of all new Parliaments, and with no statesman to guide our destinies, and no such political training as is needed to bring out such statesmanship as may exist, or to supply its place, if absent, with the conscience, the earnestness, the thoughtful habit, and the temper of deference to human nature and human interests which go far to supply the need of genius for public affairs. Lord Palmerston will be remembered with much admiration and affection ; but for national gratitude there will be, perhaps, less occasion and less room as the years pass on.

He did not claim the peculiar reverent consideration usually paid to old age ; but it will not be forgotten that he worked on to the eighty-second year of his life, with little relaxation of power, and none of will. He did his best for his country ; and the country, always sensible of his services, is not ungrateful now.

In his eighty-second year.

XI.

LORD BROUGHAM.

DIED MAY 7TH, 1868.

THE time was—and not very long ago—when the thought that Henry Brougham would die some day was depressing and terrible. It seemed as if a great light must then go out—as if one of the strong interests of life must then be extinguished. But the light so far waned during his latter years, and the interest has so long merged in a sort of pathetic curiosity, that his death is found to be a much more endurable event than it could once have been supposed.

And yet, when we read the political memoirs of the last half century, and when we think what were the hopes and the admiration entertained of the rising states-man of forty years since, we turn once more to the good words he spoke and the good things he planned in evil days, and feel once again something of the emotion that the name of Henry Brougham used to excite—something of the gratitude attendant upon social services, which we would fain cherish as the abiding sentiment connected with his remarkble image. Now that he is gone, it is fitting that we should recall what he did when he was young; and the more, if it is impossible to forget how he disappointed us when he was old.

Forty years ago.

The first glimpse we have of Brougham is as a student of the University of Edinburgh, and a member of the Juvenile Literary Society, established by the students for purposes of literary exercise and debate. He and his friend Francis Horner were distinguished members when they were only fifteen. In 1796 he instituted the Edinburgh Academy of Physics; and in the following year he and Horner were admitted together to the Speculative Society. He seems to have been the *vivida vis* of all these clubs and of some others, being the great speaker on all manner of subjects, physical, metaphysical, political, and what not. Horner early describes him as "an uncommon genius of a *composite order*," "uniting the greatest ardor for general information in every branch of knowledge, and, what is more remarkable, activity in the business and interest in the pleasures of the world, with all the powers of a mathematical intellect." This might stand as a description of him through life. In those early days he was preparing, not only his habits of mind, but his topics for future labors. In 1799 there was a capital debate between him and Jeffrey on Colonial Establishments, which appears to have occasioned his first work—still by some considered his best—on Colonial Policy. It appeared in 1803.

Meantime, that is, about February 1802, three of the young company of philosophers—Jeffrey, Sidney Smith, and Horner—had projected the *Edinburgh Review*. It was not long before Brougham was invited to join. He approved of the plan at first; soon changed his mind, and withdrew; changed again, and wrote those articles which gave the *Review* the early character so well expressed by Romilly at the time: "The editors seem to value themselves principally upon their severity; and

His early and varied accomplishments.

Joins the Edinburgh Reviewers.

[XI]

17*

[XI] they have reviewed some works seemingly with no other object than to show what their powers in this particular line of criticism are." Sydney Smith used to tell, with some playful exaggeration no doubt, how they enjoyed their power over the irritable nerves of authors. "I remember," said he, "how we got hold of a poor little vegetarian, who had put out a silly little book ; and how Brougham and I sat one night over our review of that book, looking whether there were a chink or a crevice through which we could drop" (here suiting the action to the word) "one more drop of verjuice." Sydney Smith made a noble statement (Preface to his Works) of the virtue and usefulness of the establishment of the *Review* during the days of misgovernment which overclouded the beginning of the century ; but there is no doubt that these young advocates of freedom indulged in much tyranny, and that the most vehement denouncers of oppression inflicted dreadful pain. But they were young ; and the times were hard, even exasperating to men entering life on the hopeless Liberal side in politics and political philosophy.

In 1804 Jeffrey wrote to Horner that Brougham had "emigrated." "So he writes me, but with what view he does not explain." The emigration was to London ; and his view was the practice of the Law and political life. He entered Parliament in 1810, by the assistance of Lord Holland. His friends entertained the very highest expectations of what he would achieve there ; but the more prudent of them were not sorry that he was likely to pass some years in Opposition, that his tendency to caprice might be chastened, and that he might have a chance of learning prudence in the safest school. If he could but be steadied, they said his life

Enters Parliament, 1810.

would be one of infinite service to liberty and Liberal principles. They seem not to have inquired where the steadiness was to come from, in the case of a man of constitutional want of balance. These expectations being ill-grounded, though generous, the ultimate disappointment was unjust. His alienation from his old friend Horner, as soon as they met in Parliament, and might become rivals, showed where the weakness lay which paralyzed, in after days, the action of his noble intellectual powers. Even then the vanity was apparent which became the devouring vice of his mind and character. He occasionally drew near to his unconscious rival afterward, and bore testimony, now and then, to his powers and his virtues; but the old comrades could never be again as they were before egotistical passion had begun to rule the heart of him who was to survive. Brougham's first signal triumph in the House was in his speech on the Droits of the Admiralty, in January, 1812. It was an important subject; and that speech did much to put an end to the notion that the Droits of the Admiralty were the private patrimony of the Sovereign; but what Brougham enjoyed was the opportunity for inveighing against royal vices, which were quite bad enough at that time to make it appear good patriotism to expose them. This was a function of patriotism which suited Brougham exactly, and he seized every opportunity of exercising it. At the end of the same year, on occasion of the trial of the Hunts for libel, he had a fine field for his vituperative powers, and he so applied and harped upon the words "effeminacy" and "cowardice" that Lord Ellenborough, the Judge, lost all temper, declared that the defendant's counsel was inoculated with all the poison of the libel,

[XI]

Brougham and Horner.

His first triumph in the House.

and charged the jury that the issue they had to try was whether we were to live for the future under the dominion of libellers. The taste for vituperation grows by what it feeds on; and the Opposition soon found that their splendid young advocate went too far. In 1816, when there was every chance of the Ministry being left in a minority, and going out on the question of the increase of an Admiralty salary, Brougham spoiled all by an outrageous attack upon the Regent, which emptied the House of many of the best supporters of Opposition. He was so vehemently reproached on that occasion that his personal friends began to exhibit and insist upon his services to many good causes; and truly those services were already great. Wilberforce called him "a laborer in the vineyard," on account of his effective attacks on West India slavery. He denounced the wrongs of Poland, so as to trouble the peace of the despots of Europe; and he had begun that series of appeals on behalf of popular education which will ever be his best title to grateful remembrance.

It was before this time that Mr. Brougham had entered into peculiar and personal opposition to the Regent, by espousing the cause of the Princess of Wales. When the Princess Charlotte ran away to her mother to Connaught House, and the perplexed mother drove to the House to consult her advisers what to do, Mr. Brougham, as her legal adviser, returned with her, and was engaged till three in the morning, with the Dukes of York and Sussex and Lord Eldon, in persuading the young Princess to go back to Carlton House. When the childless mother returned in 1820 as Queen Caroline, Mr. Brougham was still her adviser as her Attorney-General, and her spokesman and advocate in Parliament. He went to meet and escort her on the Continent; and he supported her cause, as did his friend Denman, with an intrepidity and disinterestedness which secured them hearty honor from the English people. The Dukes of York and Clarence voted for the Bill against the Queen: and Messrs. Brougham and Denman were therefore fully aware that they were rendering their professional advancement impossible for two or three reigns to come; yet they fearlessly brought upon themselves the vindictive displeasure of the Court and Government for a term too long for calculation. The elder Duke soon died; but the younger, when king, never got over his dislike and dread of Brougham, but was precipitated by it into some very strange political action. Meantime, the intrepid lawyers had received their due, and were enjoying the professional honors of which capable men cannot long be deprived, in a free country, by the mere discountenance of royalty. The excitement of the occasion brought out all Brougham's powers and showed his intellectual claims to honor to be as signal as the moral, in regard to this business. Lord Dudley (then Mr. Ward) wrote of him, in an enthusiasm very rare with him: "The display of his power and fertility of mind has been quite amazing; and these extraordinary efforts seem to cost him nothing."

Between that time and his accession to the Chancellorship, Mr. Brougham achieved his greatest works—the wisest and most beneficent acts of his life. He largely aided the establishment of Mechanics' Institutes, begun by Dr. Birkbeck; and to him we owe the London University and the Society for the Diffusion of Useful Knowledge. The latter has turned out, in its direct operation, a failure, from the forfeiture, on the part of Brougham

[marginal notes:]
[XI]

Displeasure of the Court.

His labors in the cause of popular education.

[XI] especially, of the original promise that political philosophy and morals should be a prominent subject.   Even
his own devoted *Edinburgh Review* slid in a hint, in
the midst of much gratulation on the usefulness of the
Society :—"We trust, however, that the appearance of
the ethical and political treatises will not be unnecessarily delayed."   They never appeared, and the classes
addressed by this Society found experimentally that
their own Harry Brougham, as well as other Liberal
leaders, had not faith enough in them to intrust them
with political knowledge, but preferred putting out, in
the most critical period of the nation's history, treatises
on physical science, as a tub to the whale.   From that
time forward it was a deep popular persuasion that the
Whigs wished to withhold political knowledge from the
people ; and the effect of the persuasion was keenly felt
by the Whig Government, after the passage of the
Reform Bill.   As to other results of the institution of
the Useful Knowledge Society, they were highly bene-
ficial.   Those publications drove a vast amount of bad
literature out of the field, and stimulated other associations to vast improvement.

Ten years after Mr. Brougham had endangered his
political prospects by his advocacy of the Queen's cause,
he received the highest honor of his life.   Under the
excitement of the French Revolution of 1830, and of
the accession of a new Sovereign at home, and in the
joy of having carried Catholic Emancipation, the men
of Yorkshire made Brougham their representative.   He

The pin-
nacle of his
fame.

said himself that he had now arrived at the pinnacle of
his fame ; and so he had.   Amidst all the popular delight
and admiration, there was no great confidence that he
would fulfil the expectations generally avowed.   It was

beginning to be understood that antagonism was his element; and it was suspected that, as usually happens with that class of minds, there was a strong personal Conservatism at bottom. There were men at that time who doubted whether Brougham would not die a Tory, and whether he would fulfil any of his virtual pledges to the people. His services were so undeniable, that men were ashamed of their doubts; but the doubts existed, and they were justified by the evidences of passion, of jealousy, of vanity, of thorough intemperance of mind, which manifested themselves more and more. Now, however, he was at the head of the representation of Great Britain, and it would be seen at last what he could and would do. It was not long before all the world agreed with him that the day of his election for Yorkshire was, as he said, that of his highest glory.

When the announcement was made, the next November, that Brougham was to be the Lord Chancellor in the Grey Administration, everybody laughed. Much of the laughter was pleasant, with exultation in it, as well as amusement; but curiosity and amusement prevailed. He had said that he would not take office, and that he was no Equity lawyer; so the anti-reformers quizzed him on account of his new trammels, and said it was a pity the new Lord Chancellor had no law; for then he would know a little of everything. His appointment was excused only on the ground of political exigency; but he disappointed expectation as much on the political as he possibly could on the legal grounds. He was Chancellor for four years; and during those four years he made no available attempts to accomplish any of the popular objects about which he had said so much before he was able to act. In the autumn of 1834, he ruined his

[XI]

Made Lord Chancellor.

[XI]

political reputation and his prospects for life by a series of eccentricities during a journey in Scotland. He mortally offended the King, and made a declaration at a public dinner at Edinburgh against strenuous reform which overthrew the last hope of his admirers. At that

His persecution of Lord Durham.

dinner began his feud with Lord Durham, whom he persecuted to death. No sort of excuse has ever, we believe, been attempted for his conduct toward that faithful reformer, nor for the temper and language which he thenceforth indulged in toward his old friends and colleagues. So vindictive and fierce were that temper and language that even Lord Melbourne, with his easy good-humor, was cowed; and the whole Ministry were fairly bullied by Lord Brougham into desertion of Lord Durham, after having upheld and thanked him for the very acts for which they extinguished him at the bidding of his cruel foe. It was a shameful chapter in the history of the Whig Government; and Lord Brougham was ever after without political character and social influence. He incurred universal reprobation by the strange offer he made to take the office of Chief Baron under Lord Lyndhurst as Chancellor. He pleaded that, as he should not take the salary, he should thus save the country 12,000*l.* a year; but the plea was a new offence. It supposed that the nation cared more for 12,000*l.* a year than for the political integrity and consistency of its high legal functionaries. Brougham had, however,

Deserts the Whigs.

already gone over to the Tories. He was on the most intimate terms with Lord Lyndhurst and the other Conservative leaders: and it was natural, for they made much of him, and nobody else did now.

His Law reforms were thenceforth his only titles to honor; and very great honor they deserve. We owe to him much of the reform which has taken place in the Court of Chancery; he gave us those local courts which go some good way toward bringing justice to every man's door. It is with these reforms that posterity, in a mood of gratitude and good-nature, will connect the name of Henry Brougham. For the last twenty years or more of his life he sighed for that simple name as for a great good that he had thrown away. He longed, as he said at public meetings, and far more pathetically in private, to "undo the patent of his nobility;" but if he could have become a Commoner again, he could never have recovered the popular confidence and admiration which endeared to him the days which he had spent in Opposition.

[XI]

His Law Reform.

When he was still a youth, his friend Horner requested a correspondent's opinion of his physiognomy. That singular physiognomy was soon familiar to all the world, in all civilized countries. Those who saw it alive and at work could not doubt that his faults had a constitutional origin which it would have required strong moral force to overcome. That moral force he had not. One of the noblest traits in his character was his attachment to his venerable mother. She deserved everything from him; and he never failed in duty and affection to her. During the busiest days of his Chancellorship he wrote to her by every post. Happily, she died before his deepest descents were made. He married a widow lady, Mrs. Spalding, by whom he had two children—one of whom died in early infancy, and the other, a daughter, in early youth, after a short life of disease. His peerage and estates, therefore, pass to the family of his brother, William Brougham, late Master in Chancery; the former under special remainder in the Patent of Creation.

His singular physiognomy.

[XI]

A blur in the picture.

Lord Brougham was at his chateau at Cannes when the first introduction of the daguerreotype process took place there; and an accomplished neighbor proposed to take a view of the chateau, with a group of guests in the balcony. The artist explained the necessity of perfect immobility. He only asked that his Lordship and friends would keep perfectly still "for five seconds;" and his Lordship vehemently promised that he would not stir. He moved about too soon, however; and the consequence was—a blur where Lord Brougham should be; and so stands the daguerreotype view to this hour. There is something mournfully typical in this. In the picture of our century, as taken from the life by History, this very man should have been a central figure; but now, owing to his want of steadfastness, there will be forever—a blur where Brougham should have been.

VI.
ROYAL.

I.

THE LAST BIRTHDAY OF THE EMPEROR NICHOLAS, July 6th, 1854.

Died March 2d, 1855.

The birthday of the Czar is just over; and surely it must have been the most anxious and dismal of his birthdays, grave as the vicissitudes of his life have been. He was born on the 6th of July (new style), 1796, and already, while only fifty-eight, he is worn, broken,—older in constitution and appearance than most men who have lived ten or fifteen years longer. His most eager enemies cannot look on such a spectacle as the decline of this man and his fortunes without a sort of grief in the midst of their satisfaction and thanksgiving :—grief that powers so considerable, and a *morale* that once had much that was fine in it, should have carried the man into a mission no higher than one of warning, after he and many others had believed it would be one of retrieval and amelioration.

There is no need to say that he was unhappy in his descent. The grandson of Catherine and the son of

Celebration of the Emperor's last birthday.

His parentage.

[I] Paul claims our pity at the outset. The mischief was, however, simply constitutional, for he was too young at the death of both to suffer by their example. He was four months old when the Empress died ; and under five years when his wretched father came to his untimely end. He was therefore exempt from the horrible imputation which rested on his elder brothers—that they knew what was doing on the night of Paul's murder, and consented to it as the only means of saving their own liberty and even life. Alexander was then four-and-twenty : but the child Nicholas, then a spirited and clever boy of four and a half, was one of the last who received a loving word and kiss from his doomed father. On that fatal evening, Paul was in one of his amiable moods ; and he went to the Empress,—that ingenuous German girl who found the greatness which had at first astonished her a miserable change from the freer and more modest life in her father's castle ;—her husband went to her drawing-room that evening ; spoke affectionately to her, and took the baby into his arms, and played with the little Nicholas. The widowed mother did the best she could for the boy, in the way of education. General

Nicholas' tutors.

Lausdorf superintended it : Adelung taught him languages, and Councillor Stork instructed him in political economy—to no great purpose, judging by the results. He was more inclined to military studies than any other ; and was almost as fond of fortification as Uncle Toby himself. He was fond of music too ; and united the two tastes by composing military marches. Though his constitutional industry manifested itself in the pursuit of such studies as he liked, he issued from the educational

Defective education.

process, ignorant—really ignorant of what it became, not only a prince, but a gentleman to know ; and not a few of the wisest men in Europe attribute his fatal errors and misfortunes to this cause, above all others.

[I]

During his youth, he was extremely unpopular. His irascibility was so great, that no one cared to approach him unnecessarily. His manners were excessively rude, and the contrast was daily pointed out, by those who dared speak to each other, between him and the affable Alexander. When he was twenty, he came to England, after the peace. He was then a tall youth, said at the time to be a stern likeness of his brother the Czar. On his return he explored his own country, and lived for some time in each of the chief provincial cities. It was then that he became interested in the condition of the lower orders of the people; and it was probably at that time that he conceived the idea of emancipating the serfs, after an interval of ameliorated condition. This was his brother's aim; and there are some enlightened Russians who believe that Alexander died broken-hearted on account of the "ingratitude" with which his efforts for his people's welfare were repaid. The words "ingratitude" and "repayment" are commonly used on such occasions; but in this case, we imagine, the hostility was on the part of one class, on account of the indulgence shown to another. It did not, and it never will, suit the nobles (in their own judgment) to have their serfs emancipated; and a somewhat recent instance of the calamities which may ensue on giving anything like hope of freedom and progress to any of the Czar's largest class of subjects, seems to explain one of the marked changes in the character and conduct of Nicholas. Seeing, as he did, that every hope held out by Alexander led to violence among the serf population—that when once assured

Unpopular in his youth.

[I] that they were regarded and pitied, they began to cut their masters to pieces, or flay them alive—he gave up the idea of regenerating the policy of the empire; and his course as Emperor shows that it suits him better to make himself a type of Russian empire, and the fufiller of the law of his predecessors, than the imitator of Alexander, in trying to make something very fine out of a mixture of the milk and honey of the Gospel with the gall and brimstone of Muscovite domination.   Alexander had, however, something more to trouble him than the failure of his benevolent schemes.   In the year 1817, when Nicholas was marrying the Prussian princess who is now nursing him in his premature old age, a secret society was formed in Russia which left not an hour's peace to Alexander for the rest of his life.   For nine years he lived in the   knowledge that a great conspiracy existed, the object of which was to form a federal union of Sclavonic republics, extending from the North Sea to the Adriatic—that object of course including the deposition of the Romanhoff family.   No means, either of fraud or force, were of any use in putting down this conspiracy; and for nine years did Alexander walk about with this fearful ghost at his heels, never knowing when the moment would come for him to feel its grasp.   This society intended to reform the political condition of Russia altogether, and to reinstate Poland. The conspiracy was a direct consequence of the war; and it is astonishing that Nicholas, who must know this very well, has not deferred to the last possible moment the sending his armies forth in European warfare.   He knows very well that the first secret society, the Alliance of the Sons of the Fatherland,

His marriage.

was conceived of and formed by young officers who [I]
had picked up ideas of a better government than the
Russian in foreign countries, and yet he offered to send
his forces into Hungary on behalf of Austria, and finds
that the same thing happens again; that the officers
and even the common soldiers have returned with some
notions in their heads which make his intervention in
Hungary more a loss to him than a gain.

The military men who returned home after the peace *Disaffection among the nobility.*
inoculated the young nobility, and the disaffection spread
through the whole class. It is an old story. The despotic monarch and unenfranchised people are one party,
and the aristocracy another, and the two are in constant
antagonism in all despotisms. It is the natural operation
of this necessity which explains every Russian problem,
past and present, and will explain every future one, as
long as despotism exists there. The singularity and
fatality of the Russian case lies in the extreme depression, brutalization, and helplessness of the popular class.
This peculiarity seems to point to a most disastrous
issue; and nothing in all the wayward conduct of the
present Czar so justifies the suspicion of his insanity as
his precipitating so unnecessarily the catastrophe which
sooner or later must come. It must be remembered,
however, that he is ignorant. He has no philosophical
insight into the principles of interpretation of history,
and he little suspects how the students and philosophers
of his day can read his horoscope, and tell his future,
or that of his family and empire, as confidently as if
they were prophets. By his best qualities,—his courage,
his energy, and devotion to a present purpose,—he
crushed the hostile enterprise at the time; and now,
nearly thirty years after, he is doing his utmost in his

18

[I]   ignorance to revive it.   One secret society after another
was discovered in Alexander's time, but, under the
appearance of suppression, each merged in the great
one which could not be traced.   It spread south and
north, comprehending nearly the whole class of nobles ;
some of whom were democratic republicans, while others
limited their demands to reform, and the deposition of
the reigning family.   It is a well-known fact that not
one distinguished family of nobles in the whole empire
was unconnected with the conspiracy.   The Czar's Committee of Inquiry ascertained this, and with it the other
all-important fact that the immense majority were the
oligarchists, and the men who desired change without
any desire to help in inducing it ; men who eschewed
the doctrinal consideration, while ready to avail themselves practically of the issue.   In other words, the
majority were found to be manageable by means of
self-interest ; and nothing could be more skilful for the
moment than the young Czar's management of them.

Alexander's decree as to the succession.   The first step of the conspirators was to create confusion as to the succession.   Alexander's will decreed
that Nicholas should succeed him, and Constantine's
Act of repudiation of the crown was sealed up with
the will.   So the conspirators declared for Constantine.
But the habit of Russian perfidy is too strong for such
dangerous occasions ; and while the conspirators were
making progress in St. Petersburg, and gaining over
the soldiers in battalions, their chief and dicator was
taking the oaths to Nicholas.   It was not safe to inflict
much punishment.   Only five men were executed, and
no more than 121 sent to Siberia.   The wisest of the
five declared to the last that nothing but a total reno-
vation of the empire, and the adoption of a free consti-

tution, could save Russsia from violent dismemberment. [I] .
When Poland arose, five years after this execution, the
Poles celebrated the death of the Russian martyrs, carrying five coffins through the streets of Warsaw, inscribed
with their names. Perhaps this may be done again, in
the same streets, when that prophesied dismemberment
of Russia is accomplished.

Though that revolution did not take place, another *Alteration*
did, far less expected. Nicholas became apparently a *in the de-*
totally altered man. The strength of his will has never *Nicholas.*
shown itself more marvellously than in the restraint
which he instantly put upon his temper and manners,
and maintained for a long course of years. Those who
happen to have watched the insane know that the most
fearful of their peculiarities, in many cases, is the in-
stantaneous transition from the brutal to the human
state. You catch their eye, and are horrified at its
expression of ferocity and cruelty; and before you can
withdraw your gaze, it is gone, and all is bland and
gracious. Thus was it with Nicholas, from the moment
when his foot touched the step of the throne. Stern
but no longer irascible, distant but never ill-mannered,
the brute part of him, known to be so largely inherited
from his ancestors, seemed to have been cast out. There
were always many who knew that it was not so ; and of
late, it is understood, his self-control has given way, and
his temper and manners are like those of his youth.

What his government of his dominions has been there *Inclination*
is no need to describe. The more hopeless he became *of his policy*
of doing effectual good at home, the more he has in- *Peter and*
clined to the policy of Peter and Catherine. He is *Catherine*
aware that the nobles regard the existing system as
doomed, and only expect or desire it to last their time.

[I]   He is aware that the host of slaves who worship him are
no power in his hand, but a mere burden.   A man might
as well be king in a wilderness peopled by sheep and
wolves as in Russia ; and no one knows this better than
Nicholas.   He is aware that he cannot reckon on the
honesty of any one functionary of his whole empire.   He
has invited and pensioned *savans* and men of letters, and
instituted schools, and toiled harder than his own slaves,
and he perceives that society grows no better, but rather
worse.   So he has recourse to schemes of territorial extension ; and there the same evils follow :—his ships are
rotten ; his cannon-balls are turned into wooden bowls ;
his quinine is found to be oak bark ; and while he is
paying enormous bread bills, his soldiers are perishing
under a bran and straw diet.

Mixture of
fanaticism
and laxity
in his
character.
Of his fanaticism one does not know what to say.
His Empress turned Greek in a day to marry him ; and
this no doubt seemed to him all right and natural.   But
when he wanted his daughter Olga to marry the Archduke Stephen, he offered that she should turn Romish
in a day—should embrace the faith of those nuns · of
Minsk who were so very displeasing to his orthodoxy.
It is probably in his case the mixture of fanaticism and
laxity which is so disgusting in the history of all Churches
at any time dominant, and involved with the State.

His family
relations.
In his family, he is no less unhappy than in other
relations.   His faithful wife, who has borne with much
from him, partly because there was no helping his
passions, and partly because he carried on his attention
to her through all his vagaries, has been wearing out for
many a dreary year under the fatigues of the life of
empty amusement which he imposes on all his family.
One favorite daughter is dead.   Another is the widow

of the Duc de Leuchtenberg; and the youngest is
Princess Royal of Wurtemberg. The two eldest sons
are always at variance, their ideas and tempers in regard
to government being wide as the poles. Their father
long repressed their feud; but it has, like his other misfortunes, become too much for him; and the scandal is
fully avowed.

Thus has the proud man, the Emperor of All the
Russias, passed his fifty-eighth birthday, sitting among
the wreck of all his idols. They are of clay; and it is
his own iron will that has shivered them all. Instead of
achieving territorial extension, he has apparently brought
on the hour of forcible dismemberment of his empire.
Instead of court gayety, his childish vanity has created
only the mirth which breaks the heart and undermines
the life. Instead of securing family peace by the com-
pressive power of his will, he has made his sons the
slaves, instead of himself the lord, of their passions.
Hated by his nobles; liked only by an ignorant
peasantry who can give him no aid, and receive no
good from him; drawn in by his own passions to
sacrifice them in hecatombs, while they fix their eyes on
him as their only hope; tricked by his servants all over
the empire; disappointed in his army and its officers;
afraid to leave his capital, because it would be laid waste
as soon as his back was turned; cursed in all directions
for the debts of his nobles, the bankruptcy of trade, and
the hunger of his people; conscious of the reprobation
of England and France, whose reprobation could be no
indifferent matter to Lucifer himself; finding himself out
in his count about Austria, and about everybody but his
despised brothers of Prussia and (as an after-thought)
Naples; and actually humbled before the Turk—what a

[I]

*The results
of his
despotism.*

[1] position for a man whose birthday once seemed to be an event in the calendar of the universe! Be it remembered the while, that he is broken in health and heart. He stoops as if burdened with years; he trembles with weakness because he cannot take sufficient food. The eagle glance has become wolfish. The proud calm of his fine face has given way to an expression of anxiety and trouble. Let him be pitied, then, and with kindness. He is perhaps the greatest sufferer in Europe, and let him be regarded accordingly. But, as we need not say, he is totally unfit for the management of human destinies. We have nothing to do with the relations between himself and his subjects; but we must see that he never again lays the weight of even his little finger on the destinies of any people beyond his own proper bounds. We have done him some harm, in the course of years, by our supineness and credulity; and we must regard ourselves, therefore, as not unconcerned in his present abasement. We must sin no more in the same way. Having thus resolved,—having made up our minds that this common foe shall do no more hurt to anybody but his own subjects,—we are at liberty to compassionate, freely and kindly, the wretched man who has declined into every other abyss before he reaches that of the grave.

II.

METTERNICH AND AUSTRIA.

1854.

THE world begins to see now that Austria is very incomprehensible; and if, in order to comprehend her,
people look back through her history for half a century,
they find her proceedings more and more difficult to
understand, while the evidences of her utter untrust-
worthiness multiply. We know of but one way of
getting any light in this manner—to review the life of
Metternich, which is the real thread of Austrian history,
from the beginning of the century—a thread now and
then snapped or worn, but knotted together again, for
more pearls of policy to be strung on. Metternich is
very old—eighty-one; and he is not in office: but, if
not in office, he is well understood to be in power; and
it may possibly be of some use to the world to see how
it has gone on while Prince Metternich was in power—
avowedly or virtually. He has been the foremost of
the Ministers of modern times in regard to the power
lodged in his hands. His means of working out his
views have been practically unlimited; and an estimate
of what he has done for human welfare, and of his success in governing on his own principles, cannot but be

[II]

instructive to us in the present moment of obscurity in regard to Austrian policy.

His birth; and introduction to Court.

Prince Metternich was born at Coblentz, in 1773, and appeared at Court when he was seventeen, in the character of Master of the Ceremonies, at the coronation of Leopold II. He saw England for the first time when he was one-and-twenty ; at which early age he was appointed Austrian Ambassador at the Hague. In the next year he married the granddaughter of Kaunitz.

His marriage.

He went from Court to Court in Germany ; and then to Paris in 1806. He saw, with his own eyes, the state of the peoples of Germany and France during the conflicts occasioned by the aggressions of Bonaparte ; he witnessed some of the noblest movements ever exhihited by nations in their hour of tribulation and peril ; he saw spectacles which stirred every other heart with admiration and joyful trust ; but he brought away from all he saw the one impression, ever deepening, that monarchs were to rule in every particular of the lives of all their subjects. His mind is narrow ; and it does not let his heart have play. So, the rally of Prussia in the expectation of invasion ; the enterprise of England in carrying the war into the Peninsula ; the virtuous efforts of Sicily before her betrayal by the Castlereagh Government ; the valor of the Swedes and the theory of the Swiss,—all appeared evil in the eyes of the wise man

Sympathies with Bonaparte and Alexander.

of Vienna. His sympathies were with Bonaparte (apart from France) on the one hand, and with Alexander of Russia on the other ; and when those two were such loving friends, on the raft in the middle of the river at Tilsit, he could have embraced them both at once, as fine specimens of the rulers of nations. It was he who gave an Austrian archduchess to Bonaparte. It was he

who was cognizant of the secret article in the Treaty of
Vienna which the Bonaparte family conveniently discovered when they met to hear that Josephine was to
be divorced; and it was Metternich who, with indecent
haste and eagerness, carried the Archduchess to France,
and gave her to Bonaparte within four months of poor
Josephine's quick apprehensions taking their first alarm.
By no one act did Austria ever lose so much, in the esti-
mation of Europe, as by the eagerness with which this
alliance was formed; and it was Metternich who conducted the whole proceeding, and infused the eagerness
into it. On the other hand, there was the other pattern
sovereign, the Czar. Alexander's Holy Alliance was
exactly the scheme for Metternich, and he turned it to
purposes of oppression and repression, which made it the
hated and despised thing it was. His admiration of Bonaparte's power and despotism did not, however, mitigate
the Austrian's dread of the revolutionary French people;
and whenever Bonaparte became in any way the representative of the nation, he became at the same moment
odious and formidable to the man who had procured
him his wife. It was Metternich who proposed an armis- *Proposes the armistice of 1813.*
tice in the summer of 1813, when Bonaparte appeared
unable to follow up his victories, won at the beginning
of the campaign; and it came out afterward that Metternich always intended that Austria should join the allies,
from the time that he knew that the allies were pledging
themselves to prosecute the war with vigor—England
furnishing the means. He and the crafty Alexander,
and the double-minded Frederick William of Prussia,
were using the armistice for the maturing of their plans;
and Metternich was preparing the Austrian declaration
of war while inducing Bonaparte to protract the interval

[II]

[II]

by an offer on the part of Austria to negotiate terms of peace.   The conference was delayed to the last moment; and the enemy was kept hanging on till the 9th of August, when, there being no more time to lose, Bonaparte wrote his conclusions.   They were received a few hours after the expiration of the armistice; and Metternich declared them to have arrived too late, unless the Czar should choose to reopen the Conference.   On the Czar's refusal, Metternich produced the Austrian declaration of war.   There it was—all ready!   Bonaparte himself, who was as well up to a trick as any man, found himself cheated by the three knaves with whom he had been treating; and dire was his wrath.   The lesson for the French and English to learn from the transaction is —to be on the watch when the Czar, and a King of Prussia, and an Austrian (and especially Metternich) are negotiating, and Austria has not declared what side she will take.

Metternich outwits Napoleon.

After the first day's battle at Leipsic, the next October, Bonaparte sent a secret offer in the night to Metternich, who was at hand, to retire beyond the Rhine, if his father-in-law would procure him terms.   No answer was returned, and on the field, after the second battle, Metternich was made a prince of the Austrian empire. His master thus honored and rewarded his minister for having outwitted his son-in-law,—a highly moral and genial state of things to precede the Holy Alliance!   A pretty set of people to exemplify the principles and precepts of the Gospel in their way of ruling the nations! Still, both master and man held themselves ready for any cheating that might be desirable on the other side. While the Treaty of Chatillon was hanging on, Austria was so undecided and incomprehensible—not choosing, in fact, either to lose the French throne for the Austrian branch, nor to leave the allies while Bonaparte might yet be dangerous—that Lord Castlereagh himself was out of patience, and urged Blucher and his Prussians forward while the great Austrian army was actually retiring. When Bonaparte had abdicated, and his wife and son were actually on their way to him to share his fortunes, as they ought, the Emperor of Austria was enlightened as to the policy of taking them home to his own Court; and the weak and shallow-minded wife was so enlightened during the journey in regard to her husband's infidelities, that she let her horses' heads be turned by the hand of the real ruler of Austria, and turned her back also on the man of sunken fortunes. She went to Vienna, and her husband never saw her again.

[II]

Metternich aided in the Treaty of Paris, and signed it. His next honor was an Oxford degree, bestowed when he came to England in 1814. For a short time—while Bonaparte was preparing his return from Elba—Metternich was in secret league with the Bourbons and the Duke of Wellington against the Czar and the King of Prussia, who seemed likely to break the Treaty of Paris. But the return from Elba cut short all that; and we next find Metternich supreme at the Vienna Congress, and entering upon that term of despotism which was comparable only to the reigns of Wolsey and Richelieu, till Canning broke it up, and gave the nations space to breathe again.

One of the signers of the Treaty of Paris.

When Metternich received (before anybody else), on the 7th of March, 1815, the news of Bonaparte's landing, he was under a signed engagement on the one hand to an "indissoluble alliance" with Russia and Prussia; and, on the other hand, was in confidential

The "indissoluble alliance."

[II]

league with England and France against those "indissoluble allies" of his, who wanted to annex Saxony to Prussia.   There is another generation now in Prussia, and something like it at St. Petersburg (for Nicholas is twenty years younger than Alexander): and thus Prince Metternich may be able to look them in the face; a thing which must have been rather difficult if these little secrets had come out during the lifetime of their predecessors.

At the height of his power, 1815-1822

Thus was the Prince Metternich at the height of his power.   His period of glory was from 1815 to 1822; and it will ever be cause of shame to England that her statesmen were during that interval the mere instruments for carrying out his policy,—a policy which has really no one characteristic of wisdom, or greatness of any sort.   It is not possible that any but the despots of Europe and their tools should point out any virtue whatever in the European policy (which was Metternich's) that prevailed from the peace till the Italian outbreaks of 1822.

Really a weakness in the Austrian administration.

Nor, with all its rigor, was there ever any strength in the Austrian administration, while he was at its head. His permitting Russia to endanger the Austrian provinces in the Turkish war was either from partiality for the despotic side, or from fear; and either way it was weakness.   He allowed the Czar to possess himself of the mouths of the Danube without opposition from the power which is dependent on the Danube.

When the French revolution of 1830 broke out, the unhappy necessity arose for Austria to take some part— to declare some opinion.   For years past the Emperor and his accomplished minister had had safe and solemn employment in playing the jailer to the revolutionists at home—in decreeing the precise badness of the air, food, and clothing of the Pellicos and Confalonieres ; and studying how to increase their torments, how to soften their brains, and break down their minds without absolutely killing their bodies. Now they must say something abroad as well as order things at home. They became more affectionate than ever with the Czar and his Prussian spaniel till a new light broke in upon Metternich. His master had cried aloud, when the news from Paris reached him, "All is lost !" But when Metternich saw that the French had taken a king after all, and that that king was as cunning and managing as himself, he took heart, and hoped that all was *not* lost. His passion for centralization was gratified by the functionarism of France under Louis Philippe ; and he evidently hoped that that restless nation, put to such a school, would come out as childish and automatic as the Austrians themselves—those dear children whom their Father Francis used to pat on the back as long as they had no ideas of their own, but whom he tied by the leg, or hung up by the neck, as soon as he caught them thinking. While the French were being put to school, Metternich was hard at work to prevent their restlessness spreading. He helped Don Carlos with money—even money, which is the scantiest of all good things in Austria. He put on Mrs. Partington's pattens, and really made her broom do wonderful service about his own door till the tide drove him in. He had now completely pledged himself to the retrograde policy of which England and France were his chief opponents. There had been a time when he had discussed the restoration of Poland ; but after this he gave way no more to any ideas of improvement. In 1810, he had enabled Gall to publish his philosophy—

[II]

His retrograde policy

[II] his view no doubt being that that philosophy would be capital, if true, as a means of managing men. Some years after he gave a gracious welcome to Robert Owen, bestowed several hours on him, and employed his secretaries for some days in copying Mr. Owen's documents. Here was centralization in its utmost perfection. Everybody laughs at the coupling of the names of Prince Metternich and Robert Owen; but, for our part, it seems to us that the men are precisely alike in their central aim, however otherwise differing in quality. Both desire to render mankind happy by transacting all their affairs for them, and pressing their minds through a mould, so that they may come out all alike. As for the rest, the one is as benevolent as the other is selfish. They differ as to what to do with the children, the one smiling upon them all, and the other frowning and punishing the best of them fearfully; but both agree upon the great practical point,—that they two are to treat all other people as children. In his countenance of the Poles, as in his graciousness to Gall and Owen, the Prince saw, for the instant, some feature available for his use. The Polish insurrection was, in his eyes, not a popular revolution, but a military rising for the restoration of aristocratic privileges. As soon as Metternich saw that it was one of the movements which threatened despotism, as well as a particular despot, he made all possible haste to the feet of the Czar, hoping that it had not been observed that he had turned his back for a moment in that presence. Graced with the smiles of all despots, obeyed by the Emperor Francis, invested with all the power that could be given to a minister, he yet accomplished none of his aims, and lost instead of augmenting his power. He utterly

His agreement with Robert Owen.

failed to amalgamate the elements of the Austrian empire. If he had desired to fit them for splitting asunder, he could not have done the work better. He has not made the Austrian portion of the people wise, strong, manly, virtuous, or happy ; and what the Italians and Hungarians are, as portions of the Austrian empire, no man living needs to be told.

At length came the year 1848. The Pope and his reforms had been a terrible preparatory trial—poor Pio Nono was so spoiling the Italian states ! Austria gained nothing by the Ferrara movement ; and when the revolutions of 1848 came, there was nothing to be attempted but to keep down Milan and Venice by force of arms. The docile children, or repressed slaves of a despotism, are the victims or the demons of a day of revolution ; and such were the citizens of the Austrian towns and the peasants of Gallicia when Vienna was up. Metternich's one idea, in the midst of his panic, was that he must keep himself ready to go on, whenever regular government should be restored. The Archduke John assured the people (through their deputation) that Prince Metternich would resign. The Prince assured them he should not. The Archduke repeated his assurance ; and Metternich retired, muttering about ingratitude for his fifty years of service ! He fled for a time, and returned ere long to his estates and his old haunts, under cover of quietness, and pretence of helplessness through extreme age. But there he is, alive and busy, though without office. If Austria is hesitating in her policy of to-day, it is because Metternich is feeling her way. If Austria is obscure, it is because Metternich is scheming. If she takes the side of the Western Powers, it will be because Metternich sees it to be the winning one ; and

[II]

Obliged to retire in 1848.

His Machiavellian policy.

if she wheels round to the side of Russia, it will be because Metternich's old eyes will fancy they see the bird of victory descending toward the Muscovite Jove whom he adores.

The question for all Englishmen to ask is whether they choose the settlement of the Eastern question to be in any way materially affected by the influence of an old man who is no sage—who has never succeeded in his own object, amidst every facility that could be given him—who has never manifested any comprehensiveness of views, any intellectual depth, any moral nobleness, any great quality whatever of statesmanship or manhood. *Metternich the representative of Austrian policy.* The day will come which will show whether Francis Joseph is worth more than his predecessors; but, while Metternich lives, Austria is Metternich; and history holds up to us, for our warning, the picture at full length of Metternich as an ally.

III.

THE DUCHESS OF GLOUCESTER.

DIED APRIL 30TH, 1857.

THE death of the last of the fifteen children of George III. carries back all minds over a large space of time, and would create an historical interest in connection with the death of the Duchess of Gloucester, if there had been much less than there is of personal interest attending the character of the amiable Princess who has just departed. Her birth, and her title by marriage, recall some associations which it may be useful to revive, under the altered circumstances of a new century and generation. The discontents which existed for a time between the father and the father-in-law of the deceased Princess produced consequences on her life—and that of most of her family—and on public morals and welfare, which ought not to be forgotten in a review of her character and position, and which are not yet extinct in regard to the existing generation.

Historical interest connected with her death.

George III. married, in 1761, the Princess Charlotte of Mecklenburg-Strelitz. He was not satisfied with pleasing himself in his own marriage, but fully expected that his brothers would please, not themselves, but him, in *their* marriages. They did not do so; and when he was a sober married man, with half-a-dozen children, he was excessively scandalized at the discovery that the Duke of Cumberland had married Mrs. Horton, and the Duke of Gloucester the Countess Dowager of Waldegrave. There were immediate political consequences arising from the family quarrel—the Opposition finding their spirits and forces at once revived; but a more permanent, and far more serious consequence was, that the Royal Marriage Act was devised by the King, and carried through Parliament with a high hand, in the midst of protests and remonstrances from Burke, Lords Camden and Rockingham, and others, and many forebodings of the mischief it would cause. Under this Act no descendant of George II. could marry under the age of twenty-five without the King's consent; nor after that age otherwise than after applying to the Privy Council (in case of the Sovereign's disapprobation), and waiting a year to see whether either House of Parliament would address the King against the marriage— which, in that case, could not take place. It was too late now, happily, to overthrow the Duke of Gloucester's marriage, which had taken place five years before. It was declared at Court in the autumn of 1772, the same year that the Royal Marriage Act passed. The fanaticism of the German Queen for royal quarterings, which even exceeded the passion of the King for prerogative, was necessarily mortified this time; but both were resolved that it should be the last. Their children should marry royalty, or not marry at all. They never doubted whether they could enforce their decision when once they had the law on their side. Certain other, prior, and greater laws of human nature they made no account of.

After the birth of two daughters, the discountenanced pair had a son, who remained the only one. He was

born at Rome, on the 15th of January, 1776; and all
the English in Rome were present at his baptism, the
next month.   On the 25th of the following April was
born the eleventh child of George III.—the Princess
Mary, who was to be the wife of the little cousin at
Rome.   The event was signalized by a rather remarkable address presented (on the day of the baptism) by
the Lord Mayor and the Corporation of London—an
address which contained a sermon on laws, liberties, and
the glorious Revolution, which did not seem to have
much to do with the infant Princess, and which got a
very short answer from the King.   That was the time
when the Americans were preparing their Declaration
of Independence, which was promulgated on the 4th of
the next July; and when M. Necker was put at the
head of French finance—a time at which King George
did not want to hear anything about liberties and revolutions, and when accordingly all manner of people
were seizing every opportunity of preaching to him
about them.

During the long course of years in which many of
the other members of the family were involved in the
penalties and perplexities of their rank, with regard to
love and marriage, it was believed that the Princess
Mary and her cousin, the Duke of Gloucester, were
attached.   She was interested in his Cambridge life (his
education being finished there); and she gloried in his
receiving the General's thanks in the field, when he was
fighting in Flanders, so early as 1794.   He proved himself both a gallant and able soldier, and really won his
rank, which rose to that of Field-Marshal in 1816.
When the young people were one-and-twenty, the Princess Charlotte was born; and as it soon became under-

[III]

Her birth,
April, 1776

[III]

stood that there would be no heir apparent if the Princess of Wales lived, the necessity was admitted of keeping the Duke of Gloucester single, to marry the presumptive heiress of the throne, in case of no eligible foreign prince appearing for that function. For twenty of their best years the Duke and the Princess were kept waiting, during which interval (in the year 1805) he succeeded to the title on his father's death. Everybody liked and loved the Princess Mary, who was a pattern of duty and sweetness through all the family trials she had to witness and share in ; and the Duke, though not a man of much political ability, was in that part of his life a Whig, and on the generous and liberal side of almost every question. We are obliged to say "almost," because he supported with his whole force the exclusion of Dissenters from the Universities, when he was Chancellor of the University of Cambridge, after the death of the Duke of Grafton. On the anti-slavery question he was as earnest in his own way as Wilberforce in his, and kind and helpful in all matters of charity that came before him. Romilly tells us a curious thing of him— that he volunteered, in a *tête-à-tête* with Sir S. Romilly, his declaration that Queen Caroline was innocent, and that her accusers were perjured. He latterly became a Tory ; but, for the greater part of his life, the same genial spirit of liberality and personal unassumingness distinguished him and the Princess Mary. As for her, she pleased old and young alike. Lord Eldon used to tell with delight a joke of Queen Charlotte's—about the last person in the world whom any one would suspect of jesting. Her Majesty used to charge the Lord Chancellor with flirting with her daughter Mary ; and the Chancellor used to reply that he was not emperor, king

General favorite with all.

or prince, and that, moreover, he was married already— [III]
a reply which reminds us of that reported by Charles
Lamb of six Scotchmen, who, on somebody wishing that
Burns was present, all started forward on their seats to
declare that that was impossible, because Burns was
dead. But we must suppose that Lord Eldon, who
really had humor in his way, considered the above as
near an approach to jocularity as could be permitted in
the presence of royalty.

In 1814, when the Prince of Orange was in England,
and his father announced his approaching marriage with
the Princess Charlotte, Princess Mary looked bright and
happy. Lord Malmesbury recorded in his Diary what *Lord*
her manners were like when the charm of youth was *Malmes-*
bury's
past, and the character of womanhood was marked. He *opinion of*
said she "was all good-humor and pleasantness;" *the Princess*
Mary.
adding, "her manners are perfect; and I never saw or
conversed with any princess so exactly what she ought
to be." And no one living, perhaps, knew more
princesses, or more of what they really were, than the
old diplomatist. The Prince of Orange went away, and
Princess Mary drooped. Everybody was saying that the
Duke of Gloucester must be the Princess Charlotte's
bridegroom after all. But a few months more put an
end to the long suspense. When the Princess Charlotte
descended the great staircase at Carlton House, that
May evening after the ceremony of her marriage, she
was met at the foot with open arms by the Princess
Mary, whose face was bathed in tears. The Duke and
Duchess of Gloucester were married in a few weeks— *Her mar-*
riage.
on the 23d of July, 1816. The bride's demeanor was
so interesting and affecting that it opened the sluices of
Lord Eldon's ready tears, which he declared ran down

[III] his cheeks; but the Chief Justice, Lord Ellenborough, also present, must have been in another mood. Some persons were talking in a corner of the crowded room; and the Chief Justice called to them, in the midst of the ceremony, "Do not make such a noise in that corner—if you do, you shall be married yourselves." It is rather pathetic now to think of the details of that marriage—the crowded saloon—the royal mother and sisters on one side the altar, and the royal brothers on the other—the bride, though no longer young, "looking very lovely," in a remarkably simple dress; to remember how the scene was related at every fireside in England; and then to think that none of the family, and probably no one who was present, survives.

No application was made to Parliament for an increase of income in this case. The benevolent habits of the Duke and Duchess had taught them in a practical way the value of money; and they arranged their plan of life so as to make their means suffice, and leave enough for much support of schools, and aid to many a good cause.

Death of the Duke. They lived together eighteen years—the Duke dying in November, 1834. It surprised no one that his wife proved herself the most assiduous and admirable of nurses during her husband's decline. After his death, she lived in as much retirement as her rank admitted, doing good where she could, and universally beloved. She saw the last of her immediate relatives drop from her side, and herself left the survivor of that long family train that used to look so royal and so graceful when returning the admiring salutations of the public on the terrace at Windsor. All that long series of heart histories was closed. The wretched avowed marriages, and the wretched, or happy, or chequered secret marriages, and

the mere formal state marriages, which took place in
consequence of the Princess Charlotte's decease, had
been alike dissolved by death. What a world of misery
could this survivor have told of, arising from the law-
made incompatibility between royalty and the natural
provision for the domestic affections! The elaborate
and public preparation required by the Marriage Act
in her own case, by which her marriage was made an act
of the State, was painful enough; but her lot, with its
one steady affection, long in suspense and late gratified,
was a happy one in comparison, perhaps, with that of
any other member of the family; and many a painful
meditation must she have had on that piece of enforced
legislation of her father's early and headstrong years.
Those various love stories are hidden now in the grave;
and she who was the depositary of so many of them has
followed them thither. There, then, let them rest.

But the lesson they yield should not be neglected.
There was a strong hope that when our young Queen
Victoria, who was at full liberty, as Sovereign, to please
herself in marriage, had made her choice, this wretched
and demoralizing Marriage Act, always reprobated by the
wisest and best men of the time, would be repealed.
There were then none left of the last generation who
could be pointed at, or in any way affected, by such a
repeal; and it was thought that it would be wise to do
the thing before there was a new generation to introduce
difficulty into the case. The opportunity has almost been
allowed to slip from us. The royal children have ceased
to be children, at least the elder ones. Meantime, there
is, as we all know, a strong and growing popular distrust, in our own country and in others, of the close
dynastic connections which are multiplying by means of

[III]

*Lesson to be
learnt from
the working
of the Royal
Marriage
Act.*

[III] the perpetual intermarriages of a very few families.
The political difficulties recently, and indeed constantly,
experienced from the complication of family interests,
involving almost every throne in Europe, are a matter of
universal feeling and conversation. There is no chance
for the physical and intellectual welfare of coming
generations when marriages take place among blood
relations; and there is no chance for morality and
happiness when, under legal or state compulsion, young
people love in one direction and marry in another. No
evils that could possibly arise from marriages out of the
royal pale can for a moment compare with the inevitable
results of a royal marriage law like ours, perpetuated
through other generations than the unhappy one that is
gone. Royalty will have quite difficulties enough to
contend with, all through Europe, in coming times,
without the perils consequent on this law. Its operation
will expose all the intermarried royal families in Europe
to criticism and ultimate rejection by peoples who will
not be governed by a coterie of persons diseased in body
through narrow intermarriage, enfeebled in mind,—strong
only in their prejudices, and large only in their self-
esteem and in their requirements. There is yet time to
save the thrones of Europe—or at least the royal palaces
of England—from the consequences of a collision between the great natural laws ordained by Providence,
and the narrow and mischievous artificial law ordained
by a wilful King of England. That King is in his grave,
and the last of his children is now gone to join him

Necessity for the re-peal of the Act. there. Let the time be laid hold of to bury his evil work
in the tomb which is now to be sealed over him and his
forever; and the act will be gratefully acknowledged by
a long line of future princes and princesses, who will be

spared the bitter suffering of those who have gone before. It can never be, as was said by wise men eighty years ago, that royal personages who are declared of age at eighteen will have no will of their own, in such a matter as marriage, at five-and-twenty. Marriage is too solemn and sacred a matter to be so treated as a piece of state politics : and the ordinance which is holy in the freedom of private life may be trusted with the domestic welfare of prince and peasant alike.

19

KING FREDERICK WILLIAM IV. OF PRUSSIA.

DIED JANUARY 2D, 1861.

KING FREDERICK WILLIAM IV. of Prussia is dead after a long period of disease of body and mind. He had become a painful spectacle in the eyes of all Europe; and at a moment when we are all disposed to regard his life and reign in the spirit of justice rather than of criticism, it is natural to review the conditions which rendered his career a disappointment to himself and his people, and a byword among the nations.

Prussia an artificial, not a natural state. Every Prussian monarch ascends the throne under the evil condition that the Prussian State in its present form is a wholly artificial one. Why the Prussia of our geographies exists as a European state, no one seems able to say. There are no natural reasons—like those of structure and conformation. On the map, Prussia looks like the Mr. Nobody of the nursery—all limbs and no trunk—all outline and no mass. Never before was there such a frontier to such a paucity of square miles. The natural weakness of Prussia in a territorial sense is a most depressing condition in the fortunes of its ruler. The population is as much an aggregation of shreds and patches as their abode. There is no dominating sense of unity among them, and the heir of any throne which is based on a loose rubble of popular materials, instead of on a sound nationality, is much to be pitied. Prussia in her present limits is an artificial state, constructed for the convenience of other states; and it cannot be well governed, nor its rulers prosperous, till some one of them shows genius of that high order which can create a nationality by animating all hearts by a common impulse. The man who can kindle such a fire of patriotism as will consume all the discrepancies which make Prussia the political riddle of the world, may make her a *bonâ fide* state, and bring her into some capacity of being well governed; but this was not done ready to the hand of Frederick William IV.; and he was not the man to do it; and whether any man can do it is as yet questionable. Thus far, therefore, to say that any King of Prussia has not made a good ruler is simply to say that he was not a genius of the highest order; and it would be hard to blame any man for that.

Again, the late King was born in 1795; and during the most impressible years of his life he was in the constant habit of hearing of the protracted fears, with short alternations of hope, in which the princes of Germany lived during the brilliant years of Bonaparte's sway. The boy lived in an atmosphere of panic. He was ten years old when the Prussian court was trimming between Bonaparte and Alexander of Russia, and keeping England quiet, and Mr. Pitt exhilarated, by promises of alliance; while the only certainty in the case was that Prussia, having deceived all parties, would be punished by whichever of them should be victorious. The boy of eleven must have shared more or less in the distress of his parents and the court when the true object of the

His birth, 1795.

[IV]

[IV]
. . . . .
· · · . .
Flight with his parents from Berlin.

Confederacy of the Rhine was revealed, and when it was discovered that Prussia was despised by every government in Europe, and delivered up by them all to the mere rapacity of France. He fled with his parents when the French swept on toward Berlin ; and he never forgot the misery of renewing the flight with every fresh arrival of bad news till they reached Memel, and held themselves ready for exile beyond the frontier. There, news was incessantly arriving of the seizure of fortresses and stores by the enemy, and at length that seven of the ministers of state had sworn allegiance to Bonaparte. The little Prince probably witnessed that pathetic scene between his parents and the Czar Alexander at Memel, in the next April, when they embraced, and kissed, and mingled their tears, and promised each other to devote their lives to the task of humbling their foe. He probably witnessed, too, the behavior of the Czar to his parents at Tilsit but a few weeks afterward, when his father was insulted in his daily rides, in the face of the assembled multitude, by the two Emperors, and when Napoleon quailed before the indignation and grief of the spirited mother of this twelve-year-old boy—so early instructed in the instability of states, and the folly of putting trust in princes. It was a melancholy childhood, it must be owned ; but, in the midst of our compassion, we cannot but wish that the boy had learned to shun instead of to follow the example of untrustworthy princes. When he returned to Berlin, his father's singularly pathetic proclamation, releasing the inhabitants of his lost provinces from their allegiance, was everywhere before his eyes ; and the French language was everywhere in his ears, from the French garrisons which were stationed all over the country. But he was still very young when the

cheering rally took place which showed what the people
were made of, and opened some brightness of prospect
to their future king. His father sent him into the field
while he was yet too young for command. He had
studied military science under Scharnhorst and Knese-
beck; and he was present in most of the great battles
of 1813 and 1814.

He had been meantime instructed in philosophy and
literature, which suited him much better than practical
military matters. He had not nerve, practical judgment,
or decision enough for action; yet he must have been
endowed with some high qualities, for his tutor, Niebuhr,
when the royal pupil was nineteen, declared that he never
met with a finer nature. It is true, Niebuhr speaks more
of feeling and fancy than of principle and judgment;
but he declares him full of the noblest gifts of nature.
The "dream" of the Crown Prince in those days (and
there was never a time when he did not dream) was of
being the ruler of Greece, "in order to wander among
the ruins, dream, and excavate." What a pity that he
was born to the throne of Prussia!

*Niebuhr's
opinion of
his pupil.*

He was a member of the Council of State when the
question of the time was the granting of a parliamentary
representation. It was a bad training for him to have
heard the reasons for giving a constitution, if reasons
there were, or to have seen what was yielded to fear, if
fear was the cause of the promise; and then to have witnessed the long delay, and the final breach of promise
on the part of his father, which must have deeply injured
either his principles or his sensibilities. Even Niebuhr,
who disliked the movements on behalf of popular freedom, never, in the days of his highest and latest conservatism, pretended to countenance the conduct of the

*His political
training.*

[IV] Princes of Germany, who promised constitutions, and then withdrew or never bestowed them. The late King seemed, however, radically unable to understand what the purpose of a constitution really was. He said he would never allow a bit of paper to interpose between him and his people ; and he evidently thought that tears, and kisses of the hand, and processions and demonstrations in the streets, were of far more weight and efficacy than constitutional provisions. He saw inscribed in the statute-book his father's promise in 1815 to develop the national representation, as soon as peace should be secured ; and he heard his father say, in 1817, and thenceforth at intervals till 1840, that "not every time is the right time ;" and that he had never mentioned the date at which he would do it. Such was the political training of the Crown Prince. It is no wonder that when he had

His marriage. married, in 1823, a Bavarian princess, he turned from politics to art, literature, and speculative philosophy. Niebuhr, on returning from Rome, met him again, a year after this marriage, and thought him "improved beyond description"—with a mind full of knowledge, and a heart full of fine sensibilities. Yet at this time the Crown Prince's notion of European politics comprehended little more than the old jealousy of Austria ; and the worship of Russia, as the only stout bulwark against Austrian supremacy. There were occasional paroxysms of fear of revolution in 1830, for instance, and whenever reform was anywhere heard of ; and there were occasional scrapes, arising from meddlings with Protestant sects, or getting into quarrels with the Pope and the clergy— scrapes incurred by the third Frederick, and affording a curious training for the fourth of the name ; but, on the whole, the Prince lived for art and literature, for dreams and sentiment, till he came to the throne in 1840. His presence in this country in the beginning of 1842, and his far-famed breakfast with Mrs. Fry, and the high hope and laudation thereby created among the Quakers, are remembered by most of our generation. He came over to stand sponsor to our Prince of Wales. He had just done a good act in issuing an amnesty for political offences, and in recalling the Grimms, Professor Arndt of Bonn, and other scholars who had been driven abroad, or displaced from their functions for political reasons. His minister at our court was then the Chevalier Bunsen, whose politics were more liberal than his own ; his apparent intention was to give his people their promised parliament ; and nothing had occurred since he became king to test the genuine worth of his sentiments ; so that he was welcomed at our court, and in some degree by the nation, as something more than a political ally. The thought was in many minds that there might hereafter be intermarriages between royal children in our country and in his ; between our Queen's children and his nephews and nieces (for he was himself childless). If times had continued quiet, and there had been no troublesome peoples to perplex royalties, such a friendship and such schemes might have prospered : but the nineteenth century is one which demands and imposes action ; and the exposure of the weakness of the poor King of Prussia, caused by the events of 1848, left no option to any who knew him about respecting or despising him. Ministers, friends, family, people could not help being ashamed of their master, friend, relative, or sovereign, after knowing the true story of March, 1848. Those who saw him in the streets of Berlin on the 21st of that March had no more hope of him.

[IV]

Godfather to the Prince of Wales.

His weakness in 1848

There had been passages in his conduct, from the day of his accession, which had reminded historical politicians of the Stuarts, though the likeness was "with a difference." No Stuart would have spontaneously promised the people, however vaguely, that their privileges should be confirmed and their institutions developed; and the King did this, on occasion of his sentimental journey through his dominions after his father's death. But when the states of Prussia Proper took him at his word, and thanked him for his purpose of fulfilling the promises of his father, he backed out of his engagements in true Stuart style. From the time of his letter to the States, reprimanding them for their expectation, his political reputation was gone. It is true he called together the provincial Estates at Berlin in 1847; but that was because he could not help it. He had impoverished himself by the vast military expenditure by which he hoped to keep down the people, and secure to himself the support of a great army, and he had given away money with both hands to Don Carlos and other hopeful followers of the Stuart example. And he wanted something else besides money. He was more thin-skinned than the Stuarts; and he was wretched under the contempt and dislike of his people. The parliament of 1847 was his method of recovering his popularity; and he boasted of having conceded all manner of valuable things, while begging the Estates to observe that he had "not surrendered one right of his crown." Well as his game of see-saw was now understood, his "beloved Berliners" were really surprised at his proclamation of the 18th of March, 1848, whereby he appeared to put himself in the very front of the revolutionists of Europe. His proposal to abolish the confederation of German States, and all the restrictions imposed by that

scheme, and to constitute one German federal state, was [IV]
almost as confounding to his own court as it must have
been to Austria.   The citizens assembled before his palace
to cheer him for his concessions ; but, unfortunately, the
soldiery were brought up by the King's order ; and, unable to bear some popular jeers, they rode in among the
crowd, and killed above sixty persons.   The groaning
and moaning proclamation of the King on the occasion
declared that the sabres were meant to be sheathed, and
that the guns of the infantry went off of themselves.
That proclamation was not the only address to the
"beloved Berliners."   The same dedication was inscribed
in chalk by night over the bullet sent into a post in the
square by one of those guns, no doubt, which went off
of themselves.

The next morning was that on which the King and *A humilia-*
Queen were compelled by the assembled friends of the *ting scene.*
murdered citizens to come down into the courtyard of
the palace, and with uncovered heads to view the corpses,
and be told that they beheld their own work.   There
was some difficulty in getting the Queen down ; but her
visitors would not depart without seeing her.   Her
husband trembled as excessively as she did.   But it was
not this which overthrew the last remains of respect in
the minds of manly observers.   It was the demeanor of
the King on the 21st, when he rode through the streets
of the city, and provoked the universal remark that he
had lost his senses.   He kissed his hand and gesticulated
like a madman, forswore all personal aims and desires,
called Heaven to witness, in the attitude of taking an
oath, that he desired nothing but the unity of Germany
and the supremacy of popular interests.   He declared
that he added another to the list of mighty princes and

[IV]

dukes who had carried the banner of freedom at the head of the nation; and that liberty and progress were the one thought that filled his mind. He liberated the Polish and other state prisoners, and declared that this day would be the great day of Prussia in future history; and in one sense, the last; as the name of Prussia should henceforth merge in that of Germany. He said nothing of who was to be emperor of this united Germany; but there were plenty of contemptuous spectators who saw that he intended to be carried into that seat of power on the shoulders of insurrectionary Germany. He declared that the people of Berlin had behaved so nobly and generously toward him as the population of no other city in the world would have done. Yet in another year

Reactionary policy.

he called (by the mouth of his minister) this movement "a street riot, disgraceful to Berlin and Prussia," and had already committed himself to the strong though shallow current of reactionary policy, checked now and then by his hankering after the Imperial crown, which he fancied to be indicated by an old monkish prophecy as reserved for him. Before the Eastern question took form, and brought in new complications, he sympathized with Austria in dread of revolution, and in precautionary and repressive measures, which secured to him the hatred of his beloved Berliners; while his occasional sentimental snatches at the crown of federal Germany prevented any cordial friendship with Austria. In this kind of employment, varied by continual attempts to retain the name of a parliament and a press while not permitting the real existence of either, and by worshipping Russia, and meddling with religion, and fiddle-faddling with art, literature, military shows, and demonstrations of other sorts, the feeble King filled up the interval between

his escapade of 1848 and the full development of the
Eastern question.

In one of his characteristics the deceased King was
unlike the Stuarts; and this quality would have entitled
him to deep and pure compassion, if it had not been
defiled by a bad admixture. His fair family affections
so implicated him with Russia that all possible allowance
would have been made for him in his difficulties during
the great Russian war, if his fair family attachments had
not been implicated with his unfair ambition and jealousy
with regard to Austria. The difficulty of his position
was indeed extreme. His people feared and abhorred
Russia, while every affection and sentiment of his own
disposed him in favor of the Romanoffs, with whom his
sister had become one. He did the worst thing possible
in that hard position; for duplicity is the lowest resource
of all: and, hard as must have been his sacrifices in any
course, the sacrifice of his integrity and royal good faith
is that which the most lenient must find it most difficult
to make allowance for. He was sufficiently punished—
punished by the loss of that public opinion of Europe
which his vanity craved; by the contempt of the Czar,
which was revealed in the secret correspondence between
Nicholas and the British Government; by his own exclusion from the councils of the Allies; and by the indignation of his own people, which would have dethroned
him if he had ruled over any but unpractical Germans.
There is little doubt that it cost him his life, for he seems
to have sunk under his pain of mind. In this country
great injustice has been done to the late King in respect
of his personal habits—and especially about the nature
and amount of his intemperance. With irritable nerves
and a feeble brain, he was in a manner intoxicated by

every sort of stimulus, as well as by wine. He was drunk at the spectacle of a moving work of art, at the sound of acclamations or execrations in the streets, at every one of the scenes which he was so fond of getting up; at pious letters from the Russian court, or at inditing one himself; at being called "the angel of peace" by the Czar Nicholas; and at the exhibition of the Czar's old uniform; at everything which in any way stimulated his sensibilities. He was truly pitiable in his *The close of* latter days. He had alienated his best friends and ser-*his reign.* vants; and when Bunsen, and Usedom, and Humboldt held aloof from him, after long forbearance, he found himself dependent on a Manteuffel, a Gerlach, and a Niebuhr, the younger—fit comrades of the Russian creatures who swarmed at his court. He could scarcely keep on decent terms with his brother and his brother's son—his two next successors. He was nicknamed by every court in Europe; and cursed, as he knew, by his people, to whom he had promised the rank of a first-class European nation. He who above all men craved sympathy on every hand, found himself a despised outcast in the crisis which an able monarch would have employed for the establishment of his kingdom in a higher position than it had ever held. He was pitiable as every man is who finds himself in the wrong place, and has no power to get in a fitter. He was not "a square man in a round hole;" and so far was he from being what the Germans so prize, "a many-sided" man, that he was not even that fewest-sided thing, a triangle in a square hole. If he had been a private citizen, he might, with his sensibility, his cultivation, and his intellectual tastes, have led a blameless, and perhaps a beneficent and happy life. He could not have been even a country

gentleman, in the continental sense, because his deficiency of will must have caused failure in the very
smallest function of administration ; but as an opulent
citizen, with his library, and chapel and music-room,
and museum of antiquities, he might have fulfilled the
anticipations of his old tutor, Niebuhr; but evil was
the destiny which made him a ruling Prince in our
revolutionary nineteenth century.

One good may live after him. He may serve as a *Lessons to*
warning to his successors. It is to be hoped that they *be learnt*
from his
are not Stuarts too—unable to take warning. The time *life.*
for Stuarts will soon be over on the Continent as completely as it has long been in England. The Prussian
people are so deficient in political education that their
political qualities have as yet been of no use to them :
but the qualities exist, and the training will come, in one
fashion or another. They will not let their Prince play
fast and loose with them for ever, nor allow their loyalty
and generosity to be made their snare in the future as
they have in the past.

V.

THE DUCHESS OF KENT.

DIED MARCH 16TH, 1861.

THIS Princess, the object of the hearty respect of the British nation as a high source of the virtues of their Sovereign, has been so exclusively regarded as the mother of the Queen as to have been little known outside of that relation. For many years she has been observed only as moving with the court—to Frogmore when the Queen was at Windsor, and to Abergeldie during the autumn holiday of the royal family at Balmoral. Yet hers was a long life of strong interests, anxieties, and responsibilities; and if we could know her experiences, we might find more romance lying between childhood and old age than is often found in the life of princes.

Her birth, Aug. 17, 1786. The Princess Maria Louisa Victoria was born on the same day that Frederick the Great died, August 17, 1786. Daughter and sister of Dukes of Saxe-Cobourg Saalfeld, she was brought up in the dulness of a little German court—as little German courts were in those days, when the invasion of French ideas, issuing from the court of Frederick, was only beginning to influence the German mind, and to create a new literary period. The small territory in which the Duke's seven children grew up (of whom the lady now deceased was the youngest but one,

and the King of Belgium the youngest), resounded with
the din of industry, but was otherwise profoundly quiet.
Ironworks and forges, spinning-wheels and looms at
which the well-known Saxony cloths and linens were
produced, saluted one sense; while others were greeted
by fumes from chemical and dye works and tanneries.
With perpetual industry of this kind before their eyes,
and a pretty country around them, and a plain and quiet
domestic life within the chateau, these children grew up
in the acquisition of the practical sense which has since
distinguished them in life. Just at the time of the
Princess's birth there was great dread in the minds of
the Opposition in our Parliament lest England should be
too much implicated with the smaller German states,
which would have jeopardized her position with the
greater Powers; and just when the infant who was to be
mother to a British Queen was seeing the light, Mr. Pitt
was agreeing with Fox as to the danger, but declaring
that it was as Elector of Hanover only that George III.
had joined the princes' league for the preservation of
the liberties of Germany. Either statesman would have
been surprised to know how near an interest would be
established between the great empire they served and
one of the smallest of the German duchies.

The Princess's first close interest in England came
through her younger brother, Leopold, who caused some
anxiety to his family by the susceptibility of his heart.
He was at Paris when he was three-and-twenty, as aide-
de-camp to the Grand Duke Constantine; and there he
fell in love with a young English lady, whose relatives
invited him to London, whither he came in the train of
the Allied Sovereigns in 1814. Supposing himself distinguished by the Princess Charlotte, he proposed, and

Her brother Prince Leopold.

[V]

[V]

was refused. Attending the sovereigns to Vienna, he was observed to be again occupied in the same way with a new object before the close of the year; but in the interval the Princess Charlotte had become free from her engagements with the Prince of Orange, and an intimation reached Prince Leopold from a friend in London that it was against his interest to be so open in his attentions to the German lady. His return to London decided the fate of other German princes and princesses *Marriage of* as well as his own. At the time of his marriage to *Prince Leopold to the Princess Charlotte.* the Princess Charlotte, in May, 1816, nothing could be further from the imagination of his sister, next above him in age, than that she should become more nearly connected with the British crown than his brother, whom all the world regarded as a favorite of fortune. She was then thirty years of age, and just two years a widow, having married in 1803 the Prince Emich Charles, of Leiningen. Her son had been declared of age at nine years old, and had succeeded his father in the Principality of Leiningen at ten. The mother was occupied in superintending his education, and that of his sister, a year younger; little imagining that her present life was a rehearsal of the lofty function of preparing another heir for a greater throne.

Death of the Princess Charlotte. Then followed the apparent overthrow of the family prospect, as far as the English throne was concerned. The dream of greatness was dissolved in tears; and the widower of our beloved Princess Charlotte was sympathized with by all, and, no doubt, eminently by his sister, as the sport, after having seemed to be the favorite, of fortune. But a few weeks proved that new entrances into our royal family were opened by the change in the prospect of the succession. The Princess Charlotte died in November, 1817; and within six months no less than four marriages were announced to Parliament, as approved by the Regent, on behalf of his brothers and one sister—the Princess Elizabeth. The Duke of Cumberland had been married three years, and his elder brother of York long before. The Dukes of Clarence, Kent, and Cambridge now announced their engagements; and the most immediately popular was undoubtedly that of the Duke of Kent. That of the Duke of Clarence was declared to be broken off, on account of the unwillingness of Parliament to grant him a larger income than his brothers; and one effect of this incident was to turn general attention to the Duke of Kent, as not only a probable successor to the throne, but the father of the future line. It soon appeared, however, that the Clarence marriage was to take place, which it did on the 13th of July, 1818. The Duke of Kent was married on the 29th of May, and the Duke of Cambridge on the 1st of June.

Marriage with the Duke of Kent, 1818.

If the Duke of Sussex was the most popular in the political world for his comparative liberalism, his brothers of Kent and Cambridge were most generally beloved for their interest in benevolent projects and informal kindliness, of the "true British" character, in which the Regent was remarkably deficient. There was a strong impression abroad, too, that the good-natured Prince Edward had been neglected first, and oppressed afterward, by his obstinate and prejudiced father; and when to these causes of interest was added that of his wife being a sister of Prince Leopold, with whom all England was still mourning, it was natural that the heart of the nation should especially follow his fortunes. There was no disposition on this account to vote him more money

[V]

[V]

than the small income given to his brothers. Parliament had refused to give 10,000*l*. a year to the Duke of Clarence; and now they were all to have an addition of 6,000*l*., and no more. Hence the load of debt which weighed upon the Duchess of Kent for many years. The Duke had shown the same lavish tendencies which made the family generally so unpopular in Parliament; and he had no opportunity of rectifying his affairs before he died. His income somewhat exceeded 30,000*l*. after his marriage; but certain loans from the Admiralty Droits had remained unpaid for above ten years; and the interest of these, and his great amount of private debts, so far hampered him that neither he nor his widow could ever have felt at ease about pecuniary affairs. Hence, perhaps, the care with which their child was trained in habits of rectitude and punctuality in money matters which have made her a noble exception to all family tradition in that branch of morals.

Re-marriage according to the rites of the English Church.

The Duke and Duchess came to England, to be re-married according to the rites of our Church, and were received by Prince Leopold at Claremont, on the 1st of July. For the sake of economy they presently returned to the residence of the Princes of Leiningen, at Amorbach, where they lived in retirement. Lord Eldon, being consulted on behalf of one or other of the royal duchesses, gave it as his opinion that it was not necessary that the expected infants should be born in England; and it was at Hanover therefore that the present Duke of Cambridge was born, on the 26th of the next March, and that a daughter to the Duke of Clarence was born and died the next day; while the present King of Hanover was born at Berlin in May. But the Duke and Duchess of Kent desired that their child should be a native of England,

and came over in April, 1819, the Princess Victoria being
born at Kensington Palace, on the 24th of the next
month. The year 1819 was full of public distress and
disturbance from end to end; but it removed all apprehension about heirs of the crown in the next generation.
There was no longer a fear that we should be governed
by a succession of childless old men.

[V]
*Birth of the
Princess
Victoria,
1819.*

For the sake of a mild winter for the infant, the Duke
removed his household to Sidmouth in November. On
the 13th of January he took a long walk with Captain
(afterward Sir John) Conroy, and both got their feet wet.
Captain Conroy entreated the Duke to change his boots,
but he was playing with his infant, and delayed too long.
He was ill at night, in a high fever the next morning, and
died on the 23d of pulmonary inflammation. For five
nights the Duchess never left his bedside, and from the
second day of the illness she was supported and aided by
Prince Leopold, who went to her at once, and relieved
her afterward of all external cares, till she was again
settled at Kensington Palace. By the Duke's will, her
duty was laid out for the best years of her life. "I do
nominate, constitute, and appoint my beloved wife
Victoire, Duchess of Kent, to be sole guardian of our
dear child, the Princess Alexandrina Victoire, to all
intents and for all purposes whatever." When she
received, by deputations, the addresses of condolence
offered by the two Houses of Parliament, the infant was
in her arms; and the study of her life from that day
forward was to establish a mutual understanding and
accord between the people of England and the Princess
who would probably stand in the closest possible relation
to them hereafter.

*Death of the
Duke,* 1820.

*The Duchess
appointed
guardian of
the Princess
Victoria.*

This was a task of extreme and extraordinary difficulty,

[V]
Difficulties of the task.

owing to the complications and uncertainties of the case. If it is difficult in a case of presumptive heirship in private life to decide how to educate a boy, whether for probable wealth or possible poverty; it is infinitely more so when the question is between the possession of a crown and the dull and aimless life of a subject Prince— and yet more, Princess. In the former case it may be said, "Educate your son thoroughly for the lower career, and he will do very well in the higher;" but to reign over a kingdom requires a training so special as to unfit the heir to enjoy the private life of princes. For many years the lot of the Princess was in suspense; and seldom has a mother undergone such wear and tear of anxiety and responsibility as the Duchess of Kent sustained on this account. The question of the succession was simplified from time to time: but it was not till within a few months of her accession that there was anything like security that the Princess would ever be Queen of England.

Death of George III.

The old King died six days after the Duke of Kent; and there was an immediate revival of the rumors about George IV. getting a divorce after all. In "Lord Eldon's Life" (ii. 305), we are shown, by a letter of the Prince Regent's, how eager he was for this divorce within two months of his daughter's death. His vehement self-will about "unshackling himself" brought matters to such a pass in 1820, that there were few people in England who did not fully expect to see Queen Caroline put away, and the King married again in the course of the year. There was, in fact, a majority of nine in favor of the Bill (which was one of divorce as well as degradation); but even the King did not venture to proceed upon this. It was only for a few months that the matter seemed settled; for the Queen

died in August of the next year, and the marriage of
the King was repeatedly rumored, before popular expectation turned to the royal brothers. At the end of
1820, another daughter, who was named Elizabeth, in
consideration of her prospects, was born to the Duke of
Clarence, but the child died in infancy. In 1827 the
Duke of York died; and in 1830, the King.

[V]

This ushered in a new period in the function of the
Duchess of Kent. For the first ten years of her child's
life she had lived retired, and had provided for the
physical health and educational training of the Princess
with all simplicity as well as completeness. All that was
known was that the Princess was met, even on cold and
windy days, dressed and in exercise in good pedestrian
style—crossing a heath perhaps, with her young companions, in thick shoes and stout duffle cloak—and that
she was reared in as much honesty and care about
money matters as any citizen's child. It became known
at Tunbridge Wells that the Princess had been unable to
buy a box at a bazaar, because she had spent her money.
At this bazaar, she had bought presents for almost all her
relations, and had laid out her last shilling, when she
remembered one cousin more, and saw a box, priced
half-a-crown, which would suit him. The shop-people
of course placed the box with the other purchases; but
the little lady's governess admonished them, by saying,
"No; you see the princess has not got the money, and
therefore, of course, she cannot buy the box." This
being perceived, the next offer was to lay by the box till
it could be purchased; and the answer was, "Oh, well,
if you will be so good as to do that—;" and the
thing was done. On quarter-day, before seven in the
morning, the Princess appeared on her donkey to claim

*The train-
ing of the
Princess
Victoria.*

[V] her purchase. Anecdotes like these, apparently small, have large meanings; and in such traits people saw promise of the rectitude and elevated economy which have made the mother of our large royal family respected by the people whose need and convenience she has so admirably respected.

She was eleven years old when William IV. sent his first message to Parliament, in which there was no allusion to the appointment of a regency. In case of his death without such a provision being made, she would have been sovereign, with full powers at once, as the minority of a sovereign is not recognized by our laws. There was another consideration which must have aggravated the anxiety of the watchful mother—that the next eldest uncle was the Duke of Cumberland. Little as could be said about this, the thought was in almost all minds that the Princess would not be altogether safe in her seat without the protection of a regency. The only apparent exceptions were the ministers, who said a great deal about the excellent health and probable long life of their master—an infirm old man of sixty-five. The danger was allowed to exist

The Regency Bill provides for the Duchess being Regent.

till the new parliament met in November, when a Regency Bill provided that, in the event of no posthumous issue of the King appearing, in which case the Queen was to be regent, the Duchess of Kent should be regent (unless she married a foreigner) till the Princess Victoria came of age. Still there were uncertainties. The King might have children; and mysterious dangers seemed to impend from the Duke of Cumberland, the extent of which became revealed to the astonished nation in 1835, when a committee of inquiry, obtained by Mr. Hume, brought to light a scheme for setting aside the succession, which it would be scarcely possible to believe now, but for the substantial documentary evidence which remains in our hands. The Orange leaders had got it into their heads that the Duke of Wellington meant to seize the crown, and that the right thing to be done in opposition was to make the Duke of Cumberland king. Letters were produced which proved that the notion of certain friends and tools of the future King of Hanover was that it would be necessary to declare King William insane, and the Princess disqualified for reigning, by being a minor and a woman. Under the explosion of loyalty thus caused on behalf of a good-natured old king and a fatherless princess, Orangeism and its leader promised whatever was required, and disappeared from public notice. All was safe after 1836 ; but the preceding five years must have been heavily weighted with care to the guardian of the presumptive heiress of the throne.

[V]

The Princess was now becoming known, more or less, to her future people. She had not appeared at the last coronation ; and the plea was that her health required her residence in the Isle of Wight at that time, when she was indeed too young for a scene where she must have filled so conspicuous a station. It was believed, too, that she had but recently become aware of her regal destination. But her guardian perceived that the time had arrived for procuring for her the advantages of travel, and of intercourse with superior minds. In 1831 began a series of tours—the first comprehending the oldest of our cities, Chester, several cathedrals, some noblemen's seats, and, finally, the University of Oxford. By degrees she became thus accustomed to the gaze of a multitude, and the homage of strangers, and formalities of processions, addresses, and, generally, the observances which

Introduction of the Princess into public life.

[V] must occupy a large portion of **her life**. At the same time the Duchess adopted **the practice of inviting to** Kensington travellers and voyagers, men of science, and other persons distinguished in the intellectual world, from whom the **Princess** might gather various information more freshly **than** from books—an experiment sometimes found rather awkward at the moment by all parties, but well intended, and probably of more or less use. The few years of the preceding reign were industriously employed.

Burdens incurred by the Duchess, They were not free from heavy and various cares. The expenses of such a method were so great that the debts of the Duchess became almost as onerous as those of her husband. Encroachments were made which she thought it more politic to yield to than to resist, and the petitions for subscriptions **for** everything, **from** blind asylums to racing-cups, **would have exhausted an income** ten times **more royal. The Duchess's reliance** (afterward justified) was that the **Queen would pay** the debts incurred in her preparation for sovereignty. After her *Honorably discharged by the Princess.* accession, **and when** nobly portioned for a maiden Queen, the dutiful daughter paid off **her** father's debts in the first year, **in** the joint names of the Duchess and herself, **and her** mother's in the next. But there were troubles more wearing than those of insufficient income. It was a matter of extreme nicety to claim due **observance** for the Princess without **insisting on too** much ; and it was inevitable that **some parties, and** probable that all, would be displeased. There was the same danger about the exercise of authority over the Princess herself ; and a long series of troubles hence arose. The free and easy style of life in the King's family, where the King and Queen and all the Fitzclarences disliked formality, and lived very much like quiet people of other ranks, did not always suit the notions of the Duchess of Kent as to the observance which her daughter's presence should command : and hence coolness arose which could not be concealed from the public. We, however, have only to bear in mind, in reviewing the life of the Duchess of Kent, that she had much to suffer in the discharge of a function by which the nation has largely benefited. When her task seemed to be closed, and she might have hoped to rest on the result of her labors and her anxieties, she had some bitter griefs to endure, some few dreary years to pass before she tasted that repose which she had so well earned and in which her latter years were passed.

The day at last dawned for which she had lived so devotedly for so many years ; and it found her wakeful and prepared. The early sun was shining in, that Midsummer morning—it was before five o'clock on the 20th of June—when the doors of the palace were thrown open to admit the Primate, the royal physician, and the Lord Chamberlain, who came to greet the Princess as Queen. The Duchess and her daughter were standing ready for the announcement, and prepared for the trying transactions of the day. From the day when Prince Albert entered upon the scene, and, yet more, from the hour when Sir Robert Peel assumed Lord Melbourne's place as the Queen's chief adviser, everything brightened to the Duchess of Kent. The Queen has never been more heartily cheered than when, instantly after the first of the silly pistol-shots which were at one time discharged at her by stupid boys to make themselves famous, she altered the course of her drive, and went to inform her mother of the attempt in person, before she could be alarmed by the rumor of

[V]

The morning of the Accession.

[V]

*Happiness
of her latter
years.*

it. That was in 1840. The latter years of the venerable Duchess have been filled with interest and with cheerfulness by the arrival of a long succession of grandchildren, by their growth and expansion into promise of various kinds, and by the early settlement in life of the eldest. At the marriage of the Princess Royal, her grandmother was observed to be much altered, and to be in very delicate health. She had sustained the shock of her son's death a year or two before, and her life had been on the whole one of wear and tear which rendered it somewhat surprising that she should have passed the old threescore years and ten. She accomplished, with little flagging, the periodical removals to Scotland, the Isle of Wight, Windsor, and London, which were as regularly established for her as for the court ; and, bodily suffering apart, her old age was a happy one, many of its hours being passed in her royal daughter's presence, and many more cheered by the affectionate attentions of her grandchildren. As for the people of England, they received her with manifest respect, wherever she appeared ; and she must have been almost tired of hearing, for many years before her death, that that respect was offered as her due for the boon she had conferred on the nation in the virtues of her daughter. The same thing must be told once more, however, though her ear is now dead to human praise. It must be told in history,

RECENT PUBLICATIONS

OF

LEYPOLDT & HOLT.

451 Broome St., N. Y.

(Copies sent by mail, postpaid, on receipt of the price.)

Taine's Italy.

(Rome and Naples.) Translated by JOHN DURAND. A new edition, with corrections and an index. 8vo. Vellum cloth. $2.50.

"One of the most powerful writers of the day—to our own taste, indeed, the most powerful—the writer of all others who throws over the reader's faculties, for the time, the most irresistible spell, and against whose influence, consequently, the mental reaction is most violent and salutary. * * * His style, literally translated (and Mr. Durand is very literal), makes very natural English. It has an energy, an impetus, a splendor to which no words of ours can do justice. * * * Finally, we cannot help laying down our conviction that M. Taine's two volumes form a truly great production; great, not in a moral sense, and very possibly not in a philosophical, but appreciably great as a contribution to literature and history. One feels at moments as if, before this writer, there had been no critics, no travellers, observers, or æsthetic inquisitors."—*Nation.*

"No one who has studied art, or speculated on history, or cultivated a love for the beautiful, or allegiance to the true, can help finding rare instruction and delight in Taine's 'Italy.' "—*Boston Transcript.*

The Myths of the New World.

A Treatise on the Symbolism and Mythology of the Red Race of America. By DANIEL G. BRINTON, A. M., M. D. 8vo. Vellum cloth, $2.50. Large-paper edition (only fifty-six copies printed), $6.00.

"Dr. Brinton is probably the first American who has specially treated the subject of Indian mythology in a thorough and scholarly way. * * * The philosophical spirit in which it is written is deserving of unstinted praise, and justifies the belief that, in whatever Dr. Brinton may in future contribute to the literature of Comparative Mythology, he will continue to reflect credit upon himself and his country."—*North American Review.*

A Psyche of To-day.

By Mrs. C. JENKIN, author of "Who Breaks Pays."
$1.25.

"After opening the pretty volume of this story, we did what a news-paper reviewer rarely finds time to do with a book to be "noticed"—read it through without stopping, from title-page to *finis.* * * * It is a book to be welcomed in any home."—*N. Y. Times.*

"A capital novel of modern French life and society. * * * The writer's method of composition, so bright, crisp, and suggestive, adds greatly to the effect of her wit, observation, and sentiment."—*Boston Transcript.*

In the Year '13.

A Historical Tale. By FRITZ REUTER. Translated from the Platt-Deutsch by CHARLES LEE LEWES (son of G. H. Lewes). 16mo. Flexible cloth, $1; paper, 75 cts.

"One of the most artistic and pleasing bits of history to be found, we think, in any literature."—*Nation.*

"One of the daintiest possible of volumes. The page is exquisite, and the binding befits it. * * * The story is full of humor, inter-mingled with strains of heroism and pathos, and sustained all the while by a noble moral of duty to man and trust in God. Of all the queer German tales which we have read, this is one of the queerest."—*New Englander.*

Mozart.   A Biographical Novel.

From the German of HERIBERT RAU, by EDWARD ROWLAND SILL. Cloth, gilt, $1.75; plain, $1.50; paper $1.00.

"A succession of beautiful pictures from the life of the sensitive and impassioned artist....The work has the charm of actual adventure and incident, without the usual waxen formality of the historical romance. The description of European social life, especially the German domes-tic sketches, are brilliant and often delightful. Mr. Sill has evidently engaged in the translation not as a task, but as a labor of love, and has admirably succeeded."—*N. Y. Tribune.*

"A story full of insight and artistic sympathy—a beautiful memorial and tribute to the life, the trials, the triumphs, and the memory of genius; and, besides all this, has the charm of a fascinating narrative and the value of a genuine memoir."—*Boston Transcript.*

"A book of rare and absorbing interest."—*Hours at Home.*

MRS. JENKIN'S NOVELS.

Just ready.

Madame de Beaupré.

By Mrs. C. JENKIN, author of "A Psyche of To-day," "Who Breaks Pays," etc. 16mo. $1.25.

In preparation.

"Once and Again."   "Cousin Stella."

Recently Published.

A Psyche of To-day.

By Mrs. C. JENKIN, author of "Who Breaks Pays." $1.25.

"After opening the pretty volume of this story, we did what a newspaper reviewer rarely finds time to do with a book to be 'noticed'—read it through without stopping, from title-page to *finis.* * * * It is a book to be welcomed in any home."— *N. Y. Times.*

"A capital novel of modern French life and society. * * * The writer's method of composition, so bright, crisp, and suggestive, adds greatly to the effect of her wit, observation, and sentiment."—*Boston Transcript.*

"Displays great delicacy of feeling and perception of character, and is written in an admirable style."—*Springfield Republican.*

"A charming Novel."—*Philadelphia Press.*

TWO NOVELS WORTH READING.—*Nation.*

"Who Breaks—Pays." By the author

of "Cousin Stella," "Skirmishing," &c. 1 vol., 12mo. Cloth. Price, $1.25.

"Who Breaks—Pays," is a love tale, told with exquisite pathos and poetry. There is a freshness and originality about the book which give it a place among the standard works of the day."—*Publishers' Circular.*

"One of the most interesting stories we have ever read. It is a love tale, but most unlike the trashy stuff published as such, and worthy the reading of intellectual people."—*Boston Saturday Evening Gazette.*

Skirmishing. By the Author of "Who

Breaks—Pays," etc. 12mo. Cloth. Price, $1.25.

"Every page tells; there is no book-making about it—no attempt to fill chapters with appropriate affections. Each sentence is written carefully, and the result is that we have a real work of art, such as the weary critic has seldom the pleasure of meeting with."—*The London Reader.*

The Annals of Rural Bengal.

By W. W. HUNTER, B. A., M. R. A. S. First American, from the second English Edition. 8vo. Cloth. $4.

Written with "the insight of Colonel Tod and the research of Mr. Duff, in prose almost as good as that of Mr. Froude." * * * If Mr. Hunter does not ultimately compel recognition from the world as an historian of the very first class, of the class to which not a score of Englishmen have ever belonged, we entirely mistake our trade. * * * He has executed with admirable industry and rare power of expression a task, which, so far as we know, has never yet been attempted—he has given life and reality and interest to the internal history of an Indian province under British rule, to a history, that is, without battles or sieges or martial deeds of any sort. * * We have given but a faint sketch of the mass of matter in this volume, the rare merit of which will sometimes only be perceptible to Anglo-Indians unaccustomed to see their dry annals made as interesting as a novel. We most cordially counsel Mr. Hunter, of whom, it is needful to repeat, the writer never heard before, to continue the career he has chalked out for himself."—*Spectator*.

"Mr. Hunter has given us a book that not only possesses sterling historical value, but is thoroughly readable * * The picture of the great famine of 1769, which did so much toward ruining the native Bengal aristocracy, is worthy of Thucydides ; and the two chapters about the Indian Aborigines, especially about the Santals, who astonished us so much in 1855, form a pleasing monograph from which the reader may learn more about the origin of Caste and the relations of the Aryan and Turanian languages, and the connection between Buddhism and Hinduism, than from a score of the old-fashioned 'authorities.'"—*Imperial Review*.

"Mr. Hunter's style is charming ; though not faultless, it is clear, direct, thoughtful, and often eloquent, and his matter is so full of varied interest, that, despite a few pages of somewhat technical discussion on a question of language, his book as a whole is fascinating to the general reader."—*N. Y. Evening Post*.

The Ideal in Art.

By H. TAINE, author of "Italy," etc. Cloth. $1.50.

"It is a classic upon its subject, and ought to be not merely read, but mastered and made familiar by all who wish to have the right to form opinions of their own on the productions of the arts of design."—*N. Y. Evening Post*.

(*See notices of* TAINE'S ITALY *on another page.*)